A MAN ALONE

Flipper felt like a condemned man, counting the days before the hangman and priest arrived at his cell. Hampton had been gone a month, but his wires offered no signs of help. Businessmen and black leaders politely declined to help, financially or otherwise, Lieutenant Henry Ossian Flipper. Perhaps they didn't believe in his innocence. Maybe they didn't care what happened on the Texas frontier. More than likely, though, they just felt it unwise to choose sides one way or the other.

Alone. The calendar showed October 17th. Two weeks before the proceedings resumed, and he had no money and no lawyer. . . .

LONELY TRUMPET

JOHNNY D. BOGGS

LEISURE BOOKS NEW YORK CITY

For David Wilkinson and Bonnie Bratton

A LEISURE BOOK®

August 2003

Published by special agreement with Golden West Literary Agency.

Dorchester Publishing Co., Inc.
276 Fifth Avenue
New York, NY 10001

ISBN 0-8439-5209-1

Visit us on the web at www.dorchesterpub.com.

LONELY TRUMPET

Alone, alone, all all alone,
Alone on a wide wide sea!
And never a saint took pity on
    My soul in agony.

        "The Rime of the Ancient Mariner"
        Samuel Taylor Coleridge

Prologue

HEADQUARTERS

General Court-Martial   **United States Army,**
Special Orders, No. 108   **Department of Texas**

San Antonio, Texas
September 3, 1881

I. A general court-martial will convene at Fort Davis, Texas, on Thursday, the 15th day of September, 1881, at 10 o'clock a.m., or as soon thereafter as practicable, for the trial of Second Lieutenant H. O. Flipper, 10th Cavalry.

Detailed for the court:

Colonel G. Pennypacker, 16th Infantry; Lieutenant Colonel J. F. Wade, 10th Cavalry; Major G. W. Schofield, 10th Cavalry; Surgeon W. E. Waters, Medical Department; Captain Fergus Walker, 1st Infantry; Captain William Fletcher, 20th Infantry; Captain W. N. Tisdale, 1st Infantry; Captain R. G. Heiner, 1st Infantry; Captain E. S. Ewing, 16th Infantry; Captain L. O. Parker, 1st Infantry; First Lieutenant W. V. Richards, Regimental Quartermaster, 16th Infantry;

Captain J. W. Clous, 24th Infantry, is appointed judge advocate of the court.

No other officers than those named can be assembled without manifest injury to the service.

By the command of Brigadier General Christopher C. Augur.

G. B. Russell,
Captain, 9th Infantry, A.D.C.

Chapter One

September 17–19, 1881

The cottonwoods looked about a month away from turning yellow. Staring out the window past the parade grounds, enlisted men's barracks, and the commissary and quartermaster buildings, he strained to see the grove just beyond the old Overland Trail. There were still no signs of autumn. He wondered if he would be around to watch the leaves turn bright yellow and feel the first hint of winter coming down Sleeping Lion Mountain. That would be a while. His duplex had already turned stifling in the early morning heat, and he wanted to open the window, but Colonel Shafter had ordered all windows in these quarters nailed shut. An armed guard stood posted in front of his door.

As the 10th Cavalry's trumpeter blared out "First Sergeants' Call" nearby, the metallic notes strangely haunting, he saw Second Lieutenant Wade Hampton, in full dress uniform, walking down the path, past the new officers' duplexes being constructed of adobe and stone next to his own quarters. He'd be here in a minute. No need in making Hampton wait, so he stepped away from the window and buckled his belt tightly across his dress blouse, making sure no dust or lint marred his appearance, an almost impossible task out here in wind-blown West Texas. Next he picked up his brand new dress helmet, with its plume of golden yak hair sprouting from the spiked top, admiring the gold cord, lines, and flounders, and a gold eagle plate with the regimental number raised above the stars and stripe shield that topped the crossed sabers.

When he placed the helmet on top of his head, Wade Hampton knocked on the door. "Lieutenant Flipper!" he called out in a polite Southern accent.

Hampton was being formal this morning.

Henry Flipper remembered the first time Wade Hampton knocked on the door to his duplex: nine months ago, New Year's Day.

That knock had surprised him as he lay on his bed reading the latest copy of *Popular Science*, which he had checked out from the post library. He had crossed the room, magazine in hand, and opened the door to see the sandy-haired junior lieutenant of the 10th Cavalry holding a tin bowl of black-eyed peas and cornbread in his left hand and a pewter flask in the right.

"Happy New Year, Mistah Flipper," Hampton had drawled out. "Since we are both Southern gentlemen on this post, I thought you might enjoy an ol' Dixie tradition." His accent had sounded of hominy and Tennessee sour mash, and, although Henry Flipper had never tasted the latter, Hampton's breath had smelled faintly of some type of liquor. "Bein' an ol' Georgia boy, you know you gotta eat black-eyed peas on New Year's Day for good luck. So I have secreted some from Missus Miller's Hotel." He had thrust out the bowl of cold peas.

"Dixie tradition . . . ol' Georgia boy." Boy! Flipper had looked into Hampton's dark eyes, expecting to find something bitter, but quickly had realized the South Carolinian meant no disrespect. That had surprised him, almost as much as the knock had. As the only black officer in the United States Army, Flipper knew all about disrespect. He had been used to it since he entered the U.S. Military Academy eight years ago. The prejudice at West Point had not shocked him then—he had expected it—but once he had graduated, fiftieth in a class of seventy-six, he had envisioned equal treatment and honor. That had rarely happened.

Flipper had been on good terms with some men. Captain Nicholas Nolan and Colonel Benjamin Grierson, for example. He had liked and respected both men, and he had felt—although he could never be certain—that they had returned his respect, trust, and admiration. But most of the officers in the United States Army were hyenas, especially that miserable Swede and Northerner who had lived just across the hall, First Lieutenant Charles Nordstrom.

Traditionally on New Year's Day, officers visited the ladies of the post, but Flipper had never felt comfortable with that and suspected most of the women, with the exception of Captain Nolan's wife, would not appreciate a "darky . . . African . . . Jim Crow . . . moke . . . brunette . . . charcoal . . . nigger"—whatever the word choice—in their house, officer or not. So he had planned to bury his nose in *Popular Science* and read.

Lieutenant Wade Hampton, however, had brought food, and although the meal hadn't fared well on the trip from town, the aroma had made Flipper realize his own hunger. So he had invited the Southern second lieutenant inside.

"Would you care for some, Mister Hampton?" Flipper had asked.

"Thank you, Mistah Flipper, but no. I have already eaten. However, I would be happy to share my flask."

Flipper had smiled. "I must decline. I do not imbibe. My apologies."

Hampton had unscrewed the cap and took a small sip. "No need to apologize, Lieutenant. That's more for me."

Although named after his famous uncle, Lieutenant

13

Wade Hampton bore little resemblance to the famous lieutenant general from South Carolina who served in the Confederacy during the late War of the Rebellion. General Hampton, the stories went, had always been a powerful man who often traveled to Mississippi to fight bears, armed only with a knife. When the war broke out, he had forked over his own money in Charleston to raise and recruit his Hampton Legion, then marched off to Virginia to fight the Federal Army. General Hampton had been wounded at First Manassas and Gettysburg, took over the Cavalry Corps of the Army of Northern Virginia after J. E. B. Stuart was killed at Yellow Tavern, and eventually surrendered with Robert E. Lee at Appomattox Court House.

Future Lieutenant Henry Ossian Flipper was nine years old when the War of the Rebellion ended. Future Lieutenant Wade Hampton was seven.

General Hampton had been elected governor of South Carolina in 1876, was reëlected two years later, and was voted into the United States Senate in 1879. As governor, he had helped secure his nephew an appointment to West Point. Odd, Flipper had thought, how a man who had done everything in his power to dissolve the Union would allow a relative to attend the military academy. Well, perhaps General Hampton was not unreconstructed.

Lieutenant Wade Hampton was a slight man, perfectly suited for cavalry duty, quiet, even charming, definitely not the kind to challenge a Mississippi black bear to a knife fight. As Flipper ate his cornbread and black-eyed peas, he and Hampton had talked about the South, the Point, the post, the commander. Hampton had drunk, but only slightly. Unlike many of the officers at Fort Davis, he hadn't appeared to be a drunk. He had been merely celebrating the new year. By the end of the day, Henry O.

Flipper had realized he had another rare friend at Fort Davis.

"How'd you like those peas, Mistah Flipper?" Hampton had asked.

"Fine, Mister Hampton. Mighty fine." They had been thick, meaty, and seasoned with fatback and bacon grease, just the way his mother had fixed them back in Georgia.

"You'll have a good year now, Henry," Hampton had said with a slight smile, "thanks to me."

Flipper thought about those words now as he let Hampton inside on this late morning.

A good year? Not hardly, and the next few days, or months, would undoubtedly be the worst.

"Capt'n Clous arrived last night," Hampton said stiffly. "I am to escort you to the post chapel, where, pursuant to General Orders One Oh Eight, you are to face a court of your peers."

Peers? No less than five, and no more than thirteen, white men.

Hampton closed the door behind him. "You need anything, Henry?" he asked, dropping the formality.

"No, thanks." Flipper took a deep breath, slowly exhaled, and forced a smile. "Best not keep the court waiting."

Wade Hampton sighed. "Henry, take it easy. This is a mere formality. Courts-martial are nothin' out of the ordinary. Hell, you were judge advocate on one yourself a few months back. You know what it's like. Besides, I'm bettin' a few members of that court have faced a court-martial before. It'll be all right."

Flipper returned Hampton's grin, but, inside, he knew better. His fellow officers, his "peers," had been laying traps for him for months now, maybe longer, and were determined to see him cashiered. Yes, he had served on courts-martial before, but always for minor offenses against enlisted men. He had never faced a court-martial himself, never faced a lengthy stay in the federal prison at Fort Leavenworth, never been shamed by the ugly charges against him.

Charge I: Embezzlement in violation of the sixtieth Article of War. Specification I: In that he, Second Lieutenant H. O. Flipper, A Troop, 10th Cavalry, being a duly commissioned officer in the service of the United States, did embezzle, knowingly and willfully misappropriate and misapply, public money of the United States, furnished and intended for the military service thereof, to wit: $3,791.77, more or less, which money came into his possession and was entrusted to him in the capacity of Acting Commissary of Subsistence at Fort Davis, Texas, this during the period of the 8th day of July, 1881, and the 13th day of August, 1881.

Charge II: Conduct unbecoming an officer and a gentleman. Five specifications of lies and misrepresentation.

"Let's go," Flipper said, and opened the door.

The guard, a 1st Infantry corporal, saluted Hampton as they walked out of the stone building, but Hampton didn't bother returning it. He and Flipper turned left and walked down Officers' Row, turning right by Colonel William R. Shafter's house, and cutting across the parade grounds, under the flag hanging limply, and to the barracks. Another left, and on they walked past the other enlisted men's barracks. Flipper looked ahead and saw the first sergeants gathered in front of the post headquarters where they were giving their morning reports.

The non-coms and officers standing on the porch stopped to watch Flipper and his escort.

"Here he comes!" a fat man in a plaid sack suit yelled. *A reporter,* Flipper thought. More civilians with note pads, pencils, and cigars appeared from inside and behind the stone building, scurrying about like Georgia cockroaches.

They went past the guardhouse, turned left in front of the post headquarters, ignoring the stares, and stopped in front of the post chapel next door.

"Good luck," Hampton whispered.

Flipper bowed his head slightly. Alone, once again. He climbed the stone steps, opened the white door, and stepped inside.

A barrel-chested German with thick spectacles and a thicker accent, Judge Advocate John W. Clous, had a black beard, its point heavily gray. His face was pale except for his veiny nose, and he seemed a contradiction, a man who looked both formidable yet sickly. Unlike the other members of the court, Clous didn't appear in his dress uniform. His blue eyes glared beneath the glass lenses as Flipper closed the door and walked down the aisle, as if Flipper were to blame for the bad weather and washed-out roads that had delayed Clous's arrival to Fort Davis.

Flipper knew Clous was his enemy. As judge advocate, he would present the Army's case against him, and those harsh eyes foretold the captain's obsession with ridding the military of another man of color. Clous served in the 24th Infantry, a black regiment like the 10th, but Flipper guessed the captain didn't care much for his enlisted men. Most white officers despised their black troops.

After saluting, Flipper stood at ease and considered his peers once more. He only knew two of the court members: Lieutenant Colonel James F. Wade and Major George W. Schofield, both of the 10th Cavalry. They served with Flipper, but that didn't necessarily help his cause. James Wade had been a hero in the Rebellion, but his reputation on the frontier was more or less nonexistent. He was Colonel Grierson's second-in-command, and any glory the 10th sowed was reaped by Grierson, not Wade. And Schofield? All he seemed to do these days was brood over the fact that the revolver he had helped Smith & Wesson develop had fallen out of favor among cavalry officers and, more importantly, the Ordnance Department. Neither had ever spoken to Flipper except when required to by duty.

The other members came from the 16th Infantry and Shafter's 1st Infantry, along with one on detached service from the 20th Infantry, all men stationed at Fort Davis but none whom Flipper could even remotely call friendly. Flipper's quick, silent head count revealed only eleven jurists.

"*Herr* Flipper," the judge advocate began in his harsh tongue. "*Kapitän* Parker has been relieved from dis court, and, because of da veather, I need more time to prepare my case. *Mit* no objections, I ask dis court be adjourned until Monday morning at ten o'clock."

That's all? Flipper couldn't tell if he felt relief or a tremendous letdown. After steeling himself for this moment, it had been postponed. He had the rest of today and all of Sunday to wait, to toss and turn, and feel the rats gnawing on his intestines. As he exited the chapel and returned to his quarters, he heard the reporters yelling: "What happened? What happened? Is it over already?"

They didn't bother talking to the subject of their articles. *Parker,* he thought. L. O. Parker was one of Shafter's officers in the 1st. Losing Parker might brighten his own chances. Flipper stopped himself. No use in getting overly excited. He really didn't have a Chinaman's chance against that stacked deck.

Monday came quickly, but Flipper had spent the weekend reading up on his rights. Again, he stood in the chapel as Clous swore in Flipper and the court. Pennypacker swore in Clous.

"*Herr* Flipper," Clous began, "do you object to anyone on dis court?"

He stood erect, proudly. "I have no objections to this glorious court," he said, daring anyone to detect his sarcasm.

"Very vell. It is so noted." Clous read the charges, then, peering above his wire glasses, asked: "You have da right to counsel, Lieutenant, if you so desire."

"I do, sir," Flipper said, introducing a three-page letter in his best handwriting to the court. "And I request sixty days or more to raise funds and find adequate representation."

Clous's frown was ugly. "Ach! Ve vill not. . . ." His eyes blazed, and his lips whitened. After a moment, the German relaxed and requested a brief adjournment. It took Flipper only a handful of seconds to realize that the judge advocate had no idea if he held the authority to grant a continuance. The brief adjournment lasted just long enough to send a telegram and receive an answer from San Antonio.

"Vell," Clous said. "If it please da court, ve vill grant a continuance."

Court would resume at 10 a.m., November 1st. The gavel's *bang* made Flipper jump.

Back in his quarters, Henry Flipper unbuttoned his

blouse and sank on his bed. He had put off the inevitable. He had less than two months to find a lawyer, but where? At least, Shafter had relented to remove the guard posted outside Flipper's quarters, and he more than likely could obtain permission to leave the post and try to get help from his friends in town.

He swung his boots onto the bed and sank into the mattress, covering his eyes with his bare arm. Who was he kidding? Who would help him? He had always been proud, and to ask men—white men—for help, that galled him. To ask them for money. . . . Hell, money had gotten him in this fix to begin with.

"God," he said softly, "oh, God, why me?"

Henry Flipper fell asleep in that position. He dreamed of home.

Chapter Two

Georgia, 1856–1864

His first memories were of his father.

"Try these on, Peanut." His father held out a pair of brogans, and Henry Flipper grabbed them and sat on the floor. He fell on his back, bending both knees to his chest, and pulled on the stiff leather, one foot at a time, then catapulted to his feet, bent to lace up the shoes, and stood with a beaming six-year-old's smile.

"You wear them shoes proudly, Henry," his mother told him. "Ain't many a boy your age gots shoes. You lucky to have a good daddy."

He leaped into his father's arms. Grinning widely, his father tossed him in the air and caught him. "That's my boy," he said. "Now run outside and break in them shoes, Peanut."

A cobbler and carriage repairman, and a good one at that, Festus Flipper was going on twenty-four when Isabella Buckhalter gave birth to their first son. Henry Ossian Flipper arrived in this world, squalling, on a beautiful spring afternoon in the ramshackle slaves' shack of the Reverend Reuben Lucky in Thomasville, Georgia. But it would be a month or so before Festus learned he was a father. He was up in Virginia at the time, learning to fix carriages.

As a child, Henry Flipper had never really resented slavery, maybe because he was so young. Years later, after he had learned to read, he recalled that being property of white folks had been nothing like UNCLE TOM'S CABIN. He would, of course, come to resent his bondage, but, growing up, slavery was all he knew, yet the Flippers were better off than many slaves, even many poor white Georgians. When Henry was born on March 21, 1856, his father was property of Thomasville alderman Ephraim G. Ponder. The Methodist minister, Lucky, owned Isabella. His parents were often separated, but Mr. Ponder let Festus work for wages, plying his trade on boots, brogans, and broken wagons. Festus must have done well, because when Henry was three years old, his father ended that forced separation.

Mr. Ponder had married the beautiful Ellen B. Gregory, rich, radiant, and fourteen years younger than Master Ephraim. Ponder planned on moving to Atlanta to be with his new bride, and that meant Festus would be forced to leave Henry, Isabella, and, now, baby brother Joseph.

"Mas'r Ephraim," Festus said, tears welling in his eyes, "I beg of you, sir, please, don't take me from my family."

Sadly shaking his head, Ponder spanged tobacco juice against the side of a brass cuspidor before answering. "It's out of my hands, Festus."

"You could buy Isabella, Henry, and Joseph from the Reverend Lucky. . . ."

"Cash is a scarce commodity, Festus. I just spent a small fortune on Ellen, built us a nice house, good quarters for you and all my niggers. You'll like Atlanta, Festus. Big city, it is, and you'll be able to save up a lot of money as a cobbler and carriage-trimmer. Maybe in a few years, you can buy your family from Lucky." He picked up a small silver bell and rang it gently. The screen door opened, and fat old Bertha stepped on the porch, saying nothing, simply waiting for her master's orders. "Bertha, bring me some tea."

He was dismissing Festus, only Festus didn't take the hint. Ponder frowned, seeing the slave still standing in front of him, and spit again. This time, he missed the spittoon.

With a sigh, he suggested that Festus ask the Reverend Lucky for help. "I'd be willin' to sell you, Festus, to a righteous Methodist like the Reverend Lucky. He'd treat you right. If memory serves, I bought you at an auction for a tad under two thousand dollars."

"Yes, sir. That's right, sir." It had actually been twenty dollars short of twelve hundred dollars.

"Well, I guess I can see if Reuben's interested."

"I already asked him, Mas'r Ephraim. He ain't got that kind of cash. He's hopin' you'd buy my Isabella and our boys. They's all good workers, Mas'r Ephraim. You won't be sorry. Mas'r Reuben, he says he'd sell 'em to you all for twelve hundred dollars. That's a good deal, sir. Henry and Joseph, they be fine workers, good, strong boys."

"No doubt. But like I said, Festus, times are hard. War talk's gettin' hotter every day. I'd like to help you, Festus. You know I've always been good to all my niggers, but I just don't have that kind of money."

White-haired Bertha opened the door again, and the wooden planks on the porch creaked underneath her weight as she carried a china tray holding a glass of mint julep tea. Ponder took the glass, dismissed his house servant, and took a deep drink, then began fanning himself in the sun.

"Mas'r Ephraim?"

"What?" Ponder's tone was sharp, annoyed at his slave's persistence.

"Suppose I was to loan you the money, sir . . . so's that you could buy my Isabella and my boys?"

Ponder sat up straight in his wicker rocker, spilling some tea on his gray trousers. "You don't have that kind of money!"

"Yes, sir. I do. Been savin'."

"Twelve hundred dollars! Good God, Festus. It would

take some white men six years to save that kind of money. Even longer. How . . . ?" His voice trailed off. He seemed to be in shock.

"Slaves ain't got much to spend money on, Mas'r Ephraim."

Ephraim Ponder smiled suddenly and set his glass on the table at his side. "Festus, you're somethin'. I supposed I could take your loan, talk to Reuben about makin' a deal. You bring me the money, and we'll see what we can do."

"I gots the money right now, Mas'r Ephraim."

Ponder laughed as Festus pulled a dingy canvas pouch from his pocket and began to count out one thousand, two hundred dollars.

Ephraim Ponder lived up to his word, too, because he bought Isabella, Henry, and Joseph from the Reverend Lucky before moving to Atlanta, although, as far as Henry knew, Ponder never paid back that loan.

The Atlanta mansion and slave quarters sat on twenty-six acres off the Marietta Road. The two-story house was made of whitewashed stone, with a beautiful verandah and an observation deck on the roof. Ponder's slaves had three wooden buildings where they lived and worked when not in the gardens. Festus Flipper continued to make shoes and work on carriages on the side, saving his money again.

To break in his new brogans, Henry ran around the square mansion, zigzagging through the lilacs and azaleas, running around and around and around until he circled the corner and slammed into a thick gray leg. A heavy paw grabbed the collar of his shirt, and Henry, dazed from the collision, felt himself being lifted.

"Watch where you're goin', you young fool!"

Henry squeezed his eyelids tighter. He felt the man's hot

breath. "I'm sorry," he managed to mumble. Eyes still closed, he heard the front door to the mansion open and figured he would be in for a beating, his first. Mrs. Ponder would have him whipped, and then Mama would peel his flesh for being a bother.

"Joshua! Don't you look magnificent." Mrs. Ponder's voice sounded musical, and the hairy paw slowly lowered Henry to the ground. His eyes opened, taking in the red-bearded man in a gray uniform with blue braid and a wide-brimmed straw hat tilted at a rakish angle. The man brushed off his hands. Henry wanted to run, but couldn't.

"Thank you, Ellen. But your colored boy here almost spilled me in the dust. He should feel the taste of leather, the whelp."

Henry waited. He looked up the stairs toward Mrs. Ponder, expecting some hideous expression, but she looked as lovely as ever. "Oh, Joshua, he's such a darling boy. And there's no harm done. Come on up, and tell me all about your brave adventures in our glorious Army. Perhaps we can take a stroll to the garden. And Henry Flipper. . . ." Putting both hands on her hips, she forced a stern expression. "You watch yourself, young man. We dare not wish to disable our brave young captain before he can give Yankee tyrants a taste of Georgia steel and shot."

Henry didn't understand the war, nor did he understand Mrs. Ponder. "Shameless," he had heard his mother call Master Ephraim's young wife back in their quarters when she thought Henry was asleep. His father's reply: "Shameless? Lord A'mighty, Mama, she's worser than a whore."

"Watch your mouth, Festus! I don't wants no blasphemy in front of my young 'uns."

Henry didn't know what "shameless" or "whore" meant, or "blasphemy" for that matter. He liked Mrs. Ponder. She

25

was always smiling, giggling, entertaining visitors. He did miss Master Ephraim, although he found it harder and harder to remember the man. His father talked fondly of him. In October of 1861, Ponder had moved back to Thomasville. Afterward, there had been more talk around the Marietta Road mansion with words Henry didn't understand.

One afternoon Henry happened upon Mrs. Ponder sitting on a porch swing, a book in her hand. She looked up and smiled.

"What are you doing, Henry Flipper?"

"Playing. What's you doing, Miz Ellen?"

"Reading."

"What's that?"

She didn't answer. Instead she asked: "How old are you?"

"Six."

"Well, reading is something white folks do."

"Can I do it?"

"You'd have to learn, Henry, and the law doesn't allow it."

"Miz Ellen?"

"Yes, Henry?"

"What's divorce?"

John Quarles might have been the biggest man Henry would ever know. His chest looked bigger than a rain barrel, and his arms bulged against his dirty muslin shirt. A young mulatto with a shaved head, he spent his days in the blacksmith shop, sweating by the forge, repairing wheels, and in the spring of 1864, he turned his wheelwright shop into a school for Henry, Joseph, and several other slave children. He had Mrs. Ponder's blessing.

They—Henry, Joseph, four other boys, and three girls—sat on a bench and watched the giant slave pull a pair of wire-rim spectacles from his vest pocket and turn up the lanterns that gave the wheelwright shop an eerie glow. Next, Mr. Quarles opened a canvas sack and pulled out a book. "This, children," he said, "is a Webster's BLUE-BACK SPELLER." Quarles laughed heartily. "Actually, it's a Confederate reprint of Mister Webster's lesson book, but I reckon it'll learn you well enough." He walked forward and handed the book to Henry. Henry had never held a book before. He didn't know what he should do.

"Open it, Henry," Quarles said lightly. "Open it and you'll find the answers to many of your questions."

Tentatively he turned the cover.

"This book," Quarles said, "will teach you the three Rs. And once you know and understand the three Rs, you can solve just about any mystery there is. Who knows what the three Rs are?"

Sally Greene's hand shot up. "I know, Mister Johnny. I know."

"What are they, Sally?"

"Readin', 'ritin' and . . . and . . . and. . . ." She pouted.

" 'Rithmetic," Quarles filled in.

" 'Rithmetic. I's plumb sorry, Mister Johnny."

The war had come to Georgia. Henry had seen the weary, gaunt men in drab gray and butternut uniforms stumbling down the Marietta Road, raising thick clouds of dust as summer dragged toward fall. He felt sorry for those men. Why, most of them didn't have any shoes, and he thought, if they just stopped to see his father, well, his father could fix them up just fine. But they seldom stopped, except the occasional straggler who wanted water. Sometimes at night he thought he heard the rumble of cannon, although he wasn't sure what a cannon sounded like. Poor Mrs. Ponder, with her forgotten husband living in Thomasville, never had many visitors any more.

A buggy pulled up. At first Henry thought the driver might want his father to fix it because the wagon stopped in front of Mr. Quarles's wheelwright shop. The pale man with the unkempt red beard wrapped the reins around the brake, grabbed a crutch, and, with a groan and an oath, stepped to the ground. Henry gawked at the man's left trouser leg pinned up above his knee.

"What you lookin' at, boy?" the man growled, and Henry ran away.

He watched the one-legged man go inside the shop. A few minutes later, the man returned, ripping one of Mr. Quarles's BLUEBACK SPELLERS in half and tossing the torn book to the dirt. He limped until he stood in front of the steps to the two-story house, reached inside his gray coat pocket, and pulled out a small bottle from which he drank. At last, the man, ignoring the slaves gathering on the grounds to watch, called out: "Ellen! Ellen Gregory Ponder, you nigger-lovin' wench. Come outside, damn you!"

She stepped onto the veranda, the screen door slamming behind her, and halted on the top step, a shotgun in her hands. Henry suddenly realized how much older Mrs. Ponder looked.

"Good day, Joshua," she said evenly.

Henry remembered the man as one of Mrs. Ponder's guests, the fellow he had charged into when he was playing two years ago. *Gosh,* he thought, *what had happened to the man's leg?*

"They told me in town," he said, his words a thick slur, "but I said, no, not my Ellen. She wouldn't break the law,

28

wouldn't teach her niggers to read and write. You pathetic little. . . ." He planted his crutch on the bottom step, but Mrs. Ponder raised the shotgun.

"Not one step farther, Joshua Wilkinson."

Captain Wilkinson glared and cursed. "You'd shoot me, after us havin' some high ol' times on those paths back of this place?"

She smiled. "Would you expect less from some 'nigger-lovin' wench' who'd dare to ignore the Georgia Penal Code?"

The visitor moved the crutch. "I ought to. . . ." He couldn't seem to think of the words, so he took another drink. "Just tell me why," he said at last.

"To help them," she said, lowering the single barrel of the long gun.

"Them?"

"They'll be free soon, Joshua. You know that as well as I."

"No!" his voice thundered. "No, I will not listen to such sedition!"

"Joshua, the war is over."

"No. Damn you. Damn it. It's not lost. Not by a damn' sight." He mumbled something else, but Henry couldn't make out the words. The man's head dropped, and he stayed in that position for a long while, chest heaving, leaning heavily on the crutch. Finally he muttered something underneath his breath and staggered back to the buggy. Once he fell, but when Mr. Quarles stepped forward to help, Captain Joshua Wilkinson slapped the wheel-wright's arm and swore savagely: "Don't touch me! Don't you never touch me."

He pulled himself up, made it to the buggy, and drove back toward the city.

★ ★ ★ ★ ★

More Confederate soldiers came the following day. These, however, stopped, and a man in a dusty gray uniform reined in a buckskin gelding in front of Mrs. Ponder's house. This time, she greeted the visitor without a shotgun.

Sweeping his hat from his steel-gray hair, the man said: "With my greatest apologies, Missus Ponder, I fear we must take residence at your estate."

"The Yankees are that close?" she asked.

"Yes, ma'am. We'll be needin' to throw up some breast-works, Missus Ponder. Likely put a sniper on your roof there."

"And what of us, Colonel?"

He shook his head. "I'd advise you to leave at once," he said softly. "Yankee vermin will be upon us quickly."

That evening, Henry's mother and father began packing their belongings in a hand-me-down carpetbag and sacks. His father removed the plank underneath his bed and pulled up a canvas bag, stuffing it in his pants pocket.

"Get your shoes on, Henry," his mother said.

"Where we going?" he asked.

"Miz Ellen's takin' us to Macon. Now do as I tells you."

"But what about my schooling?"

"Be no schoolin' tonight, dear."

"But. . . ."

"Do as you're told!" his father shouted, and his father never raised his voice.

He didn't know what a Yankee would look like. To hear Mrs. Ponder and other white folks talk, they were three-headed monsters that did bad things to women, ate babies, white and colored, and burned everything in their paths like dragons. But the way Sally Greene's mother saw them,

Yankees were tall men with white hair and flowing mustaches and goatees, honest, brave soldiers who would set the coloreds free just like Mr. Abraham Lincoln wanted. When Henry asked John Quarles about Yankees, the wheelwright merely smiled and answered: "They are just people, Henry. No different than me or you in God's eyes. No different than Master Ephraim or Captain Wilkinson. You'll find some good, some better, and just as likely some bad."

Yet the first Yankees he ever saw scared the hell out of him. He watched them stumble down the streets of Macon that winter, wretched skeletons in mere rags. For almost a year now, Henry had felt the pinch of hunger—food was scarce, the adults kept saying, because the Yankees were burning everything in their path. The cost of everything from sugar to flour to fruits and vegetables had soared, and his mother and father were burning grain and calling it coffee—but never had he seen men suffering like these. Others, too weak to walk, sat like corpses in lumbering wagons driven by somber-looking men with their heads hanging down.

"God have mercy on their souls," his mother whispered.

"Who are they, Mama?"

"Yankee soldiers," his father answered. "Just paroled from Andersonville."

A week later, he saw healthier Federals, with stained and soiled blue uniforms, dark coats and lighter pants, with unshaven faces and hard eyes. These must have been Sherman's Yankees, but they didn't look like the mutated monsters he had heard described. Neither did they resemble the seven-foot-tall heroes Mrs. Greene depicted, nor those Greek warriors Mr. Quarles told of when reading from that stirring book by Homer. One soldier, with blond hair and sky-colored eyes, kept searching in his haversack, stumbling, and stepped out of line, stopping in front of Henry and his parents. He fumbled in the sack before realizing their presence after pulling out a green apple.

"Hello," the man said, dropping to a knee and smiling at Henry. "What's your name?"

Henry stepped back toward his parents.

"I won't bite," the Yankee said. "My name's Hartsell. Henry Hartsell."

Henry looked up at his father for advice. When his father nodded, Henry faced the Yankee again and said: "My name's Henry, too."

"How 'bout that? Y'all are free now. How does that feel?"

Not knowing what to say, Henry only shrugged.

The Yankee offered the apple, but Henry shook his head. "Go ahead," Henry Hartsell said. "Take it."

Once more, Henry sought out his father's help, and, at another nod, he stepped forward and took the fruit. Smiling, the Yankee named Henry rubbed the eight-year-old's hair and marched on.

Henry followed the Yankee with his eyes until Henry Hartsell disappeared. Then he stared at the apple, not knowing if he should eat it now or later. He never got to choose.

A heavy hand snatched the apple, and Henry staggered, shocked, as a burly man with a black beard put the fruit to his mouth. The apple crunched, and, while still chewing, the Yankee said, spitting out bits of fruit as he talked: "Did you see that fool Hartsell? Sum-bitch, what's he doin' wastin' food on a darky runt?"

Chapter Three

September 20–October 17, 1881

His timing needed improvement. Flipper opened the door and stepped into the narrow hallway that divided the officers' duplex just as First Lieutenant Charles Nordstrom took Mollie Dwyer's arm. All three stood silently in the common hallway, exchanging stares. Flipper's eyes looked blank, Mollie's shamed, and Nordstrom's dulled like a rattlesnake's. The awkwardness of the moment stretched into eternity. No one knew what to say. If Nordstrom had any decency, he would escort Mollie outside, not speaking, just leaving, but God had deliberately left out any decency when He created this monster. Nordstrom stood there, inwardly gloating, enjoying this form of torture.

An eon later, Mollie broke the silence. "It's good to see you, Henry," she said, her voice soft. She looked away as soon as she finished, staring at the spur-scratched, dusty wooden floor.

"You look well, Miss Dwyer," Flipper answered, his firm voice hiding the unsettling of his stomach. "Well, I mustn't keep you from your picnic. Enjoy yourselves." He tipped his hat, smiled, and walked outside, where he turned sharply to his left and marched to Wade Hampton's quarters. He wanted to throw up. Hampton would call that love, but Flipper denied this, even after everything that had happened. They had been great friends, yet somehow he felt she was the reason for his torment. Not that Mollie had been a willing party to the traps that snared him, that threatened his military career, not Mollie. That wasn't her style. His fellow officers never could accept the fact that the lovely blonde-headed sister-in-law of Captain Nicholas Nolan, Flipper's troop commander, would make a habit of going on horseback rides with a man of color. Mollie Dwyer may have dropped the formalities, but Flipper wouldn't. "Yes, ma'am." "You're welcome, Miss Dwyer." "Allow me to saddle your horse, Miss Mollie."

He thought back to Fort Elliott up in the Texas Panhandle, and of a first sergeant's advice to a 10th Cavalry trooper who kept frequenting a certain white soiled dove in one of the dreary establishments of nearby Mobeetie. "White woman ain't nothin' but trouble for a nigger, and out here you's just a swamp-runnin' nigger no matter what uniform you wears. Even if she's a whore, you do better by stickin' to your own kind. You go to that well once too often, you be drowned."

Three weeks later, Lieutenant Flipper and First Sergeant James Watts organized a burial party for the love-struck trooper, shot dead in a Mobeetie whorehouse by party or parties unknown. Maybe Flipper should have applied the sergeant's advice to himself. Maybe he should have learned that the uniform he wore didn't hide the color of his skin. When he wore the blue for the first time, he saw himself as a man, not a black man, just a man, an officer and a gentleman, an equal to those of his grade, soldier, first and foremost. But Charles Nordstrom and others of his ilk viewed him as something lower. What was it he had heard Lieutenant Charles R. Ward say, that is before the drunken lout found himself court-martialed earlier this year and dismissed from the Army?

"Don't get me wrong, boys. I don't have a thing against darkies. Hell, I think every man should own at least one or two."

The officers listening to Ward's banter had laughed. They didn't know Flipper could hear them, but he doubted if it would have mattered if they had.

Of the entire miserable lot, Nordstrom was the worst. An unintelligent brute, the Swede had come up through the ranks, joining the 1st Maine as a private during the Civil War. After the war, he was commissioned a second lieutenant in the newly formed 10th Cavalry and promoted to first lieutenant in 1869. Gruff, shaped like a grizzly with a temperament to match, Nordstrom once clubbed First Sergeant James Watts repeatedly in a San Angelo watering hole near Fort Concho. It took one of the 10th's civilian scouts, the saloon's bouncer, and Lieutenant Leighton Finley to pull the hellion outside while he screamed: "I serve with them every damned day! I don't have to drink with the Jim Crows." It didn't matter that Sergeant Watts had been ordered to find Nordstrom and tell him to report to Colonel Grierson. Finley brought up charges of gross misconduct against Nordstrom, and, when found guilty, the wretch had been fined fifteen dollars and told to watch his temper.

Had it been the other way around—had Watts struck Nordstrom—Flipper knew the sergeant would be doing hard time at Fort Leavenworth's penitentiary. Or, in a wicked little Sodom like San Angelo, he'd be dead for striking a white man. If Henry Flipper had dared to assault a non-commissioned officer, black or white, he would have been drummed out of the service.

Wade Hampton lived in the relatively new two-story bachelors' quarters built just off the northwest corner of the parade grounds. The door was open to the lieutenant's upstairs apartment, and Hampton sat on his bunk, pulling on his boots, when Flipper tapped on the doorjamb.

"You're up early, Mistah Flipper," the Southerner drawled as he leaned back on his bed and groaned. The boot finally made a slight *whoosh*, and Hampton grunted, satisfied, and stood.

"It's nine o'clock, Wade."

"But I'm off duty." Hampton smiled.

So did Flipper.

"Let's not keep the good attorney waitin'," Hampton said. "After all, it is Sunday." His shiny boots squeaked as he crossed the room and grabbed a tan slouch hat hanging on an elk horn.

They walked downstairs, crossed the parade ground, and obtained two horses from the sprawling adobe corrals that lay just across the old Overland Trail. It felt good to be in a saddle, Flipper thought. It felt even better to be leaving the post. They gave their horses plenty of rein, moving from canter to gallop and kicking up dust as bells chimed from the Catholic chapel and a dog barked somewhere in the town of Fort Davis.

"Thank you for seeing me on the Sabbath," Flipper told Hugh Corby, attorney-at-law. The man nodded slightly, sipped his coffee, and motioned for the two officers to have a seat.

They had met in a small café across the street from the two-story Fort Davis Academy in Newtown. Only Flipper, Hampton, and Corby, plus a plump Mexican waitress and a graybeard cook, were in the adobe building.

Corby wore a suit of black broadcloth with a light blue shirt, ill-fitting paper collar, and narrow red and white polka dot necktie. Silver spectacles pinched his hawkish nose and highlighted the attorney's bloodshot gray eyes. His gray derby rested on the rough-hewn cedar table. A pale man in his mid-forties, Hugh Corby looked tall, even while slumping in the uncomfortable chair, both elbows on the table, trying to steady the tin cup with both hands. *Hung over*, Flipper thought, *or maybe still drunk*.

At last, he placed the cup on the table and ran his fingers through his greasy black hair. "I've read the charges and specifications," he said, his eyes focused on Flipper only briefly before turning toward the waitress and saying: *"Dos cafés, por favor."* Corby shook his head as the woman walked to the kitchen. "Lieutenant Hampton has filled me in on the other details. Damn' shame what they're trying to do to you, Lieutenant Flipper. But that's the Army for you."

"You served in the Army?"

Corby smiled. His white teeth surprised Flipper. Most teeth out here were a crooked yellow or brown. "Twelfth Tennessee under Colonel Samuel Marks before he was mortally wounded at Shiloh. Pittsburg Landing to you Yanks. I caught a Minié ball there myself, in my right leg. But Rebel or Yank, gray or blue, the Army's still the same. Jackasses everywhere. Not much different than Texas court-rooms."

The waitress returned with two mugs for Flipper and Hampton, then wandered away. Corby sipped some more before returning to his original position, elbows on table, slumped forward, weary, weathered, bored.

"Are you interested in taking my case, sir?" It amazed Flipper how hard it was to ask the question. He had always been a little shy, especially around white men, not to mention proud.

The attorney nodded. "I'll take it. Understand that my only dealings with military courts-martial were in the Army of the Tennessee twenty years back. And the deck's stacked against you, Lieutenant. It's a hard case to win, and it'll cost you. Plenty."

Flipper swallowed. "How much?"

"A thousand dollars. Up front."

He shook his head sadly. "I haven't that kind of money, sir."

"Good." Corby drank some, then set the coffee on the table. "If you had, I might begin to think there's some truth to that embezzlement charge. You think you can raise it?"

"Where? How?"

Corby shrugged. "You have friends in this hamlet, Mister Flipper. White men. Some of them wealthy. They've supported you since you arrived at the fort. You would think they'd ante up now to clear your name."

"You'd think." Wade Hampton didn't bother hiding the bitterness in his voice. He had already gone fishing for some financial aid in town. Some said they would gladly testify on Flipper's behalf, and Flipper hated asking them for anything else. Besides, many had loaned him money to cover the missing funds he allegedly owed the government, the missing cash and checks that led to the embezzlement charge. Although he had paid back those loans, Flipper and Hampton knew the well, for the most part, had gone dry. Times had been hard this summer, and folks were taking the wait-and-see attitude. Some money undoubtedly could be raised, but not a thousand-dollar retainer.

The room fell silent except for the lawyer's slurping. Finished, he dropped a coin on the table, picked up his hat, and stood, the interview over.

Flipper looked up. The man had to be a good six foot four.

"If you wish to obtain my services, I'll be around. If not, I understand and wish you luck. Good day, gentlemen."

Hampton pushed his cup around, eyes blank, shaking his head. Flipper knew Hampton's thoughts. Most of his civilian friends were businessmen, and helping Flipper's cause was bad business, and bad for business. After all, they were white. The support he had already received had cost some of the merchants a few customers. Flipper wondered if a thousand dollars was a fair fee, or if Hugh Corby was trying to take advantage of him.

"You can always ask an officer for help," Hampton finally said. "That won't cost you a penny. Against Army regs to charge a fee."

Shaking his head, Flipper straightened. "No. I don't think so."

"You're too damned mule-headed, Henry."

"I'll go it alone. There's few men on this post I trust."

"How 'bout me?"

Flipper forced a smile. "Thanks, Wade. But it would ruin your career."

"Yours, too, friend. 'Cause I am no lawyer. And, by the way, my career's already ruined. But I tell you what I will do, Henry. I'll request a leave. The Army owes me that much. And I'll head East, see what kind of support I can drum up for you. Money, I mean."

"From your uncle?"

Hampton's laughter rocked the rickety table. "The good senator would never get reëlected in South Carolina, Mistah Flipper, if he did that. But I might be able to track down some Negro leaders in Washington, Philadelphia, see what they can do. Don't worry, Henry. I'll try to be back before your court-martial."

They shook hands and walked outside to the hitching post. Wade Hampton was a friend, but he was leaving. Flipper would find himself alone once more.

* * * * *

He felt like a condemned man, counting the days before the hangman and priest arrived at his cell. Hampton had been gone a month, but his wires offered no signs of help. Business men and black leaders politely declined to help, financially or otherwise, Lieutenant Henry Ossian Flipper. Perhaps they didn't believe in his innocence. Maybe they didn't care what happened on the Texas frontier. More than likely, though, they just felt it unwise to choose sides one way or the other.

Alone. He had traveled that path before. Besides, who knew the truth of his case better than himself? So he immersed himself in law books, in Army manuals, poring over page after page at the post library, reading until his eyes hurt from the strain, taking notes until his fingers cramped. Sometimes he found himself sharing the library with Judge Advocate Clous. On those times he felt the tension, heavier than even when he met Lieutenant Nordstrom in the shared hall of their quarters. The German never spoke to Flipper, seldom made eye contact, and they sat in silence while pencils scratched and pages turned.

Alone. The calendar showed October 17th. Two weeks before the proceedings resumed, and he had no money and no lawyer. He sat on his bunk, shuffling through the mail, a letter from Homer Lee & Company of New York, publisher of his West Point memoirs, but it contained no royalty check, just a brief note wishing him well. Another was from his brother, Joseph Simeon Flipper, in Georgia. A third envelope, military issue, with handwriting Flipper didn't recognize, had been posted at Fort McKavett, about two hundred miles east of the Davis Mountains on the San Saba River. Flipper didn't know anyone stationed at McKavett.

He ripped open the envelope and saw the name signed in

a flowery script: **Merritt Barber, Captain, 16th U.S. Infantry**. He didn't know Barber, but he read, barely able to conceal his excitement as the words struck home.

Sir:

I have the honor to inform you that I have read with a mixture of interest and appall the charges and specifications you now face. These accusations are unjust, unbefitting an officer and a gentleman, and I am called to act.

I feel it is my duty to offer my services as a defense counsel. As you are well aware, the Army prohibits officers from accepting payment as legal counsel during a court-martial. Yet even if I could charge a fee, I would not, because I am convinced of your innocence and the injustice of these sham charges.

If you wish to accept me as your counsel, please so advise at your earliest convenience and I will join you at Fort Davis.

> I remain your obt. servant,
> Merritt Barber
> Captain
> 16th U.S. Infantry

His excitement waned, replaced by suspicion. A crank? Some white officer's idea of a joke? Maybe the letter hadn't been written by Barber, but someone else. Why would any white officer want to defend a man of color? The 16th wasn't even a Negro regiment.

Flipper thought about this only briefly before grabbing his kepi and hurrying to the post library. He located the ARMY REGISTER and looked up this Merritt Barber. A native of Vermont, Barber had enlisted in the Union Army during the Rebellion and quickly rose to the rank of major, brevetted a brigadier general, then received a commission in the regular Army after the war. He had also served as judge advocate. More research revealed that Barber studied law under Chester A. Arthur—that would now be President Arthur—and had been admitted to the bar in 1859, two years after he had been graduated from Williams College. He seemed to be a sharp administrator and sound attorney.

Still Flipper felt reserved, unsure. He returned the book to its proper place and wandered across the post, not sure where he was going until he found himself knocking on the door of Captain Nolan's quarters.

Annie Nolan opened the door. She was still in her twenties—the captain was more than twice her age—and beautiful, like her sister. At first, Annie thought Flipper had come calling on Mollie, and she started to tell him Mollie had gone horseback riding with Charles Nordstrom, but she caught herself and looked away.

"How are you holding up, Henry?" she asked.

"I'm doing fine, Miss Nolan. Is it possible to speak to the captain, ma'am?"

"Certainly. Come. Sit in the parlor. I'll tell Nicholas you're here."

Irish-born, green-eyed Nicholas Nolan had been a soldier for almost thirty years, rising from the rank of private in 1852 to lieutenant during the Civil War and now captain, commander of A Troop, 10th Cavalry. Thin, leathery, haggard, he looked much older than his fifty odd years as he entered the parlor with a tumbler half full of Irish whisky in his right hand and sat on a well-worn bed lounge across from Flipper.

"Lieutenant?" he said softly, his voice a thick brogue.

"Captain, I wonder if I can ask your advice?"

"Any time. Would you care for a whisky . . . or tea? I think Annie has made some lemonade."

"Thank you, no, sir." He cleared his throat, forced himself to meet his captain's stare. "I received a letter from a captain at Fort McKavett. He is offering to defend me at the court-martial. But I don't know this man, sir, or even if he wrote the letter. It could be a joke."

"An unfunny one if that be the case. Who is this man, Lieutenant?"

"Merritt Barber, sir. He says he's with the Sixteenth Infantry."

Nolan sipped his Jameson before answering. "Captain Barber's a good man. I dare say that letter is no joke."

"You think I should take his offer?"

The captain cleared his throat. "Lieutenant," he said, straightening on the sofa, his voice firm, powerful, honest, "Merritt Barber is likely the only chance you have of saving your career. If I were you, I'd fire off a letter to Fort McKavett and tell the captain to come quick. This is one journey you don't want to travel alone, Henry."

That last sentence echoed through Flipper's mind during the night as he lay on his cot, thinking.

Chapter Four

Georgia, 1865–1873

He woke with a start, his mother's arms tight against his chest, trying to hold him steady while the screeching of metal against metal hurt his ears, and sooty air filled with cinders teared his eyes. Clutching Joseph and the new baby, Festus Junior, his father leaned back with all his strength while the Georgia piney woods passed before them and the train squealed to a stop. As soon as all movement stopped, Isabella released Henry, who stared outside at the spindly, blackened remains of pine forest. Festus Flipper placed Joseph on the hay-covered floor. The infant—startled but quiet—was in Isabella's arms. Cautiously his father leaned out the freight car.

"Wait here," he said, and leaped outside.

Winter had passed into spring, and with the new season came word that Robert E. Lee had surrendered the Army of Northern Virginia to Grant at some courthouse in Virginia. Shortly after that, General Johnston handed his sword to Sherman in North Carolina, and General Taylor surrendered twelve thousand troops in southern Alabama. President Jefferson Davis had been captured—dressed as a woman, so the stories went. Mr. Lincoln was dead, but the war was over. Georgia, and the South, had lost.

Mrs. Ponder had told the Flippers and her other servants that they were free now. Free. Just like the Yankee soldier had said back in December. She had tried to make light of it, telling them: "I won't be able to threaten to send y'all to Red River any more." But she couldn't hide her tears, and

44

many of her slaves, even Henry's mother, had cried that day.

They packed what little they had in haversacks and two carpetbags. Festus wanted to settle in Atlanta, saying he could make a better living there, and they could catch a freight train in Macon and be on their way. He would return for his lasts and other equipment once he had the family settled in. Before they left, though, Festus handed a money belt he had made, stuffed with coins, to his oldest son. Henry took it, uncertain. His father smiled. "Strap it over your belly, Henry, an' pull your shirt down to hides it. I don't thinks we have nothin' to worry 'bout, but you never know. Anyhows, bein' a boy, you stands less of a chance of bein' searched iffen we be robbed."

Proud that his father would trust him with their fortune, he hitched up the belt, although Festus had to punch another hole in the leather so the belt would stay up. He also felt a mixture of nerves and excitement at this trip. Would they be robbed? What would he do if someone pulled a gun on him? The belt felt heavy around his body. Henry pointed to the paper money his father had left behind in a worn-out flour sack. "What about that money?" he asked.

His father laughed. "Don't think Confederate script will buy us nothin' no more," he said.

Having never been on a train, Henry couldn't help but smile as his father shoved him through the open door of the empty freight car. "Help your brother," Festus said, and Henry took Joseph's hands and pulled him inside. Next came the carpetbags and haversacks, followed by Isabella, holding the baby, and Festus. They gathered their belongings and found a spot on the rear wall.

"Best get some shut-eye, childrens," Festus said, but Henry knew he wouldn't fall asleep, especially once the car lurched, steam hissed from the ugly locomotive, and the train began belching and squeaking as it pulled out of Macon. A short while later, though, the rocking motion and easy rhythm of the train forced Henry to close his eyes. He didn't wake up until the train suddenly stopped.

His father was gone only a couple of minutes.

"What's the matter?" Isabella asked once he returned.

"Rails torn all asunder," he said grimly. "It was the Yankees that done it. Anyhows, we at Jonesboro. Reckon I can hires us a wagon to take us the rest of the way."

"Best not let your wife or young 'uns see this," the wagon driver said, and his father barked an order for Henry to cover Joseph's eyes and turn the other way.

He obeyed, even though Joseph squirmed. The mules pulling the wagon snorted, and the mulatto driver spit out a mouthful of tobacco juice. Henry held his eyes shut, facing west, until he heard his mother gasp and begin muttering a prayer. "Good God," his father said, and Henry forced himself to sneak a peek.

They were passing some sort of cemetery, only Henry had never seen one this large, or so poorly maintained. A hog rooted near one shallow grave; another gnawed on a decaying arm that protruded from the soil. Skeletons littered the ground, and the stench overpowered everyone on the wagon. Even the driver gagged. Henry fought back the bile rising in his throat, praying that the mules would hurry, but they kept their tiresome pace. His mouth fell open, despite the unpalatable odor, and his eyes widened as the wagon crawled past a grove of trees. A dozen men, maybe more, in Confederate butternut swung in the rancid breeze beneath the limbs of giant oaks. They had been hanged, not with ropes, but with grapevines.

* * * * *

Atlanta lay in ruins, nothing like the fancy city he remembered of less than a year earlier. Chimneys dotted the landscape like tombstones, towering monuments of what once had been glorious homes. Thick pine woods had been thinned out, fields laid to waste, and many wells salted. Henry wondered how his old home had fared, but they did not drive by the Ponder estate that first day. Instead, the wagon driver let them off, and they walked through the rubble toward city hall.

An American flag draped the staff in the heat of the afternoon. Tents lined up row after row along the once pristine lawn. Swallowing, his father motioned for Isabella and the children to remain while he walked toward the Yankee soldiers. Henry gasped when one of the men raised his musket at his father and yelled: "Halt!"

He couldn't hear much of the conversation, only saw his father's gestures. A minute later, the sentry yelled for an officer, and a corn-haired man, puffing on a clay pipe, joined the discussion. Another soldier approached them a short while later, said something to the other white men, and walked with Festus back toward Isabella, Joseph, Festus Junior, and Henry.

"Hey there," the Yankee said, dropping to his knee and extending his right hand toward Henry. "Remember me?"

Henry shook his head.

"Private Henry Hartsell, Second Massachusetts. I gave you an apple back in Macon around Christmas time."

Henry cowered behind his mother, but the Yankee didn't seem offended. "He's a shy one, but that's all right. I'll help find you a place to stay. You have to be careful. Lot of the buildings are barely standing, but we'll do you right."

Private Hartsell did, carrying the carpetbag Isabella had

47

been wielding, and escorting them to a fine two-story house near what once had been Atlanta's booming business district. Not only that, but once Festus had his shoe shop operating, the Massachusetts soldier began bringing others to the house. Isabella would cook them meals, and Festus would mend their brogans and boots. Henry began helping his father on the lasts. The soldiers always were polite, not like the Yankee who had stolen Henry's apple, and they paid for the meals and footwear with Yankee greenbacks.

"Hey, Top Soldier," Private Hartsell addressed Henry one morning. He held out his hand, and they shook, Henry's grin stretching across his face.

Isabella opened the screen door and smiled. "You just et less'n an hour ago, and your shoes looks fines, Mistah Private. So what brings you this way?"

As Hartsell straightened, his smile vanished. "Well, ma'am, I came to say good bye."

"Good bye?" This came from a shocked Henry.

The soldier forced a grin. "We're being transferred. Just wanted to say how much we all appreciate what you have done for us. . . ."

"You done a world for us," his mother interjected.

"Our pleasure, ma'am. We'll be moving along at first light. Anyway, we thought you might need some provisions." He faced across the street and nodded at a squad of other bluecoats. They swarmed the house, hauling barrels of flour and apples, sacks of beans and potatoes, tins of peaches, one jug of corn whisky, a cured ham, and side of bacon.

"A present," Hartsell said, "from the Volunteer Army of the United States of America."

Henry watched the soldiers march down the street as his mother cried, praising God for kind men like Private Henry

Hartsell and the Massachusetts infantrymen. Henry Ossian Flipper decided then that he would be a soldier when he grew up.

They moved to a shack on Decatur Street, where Festus began making and repairing shoes and boots in a brick shop in front of their new home. More and more people, white and black, returned to Atlanta. Saws whined and hammers pounded from sunrise to sunset. When the Flippers got neighbors, a white couple, Festus fretted, but Isabella brought them a pecan pie. "It don't matter iffen they be white or like us," she told her husband. "They be our neighbors, and I's bein' neighborly. Besides, we all free now. Mistah Lincoln made it so."

Festus grunted and reached for the brown clay jug Private Hartsell had left him. "Mama," he said, "Mistah Lincoln is gone to glory. And iffen you ain't noticed, that man of the house still be wearin' a Reb jacket."

His mother grunted something and went about her business. But when the Confederate captain knocked on the door the next morning, it was Isabella, bulging with another child on the way, who trembled.

Festus opened the door and took the proffered pie plate with trembling hands.

"That," the captain drawled, "was mighty neighborly of you. And may I say it was the best pecan pie I have ever tasted?"

Captain and Mrs. Christopher Jones would return the favor six weeks later. While Isabella and Mary Alma Jones shared coffee one morning, Henry's mother blurted out how she wished her children could get an education. Isabella had learned to read and spell, but Festus couldn't tell a number from a letter and had no inclination to learn.

If only her boys could—well, she would feel a burden lifted. She'd teach them herself, but she had not the time, what with her constantly cooking for folks in Atlanta, or the knowledge. Henry and Joseph had already had some schooling, but not since they had been forced to Macon a year ago.

Mary Alma Jones placed her coffee cup on the table. "Why, Miz Isabella, why didn't you mention this to me before? I would be quite happy to tutor your darling boys."

"Tutor?"

"Teach."

Henry didn't like Mrs. Jones as much as Mr. Quarles, but she was patient, always smiling, and she opened up a world of Dickens, Dumas, Cooper, Hawthorne, and Balzac. It was during his studies with her that they both learned that he had a head for numbers.

"You should be an engineer, Henry," she told him.

"No, ma'am," he said. "I'm going to be a soldier."

The lessons, however, ended abruptly when the Joneses moved to Augusta, and a short while later the Flippers bought a new house and shop a block east on Decatur Street. Henry figured his education was finished until his mother enrolled Joseph and him in the new American Missionary Association School, first housed in a dilapidated old church and later in an old railroad car. Two years later, Henry and Joseph entered the Storr's School, and in 1869, when Atlanta Normal School opened, they attended it.

The oldest pair of the Flipper sons, now numbering five, loved their newfound knowledge, but took separate paths. Henry enjoyed numbers, math equations, probability and percentages, logic and history. Joseph wanted Bible studies, and took to reading passages from the Good Book to his mother each night. Even though Isabella could read herself, she had to sound out the words, stumbling through Deuter-onomy, Hosea, and other Old Testament books.

He was sixteen, sorting through his father's lasts, when he overheard a customer mention an opening at West Point. "You should try to get Henry an appointment," the man said.

Festus shook his head. "Don't know nothin' 'bouts that," he said. "A Yankee soldier said the same thing to me 'bout six, seven years back, and I said no-sirree-Bob. Too far from home."

"He'd do well."

His father scoffed. "You know they won't treat coloreds right at that academy."

When the customer had gone, Henry told his father: "I think I would like to try for an appointment, Dad."

"Boy, you don't know nothin' 'bout dem things."

He held his ground, surprised at his courage. "I know I want to be a soldier."

Festus's eyes hardened. He tapped a small peg into a heel, lowered the mallet, and faced his son. "Then join up, Henry. I can't stops you. They got them colored regiments out West, fightin' Injuns and the likes."

"But an officer, Dad. I could be an officer." He liked the sound of the word. Officer. Lieutenant Flipper. General H. O. Flipper. Wouldn't that be something! He saw himself at the head of the long gray line at the United States Military Academy. Often he had listened to his teachers at the Normal School talk of West Point, say how Henry should try for an appointment. He wanted to be a soldier, desired the education, and had the right temperament for the military. Yet they cautioned him. West Point was tough on anyone, but it would be harder for him, they warned, because of his color.

Henry handed his father the last. He examined it and gave it back. "It's the wrong one, boy." The conversation was over.

For the next two nights, he poked at his supper, barely speaking to his father, until Sunday evening. "Our boy," Festus announced after grace, "wants to be a officer an' gentleman in the United States Army."

Joseph smirked, but his mother beamed. Henry looked up from his ham and cabbage, studying his father tentatively. "I'd always hoped you'd be a cobbler, like me, or somethin', but I guess that would be holdin' you back, Son. Reckon a military education is free, be goods for you." Festus paused, swallowed, pulled a piece of yellow paper from his trouser pocket, and passed it to his oldest son. "You gots to write to this here James C. Freeman. He's a Republican . . . like President Lincoln was . . . from the Fifth District. That's ourn. He can help you out, I'm told, iffen you're sure that's the way you wants to go."

Blinking, Henry tried to speak, but couldn't. His mother beamed. Tears welled in his father's eyes, in Henry's own.

"You. . . ." He tried again. "I thought you didn't want me to go."

"I don't. I thought 'bout it hard. But you's my oldest boy, Henry. You gots to follow your own path. So I got that Mistah Freeman's address for you."

Ripping open the envelope, he scanned the letter dated January 23, 1873, reading as fast as he could, his heart pounding. The beating skipped, and Henry groaned. **You are a stranger to me, and before I can comply with your request you must get your teacher and other Republicans to endorse you. Give me assurance you are**

**worthy and well qualified and I will recommend you.
Yours respectfully, J. C. Freeman.**

The correspondence, however, continued. His teachers
at the Normal School helped, as did those at Atlanta University, even a female student there named Anna White to
whom he had taken a shine. He studied as hard as he
could, reading until his eyes burned. James C. Freeman,
Henry decided, wanted to make sure that the first Negro
he recommended for appointment to the United States
Military Academy would not fail. Henry couldn't fault the
man for that. After all, he was a politician, and just
backing a boy of color would cost him votes, maybe the
next election. Freeman sent Henry a list of the physical re-
quirements and recommended a doctor to examine the
would-be cadet. That was easy. The next meetings were
harder. He was tested on history, math, geography. The
questions and answers blurred. He had to think about easy
questions like: if 48 cords of wood cost $120, how much
will 20 cords cost?—what is the sum of 1/5, 3/5 and 2/5?—
what is the capital of Mississippi, and on what river is it
situated?

When Atlanta Collector of Revenue J. A. Holtzclaw examined the papers, he looked up at Henry from his desk, removed his wire spectacles, and smiled. "You're one bright
lad, Mister Flipper."

Not everyone seemed so enthused. Henry stopped
reading the scathing editorials in the Democrat Georgia
newspapers, and ignored the taunts from whites, and some
blacks, as he walked to Atlanta University where he was
beginning his freshman collegiate studies. They would
snap their heels and fire off salutes. "Major Flipper!" the
friendlier ones would call out. "Officer Charcoal!" others
cried.

He opened one letter, postmarked in Griffin, where Mr. Freeman had a farm, and saw an anti-Flipper editorial ripped from the *Griffin News*. Scrawled in dried blood across the smeared newsprint were the words: **Die, Nigger, Die.** A week later, he found another letter waiting for him, this one from New York.

Boy:

You may be smart enough to earn an appointment to the academy, but that don't mean squat once you come up here. Just ask your buddy Cadet Smith. We don't like darkies at the Point, so do yourself a favor and go to some colored school.

Remember: Soldiers get killed. And nobody will mourn you.

> Signed,
> A Determined Cadet

He knew of James Webster Smith, the son of a former slave from Columbia, South Carolina, who had been appointed to the academy in 1870. He wondered how Smith had fared. Henry knew to expect some hazing, that he and Smith would be the only colored cadets at the Point. But once he proved himself. . . .

Henry stopped himself. He hadn't been accepted yet.

Griffin, Georgia
5 April 1873

Dear Sir:

The board of examiners pronounce you qualified to enter the Military Academy at West Point. I will appoint you, and send on the papers to the Secretary of

War, who will notify you of the same. From his letter to me you will have to be at West Point by the 25th day of May, 1873.

Yours respectfully,
J. C. Freeman

One week later, he received another notice, this one from the War Department in Washington, D.C. **Sir: You are hereby informed that the President has conditionally selected you for appointment as a Cadet of the United States Military Academy at West Point.**

The letter went on, signed by George M. Robeson, Acting Secretary of War, with an attached circular explaining the qualifications and the Method of Examining Candidates for Admission into the Military Academy.

Yet he knew he could pass any test, any physical examination. His shoulders straightened. Cadet Henry Ossian Flipper. He liked the sound of that.

Chapter Five

"The first thing my distinguished opponents will say about me," Captain Barber said, "is that, if you were to cut my throat, I would bleed acid. But others, wiser ones, know that's just malarkey. Those erudite gentlemen will argue that you have to have a heart to bleed, and I lack that particular organ." He picked up a cigar in the ashtray on Flipper's desk and took a long pull. When he exhaled, he smiled and added: "In a courtroom, that is."

Merritt Barber's blue eyes gleamed. A handsome man with a thick mustache and short, slicked-back dark hair parted in the middle, the captain had a cocksure way about him even while relaxing in Flipper's quarters, long legs stretched out and long fingers and thumb holding a fine cigar in his right hand. He set the cigar aside, smoothed his mustache, and straightened.

"We have only a short while before the court-martial resumes, Lieutenant. And you need to face a few hard facts." He paused, and Flipper nodded for him to continue. "You lied to Colonel Shafter. That can be construed as conduct unbecoming an officer and a gentleman."

Colonel William R. Shafter, bigoted, profane, spiteful— "Pecos Bill" the men called him to his face, and "martinet bastard," "fat-ass son-of-a-bitch," and "damned lout" behind his back. Yes, Flipper had lied.

"The colonel scared hell out of me, sir," Flipper shot back.

Barber raised his hand, and Flipper stopped. "Don't get defensive, Lieutenant. The members of the court won't take

56

kindly to that attitude. Look at me, Mister Flipper. I know this has been hard on you, and it will get harder. But you have to bear down once we get inside the chapel. And I'll enjoy roasting Colonel Shafter and those other bigots. We've got some pretty good ammunition."

Reaching into his saddlebags, he pulled out a newspaper and tossed it across to the lieutenant. "*The New York Globe*'s on your side. They're saying that Shafter should be on trial, not you. And maybe they're right. Unfortunately I can't enter a newspaper into evidence, and, if I could, I'm sure some colored-hating Texas excuse for journalism like the *San Antonio Daily Herald* would be called forth in rebuttal. But I will need some character witnesses."

Flipper had already drawn up a list. He walked to the far wall, rolled up the desktop, and reached inside a cubbyhole, withdrawing a sheet of paper that he handed to his attorney.

Barber examined the document while working on his cigar. At last, he stuck the paper into his saddlebag, and nodded. "You have a lot of friends, Lieutenant. Civilian friends. I don't see many fellow officers on your list."

"No, sir."

Barber didn't push further.

"All right. We're going to be in close contact, Mister Flipper, until this blows over. I hope you don't mind sharing your quarters with me."

Mouth open, Flipper looked up, shocked. "You'd . . . ?" Only one white man had ever offered to share lodging with him: Captain Nolan, back at Fort Sill, and Nolan was a different sort of man. Blacks had their places. Whites had theirs. The military, indeed the whole world, seemed to prefer such policy. The truth was many officers, especially Lieutenant Nordstrom, loathed the very fact of sharing a duplex with a man of color.

Shaking his head, Flipper found his voice. "No. I don't mind, Captain."

"Good. I detest hotel rooms, and don't plan on pitching a tent in the winter. I don't snore, and I hope to hell you don't." Barber smiled. "Now that we have my accommodations straight, let's grab some chow. You got anything in your kitchen out back?"

"Not really, sir."

"Well, what's the best place to eat in town? Or should we grab a bite here on the post?"

Flipper looked down. "You go ahead, sir. I'm not hungry."

But Captain Barber didn't move. "No secrets, Lieutenant."

Flipper sighed. "Since my arrest," he said, eyes still trained on the floor, "Colonel Shafter has denied credit at all post stores. I've been forced to pay in cash for everything, and, well, Captain, my money has quickly dwindled." Finally Flipper lifted his head up to face his attorney.

Pursing his lips, Barber stared blankly for a moment, grinding his cigar into the ashtray, powerfully, angrily. Not even aware of his action. The tobacco shredded, and the captain clenched his fists as his ears reddened. "That pathetic fat bastard," he said dryly. Just as quickly, he smiled. "Never mind. This will be my treat, Lieutenant."

"But. . . ."

"Damn it, mister," he snapped. "We're going to get along quite splendidly, and I'm going to save your career, if you do everything I say. Understand?"

"Yes, sir."

"Good. Let's eat."

November 1st came all too soon for Second Lieutenant H. O. Flipper. The coffee in his stomach rocked like waves whipped in a gale, and he found himself constantly wiping his sweaty palms against the sides of his dress trousers. Across the room, Captain Barber finished combing his mustache and turned his attention to his thin, slicked-back hair, issuing Flipper orders and advice while primping like a trooper on payday wanting to look his best for the whores, tinhorns, barkeeps, and confidence men.

"Today will probably be more formalities and such," Barber said. "You'll introduce me to the court, and we'll go from there. I want you to take charge today, Henry. Make any objections you deem proper. You've read enough with me to know what's fair and what isn't. That way, the court will see just how smart you are, that you are an officer of this man's army and not one to trifle with. If it looks like you're about to get into a sparring match with Captain Clous, I'll take over. After all, that's what I'm paid for, not that I'm getting paid." Barber placed the comb on the dresser, turned, and smiled. "How do I look?" he asked.

A mumble, something unintelligible, came out of Flipper's mouth. He knew what Barber was trying to do. Keep the mood light, take his mind off the officers gathering at the post chapel and the civilian reporters waiting at the post sutler's, permitted on military property to cover the trial, per Shafter's orders, but banned inside the chapel. Flipper had tried to smile himself and answer Barber with a quip, but he failed, sounding more like one of his troopers after a night in the saloons and a week in the guardhouse. He was worried—no, scared. To make matters worse, Wade Hampton had been delayed and would be at least another week returning to Fort Davis. The captain's smile disappeared, and he crossed the small quarters and put a hand on Flipper's shoulder.

"You ever played polo, Lieutenant?" Barber asked.

"No, sir."

"Baseball?"

"No, sir."

"Any sporting event?"

Flipper shook his head. "I helped out with a burro race here at the fort, but I never really competed." He wanted to go on, to explain that baseball and polo were team sports. Team? He never could fit in on an officer's team because of his color. If he played with enlisted men, he would be charged with fraternization. Instead, he just bit his lower lip and waited.

"Well," Barber said gently, "the few minutes, before a polo match or baseball game start, are the absolute worst. It feels like you have butterflies flying in your stomach. Butterflies?" The captain laughed. "More like turkey vultures sometimes. I've had them so bad I thought I would lose my breakfast. And Captain Ewing once sprayed his stomach contents all over his horse's withers. But once the match starts, once you're on your horse on the field, or once the pitcher throws that first ball, that quivering in your stomach disappears." He removed his hand from Flipper's shoulder and snapped a finger. "Just like that. What you have, my dear Lieutenant, is a bad case of the nerves. I don't blame you. To be honest, the reason I talk so much before a court-martial is because I have golden eagles flapping around in my gut. But I promise you, Henry, the first time you stand up to address that court this morning, you'll forget all about how sick you feel."

Flipper nodded. "Yes, sir." Strange, he thought, he already felt better. At least, he didn't think he would send his morning coffee onto the captain's spit-and-polished boots. "Reckon I've had cases of nerves before."

"Reckon so."

He reached for his dress helmet and said: "We'd best be going."

By authority of Special Order 126, T. J. Tilley of Topeka, Kansas, had been employed as the court stenographer. He filled the bill, Flipper thought, as Colonel Pennypacker swore in the rail-thin, balding, bespectacled man with stubby fingers and a nervous tic. Judge Advocate Clous proceeded to swear in the court-martial panel, and Pennypacker, once more, swore in Clous.

"I see a gentleman at your table, *Herr* Flipper," Clous said. "Your counsel, I presume."

Flipper rose sharply. "May it please the court," he began—and just like that, the dancing in his stomach stopped. He paused, fought back the urge to smile at Captain Barber, and introduced the officer as his attorney. There were no objections.

Now Clous had an introduction to make. Captain Fergus Walker, 1st Infantry, was absent today. No surprise there, Flipper thought, recalling his term as judge advocate. If an officer could find a way out of court-martial duty, he would take it. Many junior officers found the task as repulsive as an enlisted man would consider latrine duty. The court would go on despite an absence. The barrel-chested German, however, was gesturing toward another officer sitting at the table.

General Augur, he was saying, had added Colonel D. S. Stanley, 22nd Infantry, and Lieutenant Colonel James Van Voast, 16th Infantry, to the court. But Stanley couldn't make it, so he had been replaced with Lieutenant Colonel N. B. Sweitzer, 8th Cavalry, only Sweitzer had a bad case of the chills and was absent, but Colonel Van Voast was here and ready to serve.

"Objections?" Clous asked.

Flipper cast a quick glance at Barber. Van Voast was the captain's superior officer in the 16th. A good man, or another addition to a biased court? Barber stared blankly ahead, either not noticing the defendant's dilemma or simply letting Flipper call the shot. Think. What to do?

"Vell?" Clous demanded impatiently.

"Sir," Flipper said, "I must protest this addition." In the corner of his eye, he glimpsed Merritt Barber's smile.

"On vat grounds?"

He straightened, his mind racing through arguments, weeding them out like dirty laundry. "Special Orders One Oh Eight, sir," he said, "specifically state that . . ."—he quickly found the paper and read—" 'No other officers than those named can be assembled without manifest injury to the service.' " The order was returned to the table top. Flipper's eyes locked in a duel with the judge advocate's. "And may I remind the court," he said, "that those orders were from General Augur himself."

Clous looked away.

"When this court-martial began," Flipper continued, confident now, "I was asked if I had objections to anyone detailed for the court, and I said no. But now you are attempting to add a member. The time, the manner, and the circumstances of additional members are calculated to excite the greatest apprehensions . . ."—Clous mumbled something in harsh German, but Flipper didn't stop. "I had no reason to expect any new infusion to this court when I accepted y'all." *Y'all?* When was the last time his Southern accent had slipped out? He hurried on, hoping no one would notice. "I could not, and did not take this into consideration."

The chair squeaked as he sat. Clous mopped his face

with a fleshy paw. Major Schofield and Lieutenant Richards began talking in hushed tones. Colonel Pennypacker stared at Clous, and Colonel Van Voast, the subject of this argument, focused on the cracked adobe wall. Finally Clous asked for a brief recess so he could prepare his rebuttal. The gavel fell, and Flipper let out a long sigh.

Smoothing his mustache, Merritt Barber leaned toward Flipper and whispered: "Y'all?" His eyes beamed, and both officers laughed.

Captain John W. Clous's rebuttal came out forcefully and harsh, rolling his r's, chomping off syllables, and sputtering venom in a German accent that was difficult for Flipper—or, for that matter, the members of the court, especially stenographer Tilley—to grasp. The gist was that General Augur had checked with the War Department, and Washington had no problems with the addition of members to the court and that the "no other officers than those named can be assembled" was simply verbiage and irrelevant.

Merritt Barber rose stiffly from the high-backed wooden chair, running fingers through his slick hair as he moved around the table and stepped in front of the row of Army jurists. He glanced briefly at Clous, still puffing from his ranting, and shook his head.

"I don't wish to make an argument," he said deliberately, and, almost as an afterthought, turned to Tilley, his pencil hard at work scratching on paper, and added: "but will your stenographer be kind enough to take down what I may say?"

Clous shot back: "He does dat."

Barber nodded. "This matter as presented by the accused is a challenge." The captain's voice was firm, and his eyes matched Clous's intensity. "It is not argument."

Flipper watched, amazed, as Barber paced the length of the long table—actually two tables placed end-wise—where Colonel Pennypacker and the other officers of the court sat. Unlike Clous, Barber kept his voice under control. "The accused," he said, "is not aware that the War Department is authorized to have anything to do with the composition of this court," Barber continued, arguing Flipper's case. "The record shows that the accused was satisfied with the court. The department commander was satisfied when he made it, for he says no others could be assembled without manifest injury to the service. The accused was satisfied because he accepted the detail without challenge. But now . . ."— Barber shook his head—"now some motive must have influenced a change in its composition, and the accused has a right to feel that the motive must have been adverse."

It was all legalese, but it seemed powerful to Henry Flipper. Barber concluded his argument, bowed sardonically toward Clous, and settled into the chair. Colonel Pennypacker called for a closed session, so Flipper and Barber marched outside to wait.

"We done good," the captain said in a forced Southern accent. "Put a burr under the judge advocate's saddle and made our point. How are those turkey vultures in your stomach?"

Flipper smiled and said: "They have taken flight, Captain, and flown away."

"Good."

They fell silent. Flipper turned to stare at the closed door to the chapel. Barber fired up a cigar.

"It's not fair, though," Flipper said softly.

"What's that?"

Flipper nodded at the door. "Captain Clous. He gets to

sit in on all closed sessions with the court-martial board. You don't."

"He's judge advocate. That's the way this man's army works."

"It's still not fair."

"No, you're right, Henry. Clous is also the acting judge advocate of the Department of Texas. That means he'll review your case . . . his case. That definitely would not be considered ethical, or even legal, in civilian court. That's why it's imperative that we hit hard. We have to win this case here, not hope for a reversal of the board's decision."

"It's a stacked deck," Flipper said.

Even Captain Merritt Barber could not debate that point.

Chapter Six

Plebe Year, 1873-74

Leaning over the railing, he spit into the murky water as the steam-propelled ferry inched across the Hudson River. He felt sick—not seasick, but nerves. West Point, its stone buildings towering on the hills, frightened him as the boat eased into the harbor and docked. He trembled. What was he doing here? What did he know about the military? New York seemed a thousand miles from Georgia, he thought, and suddenly laughed at himself. A thousand miles? That would be just about right. Maybe not quite that far, but close enough.

It had been a long trip from Atlanta since he received the appointment. Several prominent Georgians, freedmen and radical Republicans, wanted to throw dinner parties honoring Henry O. Flipper, but the teenager politely declined. The ugly criticism in the Southern newspapers seemed harsh enough—and the pressure he felt after reading glowing praise in the Republican and black papers did not help matters—so he didn't want to call more attention to himself. He didn't want the masked cowards of the Ku Klux Klan to waylay him coming back from one of those engagements—nor did he want them to harm his family. Be quiet. Be humble.

At the post office one late April morning, a middle-aged white man wearing a fine summer suit and straw hat approached him and offered his congratulations, although not his hand. Avoiding any eye contact, the man began rambling, shuffling his feet, staring at his fingernails, and adjusting his sweat-stained paper collar as he spoke.

"It's tough, West Point is," the man said. "Many a man has failed there. No shame, but hard. Hard on a white man. 'Specially tough on colored boy like yourself. You never seen the hardships like you'll be facin' at the Academy." Flipper fought back the urge to smile. Hardships? Like being born into slavery. Like the time six years ago when nine masked white men—Army soldiers, or at least dressed in Union blue—beat up his father and several other freedmen in the colored settlement of Shermantown on the outskirts of Atlanta. Flipper waited for the stranger to make his point.

"Appointments to the Academy is hard to come by. Be a shame to waste one. Now my oldest boy, Jeff, he's smart. Has a promisin' future in the Army. I'd love to see him go to West Point. He can cut it, Jeff can. But you got the appointment from our district. Now, say you were to refuse the appointment. Like I said, ain't no shame there. Many a fella before you has declined. Tough to survive at the Point. You a Negro makes it even harder. But if you were to do something else . . . you done proved your point . . . well, then Jeff could take your place. I'd make it worth your while, boy . . . Mister Flipper." He reached inside his coat and withdrew an envelope, handing it to Flipper, who simply stared at the package.

"It's five thousand dollars. Go ahead. Count it. Take it. It's yours if you let my boy take your place."

Their eyes finally locked. "No, sir. I cannot."

"Five thousand dollars. You know how long it'd take a boy like you to earn that kinda cash money?"

"I can't take it, sir." He knew he would never get anywhere like this, so he took a different tactic. "I am only seventeen years old, sir. A minor. It's not my place to make such a decision. You would have to approach my father about this matter. Now, if you'll excuse me."

The man returned the envelope and stared blankly. He would never approach Festus Flipper. He didn't have enough guts to try bribing an adult, even a black man.

So now he was here, May 20th, 1873, West Point. He found a soldier on the docks and asked where he should go to report. "Adjutant's office," the man answered in an amiable tone that surprised Flipper, and he quickly gave directions. The man at the adjutant's office was also friendly. He glanced at Flipper's appointment certificate, then had him fill out his name, age, and other information in an enrollment book. "Report to the cadet barracks," the man said, "for assignment to your quarters." Flipper followed a redheaded orderly out of the office and across the grounds to his new home. The friendliness ended as soon as the door to the adjutant's office closed.

Pale faces lined the rear windows of the occupied barracks. Other cadets on the grounds stopped whatever they were doing and watched. The silence lasted only a minute.

"Hey, Gabe!" a voice called to the orderly. "Where you going with that black mule?"

A clamor of voices, curses, whistles, and laughs promptly followed. The orderly shook his head and smiled. Flipper bit his lip and tried not to listen to the din of insults.

"Cadet Gabriel! How come you get a nigger and we don't?"

"When the boy's done shinin' your boots, Gabe, send him up here."

"Plebe Charcoal! How long you think you'll last before you go running home to pick cotton on my daddy's plantation?"

The cadet opened a door, and Flipper walked in, removing his cap. The door shut behind him, and Flipper stared at three cadets sitting in a small office. Gabriel had not followed him in, and the heckling outside had stopped. Inside, however, came a new round of shouts as the three pockmarked men jumped up and stared at Flipper in disbelief.

"Holy Mary, Mother of God!" one barked. "What the hell are you doing?"

"Don't you know how to enter this office properly?" another shouted.

"Get the hell out of here and do it right!" the third screamed, and Flipper walked outside. The third cadet, a blond-headed lad with blue eyes and big ears, followed him. The harangue continued.

"Button your coat, fool! You're a soldier. Head up, mister. Fins and heels together."

Flipper stared dumbly.

"Fins together, damn you."

"Fins?"

"Your hands, your hands. Jesus, you're stupid. That's better. Now, sir, when you so desire to come in and address your upper classmen, you will knock at that door."

After the cadet had gone back inside, Flipper waited. Part of him briefly wanted to turn around and run like hell. But just like that he understood something. The three cadets inside were doing their job, hazing, perhaps, or maybe trying to make Appointee H. O. Flipper a cadet. The cadets outside had been nothing more than rude bigots, but these instructions were proper. His mother might not think so, but the young Union soldier he had met years ago during the war, Henry Hartsell, he would understand. Flipper smiled, quickly lost that smile, and knocked on the frame.

"Come in."

Flipper entered, shut the door, and stood in front of the three cadets.

"Heels together," the second man said. "Toes pointed out equally. Chin drawn in. You're at attention."

"Better," the third cadet muttered after Flipper corrected his stance.

"What do you want?" the first cadet asked.

"I'm Henry O. Flipper. The adjutant told me to come here."

"Report here," the blond cadet corrected. "And the proper wording is . . . 'Candidate Flipper, United States Military Academy, reports his entrance into this office, sir.' "

Flipper repeated the sentence.

"Very well. What do you want in this office, Candidate Flipper?"

"Sir." He was getting more comfortable with this. "The adjutant told me to report to be assigned quarters."

"Very well, Candidate Flipper. Corporal Andersen will take over. Welcome to the Beast Barracks."

He passed his physical, and tried to ignore the taunts and jeers of the profane white cadets. He did his best to keep his barracks to the specifications of the Corps of Cadets regulations. On the first day, Cadet Corporal Andersen ransacked Flipper's room three times until he got it right. Flipper felt like an idiot. He had to ask what "Tattoo" was. Shaking his head, Andersen told him, and went on to explain "Reveille."

A restless sleep was interrupted at five o'clock the following morning by the harsh sound of "Reveille," and an even harsher Irish brogue down the hall: "Candidates, turn out promptly!"

After roll call came barracks inspection, where Corporal

Andersen kicked Flipper's shoes across the room and ripped off the bed sheets. "Do it right, Candidate Flipper. Do it right."

Sighing, Flipper went to work. He ate alone at breakfast, listening to the grumbling of others in the dining hall. "Never seen a darky this close before."—"Hell, why do we have to eat with him? Just the sight of a damned nigger turns my stomach."—"I'll bet you five dollars that he don't last till September."

Back in his quarters after breakfast, Flipper stood at attention as Corporal Andersen walked around the room. He held his breath as the cadet stood in front of him, hands behind his back, and opened his mouth. Instead of shouts, however, the words were calm, polite. "Very well, Mister Flipper," he said. "Very well, sir, indeed."

Of course, when a second corporal inspected the same room a couple of hours later, he screamed at Flipper and told him to do it right, knocking boxes off the shelves and spitting on the floor. What he had seen that Corporal Andersen hadn't, Flipper could not even fathom a guess. The cadet corporal stopped in the doorway, spun around on his heels, and walked to the washstand. A smile cracked his ugly face as he stared at the slop bucket beside the stand, per regulations. He kicked the pail over, stepping back quickly to avoid staining his white pants, and left the room in a hurry, calling back in a vile tone: "Best clean that up, boy."

Mail came at eleven o'clock, and Flipper looked at the strange handwriting on a letter. He hadn't expected anything, not this soon, not from home. This had been posted at the Point. He opened the letter tentatively, expecting some bitter, unsigned threat, but instead found the letter encouraging, although downbeat and sad. It was signed Cadet James W. Smith. *Smith!* Flipper thought excitedly.

The only other black cadet at West Point. He read with excitement, and read the letter again and again.

Candidate Flipper:

I thought you would do well to hear from me. By now, I imagine you have borne the brunt of insults, perhaps even blows. Don't be afraid of either. And do not retaliate, even if you are beaten. The white cadets will do anything they can to drive us out of the Academy. I think you will find the instructor corps to be friendly and supportive. The cadets, however, are a different sort. Certain consequences can be avoided if you do not confront your tormentors. So I have learned from sad experience.

Three years ago, a cadet entered my room and emptied a slop jar on me and Candidate Howard, my roommate, as we slept. The cadet was caught, but not punished severely. And poor Michael Howard failed his entrance examinations and was sent back to Mississippi. I was later charged with inattention in the ranks, and, when I denied this, I was charged with lying and put back one year in the academic standings.

My father told me when I received my appointment to endure. "Don't let them run you away," he said. "Show your spunk," he told me. "Don't let them be able to say 'the nigger won't do at West Point.' Fight back." And I have fought back. My advice to you, however, is not to fight back. Go about everything with a low profile. Do your fighting later. If you fight, you can't survive the Academy. I'm not sure I will. But I hope you will.

I remain respectfully yours,
Cadet James Webster Smith

★ ★ ★ ★ ★

"Candidate Flipper, United States Military Academy, reports his entrance into this office, sir."

The dark-haired cadet with a Roman nose swore underneath his breath and muttered: "What do you want?"

"Candidate Flipper requests permission to visit James Smith, sir."

This time, the cadet officer cursed angrily and stood. "You say *Mister* Smith, you sorry-ass simpleton. Understand that Mister Smith is a cadet and you are not. I had better never hear you address a cadet with such familiarity. Understand?"

"Yes, sir."

"Well, what do you want?"

"Candidate Flipper requests permission to visit Mister Smith, sir."

"Granted. Now get out of my sight."

James Smith looked sick with melancholy, "solemncholy" they called it at the Point, maybe not dying, but defeated. Flipper remembered the looks of slaves whipped and beaten—images he had practically forgotten until now.

Scars marked Smith's freckled face, and, although he was a good four inches shorter than Flipper, the South Carolinian had the look of a pugilist, someone you wouldn't want to anger. Although both men were Negroes, Smith's olive skin was much darker than Flipper's. He had heard many stories of Smith's temper, striking fellow cadets, shouting, arguing, complaining, but although he looked physically imposing, the hurt on his face, the depression, revealed a downtrodden man.

"How'd you do on your entrance examinations?" Smith asked wearily.

Flipper answered with a sigh. "I passed, though I've never been so nervous. Didn't do too well in geology."

"Old Hanks will straighten you out there, Candidate Flipper."

"Old Hanks?"

"An instructor here. How have the other cadets treated you?"

"Some insults. Nothing terrible. I mean, no one has dumped a slop jar on me, James . . . um, Cadet Smith."

"You can call me James, Mister Flipper. When we're alone."

"I'm Henry."

Smith smiled, but it was a sad smile. "Maybe they won't hit you as hard as they hit me, Henry. You're light-skinned. That'll help. You talked to Candidate Williams?"

John Washington Williams had arrived from Virginia the previous day, increasing the number of black cadets to three. Flipper had heard the white cadets talking of the latest "black-hearted moke to stink up the place," but he had not seen Williams yet. He shook his head.

"I'll send him a letter, too. Just remember, Henry, don't fight back."

"Well, they haven't done much yet. Just called me names, kicked over a slop bucket, things like that."

"It's the summer, Henry. You go through Plebe Camp first. Once the senior cadets return, then you'll see just how much you have to take from swine."

Through manual drill, artillery instruction, policing grounds, battalion drill, guard duty—Henry learned what it meant to be a cadet. Classes began on July 1st. He pored over Legendre's GEOMETRY AND TRIGONOMETRY, Church's DESCRIPTIVE GEOMETRY, Levizac's

GRAMMAR AND VERB BOOK, PRACTICAL INSTRUCTION IN ARTILLERY, and the other textbooks he bought. He practiced French, and each night prayed that, if he was called for recital, he wouldn't make a fool of himself by botching it—"fessed cold," the cadets called it.

He thought the classroom professors would be as stimulating as John Quarles had been back in Georgia, but they proved to be as exciting as watching heat ripples in the humid afternoons. Flipper loved math, but even he found it hard to stay awake when humorless Albert Church tried to explain calculus. His instructor in French would also never be called inspiring, but the field instructors in military matters, artillery and infantry tactics and small arms, were knowledgeable and patient.

Plebe Camp ended on August 28th. Henry Flipper was no longer a candidate. He was a cadet and a gentleman. The older cadets, "furloughmen," they were called, began arriving late that morning.

"Slaker, you putrid piece of garbage, why aren't you policing the grounds?"

"I am, sir," the plebe said in a trembling voice.

"I am, Cadet Corporal, sir. Say it!"

Slaker repeated as ordered. Flipper stood underneath a maple tree only a few yards from the hazing. He busied himself picking up bits of trash and couldn't help but watch the second-year cadet, the same corporal who had overturned the slop bucket in his barracks, torment Cadet Adam Slaker.

The yearling corporal spit out his chewing tobacco, the ball landing between Slaker's shoes. "What's that I see at your feet, Slaker?"

"Tobacco, Cadet Corporal, sir."

"That's a tasty quid, you dumb plebe. Now it's dirty because I've had to hide your sorry ass. I want you to wash it off for me."

Dropping a rake, Slaker reached over and picked up the tobacco. He started to run to a water pump, but the corporal yelled for him to stop. "I don't have time for you to run to wash it off, Slaker. Put it in your mouth and chew it for me."

A crowd of older cadets, second- and first-class students, had gathered to watch, laughing as Slaker put the chaw in his mouth and began chewing tentatively.

"Don't swallow it, plebe," one onlooker said. "Make you mighty sick."

Another laughed. "How come you don't let the nigger chew that for you, Louis?"

The corporal grinned and yelled for Flipper to "hoop up and join our merry group." Flipper swallowed and sprinted to them, screaming at the top of his lungs: "Cadet Flipper reporting as ordered, Cadet Corporal, sir!"

"Plebe, I want you to relieve Cadet Slaker and chew my tasty quid of tobacco. Slaker, spit out that chaw and hand it to the darky."

Adam Slaker gagged as the moist quid dropped into his hand. He held it for Flipper to take. Flipper did as he was told. He didn't chew tobacco. He didn't smoke or drink intoxicating liquors, either, but if the cadets thought he would get sick, they had best think again. He had grown up in Georgia. He didn't care for it, but, like most Southerners, he knew how to chew tobacco, which is more than Adam Slaker could say. The poor fourth classman dropped to his knees and vomited to the delight of his senior onlookers. Flipper chewed, staring at the corporal's malevolent eyes.

"Get up, Slaker," one of the cadets ordered, and the

plebe rose, swaying on unsteady feet.

"That's enough, Flipper," one of the cadets called out, and Flipper stopped. "Take that crap out of your mouth, boy." Again, Flipper followed orders.

The senior cadet laughed. "Looks clean to me, Louis. Take your tobacco." The onlookers roared with laughter. The corporal's ears reddened. Finally he smiled and turned to Adam Slaker.

"Slaker, take that tobacco and chew some more. But don't let the commandant catch you. He frowns upon the use of tobacco." His face hardened. "I said chew, you piece of dung."

Flipper stood firm as Slaker reached for the tobacco and put the quid in his mouth. The poor kid almost vomited again, but steadied himself and worked his jaws as his face lost even more color.

The corporal laughed and turned away. "Slaker, you dumb file. Now you'll have nigger lips for the rest of your miserable life."

For the most part, the older cadets never really hazed Henry Flipper—if for no other reason than they didn't want to be seen with a black. James Smith became Flipper's roommate. Plebe John Williams might as well have roomed there, too, as often as he stayed there. Yet who else would study with them? They were ostracized. Even the sons of Abolitionists from the New England states avoided the colored cadets as they would families with yellow fever.

Reporters came and went. Flipper cut out the newspaper clippings and mailed them to his parents. He continued to ignore the taunts and jeers from the white cadets, following Cadet Smith's advice.

Summer faded to fall, and autumn gave way to the biting cold of winter on the Hudson. Christmas came unnoticed.

Williams and Smith moaned about the upcoming semi-annual examinations. Flipper wasn't worried. He had learned that the key to passing in this man's army school had little to do with knowledge and everything to do with memorizing. If you could recite from memory, you were safe. No instructor seemed to care if you didn't understand the theory of trajectory as long as you could spout it off. Flipper proudly "maxed" most of his recitations. Williams and Smith "fessed" out on most of theirs.

He stopped at his door, hearing the mumbles of Williams and oaths from Smith in another study session. He never had been much for gum games, but a practical joke suddenly struck him as too funny to pass. He knocked on the door, lowered his voice, and said: "Surprise inspection!"

Even biting his lip couldn't stop him from laughing, although he did manage to muffle his cackles, as Smith and Williams swore. A tin cup hit the floor. "Damn you, Williams!" Smith snapped. Feet scuffled. Slowly Flipper pushed open the door and stormed inside, howling.

John Washington Williams knelt, trying to mop up spilled coffee with a rag, his lips quivering. James Webster Smith busied himself smoothing out the sheets on his bed. Both men snapped to attention, realized the gag, and swore angrily. At first Flipper thought Smith might thrash him—he had that look in his eyes—but after a minute they joined the laughter. Flipper closed the door.

Smith shook his head. "You'll pay for this, Henry. You'll pay."

"Right. You think you two can fool me? Payback will be a long time coming, gents, I can assure you."

Yet they surprised him. It seems some cadet reported Henry Ossian Flipper for impersonating an officer, and in the freezing cold of January Flipper found himself walking three extra tours of guard duty and was confined to his quarters for a week. Yet all through his punishment, despite the demerits, Flipper couldn't stop laughing—at his gum game, and the brilliant retaliation of his friends.

The laughter stopped later that month. Cadet John Washington Williams failed his semi-annual examination and was forced to leave West Point. **Another darky who couldn't bear the regimen,** one newspaper reported. Six months later, Cadet James Webster Smith was found deficient in philosophy and dismissed from the Academy. In the Order of Merit, Henry O. Flipper ended his first year ranked forty-seventh in a class of one hundred. He had survived. But now he was alone.

Chapter Seven

November 3, 1881

A harsh, cold wind bit through their dress uniforms as Barber and Flipper made their way back to the post chapel. They had spent the past two days in Flipper's quarters, going over every piece of the case repeatedly, burning coal oil, trying to think ahead, to visualize what arguments Clous would use and how they could parry his blows.

After Colonel Pennypacker announced the court's ruling over Flipper's objection to Colonel Van Voast, the judge advocate had asked for a forty-eight hour adjournment to consider additional material. "What material could that be?" Barber had asked Henry back in Flipper's quarters. "I haven't a clue," Flipper had replied, and he didn't, until the following afternoon when a smiling Lieutenant Nordstrom knocked on the door and served him with additional charges.

Clous, it seemed, was doing everything to make acquittal impossible, maybe to make up for his first bloodied nose. Technically the court had ruled for Captain Clous over Lieutenant Flipper's first objection. General Augur, Colonel Pennypacker noted, had every right to appoint additional members to the court-martial board, but, he added, the accused had equal right to object to anyone subsequently added to the panel. Lieutenant Flipper had objected to Colonel Van Voast, so Van Voast could return to his duties. **The first salvo has been fired,** one Texas journalist said, **and the darky lieutenant has scored with a scratch shot**.

But the odds he faced remained overwhelming. Of that, Flipper was certain, especially now, as winter began to make its presence known in the Davis Mountains. That seemed fitting. The cold—Georgia had been bone chilling at times, and so had West Point, but not like out West. This morning was cold all right, but nothing like that wind at Fort Mobeetie way up in the Panhandle. He thought back to just before he had walked to the chapel on that first day of his court-martial, back when he had wondered if he would be around to feel winter's first breath. Well, he had, although officially it wasn't yet winter. *Small goals,* he told himself. **Now make another one. Thanksgiving. Survive until Thanksgiving.**

Head bowed, not speaking, satchel in hand, Captain Barber marched angrily to the chapel. Flipper had trouble matching the long-legged man's gait. The captain was mad. His jaw moved sideways as he ground his teeth.

"Captain . . . ," a reporter began, but Barber shoved him aside and disappeared inside the adobe building, Henry Flipper right behind him. He still didn't speak as he withdrew pencil and papers from the leather case and sat in the creaking chair. Barber hadn't said a word this morning.

The additional charges against Flipper, with four specifications, were nothing but cock and bull. Commissary Sergeant Carl Ross had loaned Flipper forty-six dollars back when Flipper's world began spinning out of control. "You just pay me when you has a mind to, Lieutenant," Ross had drawled. "I ain't in no hurry. You good for it. I knows that." Flipper couldn't see Carl Ross preferring charges. He and Ross were friends, at least as friendly as an officer and a non-com could be, and they had worked side-by-side in the Commissary Department. Flipper would pay back Sergeant Ross, as soon as this was over. Carl Ross knew that. Besides, the commissary sergeant thought of loaning money as putting it in a bank. If he didn't have it in his hand, he couldn't spend it on rotgut whisky like the other men of the 10th Cavalry. No, this was Colonel Shafter's work, or Judge Advocate Clous's.

The second "crime" blamed on Flipper was Charles Berger's theft. Just before New Year's Eve, the civilian scout had requested a ten-day leave to go to Fort Stockton. He also needed a horse to get there. Berger had been a scout for years, so Lieutenant Nordstrom gave permission, and Flipper, per orders, loaned the man a horse. Charles Berger then deserted—hadn't been seen since—and, in addition to the horse, he took off with several beef vouchers. A board had convened to investigate the matter and ruled that no one was to blame other than deserter Berger. So Flipper drew Berger's pay for January, sixty dollars, paid off the deserter's debt at the post sutler's, and kept the rest on hand to be deposited in the fort's cash accounts. The judge advocate, however, charged that Flipper had kept the money for himself.

"Dis is quite simple," Clous addressed the court calmly. "I urge da accused to have da two sets of charges disposed of in one trial." He smiled at Flipper. "It vill save him much anxiety and not cost our government so much money." Clous sighed. "*Mit* no objections, ve vill arraign da accused. . . ."

"Not so fast," Barber said, rising. He leaned on the table, palms flat, and stared angrily at the German. "The accused is not against one trial, but more information is needed. For one, when did the department learn of the new charges and specifications? Before or after this court was assembled? These are questions of legality, gentlemen. This panel was sworn in based on the original charges, not the latest bunch of poppycock."

"I object to *das Wort* . . . poppycock!" Clous snapped.

Colonel Pennypacker sighed. "Gentlemen, please."

"Well answer my question, Captain."

"*Nein*. I do not know."

"You must have some inkling."

"*Nein*."

"It's a simple question, Captain."

Clous was furious. "Da charges and specifications ver prepared and are signed by Colonel Villiam R. Shafter. Dese charges have been handed me *mit* an order to bring dem before dis court, approved and ordered for trial by da department commander. I presume dat information vill be sufficient."

"It is not sufficient," Barber fired back.

It went on like that all morning, Clous and Barber sparring, spitting, pointing fingers—hell, Flipper expected the two to come to blows. Shortly before noon, Flipper began writing a statement himself, as Barber and Clous droned on and on and on. Finally he rose timidly, and asked if he could speak. That silenced both attorneys. Flipper read his statement, saying he was agreeable to one trial on all of the charges and specifications providing the court would be sworn in again upon hearing the new charges and specifications. It sounded reasonable to him.

But not to Judge Advocate Clous. He asked for a closed session; so Flipper and Barber marched outside to wait in the cold. "Does a court-martial usually take this long to start?" Flipper asked. The one he had presided over hadn't.

"Only when you have a defense counsel as mule-headed as the judge advocate, Lieutenant."

A reporter—not the one Barber had shoved that morning, but another one with a handlebar mustache wearing a cavalry greatcoat over a broadcloth suit—made his way tentatively toward the chapel's porch. "Captain . . . Lieutenant," he began, nodding slightly at each soldier. "We've heard a lot of shouting this morning. Pretty hostile testimony, I guess?"

"Mister," Barber replied, "we haven't even begun testimony yet."

Clous announced that Lieutenant Flipper would be arraigned only on the original charges. The accused would face the other charges at a later date. Flipper didn't know how to feel about that. If he survived this court-martial, he would have to go through another, or would they drop the matter, if he were acquitted this time? Probably not. Not if Clous had his way. He rose and listened as the indictment was read to him: Embezzlement in violation of the sixtieth Article of War. One specification. Conduct unbecoming an officer and a gentleman. Five specifications.

"How does the defendant plead?"

"Not guilty," Flipper answered. "To all charges."

"*Sehr gut,*" Clous said. "Ve shall begin dis trial."

"Not quite," Barber said, and practically every member of the court sighed heavily. Flipper had to agree with them. This was getting old. For all the shouts, all the arguments, no one was accomplishing anything, except antagonizing Colonel Pennypacker and the other panelists.

"If it may please the court, the accused and I have repeatedly asked the honorable judge advocate for various items necessary for a proper and zealous defense, namely the papers and property taken from the accused's quarters when he was arrested. We would like that list so we can decide what witnesses we may call for the defense."

Clous's hammy right hand pounded on the table. "Dis

is. . . ." He sputtered something in German, then spat out in English: "Dere is no use in taking up time of dis court and lumbering up da record. If *Kapitän* Barber vants any vitnesses or papers, he can make da proper demand on me. Den vill be da proper time to bring dis matter before da court . . . if I fail to do my duty."

Shaking his head, Barber argued: "We don't know what papers you have, Captain. It is hard for us to ask for something when we don't know what you are hiding."

"I hide nothing!"

"Look, I'm sorry to go this way. But the accused has reason to believe . . . and does believe . . . that the judge advocate has in his possession documents, which are material in his defense. May it please the court, the defense asks the court to instruct the judge advocate to provide this list so that we can determine what witnesses to call."

Clous snapped again. Flipper thought the captain might die of a heart attack or a stroke right then and there. "I must protest," he said, huffing, and half ran until he stood in front of Colonel Pennypacker. "Mister president," he said, "it is not competent for dis court to take any action upon dis matter. I vould be very glad to show any papers to him at da proper time. I ask da court to be cleared so dis matter can be settled."

The court fell silent for the first time in hours. Galusha Pennypacker locked his fingers together and nodded at the sweaty German. The Philadelphian was young, not yet forty, and handsome, and he bled Army blue. His grandfather had fought in the Revolution and his father in the war with Mexico. At Fort Fisher, North Carolina, in 1865, Pennypacker had led the 97th Pennsylvania Volunteers in a brutal charge. He himself had planted the colors before falling with a serious wound. He won the Medal of Honor for his bravery. He seemed a quiet man, fair, interested. So Flipper was surprised at his angry tone.

"Mister Tilley, put down your pencil."

The stenographer looked puzzled for a second, realized what the colonel had to say was not for the record, and placed his pencil on the table. He tried to focus on the wooden cross hanging behind the pulpit as if he had no interest in what the president of the court had to say.

"This morning has been a complete waste of time, gentlemen," Colonel Pennypacker said, looking Clous in the eye until the German wilted, and then Barber, who also looked away after a couple of seconds. "If Captains Barber and Clous would care to engage in fisticuffs, they should take the matter outside. And if they would prefer a duel, although duels are prohibited in the Army of the United States of America, I am certain they could find seconds among the members of this court. Anything to shut up you two.

"This isn't some pissing match. A soldier's career is at stake here. I'm sure in some ways, his very life is at stake. And if you read the Eastern newspapers, our glorious Army is on trial. This is a most important case, yet our distinguished counsels want to drag this on for a millennium. I don't want to continue this dreary pace with a bunch of legal crud. The accused has been indicted. He has entered his plea of not guilty. It is time to start the ball, gentlemen.

"Court is adjourned until ten o'clock in the morning, tomorrow, November Fourth. At which time the judge advocate had damn' well better call his first witness." Unlocking his fingers, he reached for the gavel and shook his head.

"Pick up your pencil, Mister Tilley. Make a note that court is adjourned. We'll read over the proceedings and call the judge advocate's first witness. Ten a.m., gentlemen."

The gavel exploded. Flipper jumped.

Chapter Eight

Yearling Year, 1874–75

The explosion knocked Flipper and a half dozen cadets to the ground. He balled up like an infant for several seconds, shuddering, rolled over, and rose slightly, knees and palms on the grass, shaking his head and spitting out grass. His ears rang. Cadets helped each other off the ground, but no one came to Third Classman H. O. Flipper's assistance. Slowly he found his feet and stumbled toward the smoking mountain Howitzer. People were talking, but Flipper couldn't understand anything. Finally the ringing died down, and he made out the words of his artillery instructor: "Cadet Bigelow, run fetch a medic."

"Give them room," someone else said.

The cadets parted, and Flipper saw the ruined cannon and an instructor wiping Cadet Creel's bloody nose. The School of Battery had begun three days ago after almost a month of training in nomenclature and manual of field artillery. At light battery drill this morning, the cannon must have been improperly loaded. Anyway, something went wrong. The twelve-pounder's left wheel had been blown off, and a spoke had slammed into Cadet Creel's face, luckily catching him by the flat side and not a jagged edge. Flipper let out a sigh when he saw the ruined cannon. Only one injury, and it appeared minor. Most of the Class of 1877 could have been blown all the way to Poughkeepsie.

"I'm all right, sir," Creel said, his voice sounding even more nasal because of the busted nose.

Two other cadets laughed. The tension relaxed as the artillery captain helped Creel to his feet. "Medal of Honor, for sure," Cadet Todd said, and another chimed in: "But fifteen demerits for soiling your uniform, Cadet." The staccato of nervous jokes continued as the medics arrived to escort Creel to the hospital. Someone said something else that Flipper couldn't understand, and then another cadet, shaking his head, remarked bitterly: "Hell, I wish it had been the nigger instead of Creel, and the damned thing had killed him."

Flipper straightened, trying to control his anger. James Smith probably would have assaulted the cadet for that remark—and who could have blamed him?—but that was one reason James Smith was no longer a cadet at West Point, why Henry O. Flipper was the only black left at the Academy. **An experiment doomed to failure,** one Democrat newspaper had written. Standing just a quarter-inch under six-feet-two and weighing one hundred and seventy-five pounds, Flipper towered over the pimpled boy who had made the racist remark. He could have pounded the cadet into oblivion. He sure as hell wanted to. But, instead, he simply stared at the blackheart. At last their eyes locked. The bantering had ceased. The grounds fell silent. A second later the cadet looked away.

"All right, gentlemen," the captain said, after clearing his throat. "Now you've seen first-hand what can happen when an artillery piece is loaded improperly. Let's see if we can do it right this time."

Mathematics, French, Spanish, and drawing were the educational studies for the second-year student, plus tactics of infantry, artillery, and cavalry, along with target practice. Dancing was optional for yearlings, and Flipper, realizing he would have a hard time finding a partner, declined. Plebes were not allowed to attend dances, but yearlings were. After a year of being locked up with their hazing tormentors, they were eager to spoon a girl—"femmes," the cadets called them—and stroll along the dock hand-in-hand. Other cadets made a beeline to Benny Havens's Tavern in Highland Park for roast turkey, buckwheat cakes, and Irish whisky. Some found a parlor house or, since that five hundred dollar annual stipend the cadets received was redeemable only at the commissary and receiving money from home was prohibited, they risked demerits, and other things, by getting a loan and finding a crib girl. Rumor had it that one cadet corporal had come down with a case of an ungentlemanly disease and was forced to leave the academy.

"Can you dance?" a cadet sergeant asked him one afternoon. "Do you plan on going to the hops this summer?"

Flipper hadn't thought about the dances. He glanced at the cadet's eyes, saw their hardness, and realized the thought of a man of color attending dances thrown for the Corps of Cadets appalled him.

"No, sir," he answered at last.

So Flipper resigned himself to his studies and an existence without the off-campus company of a "spoon."

As usual, Flipper enjoyed mathematics even through Church's dry instruction, and he found he had a gift for drawing—at least, that's what instructor Robert Weir said—but, to Flipper's surprise, not to mention his teacher's, his best subject was Spanish. There was a rhythm to the language and a beauty in the words.

A Colombian who had taught fencing at West Point before Spanish was added in 1856, Patrice de Janon made his students learn the language by speaking it, not writing it. Flipper and his fellow cadets quickly learned that they had to develop an ear for Spanish if they wanted to pass, for one simple reason: when Patrice de Janon spoke in a thick, heavily accented form of bastard English, few students had a clue as to what he was saying.

With the dismissal of Smith and Williams, Flipper had no study partners. He shut himself in the room, a furnace in the summer, an icebox in winter, and studied or clipped out the latest articles on "the experiment" in the *New National Era* and *Citizen* of Washington, D.C., the *National Monitor* of Brooklyn, or the *Times*, *World* and *Bulletin* of New York. He was a national celebrity, or villain, but at the Academy he was a man without friends.

"Sunday news!" the silver-haired peddler called out. "Get your Sunday news." He pushed his cart, hawking his wares on this Sunday afternoon as he did every Sabbath at the Point. Flipper handed the man a coin and picked up the latest edition of the *Times*.

"Hey, Sunday News!" a cadet shouted. "Don't sell to that darky." Sunday News—the only name by which the peddler was known at the academy—ignored the taunt and gave Flipper his change.

"Damn it, old man, if you sell to that moke, you've lost my business."

Sunday News smiled. "As if that idiot can read. Good day, Cadet Flipper."

Flipper took the newspaper and returned to his barracks room. After reading the paper, he picked up a letter he had been saving. It had arrived earlier this week, but he had not wanted to read it until now. Every night before "Tattoo" he would pick up the envelope and savor it, staring at the flowery letters, recognizing the handwriting of Anna White, imagining that he could smell her hair.

They had met two years ago at Atlanta University. Born

into slavery, she had lived around Atlanta all of her life. Anna was a small, delicate creature, beautiful, with penetrating, dark eyes. She looked tiny, almost a foot shorter than Flipper. An odd match, Joseph Flipper had called them. But what did his stupid brother know? Now, Henry Flipper carefully opened the envelope and read:

My Dearest Henry Ossian, the letter began. Henry Ossian. He hated it when she called him that. **It is another beautiful summer night here in Atlanta, and I take pencil in hand with hope that you can say the same at West Point.**

No, Anna, he thought as sweat dampened his brow, armpits, and back, *it's another miserable night in Hades.*

Mother has planned a trip to New York City for next spring, and I hope I will be able to visit you at the Academy.

His heart skipped at the thought of seeing her again.

Funny, I have never been north of Smyrna or south of Jonesboro. You think I could find my way to West Point? I hope so. Everyone here is proud of you, especially your parents. We were saddened to read of what happened to Mr. Smith and Mr. Williams. You must feel terribly alone now. But we are sure that you can do anything you put your mind to and will become the first colored graduate of the National Military Academy. Wouldn't that be something!

I close now wishing you pleasant dreams. I wish you would write me, but I know your studies must take up a lot of your time, so don't feel obliged. But let me know if it is possible to see you at West Point. I will let you know exactly when I am to arrive.

Yours truly,
Anna

On guard duty, he had watched the photographer set up his equipment, escorted by a First Classman and the Officer of the Day. "Fall in the guard!" the Officer commanded, and Flipper grabbed his rifle, made double-quick time, coming to attention in front of the camera with his white classmates.

He had never had his photograph taken, and wondered what it would be like. Would the flash blind him? How would he look? Maybe he could buy a copy and send it home, maybe to his parents or even Anna White.

The Officer turned to the cadet corporal as the photographer ducked behind the black curtain and made some adjustments. "Get rid of the nigger, Corporal," the Officer of the Day said. "We don't want him in the picture."

Flipper bit his lower lip and tried not to shake, tried not to cry. "Run fetch us some water, Cadet Flipper," the corporal ordered, and Flipper spun around and sprinted away to find a pail, fill it with water, and bring it to his classmates. *No*, he said to himself. *Damned if I'll ever let them see me cry.*

The bitter cold caused his teeth to click uncontrollably despite everything he did to warm himself, shuffling his rifle, rubbing his hands, stamping his boots. Most cadets loathed guard duty at any time of the year, but Flipper never found it so disconcerting. After all, he was always alone. This night, however, he longed to be anywhere else, even in his dreary quarters, the temperature inside just a few degrees above freezing.

Pure black was the night, so dark Flipper couldn't see the rifle he moved from shoulder to shoulder. He walked his post and shivered.

"Flipper."

Flipper stopped. The strange voice called out again in a hoarse whisper: "Cadet Flipper."

He walked tentatively toward Post Number Four, not knowing what to expect. No one had struck him since his arrival at West Point, but that could change. As dark as it was, he would never recognize his assailants. He felt even colder walking alone—the only sound now his footsteps on the frozen ground—until he collided with the man who had called his name.

"Christ!" the man said.

"Jesus!" exclaimed Flipper.

The beckoner laughed. "Gosh, it's dark tonight. How you doing?"

"Cadet Slaker?" Flipper asked incredulously. He still couldn't see the talker's face.

"Yep. Too cold to be alone. Figured we could talk some."

Flipper laughed off his previous fright. Adam Slaker had not said ten words to him since they arrived at the Academy. He had been the victim of Cadet Corporal Louis's hazing a year ago when, sick from the malicious cadet's tobacco, he sent his breakfast onto the parade grounds. Now he risked Limbo by talking to Flipper on guard duty—not that anyone was bound to catch them on a night like this.

"How'd you do on your topog' prelims?"

"Good," Flipper answered. "You?"

"All right. Man, this is colder than a witch's teat."

Flipper snickered. He had never heard the expression. He relaxed as Adam talked about everything, from Albert Church's sleep-inducing classes to just what was it Patrice de Janon had said before dismissing class on Friday. Flipper listened with enthusiasm. He hadn't realized how starved he had been for this kind of conversation, even if Adam Slaker was doing all of the talking.

After about ten minutes, Slaker said: "Man, Flipper, I'm sorry about how you been treated. It ain't right."

"Thanks."

"I mean it. Shucks, you're a better man than half the cadets here. You already speak Spanish like you was born in Mexico. You got a career in this man's army. You just bear down. I bet things are gonna get better. You're a true gentleman, Mister Flipper. That's a fact."

Flipper didn't know what to say. He didn't have to think of anything because Cadet Slaker kept talking. Five minutes later, the two decided they had better get back to guard duty if they didn't want to get hided and loaded with a bunch of demerits.

"See you around," Slaker said as Flipper walked away.

Yet, by the time Flipper returned to Post Number Five, he knew Adam Slaker would never talk to him in daylight, not when other white men could see him, not risk being ridiculed and ostracized as Henry Flipper had been. Cadet Slaker might prove to be one of the bravest men in the United States Army, might die a hero, fighting Indians, and be awarded the Medal of Honor, but he forever would be a coward in Henry Flipper's eyes. Hell, so would all of his classmates.

"Jesus! Watch yourself!"

Cadet Charles Gatewood reached over and grabbed Flipper's arm, preventing him from falling off his horse during riding lessons. They continued at a trot until Flipper righted himself in the saddle. He nodded at the cadet, an exceptional equestrian, and Gatewood released his hold. "Be careful," he said, and rode ahead.

The riding hall at West Point was a massive gallery that attracted scores of spectators, many of them "femmes." Flipper had never been much of a horseman back in Georgia, and his cavalry instructor hadn't helped matters by putting him on a feisty bay. Twenty cadets were trotting around the gallery, some of them riding as if they were part of the horse, others pulling leather, rocking like a buoy in a cyclone. How often had he seen other cadets, seconds after the "To a trot!" command from the instructor, spin like tops and sail to the ground? The onlookers roared with laughter at the comedic spectacle of would-be soldiers of the United States Army chasing their mounts. Flipper himself had been there many a time. But today he was lucky, thanks to Cadet Gatewood. Flipper could have been trampled if Gatewood had not grabbed his arm. But what would have hurt more than horses' hoofs was the fact that Anna White sat in the gallery this afternoon.

They first strolled along the waterfront, arms locked. Anna suggested they sit down for an early supper at the Rose Hotel near the West Point Dock, but Flipper shook his head. James Smith had warned him of the Rose. Sure, the hotel was owned by the government, and technically Cadet H. O. Flipper was a ward of that government, but a Negro would never be served there. They found a place to eat in Newburgh, and Flipper walked her back to the ferry.

"I'd like to call on you when I get back to Atlanta, Anna," he said.

She smiled. "I'd like that, too."

They stared at each other blankly. Flipper didn't know what to do next. His military training was evident when he asked: "May I have permission to kiss you, Anna White."

Anna giggled. "Henry, I don't know what has become of

you. But, yes, you may kiss me."

All of the West Point slang—"femmes," "spoons"—disappeared as they embraced quickly. Flipper pulled away first. After all, he was a cadet and a gentleman.

"Your brother says you're not one to settle down, Henry Flipper." Anna's tone was mischievous. "Should I be frightened?"

Inside, Flipper seethed. That meddling, conniving little Joseph. What did he know about his intentions? For that matter, what did Joseph Flipper know about women? All he did was keep his nose buried in a Bible. It had been almost two years since they had seen each other. Not one to settle down! He might have to thrash that loud-mouthed scamp when he returned to Atlanta, Army commission in hand.

"Will you write me?" Anna asked.

"I'll try," he said.

She closed her eyes, and they kissed again. The whistle on the ferryboat screamed, and Anna pulled away, spun around, and, lifting the hems of her skirt, ran to the boat, waving at Flipper as she disappeared in the crowd on the ramp.

He watched until the boat pulled out of the harbor, then turned and walked back to the Point. At the edge of a wharf, a white-haired man of color, still wearing a faded Army blouse and stained kepi, looked Flipper's way. The old man's right pants leg was pinned up at his knee. *A casualty of the war*, Flipper thought, and was humbled. *If not for men of his valor, I would not be here today.*

Using a battered crutch, the man rose from a smelly fish bucket and pulled himself to attention. Somehow he leaned against a trash barrel and steadied himself, bringing the wooden crutch to a perfect present-arms position.

"Sergeant Jerusalem Gooding," the old-timer called out,

"Fifty-Fourth Massachusetts!"

Flipper lifted his cap to return the man's salute.

"Carry arms!" the man commanded, and moved his crutch to his shoulder. He gave a toothless grin as Flipper marched past.

"Does my heart good, Cadet," the old soldier said. "Does my heart mighty good to see this."

Me, too, Flipper said silently. *Me, too.*

Chapter Nine

November 4, 1881

"I think I discover an omission," Barber said after T. J. Tilley finished reading over the court-martial testimony and proceedings. The captain looked over his notes and slowly rose, ignoring the glares from Pennypacker, Clous, and other members of the court. Flipper really couldn't blame them, either. Barber had been warned not to drag out these proceedings any longer.

"If my memory serves me right," Barber said, "somewhere in my remarks yesterday I said substantially that it would be improper for the accused to ask to be tried by the court or express a desire to be tried by the court, because if he has any desire in the matter, it is not to be tried at all." Barber tossed his notes on the table. "It is my impression I said that. I know I had that in my mind, and I think I made that remark somewhere."

The judge advocate grunted, shaking his head. "I have no objection to having dat made a matter of record now."

"Good," Pennypacker said. "The proceedings are approved, then. Judge Advocate Clous, call your first witness."

Flipper's stomach fluttered. He had pleaded innocent to all charges and specifications. After all the legal maneuvering, all the delays, the sparring matches between Clous and Barber over nothing, the real court-martial was beginning. Flipper's future in the Army lay at stake, and Clous would bring in the heavy artillery to start his prosecution.

"I call Colonel Villam Rufus Shafter."

"Pecos Bill" 's affection for hops and barley, chocolate and pone showed. He was fat, a forty-six-year-old, two-hundred-and-fifty-pound behemoth. There was no getting around that. He sported the red, bulbous nose of a hard drinker and drooping jowls that enlisted men, and some officers, joked about behind their commander's back. His hair, white on top, dark over his large ears, was parted in the middle, thinning and well-groomed, but his mustache was brown and thick, his eyebrows even bushier. He stood an inch under six feet in his boot heels, and constantly complained of gout. Flipper had heard a few 1st infantry troopers scoff that it was hard to take a gruff walrus seriously as a soldier, but Shafter's brilliant blue eyes blazed with an intensity that had intimidated Flipper when he had first met the colonel.

Those eyes locked on Flipper as the fat man settled into an armless chair and Captain Clous rose to begin his examination.

"Please state your name, rank, regiment, command, and station."

"William R. Shafter, Colonel, First Infantry, commanding officer, post of Fort Davis, Texas, stationed at the same post."

"Ven did you assume command of da post?"

Shafter shrugged. "Twelfth or Thirteenth of March, Eighteen and Eighty-One."

"Who vas da Acting Commissary of Subsistence at da post ven you assumed command?"

"Lieutenant Flipper, Tenth Cavalry."

"Ach! I omitted to ask you if you recognized da accused?"

"I do."

"Who is he?"

99

"Second Lieutenant Henry O. Flipper, Tenth Cavalry."

Shafter sighed, bored with these seemingly meaningless questions. He shifted uncomfortably in the chair, which squeaked beneath his massive weight.

Barber leaned close to Flipper and whispered: "If I were building a house, I'd hire the man who made that chair as my carpenter. If it can support the weight of a whale. . . ."

Flipper smiled, more to appease his counsel than because he thought it funny. He doubted if he would laugh until this whole tragic affair was behind him.

"State ven or how long did Lieutenant Flipper continue under your command as Acting Commissary?"

"Until the Tenth day of August."

"I see. And vat order, if any, did you give Lieutenant Flipper on or about da Eighth of July, Eighteen-Eighty-One, in reference to da disposition of post commissary funds to be mailed by him?"

Barber cleared his throat. "Do you refer to a written order or verbal?"

The judge advocate whirled around, angered by Barber's interjection. He whipped off his wire glasses and stared impatiently at his counterpart and rival. "Just vait and see vat it is from dis testimony."

With a shrug, Captain Barber dropped his gaze to the table and began furiously working his pencil, scribbling something in an unreadable scrawl on his note pad. Clous sighed and continued asking Shafter questions.

It went on like that for most of the morning. Flipper recalled his own duty as judge advocate. He couldn't remember asking so many questions. This must be an important case to John Clous, and he would make the most of it, even if it bored "Pecos Bill" Shafter and everyone else in the chapel into a coma.

Shafter's memory became troublesome, even to Captain Clous. The colonel couldn't recall if he had checked Flipper's commissary report on July 2nd.

"Have you any means of refreshing your memory?" the judge advocate asked, trying to rein in his temper before blasting his first witness.

"I'll step over to my office and see. If I was present on that day, I know that the duty was not delegated to anyone."

"Ach! Da Second is da vell-known day dat da President vas assassinated."

"I was at the post that day. I know I was at the post that day, and I don't believe I went away the next day, though it is possible I did."

"I vish for you to refresh your memory more distinctly upon dis subject." Clous turned to Pennypacker. "Vill da vitness step out a moment or two, *Herr* president?"

The court president looked at Barber. "Objections, Captain?"

"None."

"Very well. Colonel, please go to your office and refresh your memory. Court is adjourned for five minutes." The gavel fell, and Shafter waddled out of the chapel as others rose to stretch. Surgeon Waters shook his black boot as if trying to knock off a scorpion. Apparently his foot had fallen asleep.

Barber pulled out his watch. Twelve-forty. He returned the watch and stood, patting Flipper's shoulder, and walked to the window. Suddenly he laughed.

"Vat?" Clous asked.

The captain shook his head and filled two glasses with water from a pitcher. He brought them to the defense table and sat. Flipper took a sip. "Colonel Shafter is a strange

101

bird, Mister Flipper," Barber said.

"What do you mean?"

"Well, I reckon he keeps his post records in the officer's privy. Because that's where he was running to, not headquarters."

This time Flipper's grin wasn't forced. "I guess that's why he wanted so badly to refresh his memory."

The two laughed, drawing stares from every member of the court. It felt good to laugh, after all, Flipper decided. It felt really good.

After chugging down his water, Barber tugged on the ends of his mustache. "How familiar are you with the rules of court-martial, Henry?" the captain asked.

"More now than I had ever hoped to be. I did a lot of studying before you came along. Thought I'd be representing myself."

"Then you know that under cross-examination I can only question Shafter on points Clous brings up? If I need to ask him about anything else, then I'll have to call Shafter as a defense witness. And I don't want to do that. He hates you."

"He seems to dislike all Negroes."

"There's a reason for that, Henry. You know Shafter faced a court-martial himself three or four years ago?"

Flipper's eyes widened. "I didn't know that."

"Lieutenant Edward Turner preferred charges. Nothing could be proved, and the court was dissolved. But the story goes that Shafter was seeing a Negro whore in Eagle Pass. And he also tried to charm another girl in San Antonio . . . they say she was only thirteen or fourteen years old . . . into his bedroom. When her father found out, Shafter paid him fifty dollars to keep quiet. Some say she was black. Others say she was Mexican. No matter. If those things had come out on the record, Shafter's career would have been finished. Now I don't care about the whore, but the young girl in San Antonio. . . ." Barber shook his head. "That's conduct unbecoming an officer and a gentleman, not what you did."

"Are you going to bring those up?"

"I can't. Unless I call Shafter for the defense, and, like I said, I'm not doing that. Besides, it's only character assassination, and whatever Shafter did in Eagle Pass and San Antonio is not valid to your case. And I think Clous has already brought up something I can use to pound that fat numskull."

"What's that?"

"Shafter's memory."

When Shafter returned to the witness chair, he testified that he had, indeed, signed the normal report on July 2nd and 3rd and thus was positive he had inspected the funds for the week ending July 2nd. The monotonous testimony droned on and on until finally Clous led his first witness to the point of the court-martial.

"Now, on da Eighth of July, a message arrived from Major Michael Small of the Commissary Department in San Antonio. Da major asked for all subsistence funds as of da Tirtieth of June. Is dat correct?"

"I think so. I'm not sure of the exact dates. But June Thirtieth is the close of the fiscal year."

"And vat did you do?"

"I ordered Lieutenant Flipper to submit funds for my immediate inspection, then forward them to Major Small."

"And did he?"

"I thought so at the time."

"But he did not?"

"No. About the next day, I guess, the lieutenant gave me

his statement, saying the money was in transit to San Antonio. It wasn't until early to mid-August that I learned otherwise. Lieutenant Flipper received a telegram on August Fifth from Major Small that the funds weren't there. Flipper didn't report this to me. When I found out, at first the lieutenant told me he thought it was only some temporary delay in the mail, that the funds would reach San Antonio shortly. I think that all I said to him at that time was that he should have told me."

"He lied?"

"Yes."

"Da accused said he had included a personal check for more than fourteen hundred dollars, hadn't he?"

"He did."

"Did he?"

"No."

"Ven you learned of dis, vat did you do?"

"I questioned him. He said he had simply forgotten it. I told him that was a large check to forget. I then told him that I did not believe he had ever sent the checks and I would act accordingly. I told him if I was mistaken, I would apologize."

"So you had his quarters searched?"

"Yes. By Lieutenants Wilhelmi and Edmunds."

"And vat vas discovered?"

"They found some three hundred dollars with letters of transmittal, weekly documents that I had signed . . . all of these things should have been mailed to the Commissary Department. Flipper was arrested, but at first I thought it still might be some mistake. The lieutenant had some nigger wench as his housekeeper, laundress . . . I don't know what else she did for him. I thought she might be responsible. We interrogated her in my office. I had her searched and discovered almost three thousand dollars in checks in her clothing. One was Flipper's check. The one he said he had mailed to Major Small.

"Lieutenants Wilhelmi and Edmunds also found what appeared to be the remains of checks in the fireplace of Flipper's quarters. We thought he might have had them burned in an attempt to destroy evidence once he, Flipper that is, knew we were on to him. We arrested the darky, Lucy Flip . . . I mean Smith. Charged her with theft of government property and sent her to Presidio. After further interrogation, I determined that Lieutenant Flipper had planned to abscond with those funds, maybe go down to Mexico with his mistress. You know how those people are."

"Indeed. Go on."

"Well, I had the lieutenant locked up. We sent a telegraph to the bank in San Antonio and found out that Mister Flipper had no personal account there, so his check was completely worthless. I asked him about this, and he told me that he had to deceive me in some way. He went on to say he didn't know what had happened to the money. I asked him if he thought that girl of his might have some of it. He said he didn't think so. We already knew otherwise."

"For how long vas da lieutenant in da guardhouse?"

"Well, I'm not sure. I was ordered to confine him to his quarters, get him out of the guardhouse. They wanted me to treat him like he was a white man." Shafter shook his head in disgust.

"One final question, *Herr* Colonel. Are you absolutely certain dat da accused is guilty of all charges and specifications preferred against him?"

"I am."

Clous smiled, removed his glasses, and began cleaning the lenses with a handkerchief. "I have no more questions of dis vitness. He is all yours, *Herr Kapitän*."

Shafter shifted uncomfortably in the chair as Merritt Barber rose. "Colonel, you informed Lieutenant Flipper that he would be relieved as A.C.S. after you took over as commander of Fort Davis, is that correct?"

"It is."

"Why?" Before Shafter could answer, Barber added: "Was it because you were displeased with his performance?"

The colonel had to think a moment. "It was not because I was dissatisfied with him, but it was because I thought he ought to be assisting the other cavalry officers in performance of their duties in the field."

Barber nodded. But before he could ask another question, Galusha Pennypacker cleared his throat. "It's getting late, gentlemen, and I'm sure Captain Barber has plenty of questions for Colonel Shafter. I'm going to adjourn these proceedings. Court will reconvene at ten o'clock tomorrow morning."

"Well?" Barber asked back in Flipper's quarters as he filled two cups with coffee.

Flipper shrugged. "I wasn't about to go to Mexico with all that money, with Lucy Smith or by myself."

"I know that." He handed Flipper a cup. "Shafter doesn't believe it, either."

Flipper straightened. "He said so."

"I'll nail him. Drink up, Henry, and get some sleep. It's going to be a long day tomorrow."

Steam rose from the coffee, and Flipper blew on it before taking a sip. Sleep? Who was Merritt Barber kidding? Flipper wouldn't get any sleep until this trial was over.

Chapter Ten

Second-Class Year, 1875–76

Ninety-six demerits. More than double what he had accrued as a plebe but still not enough to be kicked out of the Academy. Plebes had actually been guilty of many of the charges that had earned Flipper the demerits, but he never spoke up to defend himself or blame some inexperienced, first-year student. A cadet quickly learned to honor and respect the "code of silence" at the Point. He finished his second year ranked fiftieth out of eighty-four survivors, although he stood thirty-seventh in Spanish. Fiftieth. Some would be pleased with that, but it spelled average to Cadet Henry Flipper. He could do better than that. Yet, as he walked through the gates of West Point, he couldn't help but feel proud. He was a furloughman. When he returned to the Academy, he would be an upper-class cadet.

Strolling toward the Hudson, he suddenly felt free. Like most yearlings, he had counted the days to furlough. Now it was here. He had much of the summer to celebrate, to meet and make friends—impossible for a man of color at the Academy—and he didn't have to worry about being called in class to recite something, to determine a calculus problem's solution, or ride a galloping horse in a gallery filled with ladies only to fall from the saddle and embarrass himself. He could stay up late and not strain his vision rereading Rowan's *MORCEAUS CHOISIS DES AUTEURS MODERNES*, hoping that no one would see the candlelight and hide him for violating "lights out."

As the ferry steamed away and the walls of the Academy

diminished, Flipper thought back to that May day when he had first arrived at West Point. Now, those horrible nerves of an appointee had been replaced by the excitement of an upper classman. He had wanted to shout for joy after reading his name on the list of cadets granted furlough—the superintendent could very well have declined the leave, or reduced the number of days, because of disciplinary problems or poor academic standing, but Cadet H. O. Flipper had been given "a full pardon."

Some cadets were going home, but not Flipper. He had given much thought to a trip to Atlanta, to see his parents and brothers and, more importantly, Anna White, but he had decided against it. No, he wouldn't return to Georgia until he had been graduated from West Point. Then, commission in hand, he would walk the streets proudly with Anna on his arm. He would make history. The first Negro to survive West Point, the first black officer in the United States Army.

Two letters had come from Anna, but studies had prevented him from writing her back. He hoped to send her a note from New York City, which is where he decided to spend his furlough. He wanted to explore the city. Besides, he had also received another letter that intrigued him.

May 10, 1875
Cadet H. O. Flipper,
United States Military Academy,
West Point, New York

Dear Sir:
    The articles published recently in the city and national newspapers about your travails and successes at the prestigious United States Military Academy have

garnered the attention of everyone at our publishing house, and I would like to meet with you at your earliest convenience to discuss the possibility of you writing a book.

A book may seem daunting to many citizens, but anyone who has overcome the abject horror of slavery and the hazing from cadets can, I firmly believe, pen a splendid account of this most interesting history.

If you are interested in discussing the matter further, perhaps we can meet in the city during your furlough and talk about the book, what we think it should contain, and discuss a contract and advance. This book is sure to sell, Mister Flipper, and I think you'll find publishing pays a much tidier sum than military service.

Let me know your thoughts. We can set up a time for an interview.

> I remain
> Your obt. servant,
> Jon Markland
> Homer Lee & Company
> New York

P.S.: Please note, however, than any book contract is dependent on your graduation from the Academy in two years. JJM

Bald, bespectacled, pot-bellied Jonathan James Markland met Flipper at the train station, and hailed a hack to take them to a restaurant before going to the offices of Homer Lee & Company. He compulsively dabbed a stained white handkerchief on his perspiring brow as they settled into a corner booth, away from the windows, away from other customers. A boyish, pale waiter in a white jacket stepped up, eyed Flipper suspiciously, and stared at the sweaty white man with him.

"Can I interest you gentlemen in something to drink?" he asked.

The handkerchief disappeared into Markland's coat pocket. "Henry?" the publisher asked. "Would you like a beer, some red wine perhaps?"

He shook his head. "No thank you, sir. Coffee will do fine. Black."

"Of course," the waiter said, and grinned. Flipper didn't catch the joke until after the teenager had turned to take Markland's order, and he wondered if they had been seated here for privacy or so other customers and passers-by wouldn't see a Negro being allowed to eat here.

"Scotch," Markland ordered. "Glenlivet, if you have it. And bring us both the special of the day." Markland winked at Flipper. "The roast turkey here is divine, Henry."

The waiter quickly returned with their drinks. Flipper sipped his coffee. Markland gulped down his tumbler in four or five quick swallows and asked for a refill. "I don't see how you can drink coffee on a hot day like this," he said, and the handkerchief reappeared.

"Keeps you warm in the winter," Flipper said, recalling the saying Private Henry Hartsell had told him ten years ago. "And cools you off in the summer."

"The coffee here will take the enamel off your teeth."

"It's better than what we get at the Point, sir."

Markland laughed. "You would make a fine soldier, Henry Flipper. A mighty fine soldier."

"Thank you, sir. I hope you're right."

The food came with Markland's second drink, and he had finished a third by the time the waiter brought them cherry cobbler for desert. Afterward, the publisher leaned back in his chair and fired up a cigar. Flipper slid back in his chair, stretched out his long legs, and watched the commotion through the restaurant's plate-glass windows. The streets were crowded, men in bowlers and Irish caps, women in bonnets and straw hats, moving through Manhattan. He wondered where they were going, what they did for a living. A dirty little urchin in rags held up the latest copy of the *World* and screamed out the headlines in an Irish brogue. Blacks and whites . . . Chinese and Mexicans . . . Italians and Irish . . . Jews and Catholics . . . businessmen and the homeless . . . homemakers and whores . . . children and old-timers . . . soldiers and sailors . . . they filled New York. It was quite a city.

"Hotter than blazes," Markland commented, and mopped his face again.

Flipper had to agree. New York could rival a Georgia cotton field this time of year.

"Well, Henry, before we go to the office, do you have any questions?"

He had hundreds of them, but couldn't think of any right now.

"What we're looking for is not scandal, Henry," Markland explained. "What we want are your impressions, what you went through, what it was like." He changed his tone, curious now, not offering examples. "What do you think of hazing?"

Flipper cleared his throat, felt as if he were being called for a semiannual recital in Captain Didion's artillery class.

"It's an important part of the academy, Mister Markland. I firmly believe it makes soldiers out of boys."

"But do they take it too far on a colored boy like yourself?"

"I don't think so. At least, I don't think they hazed me unfairly as a plebe. Now some of my classmates were rude, callous apes, but that has nothing to do with hazing."

"Great, great. And what of Cadet Smith? What about him?"

Flipper looked away. Some of the usually friendly newspapers and black leaders had blamed him for Smith's dismissal, saying he should have helped his brother. But they didn't know James Webster Smith. He didn't want help, and Flipper doubted if he ever could have survived West Point if he had all the help in the world. "I'd rather not say, sir. That's for Cadet Smith to say."

"Do you think a Negro can overcome everything to become a West Point graduate?"

"You had better hope so, Mister Markland," Flipper said, smiling. "Or you will not get your book."

Markland grinned. "Excellent, Henry. Let's go up to the office. I'll show you around, let you see what Homer Lee and Company is all about. And, by the way, I am quite aware that you won't be able to write this book while you're at West Point. Your studies will prevent that. But take notes. Jot down your thoughts when something happens. Then, perhaps when you're graduated and have found a good job, perhaps here in the city, you can write, write, write. Who knows, maybe Homer Lee and Company might have a job for you."

He considered this for a moment. "Sir," he said, "when I am graduated from the Academy, my job will be as an officer in the United States Army."

The cigar dropped from Markland's mouth onto the remains of his cobbler. He picked it up, placed it in an ashtray, and found his handkerchief once again. "You're serious, Henry? You'll pursue an Army career if you are graduated?"

"Yes, sir. That's why I'm attending the Academy, Mister Markland. It isn't to prove a point. I want to be a soldier, to serve my country." That sounded corny, like a politician. He stopped himself from going further.

"Most impressive," Markland said when he rediscovered his voice. "What branch of service?"

"I'd like to try the cavalry," he said, and laughed at himself. What would Cadets Gatewood or Bigelow, two excellent equestrians, say about that? "The Ninth and Tenth regiments out West are manned by colored soldiers. I would like to be an officer with one of those."

"But those regiments are commanded by white officers, aren't they?"

Flipper gave Markland a smirk. "Well, sir, there really hasn't been a black officer to command them . . . yet."

The publisher dropped a couple of greenbacks on the table, and rose. "Why not request a commission in a white unit?"

"Mister Markland, do you really think a white soldier would take orders from me?"

Jon Markland showed Henry Flipper around as if he were royalty, introducing him to bankers, politicians, businessmen. Through the evening balls and business dinners, the tours at day and plays at night, Flipper felt like a prince. Being pampered certainly beat being hazed. Once, after three or four rounds of Scotch, Markland discretely told Flipper that, if he desired female company, Markland could have that arranged, could send a nice little chippy, black, white, or yellow, whatever he wanted, to the hotel room on Sixth Avenue. Flipper was sorely tempted to take him up on that offer, but he thought about Anna and politely declined.

He granted one more interview with a newspaper correspondent for the *New Era* before returning to West Point. It went well, Flipper thought, and, when he shook the reporter's hand and turned to board the ferry, the short, middle-aged man grabbed Flipper's shoulder, pulled him close, and whispered: "Remember, my friend, the unusual responsibility you carry on your shoulders. If you get that diploma, our enemies lose and you win us a great victory for equality. It's hard work, but after you show them you have equal powers, you will eventually win equal rights."

Chemistry and philosophy kicked him harder than the gelding had during riding lessons. Flipper quickly understood how James Webster Smith had failed his philosophy finals. A year or so ago, he had heard one cadet mention that the difference between yearling studies and second-class studies was like night and day, but Flipper had thought that meant academics got easier. Engineering and drawing were fine, but the science—well, what did a former slave know about science? John Quarles had taught him a lot about reading and math, but Quarles himself would probably be "fessed cold" in chemistry or natural and experimental philosophy.

He was thinking about that on guard duty in the barracks on a miserable December while most cadets were eating supper, when First Class Cadet Bob Stoker stopped at the post. Stoker, a slow-talking, clumsy boy from Ohio, glanced over his shoulder, made sure it was safe (no one would see him talking to a Negro), and smiled. "Man, I read a newspaper story about you last week, Mister Flipper." Another glance back. "I just want to say how sorry I am for how we've treated you. I want you to know that I ain't got nothing against coloreds . . . ,"—another look—"but I've called you a black moke, a stupid charcoal, and a damned uppity nigger to my classmates."

Flipper's eyes widened.

"It ain't that I think that, exactly, Mister Flipper," Stoker went on. "It's just that them boys that really hate you, well, they'd gut me like a bream for supper if I didn't agree with 'em, if I didn't call you them bad names." He sighed heavily, looked toward the mess hall again, and said: "They'll likely kill me if they see me talking to you. Anyway, I want you to know that, no matter what I say in front of them rubes, that I'm your friend. And I want you to know that I'm damned sorry for everything we've put you through, but I'm mighty proud to see you ride it out."

He left in a hurry. Another coward, or maybe not; Flipper never got the chance to find out. Six months before he would have graduated, Bob Stoker was found deficient in mineralogy and was dismissed from the Academy.

Somehow Flipper "maxed" his January recitals and moved forward. He suddenly found cavalry tactics and riding lessons a pleasure. No longer did his horses pitch him from the saddle. Even Charles Gatewood laughed at him as they galloped across the gallery. "You're going to be riding like Romans pretty soon, Cadet, two horses at a time," Gatewood said. "You've come a long way."

Flipper felt proud. Gatewood talked to him in public, albeit on horseback in a noisy pavilion, and on few occasions did his fellow cadets curse him or call him a nigger. Oh, certainly, most avoided him, but maybe he had earned their respect. Those thoughts, those illusions, vanished on a spring day when the cadets fell in to march on a retreat parade.

As a second-year cadet, Flipper took his place ahead of the plebes and yearlings.

"What's the brunette doing up here with the white upper classmen, Sergeant?" the cadet captain of D Company, Flipper's unit, asked.

"Because he's a second classman, sir."

The black-haired senior captain spit, looked up and down the ranks, and smiled. "I think we need to fill out the ranks in the rear, Sergeant. Don't you agree?"

"Yes, sir! Cadet Flipper, fall in to the rear."

Flipper obeyed. He had been sent to the rear before as a second classman, but always he would be returned to his proper place. He waited for this to happen as the officers inspected the formation. The cadet sergeant stared at Flipper, moved away, barked an order to a Florida third classman well in front of him. When the cadet sergeant returned, after Flipper could see the formation had filled in and his presence was no longer needed back with the plebes, he decided this time he would fight back. He was a second classman, not a plebe, and damned if he would march with them because of his color during this retreat parade.

The order sounded: "In place . . . rest!"

"Cadet Sergeant, sir?" Flipper asked.

"What is it?"

"I respectfully request that I be returned to my proper position."

The sergeant said nothing.

"The company has been formed and inspected, Sergeant, and I have a right to march ahead of plebes and yearlings as befitting a second-class cadet."

Grumbling, the sergeant nodded. "Get to it, Flipper, and be damned quick before the captain sees you."

It should have ended there—Flipper had forgotten about it—until he received notice that the sergeant had accused Cadet Flipper of speaking to him at formation. Flipper again decided to fight back. He would not receive any demerits for this so-called offense.

April 11, 1876

Sir:

In explanation of the cadet sergeant's charges, let me say that I said nothing to the sergeant about the formation of D Company. However, I was placed in the rear rank, contrary to custom. When I noted to him that junior cadets were in the front ranks and after I requested to take my proper place, the sergeant granted permission to make the change.

Respectfully submitted,
Henry O. Flipper
Cadet Private, Company D

The commandant forwarded Flipper's written defense to the cadet sergeant, who offered no resistance. The charge was dropped. No demerits. Flipper had won a victory. A minor one, perhaps, but a victory nonetheless.

Chapter Eleven

November 5–9, 1881

"Was Lieutenant Flipper a gambler?"

"Not to my knowledge."

"A habitual drunkard?"

"No, I don't think he touches liquor."

"A poor officer?"

"No." William Rufus Shafter shook his head. "By most reports, he seemed to be a fine cavalry officer."

"Yet you had him arrested?"

"Yes." The colonel's hard eyes followed Captain Barber as he paced across the chapel floor. Shafter had only been on the witness chair a few minutes, but already his flabby face shone with damp sweat despite the coldness of the morning. Someone had failed to light the stove earlier today. It would take a few hours before the chapel warmed up. Under most conditions, "Pecos Bill" would have had that man's head, but Flipper doubted if the colonel even realized that the other officers in the building shivered.

Merritt Barber walked to the table to glance at his notes. His eyes met Flipper's, and the captain winked.

"Colonel," Barber said, turning to face the witness again, "let's talk about your theory that the accused had burned the checks and stolen the money. Explain what you ordered, sir."

"I ordered the fireplace searched on that theory."

"And in giving that order, that was your theory at the time?"

"That was one of the means I took to find the checks as I

was satisfied that he had not mailed them. I took his servant over to my office and examined her, thinking that she might know something about it."

Barber nodded. "That was your theory of the disposition of the commissary money?"

"That was my theory of the way he might have disposed of it."

"You afterward found the checks?"

"I did."

"Therefore your theory was wrong."

The judge advocate rose quickly. "Dat vas one of da means or theories dat he took."

Barber shot back: "We will let the colonel testify, if you please."

Still fuming, Clous sat down. The defense counsel cleared his throat and continued his examination: "Will you please state to the court, if you know of the present whereabouts of the following articles belonging to Lucy Smith . . . one jewel box, one ring with a pearl setting, a gold ring, one gold necklace, one solid locket, one rolled plate with chain, one pair of gold Mexican earrings, one pair of gold bracelets, one gold slide for ladies?"

"I do not know."

"Hmm. Let's talk about Lieutenant Wilhelmi's report after he interrogated and then arrested Lieutenant Flipper. Did you look at the papers Wilhelmi brought to you, or did you simply take his word about the contents?"

"I do not remember." Shafter found a handkerchief and wiped his face.

"How about Lieutenant Flipper's watch . . . his West Point ring? Are those considered part of the commissary funds?"

"Of course not. They're his personal property."

"Yet they were not returned."

"I'm not sure. They should have been."

"But you don't know?"

"No."

"Did you order those officers to take possession of Lieutenant Flipper's valuables?"

Shafter answered testily: "I told them to search him and his quarters. Lieutenants Edmunds and Wilhelmi were searching for stolen government property, damn you. They brought me a lot of items, including commissary funds. Those items were locked in a safe."

With a smile, Barber shook his head. "I don't believe, sir, that you answered my question."

"I know I didn't."

"Rings, a watch, shirt studs, sleeve buttons, shoe buckles? The detectives you sent took anything they could lay their hands on. Tell me, Colonel, who looks like the thief here?"

Court member William Fletcher, a captain in the 20th Infantry, took a deep breath, slowly exhaled, and instructed Barber: "Captain, Colonel Shafter is not the one on trial here."

"He should be," Barber answered underneath his breath. "Very well. Let's talk about your interrogation of Lucy Smith, the lieutenant's housekeeper."

Now Judge Advocate Clous rose and approached the court-martial board. "If it pleases the court, I vould like a private moment with *Kapitän* Barber and da panel."

Pennypacker nodded, and Barber joined the German in front of the board members.

"*Kapitän,*" Clous whispered, "I have tried to keep scandal out of dis court-martial. Dis Lucy Smith, she could vell damage da accused's honor. It is known all over Fort

Davis dat dis girl, she has no honor. A robber. A prostitute."

"Horse apples."

Clous's eyes flamed. He barked something in German, jerked off his glasses, and tried to stare down Barber, but couldn't. When he realized this, he turned to Pennypacker. "Ach. I try to help, and dis is vat *Kapitän* Barber fires back at me. Insults. Commandant Shafter should not be allowed to testify about dis housekeeper."

"You brought Miss Smith up, Captain," Pennypacker said. "It's Captain Barber's right to cross-examine the witness."

"Ach!" Clous positioned his glasses on his nose. He shook his head, mumbling something in his native tongue.

Barber grinned. "The German and American slang are uncommonly similar. You say ach. We say god damn."

"Vat is dis?"

With a shrug, Barber said: "Just paraphrasing Mark Twain."

Clous stared at him for a second, shook his head again, and walked back to his desk. "Ach," he said, waving his right hand as if swatting at a bothersome fly.

Said Barber: "God damn."

Court was adjourned until Monday morning. Barber said he thought the cross went well. He had called into question both Shafter's memory, his aimless running of the post, and his lack of reason for holding Flipper's valuables. Come Monday, Barber would hit the colonel with his interrogation about Lucy Smith. The captain fired up a cigar.

"Lucy Smith was my housekeeper, Captain." The words shot out of Flipper's mouth. "Well, maybe more than that, but. . . ."

Barber pulled the cigar from his mouth. "You don't have to explain that to me."

"But I feel I have to. I know what everyone's saying. We danced some and . . . well. . . . But about the clothes. I let Lucy keep clothes here because she asked if it would be all right. She wanted something to wear while cleaning."

"Sounds reasonable. Except she pitched a tent behind your quarters."

"Before that, sir. Yeah, we liked each other. Sure. And after she moved behind me, she was concerned about her jewelry and things. Wouldn't be safe in a tent. I told her to put the stuff in my trunk. I told her not to touch those government funds. She promised me she wouldn't."

The captain closed her eyes. "Henry," he said with a sigh, "you're way too trusting. Didn't you think she might steal that money?"

"No, sir." He was near tears now. "I thought I could trust her. I thought. . . ." He exhaled. "I've never had much luck with women, Captain."

"It's Merritt. Remember?"

"Yes, sir. Merritt. I know I made a lot of mistakes. Handling money never was my strong suit, anyway. I'll be the first to admit that I make a poor A.C.S., but I'm a damned good soldier."

Barber smiled. "Poor judgment is not a crime, Henry."

"It can be," Flipper said hoarsely. "In the Army, it can be."

When the court-martial board reconvened Monday morning, John Clous complained of a headache and requested a brief recess. That break dragged on till noon, and Barber resumed his cross-examination of Colonel Shafter. At least today the chapel was heated.

Lucy Smith, "Pecos Bill" said, had been questioned intensely, and afterward he evicted her from the post. As she was leaving his office, however, Lieutenant Wilhelmi noticed she had something concealed in her dress.

"I called her back and asked her if she was hiding something. She said no. The trollop even lifted up her dress on one side to show me. So I told her to get out of my sight. Lieutenant Wilhelmi, he insisted she was hiding something. He searched the other side of her dress, the one she hadn't lifted. Found an envelope. We searched it, found checks and cash, all property of the government . . . all funds Flipper said he had sent to San Antonio. We questioned her more after that discovery."

"Did you threaten her?"

"No."

"Use ungentlemanly language?"

"I don't think so."

Barber shook his head. When he spoke again, his tone had turned loud, angry: "Colonel, isn't it true that you told Lucy Smith . . . 'God damn you, you'll go to prison, and Mister Flipper, god damn him, I have got him, too'?"

"No, sir. I would never use such profanity. And I don't think you should be using it here. This is a house of God."

The counsel scoffed and continued. "Your female servant, the one you had search Lucy Smith, she says otherwise."

"She's mistaken."

"She's a god-fearing, Christian woman."

"She's a god-damn' nig. . . ." Shafter caught himself. He leaned back in the chair and mopped his sweaty, crimson face again. Barber kept coming. No pause. No quarter. Charge and attack. Charge and attack.

"You did order your servant to search Lucy Smith?"

"I did." The colonel's reply was barely audible.

"A strip search?"

"I told her to search her."

"Didn't you tell her to strip Lucy naked?"

"I said search her. I said I wanted a thorough search."

"Who was in the office when this search was done?"

"No one in that room. Only the two colored women."

"Who was around the building?"

"I can't recall. Myself. Lieutenants Wilhelmi and Nordstrom. Captain Bates. My orderly. The sergeant major. Regimental quartermaster probably. A few others."

"How many of those were peeping in the open window? Spying on poor Lucy Smith?"

Judge Advocate Clous flew out of his chair in a rage. *"Warten Sie einen Augenblick! Unrecht!* I must protest! Dis is outrageous! *Genug davon hab' ich!"*

The room fell silent, the only sound the hard puffing from a vehement William Shafter. Barber turned sharply and headed for his table, flipping through pages of his notes.

Clous continued: "I object. I must ask dis court, who is on trial, dis vitness or da accused?"

Merritt Barber whirled for his desk, reined in his temper, and turned to the court panel. "Gentlemen, I am not putting Colonel Shafter on trial, but I am showing that the treatment he administered against Lieutenant Flipper has been the most severe ever administered to an officer of the Army since its organization."

"Dis is a travesty!"

Pennypacker shook his head. "Sit down, Judge Advocate. Your objection is overruled. Continue your cross, Captain Barber."

Flipper couldn't believe it.

For two more days, Barber lambasted Shafter in the chapel. Flipper had never seen a lawyer like Merritt Barber. He was relentless. What was it the captain had said when they first met? If you were to cut my throat, I would bleed acid? Yes, that was it. Flipper smiled, then remembered Barber had added that he didn't have a heart . . . in a courtroom. He hadn't exaggerated.

"Did you not make statements," Barber asked Shafter, "based on your own knowledge, or those reports, that Lieutenant Flipper was going to run to Mexico, and that was the reason you sent officers to detain him and bring him to your quarters?"

Shafter sighed, bored after hours of answering Barber's pesky questions. "Are you asking if I said I thought he was going to Mexico?"

"Yes." He did not bother to add "sir."

"I do not think I ever said so. I was getting worried about the loss of the money. I heard Mister Flipper was in town and. . . ."

Barber stopped him by holding up his right hand. "Excuse me, Colonel, but the loss of the money had not yet been discovered."

"No, damn it, but I knew Major Small had not received the money in San Antonio. I thought that if Flipper had anything to do with it, well, anyway, I learned he was in town with his horse saddled, saddlebags on the animal. I thought he could go to Mexico if he wanted to, so I determined to have him returned."

"You had heard rumors that Flipper was going to make a run for the border. Where did those rumors come from?"

"I'm not responsible for any rumors, Captain."

Flipper watched Barber pace across the floor a few times. The captain ran his fingers through his hair and shrugged. "I guess not, Colonel." He checked his pocket watch, nodded, and smiled. "I shall suspend the cross-examination of this witness for the present. That is all I have to ask for the time being."

Judge Advocate Clous blinked. "Do I understand da defense to say dat dey have concluded da cross-examination upon da post commandant?"

"I do, sir." He waited until Shafter had risen. "But just one more question." Shafter glared and settled his ample frame back into the chair.

"Why did you confine Lieutenant Flipper to the post guardhouse?"

"I considered him a thief, a traitor."

"But you had little evidence."

"I thought I had enough." He leaned forward. "And I thought, sir, that you had only one more question for me."

The attorney beamed. "I ask only for your patience, Colonel. Would you have put a white officer in the guardhouse under similar circumstances?"

"I. . . ." Shafter leaned back. "Each case is different."

"Indeed. In fact, you had to be ordered to release Lieutenant Flipper and have him confined to quarters, which is what you should have done in the first place, isn't that true? And isn't it true that soldiers under your command said they were ashamed of the treatment being visited upon my client?"

When Shafter didn't answer and Clous shouted an objection, Barber simply smiled. "He doesn't have to answer that. And this time I *am* finished with the witness."

Pennypacker nodded and asked: "Does any member of the court have any questions for this witness?"

R. G. Heiner, a captain with Shafter's 1st Infantry, raised his right hand. "I don't have a question of Colonel Shafter, but I'd like to say a few things." Heiner stood, inhaled, and tugged on his goatee, collecting his thoughts.

"I dislike very much to make the remarks that I am going to make," he said at last, "but I feel compelled to do it. I, for one member of this court . . ."—he looked from side to side at the other panelists—"feel that I have other duties to perform for the government, but I'm here trying Lieutenant Flipper for certain offenses. I make this remark in open court because I wish to ask the accused's counsel to remove an opinion from my mind which now prevails." He glanced at the stenographer, made sure Tilley was taking everything down. "Captain Barber's cross-examination since Saturday has nothing whatever to do with the case we are called upon to try." Heiner let that sink in before continuing.

"If there is an attempt to make out here a case of persecution, I think it should stop. This is the Army, sir. The Army of the United States of America. That should mean something."

Barber smoothed his mustache after Heiner took his seat. "It means a great deal to me, Captain," Barber said. "And I suspect that it means even more to Lieutenant Flipper. But to respond to your suggestion, I desire that every single thing, every act of Lieutenant Flipper and all of those connected with him be brought forth to this court. If I find that persecution exists in this man's army, so be it. And, for the record, sir, I hope that no member of this court will feel that he has any other duties more important than to defend and guard the integrity and honor of a soldier and an officer in this Army."

"That little son-of-a-bitch," Barber said back in Flipper's duplex. "I haven't figured out if Heiner really thinks there's no such thing as persecution in this man's army, or if he is just pissed off at me for persecuting his fat-ass commanding officer." Barber took a quick pull from a bottle of brandy he had bought at Lightner's Saloon. "Jesus, persecution. All he has to do is ask any of the Irish in the Army, or Italians. They. . . ."

He looked at Flipper, swallowed, suddenly ashamed. He returned the cork to the bottle and placed the brandy on Flipper's sideboard. "Sorry, Henry. I'm just irritated at that . . . well, I mean, if anyone knows about persecution, it's you."

Flipper returned a smile. "Forget it, Merritt. Now, do you plan on drinking your supper, or should we get something solid to eat?"

"All right, Henry. Let me make a trip to the privy and we shall fill our stomachs." He went out the door, down the hall separating Flipper's and Nordstrom's quarters, and out back.

Forget it, Flipper said again, this time to himself. Yeah, Merritt Barber had been right. He knew all about persecution.

Chapter Twelve

First-Class Year, 1876–77

They streamed to Philadelphia in the summer of 1876, coming from all over the United States, even across the globe. A family from Skowhegan, a priest from Paris, school kids from Harrisburg, professors from Albany, planters from Alabama, sailors from Liverpool, a fisherman from Greece, nuns from Saint Augustine, a miner from Nevada, merchants from San Francisco, a gambler from Baton Rouge, a widow from Chattanooga. It seemed that everyone journeyed to the confluence of the Delaware and Schuykill rivers for the Philadelphia Centennial Exposition. For ten days practically the entire Corps of Cadets and instructors from the United States Military Academy camped near George's Hill, forming a military village of canvas tents that turned almost as popular with tourists as Mr. Alexander Graham Bell's invention called a telephone displayed at Machinery Hall.

When not on duty at the makeshift, but immaculate camp, the cadets roamed the streets of the beautiful city, looking in awe at the wonders of technology, and generally feeling like eight-year-olds attending their first county fair. Flipper had never seen anything like the myriad displays, from the typewriter to the Corliss Steam Engine, which someone said had more power than fifteen hundred horses combined.

"Would those fifteen hundred horses be Morgan stallions or the nags Flipper rides?" Charles Gatewood asked, and everyone, Flipper included, laughed.

For once, he was part of the Corps. Here, away from the portentous walls of West Point, Flipper felt welcome, not like some leper. Maybe it was because of all the excitement around them, or perhaps it was because Henry O. Flipper had proved his worth. He was a first classman now, standing sixty-fourth in the Order of General Merit, not excellent by any means, but he would have ranked higher if not for chemistry and philosophy.

Gatewood had invited Flipper to join a group determined to see everything the Centennial had to offer. Adam Slaker was with them, and so were Benjamin Butler and highbrow John Bigelow, Jr. Of course, those cadets had never been unkind to Flipper, although they hadn't been remotely social. At least four other cadets had bowed out of Gatewood's reconnaissance party when Flipper joined the group. "To hell with them," Butler had said, and asked Flipper if he wanted some lemonade.

Bigelow soon left the group for one of the city's lovely blonde-haired debutantes who desired to see stereocards in a booth before sampling an ice cream soda. He said he would meet up with the others later in the art exhibits at the Memorial Hall annex. None of the remaining cadets believed him.

"Popcorn!" a vendor cried. "Popcorn right here, folks! Come, get a bag!"

Slaker and Gatewood each bought a bag, while Butler coaxed Flipper to try something else. The two cadets plunked down a nickel and were given a long fruit wrapped in silver foil. Butler peeled away the aluminum and stared tentatively at the white, pulpy thing shaped like a misformed crescent. He watched as Flipper took a bite.

"How is it?" Butler asked.

Flipper swallowed. "Good. Really good."

Gatewood and Slaker had returned, popping kernels in their mouth one at a time. Butler sniffed the fruit in his hand before reluctantly following Flipper's example.

"What the hell is that thing?" Gatewood asked.

Since he was off duty, and didn't think he would be issued any demerits, Flipper answered with his mouth full. "Banana. Comes from the tropics. Good stuff."

"I'll be damned," Slaker commented.

They traded snacks. Butler pinched off a piece of his banana for Slaker and Gatewood—Flipper realized they had yet to come far enough where the white cadets would eat after a black man—and Slaker handed Flipper a small bag of popcorn.

"Finish that off, Henry," he said. "I don't want no more."

After eating, they pushed their way through the throngs to see the towering hand and torch that would be part of the Statue of Liberty in New York, and each cadet chipped in a couple of coins to help fund the project. Next, they toured the halls lined with life-like mannequins dressed in buckskins, breechcloths, bone breastplates, and magnificent beaded dresses.

"You ever seen an Indian?" Gatewood asked.

"No," Flipper answered. "Not a wild one. I once saw a Cherokee in a stovepipe hat in Atlanta. My daddy made him a pair of shoes. I reckon he doesn't count."

Gatewood shook his head. "I wonder what it'll be like . . . fighting Indians."

"I don't know. Haven't thought about it much."

"You'd best think about it some, Henry. We'll be soldiers soon."

They both turned at the sound of a man running down the hall. It was John Bigelow. "Charles!" he screamed, almost trampling a mother and her infant and mumbling some apology as he ran past the dummy figures of Apaches, Comanches, Kiowas, and Cheyennes. Most visitors at the exhibit stared at the charging cadet in anger. A few looked at Flipper as if he were to blame; he simply shrugged.

"Charles!" Bigelow shouted again. He was waving a folded newspaper over his head as if he were back at First Class Camp at the Point with a torch in night-signaling demonstrations. Bigelow was out of breath by the time he reached the Kiowa display. The onlookers shook their heads and resumed sightseeing.

"I thought you were going to meet us at the art exhibit," said Slaker, who had walked over with Butler to join his fellow cadets.

Hands on his knees, Bigelow continued panting.

"That blonde realize you are not an officer and a gentleman even though your papa is the New York Secretary of State?" Butler said with a grin.

Bigelow ignored the teasing and straightened. He handed Gatewood the newspaper, the *Philadelphia Times*, and said: "Boys, you're not going to believe this. And it's pretty ironic that I found you all here."

Flipper stood slightly behind Gatewood, so he read the multi-stacked two-column headline over the cadet's shoulder. His eyes widened at the news. "Holy Mary, Mother of God," Gatewood said, and lowered the paper.

The smiles had left Slaker and Butler. "What is it?" Butler asked.

Charles handed his friend the newspaper. "Custer," he said hollowly. "He and his whole command were wiped out at a place called the Little Bighorn."

Back at West Point, the camaraderie Flipper had experienced at the Centennial Exposition vanished. He lay in his tent at First Class Camp, listening to a cadet moan to his friends about being assigned guard duty with Flipper.

"He's the senior officer, damn it," the New Yorker said. "That means I have to answer to the black ape."

Another cadet laughed. "Admit it. Flipper's a better soldier than you."

"Not by a damned sight. Way that nigger swings his arms when he's marching, he's bound to clobber some fool. But he never gets skinned the way a white cadet would."

"Better watch it. Cadet Flipper might order you to. . . ."

"Shut up. Hell, why couldn't that moke have been with Custer? At least some good would have come out of the affair then."

There were other cases, too. Once, during camp, a cadet asked to borrow some ink. Flipper gave him a stick of India ink without a second thought, and the cadet returned it promptly—only Flipper found it inside his tent, on the grass, in the back. The coward had sneaked around the back, lifted the canvas, and shoved the remains of the ink inside so he wouldn't be seen entering Flipper's quarters.

Maybe the worse case came when a timid plebe from Wisconsin asked to borrow Flipper's algebra textbook. That was common during the summer, before cadets were forced to buy their own books from the commissary. They were standing outside Flipper's room, alone.

"Gotta bone up, eh?" Flipper said jokingly.

"Yeah. Can I have it? I'll give it back. Promise."

Flipper reached into his trouser pocket and withdrew the key to his trunk. "It's in my trunk. I've saved all of my books. But I've got to get to Kendrick's class on time or I'll be hided like there's no tomorrow. Take the book, lock the trunk, and put the key underneath my clothes bag."

The kid took the key with some reluctance. Flipper frowned. "Don't worry, plebe. No one's gonna see you in my room."

"It ain't that," the boy said, although Flipper knew he was lying. "It's just that . . . you'd trust me?"

He smiled. "You're a cadet and a gentleman, aren't you?"

At the end of August, Flipper found the book on his bunk. He picked it up and cursed the Wisconsin plebe. Flipper had bought that book during his plebe year, had proudly written his name on the inside front and back covers, and scratched an "F" on the cover. The plebe apparently had not wanted anyone to know he had borrowed a book from Flipper, so he had cut the letter from the calfskin cover.

It wasn't always like that. Bigelow and Butler treated him decently. His instructors were fair. In September, Johnson Chestnut Whittaker of Camden, South Carolina, joined the Corps of Cadets. Flipper no longer was the only black cadet, and for the first time since James Webster Smith had been dismissed, he had a roommate.

A Bible-thumper, that's what Whittaker seemed to be. West Point demanded morality, demanded religious worship. You attended chapel regularly, for two dismal hours on Sunday mornings, not to mention prayer services Sunday afternoons and Wednesday evenings. But Flipper had learned quickly that God did not exist inside the Academy's gates, at least not in the minds of most cadets. God would not help you survive Old Hanks Kendrick's mineralogy classes. God, like yearlings, despised plebes, and anyone who turned the other cheek was a damned coward.

Whittaker was kneeling in front of his cot, clutching a Bible to his chest with his left hand and mumbling a prayer when Flipper walked in. He turned slowly, scared, not knowing his roommate had entered. One look at the plebe's face told Flipper that the poor boy had reason to be afraid. His right hand clutched a bloody handkerchief, and blood seeped from both nostrils as well as a cut on the bridge. His left eye was partly swollen shut.

"Jesus," Flipper said, tossed his books aside, and dropped beside Whittaker. "You need to go to the infirmary."

The boy shook his head.

"Who did this to you?"

Whittaker wouldn't answer.

"Johnson, you can't let them beat you like this. Calling you names is one thing, but this is wrong. Who did it?"

"God will . . . ," Whittaker began, but Flipper cut him off.

"Don't hide behind God, Johnson. They'll hate you for it, think you're yellow, and you'll never make it here."

"It don't. . . ."

Flipper swore now, had to hold back from hitting Whittaker himself. He shot up, kicked an iron leg of his bunk, and screamed at his roommate: "Damn it, Johnson! We are not slaves any more. We are men. Cadets. They cannot lay a hand on us, damn it. If you don't speak up now, they'll be able to whip any colored cadet. I'm not letting you do that. Now, who hit you?"

Whittaker was crying. "McDonald," he said through his sobs, and Flipper cursed the son-of-a-bitch from Alabama. J. B. McDonald, a cadet and a gentleman. Like hell. Well, that rogue had gone too far now.

"He said I gave him an uppity sneer," Whittaker choked out between sobs. "Said he didn't have to take that from no damn' Carolina nigger."

"I want you to press charges, Johnson," Flipper said, calmer now. "You have to."

His roommate nodded.

Cadet J. B. McDonald was court-martialed, found guilty, and suspended from the Academy for more than six months. Flipper wondered if Whittaker or himself would have been given such a light sentence if they had assaulted a fellow cadet.

Recitations were over. On June 1, 1877, final examinations began. Geology and mineralogy came first, and Flipper felt like a scholar as the words flowed from his mouth. John Quarles would have been proud of him. Even Old Hanks Kendrick smiled, the rest of the board members nodded, and the *New York Herald* wrote: **There is no doubt that he will pass. . . .**

In law, he "maxed" his recital on Domicile. In fact, he did so well the Bishop Quintard of Tennessee, who was on the Board of Visitors, stepped outside after the examination and shook Flipper's hand. Flipper continued his run in civil and military engineering, expertly explaining "order of battle" and using the battles of Zama, Pharsalia, and Leuctra as examples.

But then came ordnance and gunnery, and the equation scratched on the blackboard might as well have been written in Chinese. "Determine the angle of trajectory and the range," said Senator Maxey, another board member, and Flipper knew he should have studied Benton's ORDNANCE AND GUNNERY a lot more thoroughly.

He finished, knowing he should have done better. A captain shook his head and said: "Cadet Flipper, I'm disappointed."

"So am I, sir."

Bishop Quintard, however, laughed. "Well, I understand Cadet Flipper is interested in a cavalry career, Captain, not artillery."

Senator Maxey didn't find any humor in examinations. "Cadet Flipper," he said, "you are dismissed."

He had slightly "fessed" one of his recitals. It would cost him a few places in the Order of Merit, but it wouldn't prevent one thing. One June 14th, Henry O. Flipper would get his "sheepskin" from the Point. He would be Henry Ossian Flipper, Second Lieutenant, awaiting assignment. He would be the first man of color to be graduated from West Point, the first black officer in the United States Army.

"Young gentlemen of the graduating class," began Professor C. O. Thompson, Board of Visitors president, and Flipper stifled a yawn. Ben Butler saw him and smiled. Embarrassed, Flipper tried to listen to Thompson's speech. A lifetime later, he craned his neck and caught Lieutenant Ben I. Butler, mouth open, head tilted back, letting loose the biggest yawn he had ever seen.

"Young gentleman," Thompson droned, and John Bigelow rolled his right forearm in a circular motion, whispering sarcastically: "And in conclusion. . . ."

Thompson's speech finally ended to scattering applause, and Major General W. S. Hancock stood up to make his speech, followed by another long-winded affair from Secretary of War G. W. McCrary, followed by Major General John M. Schofield's address, the "supe," West Point's superintendent. His speech grabbed the interest of the Class of 1877—and it was relatively short.

When he finished, the crowd applauded with enthusiasm. William M. Black of Lancaster, Pennsylvania, stepped forward to graduate at the top of his class. Forty-eight more names were called, and the cadets—no, soldiers about to become commissioned officers—stepped up to shake hands and take their diplomas.

"Henry . . ."—Schofield's words sounded so far away— "O . . . Flipper." Someone nudged him. Flipper stepped forward, dazed. He was graduating fiftieth in a class of seventy-six, but had stood fifteenth in discipline. He had made it.

As he shook the superintendent's hand and received the diploma, he turned to face the crowd—cadets, newspapermen, parents and relatives, soldiers, everyone—but not his parents, not his brothers, not Anna. They couldn't afford the trip to New York. Flipper didn't let that trouble him. They were proud of him. He was proud of himself. Ben Butler cut loose with a Rebel yell, and everyone must have joined in. The applause deafened him. Butler, Gatewood, Slaker, Bigelow—even the men who had despised him for four years—they were stomping their feet, pounding their palms. A beaming General Hancock clapped excitedly. Someone let loose with a shrill whistle. "Supe" Schofield shook his head and had to wait for the celebration to die down before calling forth the next graduating cadet.

Eyes welling, Second Lieutenant H. O. Flipper couldn't help but grin as he walked back toward his fellow officers. They slapped his back, praised him, pumped his hand in plaudits until his arm ached. After four years, they had finally accepted him. As an officer and a gentleman, as an equal, as a man.

Chapter Thirteen

November 10, 1881

The hardest part of a court-martial came during the mornings when T. J. Tilley read back the transcripts of the previous day's testimony. Flipper had to hear again the words of Shafter, only this time in the Topeka stenographer's dreary monotone. Afterward anyone could change or correct his remarks for the record. Once approved, the trial would continue.

"Call your next witness, Captain Clous," Pennypacker said, and the judge advocate asked Major Small to come forward.

"Michael P. Small, Major, Commissary of Subsistence. My duties are Chief Commissary of Subsistence of the Department of Texas, Purchasing and Depot Commissary, San Antonio, Texas. Station, San Antonio."

Flipper heard the words as Small introduced himself for the court record. He had communicated with the man by letter and telegram since he had taken over as Fort Davis' Acting Commissary of Subsistence but had never seen Small until now. He had pictured the major as a tiny, balding man with a pale face and thick-lens glasses that pinched the bridge of his nose. But Michael Small was as tall as Flipper, maybe even an inch taller, with a bronze face, Roman nose, thick black hair, and no glasses. He spoke strongly, full of confidence, and looked sharp in his dress uniform.

Clous led his witness through a review of Flipper's actions, and irregularities, between July 4th and July 24th, when the major was on furlough. Flipper found Small's answers, unlike Shafter's testimony, to be accurate, knowledgeable, thorough, and not racist. The man was a professional, but Flipper also knew that the court-martial panel might find the major's words damning: shortage of funds; Small's concern over the matter; trouble communicating with Flipper. The judge advocate seemed pleased when he relinquished his witness to Merritt Barber.

"Major," Barber began, remaining seated beside Flipper, "when did you become Chief Commissary?"

"December Twentieth, Eighteen-Eighty."

"And was Lieutenant Flipper the Acting Commissary of Subsistence at Fort Davis when you began your duties?"

"Yes, Captain, he was."

"You served as an A.C.S. before, haven't you, Major?"

"Indeed."

"Is it a difficult assignment?"

Small nodded. "It can be. You have to be well-organized. And it can be tough collecting money. Soldiers may be away from the post, hundreds of miles away."

"So, one shouldn't be overly concerned if a few dollars are missing?"

"Well, there's always a reason for concern if the books don't add up, Captain. And three thousand, seven hundred, ninety-one dollars, and change is not a few dollars."

Flipper sucked in air at that reply, but Barber seemed unconcerned. "True," the captain went on, "but there is a difference between embezzlement and poor bookkeeping, isn't that so?"

"Of course."

"And if, say, a paymaster were robbed by bandits and relieved of his funds, would he be charged with embezzlement?"

"No. Of course not."

"Thank you, Major. One final question. What was your opinion, as the Chief Commissary for the Department of Texas, of Henry Flipper's job as A.C.S.?"

Clous objected. Why, Flipper had no idea, and the court almost immediately overruled the judge advocate. Barber nodded at the witness, signaling him to continue.

"To the best of my knowledge," Small said, "up to the time Lieutenant Flipper got in this trouble, it was well conducted. I had no reason to be dissatisfied with his administration of the post subsistence affairs."

"Thank you, Major."

Neither the judge advocate nor the court had further questions for Small, so he was dismissed. Pennypacker checked his watch and suggested a recess for dinner, but Clous rose and said: "Gentlemen, I vish to call da court's attention to *ein* particular item."

The court president looked hungry and irritated. "Is it a brief item, Captain?"

"*Ja.*"

"Proceed."

"Under the United States Revised Statutes"—Clous held up a thick, leather-bound book—"if a person is charged *mit* embezzlement, da prosecution must only prove dis . . . as Major Small said, da books do not add up. All I have to do is show documentation, da books, and prove a deficiency in da proceedings. Da prosecution does not have to show dat da accused did dis for profit."

Barber's nostrils flared as he rose. "May I remind the judge advocate and the court that Lieutenant Flipper has been charged with embezzlement under the Sixtieth Article of War. That means that the judge advocate must prove to the court's satisfaction that Lieutenant Flipper embezzled those funds by fraudulent means and for personal gain."

Pennypacker shot back: "Sit down, the both of you."

The officer-jurists huddled together for three or four minutes. Flipper caught himself holding his breath until Pennypacker addressed the court. "Captain Clous, we will discuss this further in closed session. Captain Barber, you and the accused shall wait outside until summoned."

Barber remained agitated once they were on the chapel's porch. He ran down the steps, kicked the dirt, swore, and slammed his right fist into the open palm of his left hand. The newspaper reporters wisely kept their distance. "That Clous, I bet his bloodline traces back to Attila the Hun, the Scourge of God." His fist connected again. "And Pennypacker and the rest of those bastards. The Article of War should take precedent. There shouldn't be any discussion. Son-of-a-bitch!"

The captain's tirade continued, but Flipper lost interest. Instead, he concentrated on the slender, sandy-haired second lieutenant in campaign clothes and a brownish-red slouch hat making a beeline for the chapel. Suddenly Flipper smiled. Merritt Barber must have noticed that because he shut up, stared at Flipper for a second, then focused on the approaching officer.

"Hello, Henry," Wade Hampton said. "Miss me?"

"Welcome back to Fort Davis, Wade," Flipper said. "How was your furlough?"

The Southerner frowned and shrugged. Flipper didn't lose his smile. He already knew that his friend's efforts to drum up support by important black political figures in the East had failed, but it was good to have Hampton back. It was good to have another officer on his side.

The reunion was short-lived. Clous opened the door and asked Barber and Flipper to come back inside. The smile appearing between the big German's mustache and beard told the attorney and defendant that the court had ruled in favor of the judge advocate.

"Exception," Barber said after the formal announcement.

"Noted," Pennypacker responded. "Instead of recessing for dinner, we'll adjourn for the day, reconvene at ten o'clock tomorrow morning."

They sat on the porch outside Flipper's quarters, sipping coffee as Barber explained to Hampton what all had happened during the first few days of the court-martial. Hampton's only comment was to shake his head and murmur: "That ain't right."

Merritt Barber let out a long sigh when he had finished. "Don't get me wrong, Henry," he said as if trying to restore lost confidence. "I still think we have a good chance of acquittal on all charges and specifications. We have shown that Shafter wasn't an exemplary leader, though I honestly don't think he tried to frame you. Wilhelmi and Nordstrom perhaps. But Shafter? He's too stupid to frame anyone. And Major Small had no complaints about your effectiveness as A.C.S. So when Lieutenant Wilhelmi testifies, I'll gut him and his pack of lies like I would a perch."

"Who testifies before Wilhelmi?" Hampton asked.

"George Davidson and John Withers. Their testimony should be harmless."

Hampton blinked and stared, waiting for an explanation. He didn't know either man. Flipper understood the expression and said: "Davidson is the chief clerk for the Commissary Department in San Antonio. Withers works for the San Antonio National Bank."

The incredulous Southerner shook his head. "The

Army's bringing in a banker some four hundred miles?"

"Captain Clous is," Barber replied. "And Withers is only a cashier there."

"Seems to me to be a waste of government funds." Hampton drained his coffee.

"I'd agree with you, Lieutenant, but the judge advocate is bound and determined to present a thorough case to get a guilty verdict. He's a good lawyer, tough, smart, relentless. And he'll break any rule if it favors his end. He's a bigger arse than I am."

"Yeah," Hampton said, "but would he go to that trouble if Henry was a white man?"

No one bothered to answer that, but the conversation continued, mostly planning for the next day's testimony and tactics. The three officers were so involved in their discussion that they failed to notice the woman until she stood on the porch and cleared her throat. Hampton, Flipper, and Barber turned and stared, no one saying anything, like schoolboys who couldn't believe they had been caught in the act of some nefarious deed, or maybe simply officers gawking a beautiful woman.

Mollie Dwyer pushed her blonde bangs from her eyes and broke the silence. "Hello," was all she said.

"Miss Dwyer," Hampton said, at last remembering his South Carolina upbringing, and swept off his hat. Flipper and Barber quickly followed his example.

"Is Charles inside?" she asked.

"I haven't seen him, ma'am," Hampton answered. "He's probably at headquarters. I can send an orderly to fetch him."

She shook her head. "It's all right. He's supposed to take me to supper, but I'm early. I'll wait. Don't let me interrupt you gentlemen. I'll just step inside the foyer and wait by his door."

"It's not necessary, ma'am." Merritt Barber had found his voice. "We're all done here. The three of us were going to town for supper. I'll just get my coat."

Hampton nodded. "And I'll grab us three horses from the corrals. I'll meet you there."

Supper in town? That was news to Flipper, but by the time he blinked and tried to comprehend what was happening, Hampton was running across the parade grounds, and Barber had disappeared inside the duplex. He stood alone, kepi in hand, staring at Mollie Dwyer.

"It's good to see you, Henry. I've been meaning to talk to you, if I could find you alone."

Flipper nodded. *Talk, you dumb oaf. Tell her something. Don't just stand here like a knot on a log.*

"Henry. . . ." Mollie spoke his name in a heavy sigh. She closed her eyes and stepped closer. "Henry, somehow I think I'm to blame for all of your troubles."

He moved toward her but stopped himself from getting too close. In a way she was right. Flipper wouldn't blame her for anything, but if they hadn't been too friendly—a white woman and a black man—he doubted if Lieutenant Charles Nordstrom and Louis Wilhelmi, among others, would have hated him as much as they did, hated him enough to frame him for embezzlement.

"It's not your fault," he said at last, and waited for Mollie to open her eyes. When she did, he saw the tears.

"Thanks for saying that." She took his proffered handkerchief. "I hope everything works out for you."

"So do I."

"Maybe, when this is all over, we could go riding again."

He shook his head. "Lieutenant Nordstrom wouldn't like that." There was no hiding his bitterness.

Mollie looked down. "Henry, I know you don't like

Charles, and I know the two of you have had some problems, but he wouldn't. . . ." She couldn't finish. Maybe she couldn't convince herself that her beau was a lout, a liar, and, if only Flipper could prove it, a sneak thief, and disgrace to his uniform.

"Here comes your date," he said evenly, trying not to sound hateful, hurtful. Nordstrom hurried from headquarters. Flipper recognized the Swede's awkward gait. He could almost make out the glare on Nordstrom's face, angrier than a hornet that his girl was talking to Flipper again. She dabbed her eyes again and returned Flipper's white handkerchief.

"I'll pray for you," she whispered as he passed her. The wind caught the door and slammed it as he went inside. Barber glanced at him through a mirror while combing his hair. Flipper said nothing. He sank into a chair and dropped his head, trying not to listen to Nordstrom or Mollie, but that was impossible as the brute raised his voice. She yelled back. Nordstrom tried to counterattack, but Mollie made some final curt comment, and left him standing by himself. Flipper caught a glimpse of her as she hurried past his window, heading toward Captain Nolan's house.

Charles Nordstrom stormed inside the duplex and yelled at Flipper's closed door. "You stay away from Mollie, you hear me, Flipper? She's not for the likes of you, you . . . !" He stopped himself, probably remembering Barber was inside and could prefer charges of conduct unbecoming an officer and a gentleman. "You . . . you just keep your place, Lieutenant." The slamming door rocked the duplex.

Tossing the comb aside, Barber reached for his hat and coat. "Let's go meet Lieutenant Hampton, Henry, and get something to eat."

Flipper nodded, but didn't move. He didn't feel much like eating. He thought briefly of his rides with Mollie Dwyer, but his mind kept racing back to Anna White, Anna and Atlanta.

Chapter Fourteen

Furlough, 1877

"So, I was thinking that maybe, if you think it would be all right, that we could get married . . . someday, that is. No sense in rushing things. I mean, if you think that's all right, if your daddy don't object. I mean we could have a long engagement. Don't know where I'll be stationed, Texas most likely."

A cadet, he thought, who had survived Old Hanks Kendrick's mineralogy classes should be able to make a better proposal than that. He was on his knee, trying not to shake too much, and holding Anna White's gloved hands— at least he had that much right—but staring nervously at her tan button shoes, afraid to look up. She had small feet. Her shoes were well-made. Yes, he thought, I am the son of a cobbler. He relaxed then and risked embarrassment and heartbreak by glancing up. Their eyes met, and he almost immediately looked away. But his West Point-educated brain quickly registered that the look on Anna's face was not one of "I'm sorry, Henry" or "Are you kidding?" Her face and eyes beamed. He looked at her again.

Anna White dropped beside him, hugged him tightly, pulled away, nodded, and kissed him. When she broke the embrace a second time, Flipper saw tears streaming down her cheeks. "Henry Ossian," she whispered, "any woman would be honored to have you for a husband. Of course, I will marry you."

"Really?" He looked as if struck dumb.

"You have to see my daddy, though."

The pounding in his chest picked up speed, but the churning in his stomach began to lessen. He had done it. He had proposed to Anna White, and, glory to God, she had said yes. Yes. Flipper couldn't believe it. He thought about brother Joseph. What was that he had told Anna? Henry wasn't one to marry. Something like that. Well, he wondered, what would Joe would have to say now? He kissed Anna again, his mind racing, fantasizing about Mrs. Henry O. Flipper on his arm, himself dressed in his best uniform, the husband and wife guests of honor at some frontier fort in the Southwest. White officers and their spouses clapping for the handsome couple, making room on some dance floor as Flipper and Anna waltzed to the music of the regimental band.

Upon his graduation from the Academy, Flipper had quickly grown accustomed to being entertained by just about everyone: senators and soldiers, hotel clerks and stagecoach passengers. Women and children—white and black—had asked for his autograph. Frederick Douglass's son had been host of a reception for the gallant Mr. Flipper in New York City. He had been filled with wine and cheese. The wine had traveled straight to his head, and he had felt giddy. But he hadn't been so drunk that he would accept an invitation to speak. He had politely declined, saying that he was a soldier, not an orator. The guests had laughed and politely clapped.

Back in the South, however, his celebrity status forced him to make speeches. So he tried his best, but always kept those affairs short. On July 21st in Atlanta, he took his oath as an Army officer. That was cause for celebration and a speech, and Flipper knew he couldn't get out of that, nor could he decline Joseph's invitation to an August reception at the African Methodist Episcopal Church. Joseph Flipper was the bishop there and would make the main speech. All Flipper had to do was stand up, say a few words, and take a bow.

"Make sure you wear your dress uniform," Bishop Flipper said.

"Anything you say, Brother," Lieutenant Flipper agreed.

Anna squeezed his hand as they sat together in the uncomfortable pew with Henry's parents and other brothers. She leaned close to him and whispered: "You should have asked Joseph for a cut of the profits. I've never seen so many people."

That didn't help soothe Henry Flipper's nerves. He had expected only a few church members, family, and friends to show up. After all, admission was two bits. But people crowded into the stifling building. They stood along the walls, sat on windowsills, crowded the doorway, and jammed together in the pews. The choir sang, children put on a short play, elders read passages from the Bible, a man with the United States Attorney's office made a speech, followed by other speeches. Finally Bishop Joseph Flipper gave the keynote sermon-lecture-speech, and an eternity later called up policeman J. O. Wimbish, who gave some long-winded oratory full of praise for Henry Ossian Flipper and introduced Georgia's favorite son, black or white.

Henry Flipper rose. He felt wobbly from the heat. The applause was deafening. He forced a smile, wiped his sweaty face with a handkerchief, and cleared his throat.

"Ladies and gentlemen," he said, "I've been away from home four years, and a lot has changed. When I left here in Eighteen Seventy-Three, Atlanta, Georgia was a southern town trying to recover from the trauma of civil war. Now it is a booming metropolis where all men, white and black, are free to pursue their goals." He listened to the clapping, saw his father and mother smiling, and risked a glance at Anna White. She was beaming proudly.

"When I left here, I could not even imagine the marvels of technology. Now I have seen with my own eyes the typewriter and the telephone." More clapping, although he guessed few in the crowd had ever heard of those inventions. "When I left here, my brother Joseph was a pest and a bother." Laughter. "Now he is a respected man of God, a bishop, a servant to the Lord Almighty, and following the path we all should hope to travel." Loud clapping. "And when I left here, a colored graduate of the United States Military Academy was only a dream. Now it is reality."

Cheers, amens, and heavy clapping made him straighten. He could make a speech, after all.

"Yes, much has changed. Yet one thing remains the same." He paused. "The African Methodist Episcopal Church of Atlanta is still the hottest place to be in August." Laughter. "With that in mind, I shall keep this speech short. I thank you for your kindness, your hospitality. I thank my parents, my brothers, and Miss Anna White for their unconditional love and support. I thank God for His guidance. And I thank the United States of America."

H. Flipper Makes Ass of Himself

He stared with disbelief at the headline in the Atlanta *Constitution*. Henry O. Flipper was high-toned, a colored boy with a cloven foot, and the entire affair at the nigger church was an embarrassment. Flipper was uppity and a braggart, and the reporter looked forward to the day when the darky soldier would leave Atlanta for good, never to return.

"Don't pay no attention to that trash," Joseph told him.

Nodding silently, Flipper folded the paper and placed it on the table. His brother snatched it up, wadded it into a ball, and headed for the cook stove. Flipper tried to sip his coffee, but his appetite had vanished. So this was his homecoming. *Forget about what some white reporter has to say in some Democratic newspaper. Remember the applause in the church, the look on the faces of Anna and your parents.*

Yet other newspapers were just as harsh. A writer in Warrentown suggested that Henry O. Flipper thought he was bigger than General Grant and would soon be running for President himself. It was up to good Southerners like the Ku Klux Klan to band together to prevent such atrocities. In Thomasville, a newspaper raged over how well many whites approved of Flipper, that they looked at him as a celebrity and even treated him as if he were white himself. They seemed to forget that coloreds were running wild. Another Atlanta paper blasted a white drugstore clerk who had sold Flipper a sarsaparilla.

The letter came from Pastor B. F. Porter of the Morris Brown African Methodist Episcopalian church of Charleston, South Carolina. He pleaded with Flipper to join his cause and accept a commission as general of the Liberian Exodus Army, return to the homeland, Africa. Porter went on to state that thousands of Negroes wanted to leave the oppression of the United States and join their free brothers who had immigrated back to Africa since the American Colonization Society began returning freedmen and runaway slaves to their mother country in 1820. General? Flipper reread the letter.

General Flipper would be the commander in chief, responsible for building forts in the new country as well as training soldiers and recruiting black officers from West

Point and the Naval Academy. Porter must have mentioned his plan to newspaper reporters because Flipper was soon reading about his involvement in the Liberian Exodus Army. To his surprise, many blacks in Georgia and across America wanted Flipper to accept the commission, and, naturally, white leaders and newspapers encouraged him to go to Africa, go anywhere but here.

"Do you want to go to Liberia?" he asked Anna.

She finished chewing a piece of bread, washed it down with water, and said: "You don't."

"No," he agreed, sighing heavily. He felt a need to explain. "That's like running away. Grasping at straws. I worked too much to get where I am now. I'm not about to resign my commission. It's all I ever wanted."

"All?" Anna asked.

He nodded and didn't notice her turn away. Months passed before the scene flashed through Flipper's mind again, and only then did he realize his terrible mistake. By then, though, it was too late. So he kept on talking. He told her he had no idea when he would receive an assignment in the Army. Since his graduation, he had been on an extended furlough. The United States Army had its first black officer but no place, it seemed, for him. But he couldn't desert the Army, not now, never.

They finished their meal in silence.

The pressure built. He felt like an overheated boiler in a locomotive about to explode. Africa. Africa. Africa. More letters came, urging him to accept the general's job. But nothing from the War Department. Flipper felt as if the Army hoped he would go to Liberia. Even Joseph suggested that he depart for Africa. "You wanted to be a soldier, Henry, and it doesn't look like you'll ever get that opportunity here," he said.

Maybe that's what's holding me back, Flipper thought, and went home to write a letter to the *News and Courier,* Charleston's biggest newspaper. He explained that he was flattered with the unique opportunity offered by Pastor Porter, but that he must politely, yet firmly, decline. Fleeing was not his nature, and he would never resign from the United States Army. The newspaper published his letter verbatim. Other newspapers, including the *Army and Navy Journal,* picked up the story.

Liberia, like autumn, faded away. But still no news came from Washington.

Mr. White was an imposing man with a fierce white beard, intense eyes, knuckles raised like humps, and a chest shaped like a rain barrel. Back in the Atlanta Normal School, Flipper's classmates had said that Mr. White had been the strongest field hand in all of Georgia, and no one argued the matter. Flipper towered over most men he came across, but as he sat on the verandah beside Anna's father in front of the White's home, he felt like an ant.

"Papers been writin' lots of bad stuff 'bout you," White boomed while rocking in a huge chair and stuffing tobacco in a clay pipe.

"Heré," Flipper stressed. "Most of the other places I've been have been kind to me, sir."

"Northern papers, I reckon."

"No, sir. Charleston. Richmond." He tried to laugh. "It seems everywhere but Atlanta, sir, and a few neighboring cities."

White nodded slightly—the man didn't appear to have a neck, just muscle connecting his enormous head to a muscular torso—and fired up the pipe, tossing the match into an Arbuckle's coffee can that served as a cuspidor.

"So you here's to ax fer my baby's hand?"

"I've already done that, Mister White. You said you'd have to think it over."

"You respect her daddy's wishes?"

He had to think about that. His stomach began to churn uneasily. His palms felt clammy. Rather than answer, Flipper cleared his throat and said: "Sir, I can support Anna. I'll be an officer in the Army, plus a firm in New York City wants me to write a book. I'll be receiving royalties once it's published, in addition to my salary as a second lieutenant."

"Yeah, I hears you. But you be sent out a right fur piece from 'ere. Dis be all my Anna ever knowed, 'ceptin' that time she and her mama visited you up North. An' I hear tell of the West. It be a land of hardships for anyone, colored or lily white. You likely be goin' from one post to 'nother. Dis da kind of life you wants fer my girl?"

"I love her."

"So do I."

Flipper felt sick now.

"Son, you's a good boy. I knowed you a long time. An' I reckon I knows Anna loves you a lot. But, Henry, all you ever concerned yourself with has been you. I ain't sayin' you bad, ain't sayin' you neglects yer family. You a good lad. But all you ever wanted, long as I recollects, is to be a soldier boy. Now you one. You soon be fightin' Indians, I guess. Mights even gets yerself kilt. So what's my baby gonna be doin' all dis time? You ever think 'bout her, Henry?"

He closed his eyes. Flipper could see her now, but no longer at some Army ball. Anna looked worn, aged, kneeling by a rocky streambed with a load of clothes, pounding laundry until her fingers bled.

The chair and wooden porch creaked as Anna's father stood. He took a long drag on the pipe stem and slowly exhaled. "You ax yerself dat, Henry Flipper. You an' Anna thinks long an' hard 'bout what's to become of you after you leaves Atlanta."

He rented a road wagon from a livery, picked up Anna, and, despite the cold of December, drove all the way to the Chattahooche River. She had asked to see him, alone, and a foreboding overcame him as the mule clopped along and Anna didn't speak.

The river looked icy, leafless trees gloomy, towering pines swaying eerily. Flipper set the wagon's brake, jumped down, and helped Anna from the seat. He reached for the picnic basket his mother had fixed, but Anna quickly said: "I'm not hungry, Henry."

Henry, she had said. Not Henry Ossian. She stared at the river.

Let's end this now, he said to himself. Waiting, knowing what was coming but not wanting to know, was killing him. "You want to get married, or not?" he said, trying, but failing, to hold back his anger.

Anna looked down. "Henry, this is hard to say."

He turned from her. "You just said it!" he shot out, and walked hurriedly to the slick riverbank. Grinding his teeth, he picked up a rock and sent it sailing. It splashed in the river. He saw another rock, this one submerged, and snatched it up, threw it even harder. The cold water stung his fingers. He didn't care.

"Henry."

Anna stood behind him. Flipper wiped his eyes, refused to turn around.

"Henry," she whispered. "I'm sorry."

156

Then she was crying. He turned now, saw Anna on her knees, ruining her pretty dress, sobbing uncontrollably. Flipper forced down the bile that had begun to rise in his throat, forgot about his anger, the cold, the bitterness of rejection, betrayal. He couldn't hate Anna White, or her father, as much as he tried. He reached to help her up, but tears blinded her. "Don't," he pleaded. "Don't cry."

"I . . . can't . . . help . . . it." Her words came out in broken sobs, like a wailing hound. "I . . . love you . . . so much." Flipper dropped beside her, pulled her close, kissed her hair as she cried on his shoulder.

"It's all right," he whispered.

Later, they held each other underneath a pine, watching the Chattahooche roll. A few ducks landed near the far shore and briefly quacked, the only sound except the rippling water and rustling pines.

"Your father's right. So's Joseph, I guess." Flipper couldn't believe his own words, yet he continued: "Army life's no good for you, Anna. And when Joseph said I wasn't the marrying kind, I guess he was right, too. I'm not sure I'd make a good husband. All I ever wanted was to be in the Army. Be an officer. Career soldiers don't make good husbands, good fathers."

Anna sniffed. "Maybe," she said. "Maybe I could wait. Maybe you'd come back after you finished soldiering. Maybe then. . . ." Her words trailed off. After a long time she said: "You know I'll always love you, Henry Ossian Flipper."

"And I'll always love you."

She broke his embrace and rose slowly, standing in front of him. He remained seated. Their eyes locked. They would never see each other again. Waiting? Marriage later? Dreams, only fanciful dreams. Those things would never happen. He had his own world to discover, and Anna White would be stuck forever in hers, and maybe it was better this way. Lieutenant Flipper would never fit into Georgia society, white or black. Life as a military wife would destroy Anna White. Yet, as he stared into her beautiful dark eyes, Henry Flipper knew he would never know or love a woman like Anna White. After today, she would be a memory, gone forever. Anna must have known that, too.

Slowly she began unbuttoning her dress.

Festus Flipper handed the telegram to his son.

WAR DEPARTMENT WASHINGTON D.C. STOP. TO 2nd LT HO FLIPPER. STOP. YOU ARE HEREBY ORDERED TO USE FASTEST MEANS OF CONVEYANCE AND REPORT TO "A" TROOP 10th US CAVALRY AT FORT CONCHO TEXAS FOR FURTHER ORDERS. STOP. ACKNOWLEDGE RECEIPT BY TELEGRAPH IMMEDIATELY. STOP.

Flipper read the telegram a second time, finding his emotions mixed. He was going to the Army, heading West, realizing his dream at last, but he was going alone.

Chapter Fifteen

November 11, 1881

George Davidson, Clerk for the Chief Commissary of the Department of Texas, basically verified everything that Major Small had said under oath regarding the problems collecting subsistence funds from Fort Davis and A.C.S. Flipper. The only reason Clous had Davidson testify, Flipper guessed, was because the judge advocate was meticulous and zealous and wanted to hammer his protocol point home.

"Any questions, Captain Barber?"

The defense counsel looked up at Colonel Pennypacker and shook his head, then quickly changed his mind. "On second thought, just a couple or so. Whose responsibility is it to mail commissary funds from a post to the department headquarters?"

Davidson pursed his lips and thought. "Well, under Army regulations, it should be done by the post adjutant." He spoke rapidly with an accent Flipper had not heard since his furlough to New York City while a cadet at West Point.

A smile replaced the bored look on Merritt Barber's face. "Not the Acting Commissary of Subsistence?"

"No, sir."

"Therefore, it was up to the adjutant to make sure those funds were mailed? It really wasn't Lieutenant Flipper's responsibility?"

Davidson shook his head. "According to Army regs, sir. But each post commander has his own way of handling things like that."

"I see." Barber looked across the room and stared at John Clous while addressing his final question to Davidson. "And do you have any idea who is the post adjutant at Fort Davis?"

Clous scowled even before Davidson answered. "I believe, sir, that it is First Lieutenant Louis Wilhelmi, First Infantry."

With a smile, Barber looked at the witness again. "Wilhelmi? That's very interesting. Thank you, Mister Davidson. That is all I have."

The commissary clerk was dismissed, and John Withers was called forward by Captain Clous. Withers looked like a bank cashier: small, balding, bespectacled, with a pale, freckled face and nervous twitch. He seemed to sweat more than Colonel Shafter, and the temperature had hit only 41° this morning, although it was slightly warmer in the chapel.

After being sworn in and stating his name, residence, occupation, and place of employment, Withers began his testimony, being guided by the German captain.

"*Herr* Viters," Clous said with a harsh smile, "did da accused ever open a personal account at da San Antonio National Bank?"

"Personal? No, sir."

Next, Clous picked up a check from his table, crossed the room, and handed it to the witness. "Dis is a check from da accused. Vould you read da amount?"

"One thousand four hundred forty dollars and forty-three cents."

"*Ja*. But Lieutenant Flipper, he had no personal account. Did he have an account as Acting Commissary of Subsistence at your bank at dat time?"

"No, sir."

Clous took the check and handed it to Captain E. S. Ewing, the closest member of the court-martial board, to pass around to the other officers. "So dis check, it is fraudulent, no?"

"Well, Lieutenant Flipper hadn't the funds to cover it when it was written."

"*Danke.* I have no more questions."

The judge advocate settled into his chair, quite pleased with himself. Flipper whispered into Barber's ear, and the attorney nodded. "He's a sneaky reprobate," Barber told Flipper in a hushed tone before standing.

"Mister Withers, you testified that Lieutenant Flipper had not opened a personal account at the time, is that correct?"

"Yes." The cashier wiped his brow with the back of his hand.

"How about another kind of account? Did he have an account in the name of the Fort Davis quartermaster?"

Withers blinked. "Yes, for a while. He closed it in March."

"So you must be familiar with the lieutenant."

The clerk's head bobbed slightly, and he glanced briefly at Flipper. "I've never met him personally, but I've heard about him. And Mister Sweeney, the bank's vice president, speaks highly of him."

"Now, when you say Lieutenant Flipper had never opened a personal account, does that mean he didn't have an account at the bank at the time he wrote that check?"

Withers hesitated. When he looked to Clous for help, Barber shot out: "Look at me, sir! The judge advocate can't tell you what to say now."

"I protest!" Clous yelled, but Pennypacker ignored him and told the witness to answer the question.

"Well, a firm out of state had sent a certificate of deposit in Mister . . . Lieutenant Flipper's name. The bank was holding it for him."

"Do you know the name of this firm?"

"Homer Lee and Company."

"Thank you, Mister Withers." Barber sat down.

"Redirect, Captain Clous?" Pennypacker asked.

"*Ja*. Dis certificate of deposit. How much vas it for?"

"Seventy-four dollars."

"Seventy-four dollars. Dat is far from fourteen hundred dollars, isn't dat so?"

"Yes, sir."

"I have no more questions." Clous's smile had returned as he sat back in his chair.

"Seventy-four dollars," Flipper said bitterly. "That Markland fellow told me I would have substantial royalties coming, a few thousand dollars. I swear to God I thought I could cover that check by the time it arrived."

Barber nodded sympathetically. "Never trust a publisher, Henry," he said. "Don't worry yourself sick. I think we held our own today, even made some valid points. Withers and Davidson are minor witnesses. Tomorrow Clous will bring Wilhelmi to the stand, and when I get my turn at that lying little snake. . . ." He didn't bother to finish the sentence. Instead, he switched topics. "The one thing we need to do now is start adding to our plan of defense. We need someone with a lot of clout as a character witness." Barber ran through his notes. "Town merchants we've got. Wade Hampton said he'd testify. But I want somebody big."

"Captain Nolan?" Flipper suggested.

"Bigger."

"Maybe Colonel Grierson."

Snapping his fingers, Barber said: "He's the one."

Flipper frowned. "But Colonel Grierson left for Fort Concho the First of this month. And as busy as he is, I don't think he could get back to Fort Davis in time."

"We don't need him, Henry. A letter from him will serve as an affidavit. I'll write him myself, ask him for a written character reference to be used in your defense. Grierson's a good man . . . and a fine officer. He'd be glad to help."

"Yes," Flipper agreed. "The colonel's one of the finest men I've ever met. He and Captain Nolan." He looked up at Barber and smiled. "And you, Merritt. And Wade."

The mood turned somber. Barber reached for his bottle of brandy and filled a tin cup. He didn't bother to offer Flipper the liquor, knowing he wouldn't accept.

"How long have you known Lieutenant Hampton, Henry? I don't think I ever asked you that."

"Less than a year," Flipper said, and told Barber how Wade, perhaps slightly in his cups, had banged on his door that New Year's Day and shared black-eyed peas.

"Black-eyed peas?" Barber asked after another sip of brandy.

"It's a Southern thing, Merritt. Brings good luck for the rest of the year if you have them on New Year's Day."

"I didn't know that. I'm from Vermont, remember. In fact, I don't think I've ever had a black-eyed pea."

"They're pretty good. At least, I think so. My mother made them all the time. Black-eyed peas, corn pone, ham, and grits. Maybe some greens. Mighty good eating on January First. We don't get fed like that in the Army."

"I guess not." And Barber added softly: "Thank God." He drained the cup and asked: "How about Captain Nolan? How long have you known him?"

"A long time," Flipper replied. "Well," he added after a pause, "I guess not a long time. But since I joined the Tenth. January of 'Seventy-Eight. It seems a lot longer." His voice trailed off. "It seems a long, long time ago."

Chapter Sixteen

Fort Sill, 1878

Fort Concho lay somewhere out in West Texas along the Middle Concho River, but Henry Flipper got only as far as Houston. Major J. F. Wade met him at the train depot with a change of orders. Instead of being stationed at Concho, A Troop of the 10th Cavalry was on its way to Fort Sill. Second Lieutenant H. O. Flipper thus was ordered to proceed by means of fastest conveyance and with due haste to report to the troop in the Indian Nations. Major Wade was not the only person waiting for Flipper at the depot. Reporters from the Houston newspapers requested interviews with the sudden celebrity, and the *Age* editor himself whisked young Mr. Flipper to the editorial offices while an assistant went to learn when the next northbound stage was leaving the city.

Houston seemed another country and years removed from Atlanta, Georgia. That surprised Flipper. Texas, or at least Houston, was definitely a Southern city, but everyone he met treated him with respect. The newspapermen wrote kind words and phrases about the colored officer. They shook his hand, offered him cigars, and recommended a boarding house where he could spend the night before lighting off to Fort Sill and his obligations to duty, honor, and country.

The swaying motion of the coach—swaying, that is, when not jarring after striking a pothole, ham-size rock, or whatever trap had been left on these frontier roads—made

Flipper glad he had never dreamed of becoming a sailor and opted for Annapolis. He had traveled by rail to Indian Territory, but that left another one hundred sixty miles via stagecoach. Somehow he managed to steady his stomach, which is more than he could say about his fellow passenger, who twice hung his head out the window and sprayed the side of the Concord, once outside of Caddo, and again this morning.

After losing his breakfast the second time, the frontiersman took a deep breath and leaned back on his bench, wiping his mouth with the back of a gloved right hand. He smiled at Flipper and fired up a six-inch cigar that cost less than a penny per inch and stank worse than Isabella Buckhalter Flipper's chitlins. Flipper had to wonder if the man hoped the cigar smoke, coupled with the stagecoach ride, would force the green officer to follow suit and purge his stomach.

Ben Clark was a leathery-looking sort, with a hard, bronzed face and eyes darker than any Cherokee's. His sandy hair hung to his shoulders, upper lip hidden by a bushy mustache and a week's worth of whiskers over the rest of his face. He wore Army-issue trousers tucked in calf-high moccasins, dark flannel shirt, buckskin jacket, and a brown bowler. A shell belt held a pistol and the biggest knife Flipper had ever seen. He wondered if it was a Bowie.

"You'd be the darky lieutenant I read about," Clark said. Those were the first words the man had spoken to Flipper since Caddo. He knew Clark's name from overhearing a conversation with two stable hands at one of the swing stations along the route. Clark didn't say "darky" with any bitterness or disrespect. It just flowed as normal, everyday language. Still, Flipper thought about replying with surprise that Ben Clark could read but decided against it. "Second Lieutenant Henry Ossian Flipper, A Troop, Tenth Cavalry," he said.

Clark nodded, pulled on his cigar, and blew the smoke out the window. "Fort Sill, then," he said. "Looks like the two of us'll be workin' together a spell. I'm a scout and interpreter for you boys." Ben Clark then did something that utterly surprised Flipper.

He held out his hand and said: "Name's Ben Clark. Pleasure to meet you, Lieutenant."

Fort Sill's stone, adobe, and wooden buildings sprawled throughout the military reservation at the confluence of Cache and Medicine Bluff creeks. The stagecoach pulled to a stop in front of the massive corrals, and Flipper followed Ben Clark into the frigid December air. A thin layer of snow dusted the ground. Flipper stared at his new post, less than ten years old, amazed at the bustling of activity even though it was New Year's Day. He looked awestricken at the soldiers in drill formation: black men, with the exception of a red-headed officer barking out orders. Buffalo soldiers, they were called, a name the Plains Indians had given them and one the troopers, most of them former slaves, had latched onto with pride. Men of the 10th Cavalry. Flipper's regiment.

"Lieutenant?"

Ben Clark pulled a glove onto his right hand and nodded toward the parade grounds northwest of the quartermaster corral. "You'd best report to HQ, sir. Second buildin' on the south side of the parade grounds, right next to a long buildin' that looks like a warehouse. That's the infantry barracks. A Troop's captain is Nolan. Don't know if he's here yet. The post commander is Jack Davidson, your lieutenant colonel. Henpecked, but he ain't a bad hand. I'll fetch an orderly and send your trunks on to your quarters."

Flipper nodded. "Thanks, Mister Clark."

"Good luck to you, Lieutenant."

Second Lieutenant H. O. Flipper took a deep breath on the wooden porch of the headquarters building and pounded on the door. "Yeah?" came a surly response from within. "Open the damn' door. 'Tain't locked."

Flipper entered sharply, saw a black sergeant major with a gray beard and tiny spectacles sitting behind a paper-cluttered desk. Without thinking, Flipper saluted and shouted: "Second Lieutenant Flipper, A Troop, Tenth Cavalry, reports his entrance into this office, sir!"

The sergeant major stared at him blankly.

No one spoke for half a minute. Flipper stood erect, unmoving, scarcely breathing. Loud squeaks announced the opening of the door to Flipper's left, and a handsome man with curly hair, Roman nose, and well-groomed mustache and goatee stepped into the room. The officer smiled. "Lieutenant Flipper, I presume," he said.

"Yes, sir," Flipper fired back.

He immediately liked Lieutenant Colonel J. W. Davidson. The post commander had graduated from West Point and risen to the rank of lieutenant colonel. On the other hand, the regiment's colonel, Benjamin Grierson, had been teaching music up in Illinois when the war began, enlisted as a private in the 6th Illinois Cavalry, and been promoted to colonel in a year. After the surrender, Grierson organized the 10th Horse and in fact had helped established this very post near the Wichita Mountains. Often Flipper had heard that soldiers like Grierson who came up through the ranks harbored nothing but rancor toward West Pointers such as Davidson and Flipper—and vice versa—but Davidson praised Grierson to no end after they left the sergeant major struck dumb at his desk and entered the adjoining office.

"You'll like the colonel," Davidson told Flipper. "He's down at Fort Concho, but sends his compliments and looks forward to meeting you. Captain Nolan is a fine man, too, Lieutenant, and I'm sure you'll enjoy serving under him. He's still *en route* here. Should arrive any day now."

"Yes, sir! In the meantime, sir, what are my duties?"

A smile formed somewhere between Davidson's black mustache and pointed goatee. "Full of brass, you are, eh, Lieutenant? Rearing to go. Well, that's great. Lieutenant Lawton will assign you quarters. He's the post quartermaster, so, if you need anything, see him. Lieutenant Pratt is the senior lieutenant of A Troop, and he's on this post. He'll show you around the fort. In the meantime, I'm assigning you duty as post signal officer. You will instruct troops in proper techniques."

"Very good, sir! Anything else, sir?"

The smile widened. "Yes, Lieutenant, there is. Lower your voice, son. This isn't the Point, and you aren't a plebe. You don't have to try to shatter every window in headquarters when you enter this building. And in this man's army, Mister Flipper, officers do not salute sergeant majors unless returning a salute, and officers do not call enlisted men 'sir'."

He felt like an utter fool. Davidson laughed out loud and planted a firm hand on Flipper's shoulder. "You'll do fine, Lieutenant. It's a privilege to have you on my post. You'll honor me and my family by dining with us Thursday evening. That, too, is an order."

"Very good, sir," he said, softly this time.

"Carry on, Mister Flipper."

He dined with Colonel Davidson. He dined with Lieutenant Lawton. He dined with Lieutenant Pratt. Flipper felt uneasy about his celebrity status, yet he didn't know what he should do. So he accepted it. He never appeared like some braggart, and tried not to think about the eyes staring at him just about everywhere he went at Fort Sill. While waiting for A Troop's arrival, Flipper fell into a routine: signal drill followed by someone's dinner party and at night, alone in his quarters, writing his memoirs for Homer Lee & Company.

Not that everyone liked and admired him, or simply pretended to, or thought it capital to be seen with the first colored graduate of the United States Military Academy. The post adjutant, an infantry lieutenant named S. R. Whithall, assumed no façade to mask his hatred and bigotry. While the black troopers of the 10th loved being directed by a black officer—even in something as dull as semaphore and heliograph methodology—the white infantry soldiers took Flipper's instructions and orders with bitter distaste. Perhaps they despised the color of his skin and hated taking his orders, but they were soldiers, and did what he said.

They were the first wild Indians he had ever seen. Well, maybe not so wild, but they were Comanches. Half a dozen rode proudly on weary nags to the store, five men, with glistening black hair, and one silver-haired woman. Cheap bells, woven into one man's leggings, jingled. Most of them wore shabby Army-rejected blankets, and their clothing was a blend of cultures: some feathers, doe and buffalo skins, bright beads—muslin shirts, one filthy pair of Levi's, bandannas, belts, and an assortment of hats. One man even carried a gaudy carpetbag. Flipper looked for weapons, but saw none. He knew the Comanches lived on the nearby reservation, but it hadn't been that many years ago that they were being called the "Cossacks of the Plains" and terrorizing settlers from Kansas to Mexico.

"Your in-laws, Ben?" Lieutenant Henry W. Lawton asked the government scout and interpreter.

"Nah. My squaw's Kiowa. Them's Comanch'."

Lawton, Flipper, and Richard Pratt had set up a telescope to watch the eclipse of the sun. Ben Clark was just loafing around the store, smoking one of his miserable cigars and playing dominoes with rawboned Horace Jones, another post interpreter. As the Indians dismounted, Clark pitched away his cigar and called out to the officers. "Hey, how much longer till that eclipse?"

"Just a couple of minutes," Pratt answered.

"Watch this, gents," Clark said, and rolled a cracker barrel down the steps in front of the approaching Comanches. The Indians stopped, staring at the scout suspiciously as he righted the wooden barrel and climbed on top. He began shouting, maybe singing, something in a guttural language, pointing to the sun and dancing, or rather hopping on the barrel.

Flipper stared at the scout before glancing at Pratt and Lawton. The two officers scratched their heads.

"What's he doing?" Pratt called out.

Horace Jones shrugged. "Telling them that he's going to make the sun disappear. Telling them that they think he's just a dumb white-eye who can speak Comanche and has a Kiowa woman, but he's about to show them his power. Tells them it'll be dark forever and some other bosh."

The Indians began talking among themselves. The old woman spit at the barrel. Flipper looked at the sky. The eclipse had begun.

"Is this smart?" Lawton asked.

"Nope," Jones replied, and slipped inside the store.

The sky darkened, and the Indians shouted among themselves. One fell to his knees and began singing what Pratt said was his death song. The others weren't so timid.

The old woman reached Clark first and, in the middle of his gesturing, grabbed his gun belt and jerked him off the barrel. Ben Clark laughed at first, then screamed as the Comanches leaped upon him, pounding him with fists and one green and gold carpetbag.

"Dear Lord," Pratt said, and raced to the scout's rescue. Flipper and Lawton followed.

"Niatz! Niatz!" Pratt shouted as he shoved Old Carpetbag aside and pushed Dirty Levi's away. *"Niatz. Niatz."*

Lawton did a flying leap and took out the two other men, pinning them temporarily as the hens scurried about the yard, heading for the roosts, and roosters crowed as if there would be no tomorrow.

That left the woman for Flipper, and he quickly grabbed her right hand, which held Ben Clark's Bowie knife and was about to be used to cut his throat or lift his scalp, probably both. She elbowed Flipper's thigh with her free arm, but he held his grip, squeezed and twisted until the knife fell to the ground. Pratt pulled the scout to his feet and shoved him toward the store. Flipper released his hold on the screaming woman, and the three officers led a not-so-organized retreat.

Horace Jones opened the door as Clark, bloodied but laughing, tumbled inside. The door slammed, and the lock caught, leaving Lieutenants Pratt, Lawton, and Flipper to face five angry Comanches and another one resigned to his death in a world of darkness.

Pratt slammed his fist against the locked door and mumbled: *"Suapuat."* The word, Flipper guessed, was Comanche but directed at Ben Clark.

172

The three men turned to face the gathering Indians. The Comanche death song blended with squawking poultry until the woman stepped forward and blurted out something. The singing stopped. Even the hens and roosters fell quiet.

Pratt took over negotiations. He spoke mostly in English, using a few Comanche words, but most of the communication was made with hand gestures. The first thing Pratt requested was the return of the scout's knife. The old woman had picked it up. She muttered something, stared at Flipper with malevolent eyes while rubbing her wrist, and reluctantly handed the Bowie to Flipper, handle first. Pratt glanced at the darkened sun and somehow explained to the Indians that, if they promised to behave, gave their word they would not draw and quarter Ben Clark, then the scout would in turn promise to come outside and make the sun reappear. The Comanches talked this over among themselves, and finally the woman and Old Carpetbag nodded.

"All right, Mister Clark," Lawton said. "Mister Pratt has negotiated a truce. Come on out and perform your magic."

The door opened. Ben Clark wiped his bloody nose with a gloved right hand and walked drunkenly to the cracker barrel. He started laughing so hard that he overturned the barrel once before he climbed on top and resumed his sun dance. Flipper sighed in relief as the eclipse passed and the sun reappeared. The Comanches said a few words, made a few gestures, and left, forgetting whatever they had come to the store to buy. Only then did Horace Jones step out of the safety of the store. Flipper handed him Clark's massive knife.

Once the Comanches had disappeared, Clark sank onto the keg and laughed some more. "Boys," he said, "I've got me a new Comanche name . . . Bad Medicine."

* * * * *

Captain Nicholas Nolan was a fine man. Born in Kilkenny, he still spoke with a thick Irish brogue, sported black hair, brown eyes, fair skin, and stood a couple of inches shorter than Flipper. As soon as he arrived with A Troop, he invited Flipper to dinner.

"I'm glad to have you in my troop, lad," Nolan said after his cook had carted off the dirty plates and left the officers alone. Flipper sipped black coffee. Nolan took his Jameson neat.

A widower, Nicholas Nolan had been in the Army for twenty-five years, and to show for it he had a captain's pay, two brevets during the late war, a bullet wound from Virginia, and a young son and daughter without a mother. "You and I are a lot alike," the captain said as the whisky took hold.

"How's that, sir?"

"We both know of persecution. The Irish. The Negro. I can't promise you glory, Mister Flipper, nor lovely assignments or anything but a sore backside and a lack of sleep, but I will make you this solemn vow. As long as you serve with me, lad, you'll get a fair shake. You deserve that, more than anyone in this Grand Army that I've ever served with."

Nolan placed his empty glass aside and smiled. "This is not turning into a wake. We're here to celebrate, Mister Flipper. To honor your commission, to celebrate my upcoming nuptials, and to toast our glorious Army and the United States of America." He poured two fingers of Irish into the glass and raised it. Shot glass and China cup clinked.

"May you be in heaven ten minutes before the Devil knows you're dead," Nolan said.

Flipper responded: "Go *raibh míle maith agat*." An instructor at the Point had taught the cadets that, along with *Céad Míle Fáilte* and a few choice Gaelic curses.

Nolan's eyes gleamed, and he polished off his whisky. "The Irish. You spoke the Irish. Mister Flipper, you and I shall get along gloriously."

A week after arriving with A Troop, Nolan departed for San Antonio to marry Annie Dwyer. He left Lieutenant Pratt in charge of A Troop while Flipper served as Acting Captain of G Troop. Winter left the Indian Territory, and spring blew in like a gale. Forty-seven-year-old Nicholas Nolan soon returned with his twenty-one-year-old bride. Not only that, but the captain's sister-in-law joined the newlyweds.

"Mister Flipper, this is my wife, Annie." Flipper bowed. Annie Dwyer Nolan smiled and held out a delicate right hand. That left Flipper awkward, unsure of protocol, etiquette, and everything else. He kissed the hand briefly and stepped back, half-expecting a court-martial or at least a haymaker from his captain.

Mrs. Nolan, however, simply beamed and said: "I'm so glad to finally meet you, Mister Flipper. Nicholas has told me so much about you, and it isn't every day that I get to meet a national celebrity."

After another bow, Flipper faced another woman, a radiant creature with blonde hair and a Bloomingdale dress. This would be Annie's sister, but she looked far from fragile. Her features revealed strength, especially those independent eyes.

"And my sister-in-law, Mollie Dwyer."

"A pleasure, miss," Flipper said.

Mollie laughed and held out her hand, not to be kissed, but shaken. "It's my pleasure, Mister Flipper."

Before Flipper could even think, he had blurted out: "Call me Henry."

Stupid, he thought, or the Comanche word: *suapuat*. Officer or not, you didn't go around telling a white woman that. A black man that forward could foresee a hemp rope and a burning cross, or at the least a severe beating. He wouldn't make that mistake again, if he lived past this night.

"Henry," Mollie said, and, instead of outrage, everyone laughed and retired to the Nolan family parlor. Annie described the wedding for Flipper, the captain told fanciful war stories to his children, and Flipper and Mollie sat quietly, munching on lemon cookies and sipping punch. An hour or so later, the little Nolan girl asked Mr. Flipper to tell her a war story.

He brushed the crumbs off his lap and apologized. "Missie," he said, "I really don't have any good stories to tell you. Your daddy's the one to. . . ."

"Biodh ciall agat," Captain Nolan said in mock anger. "Tell the child a story, Mister Flipper. You're practically part of the family."

Part of the family—Flipper didn't know how to take that. Yet it was true. The Nolans asked him to share their quarters. Flipper certainly felt at home with the Nolans, so he requested permission from Colonel Davidson, got it, dismissed his cook, and moved his gear into a small room in the Nolan quarters.

He often found Mollie Dwyer at the stone quartermaster corral, and learned she enjoyed horseback rides. It was Mollie Dwyer who asked Flipper to join her on one Sunday afternoon excursion. That, too, caught the junior lieutenant by surprise. He thought about it, thought hard about making up some excuse, but he suddenly said to himself:

What the hell. He hadn't been lynched for kissing Annie Nolan's hand. He hadn't been victim of a mutiny during signal instruction. Colonel Davidson liked him. So did most of the officers at Fort Sill. He wasn't sexually interested in Mollie—at least, he told himself that—they were simply friends. She would need an escort, and Henry O. Flipper was an officer and a gentleman.

"I'll get two horses, Miss Dwyer."

"It's Mollie, Henry. Call me Mollie."

He left without responding to that, found a saddler, and requested his mount and a gentle mare for Miss Dwyer, with sidesaddle. Mollie laughed at the sidesaddle when she saw it.

"Henry Flipper, I plan on racing you up Cache Creek, and I'm not letting you cheat me by making me ride one of those silly things. Bring me a real saddle, sir. A McClellan like yours."

"Is there a problem here, Mollie?"

Both turned to face the post adjutant. Lieutenant Whithall scratched his hawkish nose and stared angrily at Flipper and the two horses.

"Not at all," Mollie replied. "Henry and I were just going out for a ride. Only I don't like sidesaddles."

"I see," Whithall replied, but Flipper knew he didn't. "It's dangerous, Mollie. If you'd like me to accompany you, it would be my honor, miss."

"I'm sure it would," she said haughtily. "But Henry and I will make out fine. Right, Henry?"

He didn't answer. He was too busy leading Mollie's horse back to the stables to find a McClellan saddle.

Summer turned the fort into a malarial swamp. Troopers, white and black, became sick. More than a handful died. The temperature crept toward 100°, and Flipper was glad to be given duties other than signal instruction and cavalry drill. He oversaw a detail stringing telegraph lines and another building a road from the Red River to Gainesville, Texas. Twice he brought food to the Comanche-Kiowa Agency, and once oversaw guard duty for Indian prisoners.

Even the troopers liked getting out of Sill. They would prefer fighting Comanches for six months in the field to one day of drill.

Later that year, he led G Troop as the buffalo soldiers escorted a wagon train to Fort Concho to pick up supplies. Flipper had hoped to meet Colonel Grierson there, but the regimental leader was in St. Louis at the time.

He didn't know what to make of San Angelo, the parasite town of whores, gamblers, and mountebanks who did their damnedest to siphon United States script from the soldiers stationed at the post. Nor did Flipper know what to make of the fort, or the people there. His troop pitched camp along the North Concho River, and watched in amazement as just about every laundress, every servant, every wife from Concho—and more than a handful of prostitutes from San Angelo—paraded through the camp to catch a glimpse of the colored officer.

"You should be chargin' two bits admission, Lieutenant," Sergeant Brand told him. "Be able to retire by the time we leave this here post."

One tiny, silver-haired laundress summoned up enough courage to run to Flipper and kneel before him. Tears streamed down her ancient face as she said: "You's the most famous man I've ever met, Mister Lieutenant. You make all us Negroes proud." She pressed a tiny stone into Flipper's hand and ran away. Several women cheered, either for Flipper or the woman. Flipper brushed away a tear of his own and stared at the shiny white gem the ancient laundress had given him.

"Concho River pearl, sir," Sergeant Brand said.

Back at Fort Sill, Flipper relished the coming of fall. His Sunday rides with Mollie Dwyer became frequent, and still no one complained—at least to Flipper's face. He had grown accustomed to his celebrity status and felt that he had earned some respect, although he knew he would never deserve a West Texas pearl bestowed on him by a weary woman old enough to be his great-grandmother. He carried that gem as a reminder. Henry Ossian Flipper had a standard to bear. He could never disappoint them, never let them down.

Chapter Seventeen

November 12–14, 1881

"Louis Wilhelmi, First Lieutenant and adjutant, First Infantry. . . ."

Flipper seethed as the judge advocate began questioning the bigoted lieutenant, taking him through his Army career before beginning a biased account of the events preceding Flipper's arrest. Flipper wondered who hated him the most: Wilhelmi, Nordstrom, Shafter, or Clous?

The Prussian-born Wilhelmi cleared his throat. He was a thin, pale, pockmarked man with a hawkish nose that had been bent and broken several times. Suddenly Flipper remembered Cadet Corporal Louis Wilhelmi, from the Point, and he sank back in his chair. He had been the obdurate cad who had forced Cadet Slaker and Flipper to chew that quid of tobacco during their plebe year. Strange, he thought, how he hadn't placed the face until now. But Wilhelmi hadn't been at West Point for long. Sometime during Flipper's yearling year, the cadet corporal had disappeared. Wilhelmi was now telling the court that he had gotten sick and had been forced to withdraw from the Academy. Pneumonia, Wilhelmi was saying, but Flipper wondered, his mind racing, recalling the rumor going around the barracks of a certain cadet corporal who had come down with a dose of the clap and had to leave the Point. Could it be?

"Tell us about da events of July Tird, dis year," Clous said.

"I was at headquarters and overheard a conversation between Lieutenant Flipper and Colonel Shafter," the lieutenant said in his irritating nasal drawl.

"Vat did dis conversation regard?"

"They were talking about a check for fourteen hundred and forty dollars. I remember Colonel Shafter asking . . . 'Isn't that a rather large check for a junior officer to have?' Or words to that effect. And Lieutenant Flipper said he had a lot of small checks which he didn't want to transmit to the chief commissary, so he sent them to the San Antonio National Bank. Flipper told the colonel that the fourteen hundred dollar check represented that amount."

Clous nodded. "How do you remember da date of dis dialogue?"

"The Third of July is clearly fixed in my mind because the following day was the Fourth, and Lieutenant Flipper had issued a circular asking the Mexicans at Fort Davis. . . ."

Barber shot out of his chair and objected, but that didn't stop Wilhelmi.

". . . to bring their burros here for a race."

"I objected, gentleman of this court," Barber said.

The judge advocate shook his head. "Da question is valid. I simply vanted da vitness to explain how he remembered dis date."

"No," Barber argued, "you're trying to imply that Lieutenant Flipper planned to take off for Mexico with the missing money. The fact that Lieutenant Flipper issued a circular about a burro race is irrelevant and immaterial."

"It is perfectly competent for Lieutenant Wilhelmi to recall dis conversation with da accused. I presume he is simply giving the introductory remarks."

Barber shot back: "It is perfectly evident what he is trying to give."

Colonel Pennypacker grunted. "Gentlemen," he said mildly, "the witness may continue his statement, and the defense counsel can object to any part of the testimony as he sees fit."

Shaking his head, Captain Barber sat down. "No," he said, "I will not take up the court's time. Let the witness slash it all in, if that's what he wants to do."

The judge advocate seemed pleased. "Go on, Lieutenant."

Wilhelmi didn't need any encouragement. "Well, after the colonel and Lieutenant Flipper finished talking, the lieutenant talked about the race planned for the Fourth. He seemed quite taken with the Mexicans, always chatting them up, usually in Spanish. I kinda thought that maybe the lieutenant was asking them about the country, as if he was planning to desert and. . . ."

"Objection."

"Sustained. The witness does not know what the defendant was thinking or planning."

Clous quickly changed the line of questioning. He had already raised his damning point that Flipper might have been plotting a trip across the border. "As post adjutant, you are familiar *mit* da duties of Commissary of Subsistence, *ja?*"

"I am."

"Tell us vat led to da accused's arrest?"

Wilhelmi went on, talking through his ugly nose, rehashing previous testimony about the communication problems between Flipper and San Antonio. "We thought there was a problem with the books, thought that Flipper might be planning to desert with that money."

Clous waited for an objection, but when Barber remained silently, he pulled off his glasses, fogged the lenses with his breath, and wiped them with a handkerchief. After repositioning the small glasses, he smiled and asked: "Let me save da defense counsel from having to ask dis question. Do you have, or have you ever, shown any prejudice toward da accused?"

"No," Wilhelmi lied. "I'll admit that I didn't socialize much with Lieutenant Flipper, but I wasn't like some whites who just don't like to be brought together with them."

Them. Flipper forced down the bile rising in his throat.

"If Lieutenant Flipper ever felt ostracized, it wasn't on my account."

With the court adjourned, Flipper and Barber retired to the duplex where Flipper told him about his dealings with Wilhelmi back at West Point.

"Are you sure?"

"I'm certain it was Wilhelmi on the parade grounds that time with the chewing tobacco. Now, I can't honestly say that he was the cadet corporal who had to leave the Academy because of. . . ." He paused, slightly embarrassed.

Merritt Barber smiled. "I did not go to West Point, as you know. My education came at Williams College, Ohio State Law College, and the Tenth Vermont. But I have heard stories of more than a handful of former cadets who wished they had practiced discretion if not abstinence. And quite a few officers on the frontier, as well."

"Can you use it?"

He lit a cigar before answering. "The rumors are hearsay, and even you can't confirm why Wilhelmi left West Point. Clous will object, and, even if I asked about it, I think it would reflect badly on you, Henry." Barber paused, uncertain. He took a deep breath, exhaled, and explained:

"Deep down, the officers we're facing would say . . . 'That uppity little darky is besmirching Wilhelmi's good name. No proof at all.' I think that would all but convict you of conduct unbecoming an officer and a gentleman."

Flipper took it all in without speaking. At last he nodded. "You're right. And I don't want to sink to the level of Clous, Wilhelmi, or Shafter."

"But I can bring up the fact that he knew you at the Academy, that he might have resented you," the captain continued. "You were graduated. He wasn't. That's worth something." He took a long pull on the cigar, tilted his head back, and blew a stream of smoke toward the ceiling. "Now, tell me about this burro race."

Flipper shrugged. "Not much to tell. Captains Bates and Veile wanted to do something special for the Fourth of July and decided on a burro race. They asked me to get local Mexicans because I speak Spanish better than any officer at the post."

"Kinzie Bates is going to testify for the prosecution," Barber said, lifting his head to face Flipper. "I know he'll talk about the embezzlement charges, but what can he say about the burro race that'll potentially hurt us?"

"I don't know. Like I said, I made up the circulars for the race, and wrote them in Spanish. We had a lot of folks up from Chihuahua. On the Fourth, I explained the rules to them. I mean there was nothing to it, Captain. The total pay-off was only fourteen *pesos*."

"Any wagering?"

"Certainly. It was a race, and this is an Army post in Texas."

"How did you make out?"

"I don't gamble. Horses or cards. Not even mumblety-peg."

A minute, maybe more, passed in silence. Barber leaned back again, closed his eyes, and enjoyed his smoke. Finally he removed the cigar and said easily: "A burro race."

Flipper nodded. "Burro race."

"Hardly what I'd call damning."

"No, sir."

"But tomorrow's testimony from Wilhelmi might be. Clous is going to play up this idiotic idea that you planned to take off for Mexico. And that, Lieutenant, you can bet on."

There was no testimony the next day, however, as Captain Barber came down with a delicate illness himself. Court was adjourned until November 14th, only then stenographer Tilley was sick.

"God help him," Barber whispered, "if he's got the trots. Damned Army food."

Flipper smiled. "It's better than what Wilhelmi had at West Point. . . . I don't mean the food."

Merritt Barber grinned widely.

The court permitted Judge Advocate Clous to record the testimony, but first he read back the previous transcripts involving Small, Davidson, Withers, and Wilhelmi. Listening to testimony spoken in Tilley's somnolent monotone had been bad enough, but Clous's harsh German accent proved hellish. It was mid-afternoon before the proceedings were approved and the judge advocate could resume questioning Wilhelmi.

"Lieutenant, vat happened on da Tent of August?"

"It was shortly before retreat, and I noticed Lieutenant Flipper's horse tied up at the hitching rail in front of Sender and Siebenborn in town."

"Sender and Siebenborn, da mercantile, *ja?*"

"Yes, sir."

"*Sehr gut.* Go on, Lieutenant."

"Well, I noticed that the lieutenant's saddlebags were on the horse. That struck me as strange. Why would Flipper throw saddlebags on his horse just to ride to town? I immediately returned to the post and reported my observations to Colonel Shafter. I told the colonel that I was afraid Lieutenant Flipper might be planning to leave the post, perhaps even the country."

"I see. And did Colonel Shafter give you any orders?"

"He did. He told me to ride to the mercantile, find Lieutenant Flipper, and inform him that he was being relieved as A.C.S. and bring him back to the post. I followed my orders and brought Lieutenant Flipper back to headquarters. Colonel Shafter questioned him some, then I went with Lieutenant Edmunds to search Flipper's quarters. Lieutenant Flipper went with us."

"Continue."

"His place was a mess, what you'd expect from some darky laundress, not an officer. His clothes were all mixed up with Lucy Smith's, his concubine."

"Objection!" Barber slammed his fist on the wooden table.

"Sustained."

"His housekeeper," Wilhelmi corrected with sarcasm. "Her skirt was hanging over his trousers. We found a lot of women's stuff on a bed. Old toothbrush . . . comb . . . things like that. Colonel Shafter had wanted to believe that if anyone had stolen government funds, it would have been that black wench, but upon examining Lieutenant Flipper's quarters, Lieutenant Edmunds and I believed that they had been in this together."

"Vat did you do next?"

"We asked Lieutenant Flipper to empty his pockets."

"And?"

"He pulled out a handkerchief from the pocket on the right-hand side of his blouse. A check . . . for fifty-six dollars . . . flew out."

"You recognized dis check?"

"Most certainly. It was a check I had given him personally. It was for my commissary bill for July, that of the band and the post bakery."

"Most damning," Clous said softly. Instead of objecting, Barber just rolled his eyes.

"Captain Clous," Colonel Pennypacker said, objecting for the defense counsel. "Refrain yourself, sir."

The judge advocate smiled. "Continue, Lieutenant. I find dis fascinating."

Wilhelmi went on. He and Edmunds had found more checks in Flipper's quarters, plus some silver. Edmunds went through a trunk and pulled out a pocketbook. Inside he discovered more currency and a twenty-dollar gold piece. More money was found hidden inside copies of *Appleton's* and *Scribner's*, all checked out from the post library, and inside a copy of *Popular Science*, also from the library, he discovered sales accounts and letters of transmittal Flipper said he had already sent to San Antonio.

"Lieutenant Edmunds also pointed out the ashes in the fireplace. We thought Lieutenant Flipper might have burned the remaining checks he claimed to have sent to San Antonio."

"At dis point, did you arrest Lieutenant Flipper?"

"I did, sir."

"How did he react?"

Wilhelmi shrugged. "He said . . . 'Very well'."

"Tough day," Wade Hampton commented as the three officers dined at the café in Newtown.

"We get our turn tomorrow," Barber said. "I don't think Mister Wilhelmi will sound quite so competent during my cross-examination."

Hampton and Barber continued their conversation, talking about strategy for the following day. Flipper sat across from them, staring at the rough-hewn table, holding the cup of coffee, now cold. He hadn't even tasted it.

He felt alone again, even among two men he considered friends. Hampton and Barber were so busy talking about the court-martial, they didn't seem to remember that Flipper sat with them. The Mexican waitress came by and offered to refresh Flipper's cup, although it was still full. He shook his head, and the rotund lady walked away.

Portions of Wilhelmi's testimony played through his mind, over and over like one of Albert Church's mathematics lectures at the Academy. *If Lieutenant Flipper ever felt ostracized, it wasn't on my account.* Louis Wilhelmi was a liar. Flipper didn't know if Merritt Barber would be able to prove this tomorrow, but he knew. He did feel ostracized at Fort Davis. He had felt that way for much of his career in the Army, but not always.

Chapter Eighteen

Fort Elliott, 1879

"Tell us a story, Lieutenant Flipper."

A first lieutenant stuck a bottle of rye in Flipper's right hand. Another slid a handful of cigars into his blouse pocket. Ten pairs of bloodshot eyes trained on him in the dim light of the makeshift dance hall. Flipper passed the bottle without drinking, shook his head, and stifled a yawn.

"Gentleman," he began, but the loud sawing of a fiddle and plucking of banjo strings cut short his protest. Mrs. Maney ran forward, grasped Flipper's hands, and pulled him to the dance floor, one more time, while the white officers and their partners cheered.

Flipper had been at Fort Elliott for two days. If most of Fort Sill's officers had treated him like General Sherman, the garrison at Elliott toasted him more than they would George Washington. His duties as G Troop's Acting Captain had ended, and he had returned to A Troop, continuing on as signal officer. He had finished his memoirs, mailed them to Mr. Markland, and held the book in his hands before 1878 drew to a close. **The following pages were written by request,** the book began, and Flipper's status had gained new heights as his fellow officers and quite a few civilians asked him to autograph copies of THE COLORED CADET AT WEST POINT: AUTOBIOGRAPHY OF LIEUTENANT HENRY OSSIAN FLIPPER, U.S.A.

Early the following year, however, A Troop had been transferred from Fort Sill to this desolate post near the des-

189

olate town of Mobeetie in the desolate Texas Panhandle. "Fort Elliott's not the end of the world," Colonel Davidson had told Flipper before the troop pulled out of Sill, "but you can see it from there."

Flipper had cried unashamedly when he had left Sill. Davidson, Lawton, Pratt, they were good men, and they had treated him as an equal, as a man. He had felt at home there, but that was the Army for you. At least Pratt and Nolan would be with him in Texas, but he would miss Mrs. Nolan and, especially, his rides with Mollie Dwyer. He didn't know what he would find at Fort Elliott, or how the all-white soldiers stationed there—one 4th Cavalry troop and two companies of the 23rd Infantry—would accept him. When Captain Nolan took command of the fort and made Flipper the post adjutant, Flipper's fears were heightened.

Yet Flipper had been invited to the post dance. He had politely declined the invitation and retired to his quarters only to be wakened from a sound sleep by Lieutenant J. A. Maney of the 23rd. Maney had insisted that Flipper join the officers and would not take no for an answer. So here was Henry Flipper, dancing with the white man's wife.

The dance ended, and Flipper was forced to tell a story.

"I, um . . . let's see." He caught the bottle of rye and laughed, tossing it to Lieutenant Pratt. "No, thanks," he said.

"It'll loosen your tongue some, Mister Flipper," a 4th Cavalry captain suggested.

"It would loosen my stomach," Henry said, and the officers hooted.

"Colonel Davidson," Flipper began, "ordered me to the Wichita Agency to inspect cattle being delivered by some Texans. This was last fall, but it was warm. No one told me about these blue northers you have in this part of the country, so like a green lieutenant I took off for the agency with my orderly, who also must have never heard of changing weather. We made the thirty-two miles without a problem, and I took the only room available. The storm blew in that night, and, when the Texas cowboys arrived and found out they had to sleep on the floor, or in the grain room in the stables, they weren't too happy about it. They bawled more than the cattle."

They weren't happy about anything, Flipper recalled, but did not include this in his story. They had screamed about being put out by a nigger, and complained that a Georgia darky didn't know a damned thing about cattle. Flipper had held his tongue and the following morning had inspected the cattle in freezing cold and handed the Texas *segundo* a receipt.

"Anyway, I inspected the cattle. No problems. And wanting to get back to Sill in a hurry, I rode off, hoping it wouldn't snow any more. Naturally it did. I've never been so cold in my life. I don't think my orderly would ever ride with me again. Four hours again, thirty-two miles, only this time the wind was blowing like mad and the temperature had dropped into the twenties. Felt colder, too. Anyway, by the time I got back to Fort Sill, I had to get Captain Nolan's cook, Missus Matthews, to cut off my boots with a pair of scissors. I took a bath and don't think I woke up for a week."

"I've got a Flipper story for you," Lieutenant Pratt said with a smile. "We're getting ready to leave Fort Sill. Packs are being put on the mules, and one of the 'skinners, he's a greenhorn, asks of no one in particular . . . 'How long will it take us to get to Fort Elliott?' Lieutenant Flipper comes up to the boy and says . . . and this is exactly what he tells him . . . 'It's one hundred thirty-five miles, I'm told, to Fort

Elliott.' Now, that should be all the 'skinner needs to know, but Mister Flipper keeps going. 'A mule can go forty-five miles a day with no load, but twenty miles a day if he has a two-hundred-pound load. So if the mule is thus packed, we can divide one-thirty-five by twenty and deduce that we should make it to Fort Elliott in six-point-seven-five days.' I swear, I thought the muleskinner would up and quit right then and there."

"How long did it take y'all?" Lieutenant Maney asked.

"Six days," Pratt answered.

Not to be outdone, Flipper said: "Obviously the packs on those mules weighed less than two hundred pounds, thus allowing the animals to travel twenty-two-point-five miles per day."

The room exploded with laughter, the band started playing again, and Mrs. Maney latched onto Flipper for yet another dance.

Life at Fort Elliott, however, soon became more than dances and dinners. Post adjutant duties took up much of his time, but he enjoyed working closely with Captain Nolan. His one break from paperwork came when Nolan ordered him to map the reservation boundaries. By the time Flipper came back, Lieutenant Colonel John W. Hatch of the 4th Cavalry had assumed command of Fort Elliott. Nolan returned to A Troop, and Hatch named his own adjutant. Flipper didn't mind. This was also the way of the Army.

A West Pointer, Hatch also took an immediate liking to the celebrity lieutenant. Flipper continued to find himself the guest of officers' parties, resigning himself to an enjoyable, if not overly exciting, career in the 10th Cavalry. But later that month, a handful of Comanches fled the reservation, and Lieutenant Henry O. Flipper wondered if he would get his first taste of combat.

With fifty-four men, Nolan and Flipper pressed hard for three days until they reached Blanco Cañon, where they set up base camp and prepared scouting duties to find the Comanches. They would send patrols out in each direction, covering a hundred-mile radius from the cañon in the Llano Estacado.

Come first light, Lieutenant Henry Flipper would lead his first assignment in a hostile situation. He felt sick to his stomach.

"I'm sending Ben Clark with you," Nolan told him that night. "He knows this part of the country better than most. You know your orders, Henry. Capture any hostiles. Fire upon them if need be. They'll kill you if they have the chance." Nolan smiled, tried to change the topic. "Don't worry yourself sick, son. Pretend you're taking a Sunday afternoon ride with Mollie."

"Ben Clark does not look like Miss Dwyer," Flipper said.

"Thank God for that."

His tension eased over the next few days, mainly because his patrol failed to find any sign of Indians. "Comanch' can disappear in the Staked Plains," Clark told him. "I'd bet two or three of your books that we don't even spot Comanch' horse apples, let alone a buck with a Winchester."

Clark was right. For a month, patrols failed to find one Comanche. The Texas sun blasted men and livestock like a prairie fire. Sunstroke left many of the black troopers unable to ride. Two men came down with dysentery. The Blanco Cañon source of drinking water dried up. One man deserted. The Comanches didn't have to fight the Army,

Flipper thought. Texas did a pretty good job of putting the 10th Horse out of commission.

"We need to find water," Nolan said.

"Yes, sir," Flipper answered through cracked, bleeding lips.

"We'll break camp at first light. I'll take half the men north, you go east. If you find water, send a galloper after us. I'll do the same. If neither of us finds water, you will proceed back to Fort Elliott. I'll turn east and also strike a course for Elliott."

Flipper nodded. "Very good, sir."

Shaking his head, Nolan turned and walked to his tent. "It's one hell of a way to fight a war, Lieutenant."

His legs couldn't support him. He realized that as soon as he slid from the saddle, and reached out frantically for support, but his hands slipped on the sweat-dampened leather and he sprawled on the sun-baked ground. The big gray gelding stared at him and snorted, too weary to do anything else.

Ben Clark and Corporal Erskine King reached him first. Flipper heard their questions, but couldn't get his mouth and throat to work. Quickly they dragged him away from the horse. He felt the shade, thought he must be under a tree, although he hadn't seen a tree in days, and opened his eyes to see two of his troopers holding their dusty campaign hats, shielding the sun off their lieutenant's face.

Flipper cursed himself for his weakness.

"Open that can, damn you!" Clark snapped to someone.

He felt his head being lifted, tasted something wet on his lips. He tried to swallow, couldn't, finally managed it. Tomato juice. Canned tomatoes.

"It's the best we can do, Lieutenant," the scout said, and

forced another mouthful into Flipper.

Corporal King shook his head. "He up an' given his canteen to Evans and Browne," the former Tennessee slave told Clark. "Don't thinks the lieutenant had no water since yesterday morn."

Troopers Evans and Browne were played out. Too weak to ride, they now followed Flipper's command in a pair of travois manufactured out of bedrolls, latigo strings, and carbines. Flipper had not found even a trace of water since leaving Blanco Cañon, and had not heard from Captain Nolan's patrol. For all he knew, Nicholas Nolan's bones lay somewhere on the Llano with the rest of his men.

He tried to remember. It had taken A Troop three days to reach the cañon from Fort Elliott, but the men and animals had been fresh then. He had no idea how long they had been riding. He figured they were lost, figured Ben Clark knew that, too, only he wouldn't tell anyone—not even Flipper.

Grunting, he forced himself to sit up. He fought of a wave of dizziness and pushed away the can of tomatoes, glanced at the sun, tried to think. "Does it ever rain in this state?" he asked Ben Clark.

"As often as it rains in hell," the scout answered. "We're out of water. If we don't find water soon, I'd like your permission to kill one of our mounts."

Flipper blinked. "What for?"

"Drink its blood, Lieutenant. We might be drinkin' hoss piss before we're out of this mess."

What next? He stood weakly, leaning on the scout for support. Slowly he remembered his orders. *Dismount. We'll walk the horses for the rest of the day.* "Bad Medicine," he said with a feeble smile, "I wish you'd make your medicine and make that sun disappear."

"Me, too, Lieutenant."

It hurt to talk, yet he had to. He didn't want his men to see him like this again: falling into the dust, unable to stand, delirious. "We'll walk the horses for the rest of the day," he said, and, leaving the scout's support, weaved a roundabout path to the waiting horse. He grabbed the reins, patted the gelding's neck, and took a step east.

One step forward. Then another. You can do this, Henry Ossian Flipper. Another step. That's right.

"Lieutenant!" Clark called out. "Let me help you up there, sir. You ride. Your horse is stronger than the rest of these nags. He'll carry you."

"No."

"No shame, Lieutenant."

"I'll walk. We'll all walk, Mister Clark. That's an order."

They walked. For two more days, without water, the men staggered along. No one spoke unless necessary. They rose early in the morning, marched until it got too hot, then rested until late afternoon, when they continued until well past dark.

On the third morning, Ben Clark found a wagon trail made by buffalo hunters, and quickly reported the good news. The men were too weak to shout with joy. Those that could mounted their horses and shortly before noon Flipper's command entered Fort Elliott. The first man Flipper saw was Captain Nicholas Nolan.

"Céad míle fáilte," the Irishman said, grabbing the gray horse's reins. "I thought you were a goner for sure. We've had patrols searching for you the past three days. Lose any men?"

"None dead, sir," he answered weakly. "I'll make my report at. . . ."

"You'll make your report after you've slept, Lieutenant.

After you've bathed, eaten, and had water. You look half dead, son." Nolan turned. "Trooper!" he shouted. "Take care of Mister Flipper's horse." Facing Flipper again, Captain Nolan winked. "You're a hero, Henry. An honest-to-god hero."

Staggering to his quarters, Flipper didn't feel like a hero. He didn't like everyone looking at him. These stares weren't worshipful. Far from it. He felt like he did on that first day at West Point, hearing the taunts, the jeers. Only a few onlookers said anything. They just looked, pointed, shook their heads. Flipper tried to ignore two 4th Cavalry troopers, a mustached, husky sergeant, and a string bean corporal, in front of headquarters. The corporal crushed out a cigarette butt with the toe of his boot.

"Son-of-a-bitch," the sergeant swore with contempt. "The damned moke made it back alive."

Chapter Nineteen

November 15–18, 1881

Where to start? Barber and Flipper had debated that for hours. Louis Wilhelmi had made a lot of suggestions, and told more than his share of lies. So much for taking the oath to tell the whole truth and nothing but the truth. Eventually, they had decided to begin the cross-examination with the burro race. At first it had seemed silly to Flipper, but Barber explained that they had to dispel any thoughts that he actually might have been planning to escape across the border.

"Refresh my memory, Lieutenant," Barber said, still seated beside Flipper on the wintry Tuesday morning as he began his interrogation. "At the time, you thought Lieutenant Flipper was the originator of this burro race?"

"I did."

"But do you now know that he did not get the race up, but that Captain Bates and Captain Veile got it up and engaged Lieutenant Flipper to post the notices in Spanish?"

"Don't know nothing of the kind."

Flipper shook his head. A first lieutenant could at least speak proper English, especially during a court-martial.

"Very well, then. How many officers contributed to the prize money?"

"I don't know exactly."

"Did Lieutenant Flipper?"

Wilhelmi scowled. "Not to my knowledge."

"Did you?"

Silence.

Barber raised his voice. "Did you, Lieutenant?"

"Yes." Wilhelmi couldn't mask his bitterness.

"In fact, you knew that Lieutenant Flipper had almost nothing to do with this race, and that your previous testimony was ridiculous." Barber waved his hand at the judge advocate before Clous could rise to object. "I withdraw that statement, gentlemen." He stood, smoothed his dress blouse, picked up his note pad, and approached the witness.

"When did Colonel Shafter say he was afraid Lieutenant Flipper might leave the country?"

"I think it was after Lieutenant Flipper's arrest." The nasal whine sounded like fingernails on a chalkboard. "He said how easy it would have been for Lieutenant Flipper to escape into Mexico."

"But you said in previous testimony"—Barber flipped through a few pages of his pad and read—" 'I told the colonel that I was afraid Lieutenant Flipper might be planning to leave the post, perhaps even the country.' Colonel Shafter had not expressed any such concern before this incident?"

"I don't remember."

"How about those saddlebags you testified about? You said they struck you as strange, that seeing them prompted you to think the lieutenant was about to desert. Correct?"

"Yes."

Barber lowered the note pad to his side, and paused before speaking firmly, his eyes boring into the witness. "Mister Wilhelmi, a first lieutenant addresses a captain as sir."

"Yes, sir."

"Didn't you know, mister, that it was the custom of Lieutenant Flipper to ride with those saddlebags?"

"I did not know anything of the kind, sir."

"You've seen Lieutenant Flipper's horse before? An Andalusian stallion, the only one in the Tenth Regiment."

"Often, sir."

"And never recalled the saddlebags?"

"No, sir."

Barber laughed. "Really, Lieutenant, your memory is somewhat selective. When you arrested Lieutenant Flipper, how was he dressed?"

"In his uniform, sir."

"Was he wearing a cap?"

"Yes, sir. He had on his coat, too," Wilhelmi said mockingly, and added insultingly, "and a pair of pants. Sir."

Merritt Barber ignored the caustic sarcasm. "Shoulder straps?"

"Yes, sir."

Among the court-martial board members, Lieutenant Colonel James F. Wade cleared his throat, leaned forward, and spoke to the witness. "Mister Wilhelmi, if I detect one more 'sir' uttered in a disrespectful tone, I shall prefer court-martial charges against you. Is that clear?"

"Yes, sir," the lieutenant replied meekly.

"Carry on with your questioning, Captain Barber."

Good old Colonel Wade, Flipper thought. He had been the first officer of the 10th Horse that he had met, back at the train depot in Houston when he had informed Flipper that A Troop was on its way from Fort Concho to Fort Sill. The feeling was fleeting, though. Flipper quickly realized Colonel Wade was demanding respect for Merritt Barber, a white man, an officer who just happened to be defending a black man. If Flipper had been asking the questions himself, the colonel would have let Wilhelmi mock him for as long as he desired.

Barber thanked the Colonel Wade and approached Wilhelmi. "In short," he said, "Lieutenant Flipper was dressed in the ordinary riding dress of an officer."

"I do not know whether it is the ordinary riding dress or not."

"His ordinary riding dress, then?"

"I do not know whether it was his ordinary riding dress. I never took notice what his ordinary riding dress was."

It went on like this, but by the end of the day, Flipper thought his attorney had done a fine job. He had brought Wilhelmi's selective memory into focus, and had pointed out that Flipper rode with his saddlebags all the time, and had been dressed in typical uniform at the time of his arrest, not the outfit one would likely wear if he planned on deserting.

"You are the originator of this theory that Lieutenant Flipper planned to leave for Mexico, aren't you?" Barber asked.

"I am not."

Flipper looked at the faces of the court-martial board. Barber had done his job. They didn't believe Wilhelmi—but would that be enough?

Over the following two days, Barber questioned Wilhelmi about the arrest and other details—the search of Lucy Smith, the missing checks. To drag things out, or so it seemed to Flipper, Barber made Colonel Shafter and Wilhelmi bring all of the confiscated items to the chapel for an inventory. By the time that was complete, Colonel Pennypacker had had enough and called for an adjournment until the following day.

"What was that all about?" Flipper asked his friend and counsel in the kitchen behind his duplex.

"Feint, Henry, just a feint. No feints tomorrow,

though." Barber grinned. "No, tomorrow, I'll knock the hell out of Louis Wilhelmi."

Merritt Barber smoothed his mustache before standing to face the witness for the fourth day in the chilly post chapel. "How long have you known Lieutenant Flipper?" He held up his hand before Wilhelmi could answer. "Let me rephrase that. When did you first see Mister Flipper?"

Wilhelmi's eyes narrowed, and he hesitated before answering. When he finally spoke, he lowered his voice to almost a whisper. "I first saw him in June of Eighteen Seventy-Three."

"Where?"

There was another pause. "At West Point, New York."

Barber smiled. "You were in the Academy with him, then?"

"I was."

"But you had to leave the Academy? And speak up, Lieutenant, so Mister Tilley can take down your testimony without straining his ears."

Captain Clous had heard enough. He grunted, almost upending both chair and table, and shot out: "I object to dat question as irrelevant and immaterial."

Turning to face the judge advocate, Barber responded: "I have a right to ask him for a record of every part of his life. Remember, Captain, that you brought up Mister Wilhelmi's background during your examination of this witness. He himself testified that he had been forced to leave West Point. If he had been in state prison, I would have a right to ask him about that."

For once, Clous looked speechless. Pennypacker overruled the judge advocate's objection and told Wilhelmi to answer the question, and to speak so that everyone in the court could hear.

"I resigned sometime in December of that year."

Flipper beamed. *Because you dipped your wick where you shouldn't have.*

"Because you were sick? Pneumonia, you told the court."

"Yes, sir."

"What did you then do?"

"I went to Philadelphia, and after I was well enough from my sickness I found employment at an insurance company and engaged in obtaining an appointment to the Army, which I received on the Fifteenth of October, Eighteen Seventy-Five." He looked at Flipper and added: "That was nearly two years before Lieutenant Flipper was graduated."

He was making his point, showing the court that he had been serving in this man's army two years before Henry Flipper ever received a commission, showing how he was determined to be a soldier even after he had been forced to leave West Point.

"After you left the Point, were you at any time engaged in any detection business?"

"No, sir."

"Nor any business of a detective character?"

"No, sir."

"This matter, then, was your first experience?"

"Which matter?"

"The matter of Lieutenant Flipper."

Again, Clous rose to object. "*Kapitän* Barber calls da search of Lieutenant Flipper's quarters 'detective' business, and I must protest against it."

With a smirk, Barber returned to his chair beside Flipper. "The question is withdrawn," he said, and added his own sarcasm: "I hope the judge advocate will not scold me any more than he can help it and not take up the time of the court."

"*Ein* moment! I am not scolding."

"Enough, please," Pennypacker said wearily, and at least two members of the board also sighed heavily.

"One more question, Mister Wilhelmi. You said you never felt any prejudice toward Lieutenant Flipper. Did you ever visit Mister Flipper, or ask him to visit you?"

The lieutenant shook his head. "I have never asked him to visit my house, nor have I visited his house. . . ." He grinned, remembering the arrest, and added: "Except, officially."

"Yes. I guess Colonel Grierson, Captain Nolan, and Lieutenant Hampton were the only officers who welcomed Lieutenant Flipper at this post."

Wilhelmi laughed out loud. No one in the court had expected that. "Colonel Grierson and Captain Nolan were Lieutenant Flipper's commanders. I expect they were bound by duty to entertain him. As for Lieutenant Hampton, why don't you ask him?"

Barber glared at the lieutenant. Wilhelmi tried to match the captain's stare, but finally looked out the window. "I'm finished with this witness," Barber said.

They stood in front of the chapel after court was adjourned. Barber answered some questions from the reporters, and, when the pack left to hound Clous and Wilhelmi, the captain scanned the parade grounds. "Have you seen Mister Hampton, Henry?"

"Last night. Captain Bates ordered him to leave this morning for Fort Quitman. Don't worry. Wade said he'd only be gone a week or so. He promised to be back shortly after Thanksgiving and testify on my behalf."

Barber nodded quietly. "Why did Wilhelmi say that?"

"What?"

" 'Why don't you ask him'? What could he mean?"

Flipper spat. "I took it as why don't you ask him why he's a nigger-lover?"

"Maybe. We'll see." Barber shrugged and patted his pockets, searching for a cigar. He came up empty. With a smile, Barber put his hand on Flipper's shoulder. "Anyway, we had a good day in court. Let's go home," he said, and began walking toward Flipper's quarters.

Flipper fell in behind. Home? Where was home? Atlanta . . . no, not any more, not for a while. He remembered November in Georgia, his favorite time of year. The pecans would be ripe, falling off the trees, ready to be picked up. His mother would bake a pie for Thanksgiving, and sometimes chop up the nuts to put in biscuits. But if the worst happened, if he had to leave the Army, he wouldn't return to Georgia. That would be like admitting failure. Atlanta didn't hold any promise for Henry Flipper.

Was he a man without a home? Flipper didn't know for sure. Soldiers often had no real home. The Army instills that in you, prepares you for life in the field, transferring you from one place to the other. It wasn't a bad life, really. Flipper had always felt sort of footloose. Fort Davis certainly hadn't felt like home, nor had Fort Concho. But Fort Sill had. To Lieutenant H. O. Flipper, it was home—at least, for a while.

Chapter Twenty

Fort Sill, 1879–1880

It felt great to be back home. Home. Indian Territory would never be Georgia, but Fort Sill felt like more than just a place for Lieutenant Henry O. Flipper to hang his hat. It had been his first post, and he couldn't conceal his happiness when the orders came in October to leave Fort Elliott for Sill. *Maybe this is home,* Flipper had thought. He realized that Georgia no longer held any appeal to him, although sometimes he longed for Anna White, but Anna's lure had lessened. She seemed farther away than Atlanta, far, far away, out of his reach.

18 September 1879
Atlanta

Dear Henry:

I take pencil in hand and pray that this letter finds you in good health and spirits. All is well in Georgia and with our parents and siblings. We have read about your accomplishments in the local papers, and you can guess what those Democrat editors think. I am happy to inform you that your success in the Army leaves them frustrated and angry. Keep up the good work.

Alas, I also thought I should inform you of some news. I'm not sure if you have heard that Anna White recently married Mr. Augustus Shaw of Brunswick. He's a gentleman, a hard worker, and promises to be a good provider, so I hope that you will not take this news with a heavy heart and wish Anna and Mr. Shaw a rich life together.

I am asked about you every Sunday after services. The entire congregation and much of Atlanta are so proud of you. Of course, I am running out of things to say (not really) and, if you don't write soon, I may have to start lying and inventing stories about your frontier exploits. You wouldn't want your brother, a bishop in the church, to start sinning, would you?

I close now, wishing you all the best.
Yours in Christ,
Joseph S. Flipper

His brother had written him, not Anna. She could have at least explained her reasons. Flipper laughed at himself. What was he thinking? He had no claim to Anna. He should be happy for her. She had found someone. A good man, Joseph said. A better husband than Henry Ossian Flipper could ever hope to be. "Soldiers make poor husbands," Captain Nolan had once told him. Of course, that hadn't stopped the Irishman from twice marrying. Maybe he'd write her when he found the time, tell her how happy he was for her, wish them a great life together, that kind of thing.

Most of the troopers of the 10th had been glad to bid good riddance to the Panhandle. The orders were delivered in person by newly promoted and transferred Captain Henry Ware Lawton, who was replacing retired Captain Clarence Mauck of B Troop, 4th Cavalry. To celebrate Mauck's retirement, Lawton's promotion, and A Troop's return to Sill, Lawton bought a keg of beer from the post sutler and invited Flipper and a 23rd Infantry officer named T. M. Wenie. The four of them drained the keg dry. It was the first time Flipper had ever tasted beer. It was the first time he had ever been drunk. It was the last time he would ever do either. He nursed the hangover most of the way from Texas to Fort Sill, but he did gain something other than a temperance lesson from the experience. Captain Mauck sold Flipper his Andalusian stallion for two hundred dollars.

He had arrived at Fort Sill with an advance party and went straight to work, immersing himself in his duties as post signal officer and instructing his troop in cavalry drill, blocking the hurt of Anna White's marriage from his mind. He soon fell into a routine, coping, as all soldiers had to do, with the tedium of post duty. Flipper could say one thing about his tour at Fort Elliott: it had never been dull, especially the assignments in the field.

"Mister Flipper," Lieutenant Colonel Davidson said one evening after they had supped together at the commanding officer's quarters, "I wonder if you could handle a rather ticklish assignment for me."

"Certainly, sir." Flipper straightened, excited, waiting as the officer clipped and lighted a long cigar. The two men sat on the verandah, enjoying the late autumn wind. Flipper wondered what kind of assignment would be considered ticklish. Certainly nothing he had done so far at Sill—not providing mail escort, overseeing Indian work details, or leading pointless reconnaissance missions—and there was nothing out of the ordinary about showing white and black soldiers proper signal methods.

The CO had invited Flipper to supper to make up for a ticklish situation in which the junior officer had been

Join the Western Book Club
and GET 4 FREE* BOOKS NOW!
A $19.96 VALUE!

Yes! I want to subscribe to the Western Book Club.

Please send me my **4 FREE* BOOKS**. I have enclosed $2.00 for shipping/handling. Each month I'll receive the four newest Leisure Western selections to preview for 10 days. If I decide to keep them, I will pay the Special Members Only discounted price of just $3.36 each, a total of $13.44, plus $2.00 shipping/handling ($19.50 US in Canada). This is a **SAVINGS OF AT LEAST $6.00** off the bookstore price. There is no minimum number of books I must buy, and I may cancel the program at any time. In any case, the **4 FREE* BOOKS** are mine to keep.

*In Canada, add $5.00 shipping/handling per order for the first shipment. For all future shipments to Canada, the cost of membership is $16.25 US, which includes shipping and handling. (All payments must be made in US dollars.)

NAME: _____

ADDRESS: _____

CITY: _____ **STATE:** _____

COUNTRY: _____ **ZIP:** _____

TELEPHONE: _____

E-MAIL: _____

SIGNATURE: _____

**PLEASE RUSH
MY TWO FREE
BOOKS TO ME
RIGHT AWAY!**

ENCLOSE THIS CARD WITH $2.00
IN AN ENVELOPE AND SEND TO:

Leisure Western Book Club
P.O. Box 6640
Wayne, PA 19087-8640

caught in the middle. Earlier in the week, when Flipper had been Officer of the Day, Corporal Erskine King had arrested the colonel's teenage son for walking on the parade ground grass. Following Davidson's explicit orders, King locked the boy in the post guardhouse and reported the incident to Flipper, and Flipper in turn went to tell the boy's dad.

He had stood on this very porch and felt Mrs. Davidson's wrath. "You turn my son loose immediately, Lieutenant Flipper!" she had snapped, hands on her hips, face flushed, eyes like a viper's. Davidson had barked right back: "He stays there till I order his release, Mister Flipper." Then he had turned and scolded her: "Madam, I'll have you know I'm the commanding officer of this post." But Mrs. Davidson had counterattacked: "Sir, I'll have you know that I'm *your* commanding officer." Flipper had left with orders to release the boy forthwith. Now he wondered if this new assignment might have something to do with the marital spat he had witnessed.

When the cigar was lit to his satisfaction, Davidson looked around the grounds to make sure no one was eavesdropping and moved closer to Flipper. "The men are gambling, Mister Flipper. I know this, but I can't prove it. I've assigned every officer here to look into the matter, and every single one of them has failed me." Davidson sighed. "I even asked Ben Clark to spy around."

Flipper refrained from chuckling. If that rapscallion and scout had discovered a card game going on after hours, he would have joined it.

"Nothing," Davidson continued. "I've even walked around late at night like some miscreant, sneaking into the barracks, looking through the windows of the servants' quarters." He stifled a yawn. "And I'm not cut out to be a detective, Lieutenant. I'd like you to take charge of this matter, Mister Flipper. See if you can't find where they're hiding their game. If you find anyone gambling on this post, I want you to arrest them and then report to me. Understood?"

Flipper smiled. "Yes, sir," he said, snapping a keen salute.

In his quarters, Flipper pulled off his boots and opened the trunk he kept unlocked at the foot of his bed. On top of his scrapbooks he found the pair of Kiowa moccasins Ben Clark had sold him back at Fort Elliott. They were made of soft deerskin, unbelievably comfortable, and didn't squeak like those stiff leather cavalry boots. To capture some gambling soldiers, he would have to be quiet.

Outside, he crossed the grounds and began scouting out the suspected buildings. The servants' quarters were too small, not a likely house of chance for a cavalry troop. Besides, the soldiers would risk arrest, or even being shot by a jumpy sentry, if they left the barracks. So they had to be gambling in the barracks. He had to catch them. First, he looked for signs of light, but saw nothing through the windows, so he crept up to the door, put his gloved hand on the knob, and listened. Nothing. He opened the door anyway, and stepped inside. He heard a few snores, saw the forms of men in their bunks. Quietly he walked through the barracks, stopping occasionally, but spotting nothing out of the ordinary. This wasn't going to be as easy as he hoped, and he walked out of the building.

For two consecutive nights, Flipper continued his secret mission with nothing more to show for it than bloodshot eyes and a cranky disposition during signal instruction the following mornings. He was about ready to report his failure to Lieutenant Colonel Davidson as he walked through the barracks a final time, listening to the snores, when he stopped. He thought he had heard something. But what? He squatted and ducked beside a bunk in case someone was entering the barracks. Seconds later he glanced at the sleeping man in the bunk. Man? Not hardly. He carefully pulled back the wool blanket and saw in the darkness the form of a pillow and bedroll.

Excited, Flipper stood and scanned the darkness. The trooper across the room was a real person, and those snores weren't the work of some Thespian. The man was really asleep. He picked up a Spencer and poked another form with the carbine's barrel, and when the man didn't move, Flipper discovered another bedroll and pillow. But where were they? He tossed the weapon on the bed and took a few more steps, stopping when one of the real soldiers snorted, mumbled something, and quickly fell back asleep.

Another minute passed before Flipper moved. His excitement waned. The games of chance weren't going on in the barracks, so where had the men gone? He had watched this building for three hours before going inside, as he had every night since receiving this assignment. With a heavy sigh, Flipper looked up and stared at the ceiling, ready to pray. It was at that moment that he saw the light, shining through a small crack in the barrack's ceiling.

"So what happened next?" Richard Pratt asked.

They sat at headquarters, Lieutenants Pratt, Colladay, Slater, Moore, and Whitall; Captains Nolan, Hodgson, and Lee; Major Wade, First Sergeant Watts, Sergeant Major Dover, Ben Clark, Flipper, and Lieutenant Colonel Davidson, sipping coffee and snacking on Mrs. Davidson's lemon cookies while Flipper related his successful mission that had led to the arrest of seventeen troopers.

"I looked for a ladder, but couldn't find one," he said after swallowing the last bite of cookie. "So I grabbed the Spencer carbine again and poked the barrel against a plank in the ceiling. Sure enough, it was loose. Then I quietly moved a trunk to stand on, pushed away two planks, and pulled myself into the garret. Those boys were rolling dice, didn't even notice me."

A few officers laughed.

"How'd they get up there?" Captain Nolan asked.

"That's why I couldn't find the ladder. They used it, then pulled it up behind them, and put the planks back in place. I barked out an order, and I wish you could have seen their faces . . . I almost doubled over myself . . . and told them they were under arrest, that they had just rolled blackjack."

Nolan spit out his coffee, and the room erupted with guffaws, although S. R. Whitall remained stone-face silent. "Henry," Nolan said with a smile, "you don't gamble, do you? You roll snake eyes when playing craps, me lad. Blackjack's a card game."

Spring felt like midsummer along Cache and Medicine Bluff Creeks, unseasonably hot before the rainy season. Sundays became Flipper's favorite. Each afternoon, after services, Fort Sill's officers would escort their favorite ladies away from the post for a picnic and Indian Territory's version of a fox hunt. Of course, there were few hounds to run few foxes, so, to the cheers of women, the fort's finest on horseback would chase jack rabbits and coyotes and anything else that seemed sporting.

Yet what Flipper enjoyed more were his horseback rides, after the festivities, with Mollie Dwyer. She rode well, perhaps even better than Henry Flipper, and he loved her company, her musical Irish brogue, the way she treated him as a friend—not a friend of her brother-in-law's, not a black friend, but simply a friend. The only arguments came over Mollie's pleading to ride Flipper's gray Andalusian stallion, and his quiet but firm noes.

Captain Clarence Mauck had been a fine judge of horse-flesh. The Spanish-bred stallion stood a good fifteen and a half hands, with an arched neck, short body, and powerful legs. His large eyes bespoke of a mild personality, and Flipper knew the stallion, like most Andalusians, was gentle. But the horse that Flipper had named Abraham had been trained for the *rejoneadores,* Spain's mounted bull-fighters, and he wasn't sure Mollie could handle the high-step, swinging gait if Abraham suddenly wanted to show just how proud and eager he could be.

They stopped this Sunday afternoon to rest under some elms. Mollie pulled wrapped sandwiches from Flipper's saddlebags and tossed him one while she pulled off her boots and socks and soaked her feet in the flowing creek. Flipper, ever the gentleman, averted his eyes.

"Have you ever been in love, Henry?" she asked out of nowhere.

He sat still, unsure how to reply. "Once," he finally said. "Back in Georgia."

"What happened?"

"Candles burn out sometimes, Miss Mollie. I guess that's what happened with me and Anna."

"Anna. Nice name."

"Yes'm. Anyway, I got orders to report to the Tenth. She stayed in Atlanta. Got married sometime last year."

"Are you over it?"

"I think so." He pinched off a piece of bread and tossed it to a school of ants. "How about you, Miss Mollie. Has

Cupid ever aimed an arrow at your heart?"

Mollie laughed. She had a rich voice, and, whenever she laughed, her entire face radiated with beauty. "Lots of times, Henry. I'm in love now."

He quickly finished his sandwich, not knowing where Mollie was heading and not wanting to find out. He remembered the black trooper shot dead in that whorehouse back in Mobeetie, recalled Sergeant Watts's words again and again: white women ain't nothin' but trouble for a nigger. . . . He stopped himself. Mollie couldn't be in love with him. They were only friends. *Stop acting like a schoolboy,* he chided himself. But still, he said—"We'd best be getting back to the post, Miss Mollie."—washed down his sandwich, and began tightening the cinches on both saddles.

"Aren't you going to ask me who I'm sporting, Lieutenant Flipper?" Mollie said as she pulled on her socks and boots.

"No, Miss Mollie," he answered, and surprised himself with his banter. "Might make me jealous."

She laughed, and grabbed the reins to both horses. "You're not the jealous type, Henry."

"Well," he admitted, "maybe. As long as it's not Lieutenant Whitall."

"That ogre?" Mollie scoffed. "Not hardly." She pointed her chin toward the elm. "Pick up my quirt, Henry, please. It's behind that big elm."

"Yes, Miss Mollie," he said, and left the horses with her. He had just stuck his head around the tree when he heard the creaking of leather, the snorting of Abraham, and, above it all, Mollie's boisterous laughter. He saw no quirt on the ground, realized he had been duped, straightened, and whipped around to see Mollie, riding his stallion pell-mell for Fort Sill, her dun-colored hat bouncing across her small back, held only by the horsehair stampede string he had braided for her.

"Lordy, lordy," he whispered before screaming Mollie's name, begging her to come back. She disappeared over a rise, and Mollie's gelding began to trot along after the stallion. He had to hurry up, or he'd be walking back to the post.

"Took you long enough," she told him from her perch on the stone corral.

His anger vanished. At least, she hadn't been hurt. "I had trouble catching your horse," he said as he swung down from the saddle and handed the reins to an orderly. "He wanted to run after Abraham."

Mollie giggled. "Abraham has a smooth gait, Henry. And he's gentle as a lamb."

"That's why I ride him," he said honestly. "Horsemanship was never my best subject at the Academy."

She jumped from the corral, offered her hand in truce, and they shook. "See you later, Henry Ossian," Mollie said, and took off at a lope, still giggling.

Flipper shook his head.

"Enjoy your ride, Lieutenant?" a cruel voice sounded to his right. Flipper turned to spot Lieutenant Whitall. He decided not to answer the lout and instead headed to the stall where a trooper was grooming Abraham.

"Don't you worry none, Mister Flipper. I hear tell the colonel's got another mission for you, one that suits a Jim Crow."

The water from Cache and Medicine Bluff Creeks could be the best tasting in the world, Flipper thought, yet the post cemetery was filled with men, women, and children who succumbed to malaria or dysentery. Several ponds, not too deep, stretched from the Army post all the way to the Red River and beyond, and, when the rains came, these filled up and became foul-smelling cesspools that mosquitoes loved.

Lieutenant Colonel Davidson, noting Flipper's engineering experience, asked him to tackle another ticklish assignment. Others had tried to remedy Fort Sill's sanitation problems, but, always, when the rains returned, malaria and death followed closely behind. Flipper scouted the series of ponds that week and reported that he could oversee a drainage ditch that would remedy the situation—but they needed to complete the project before the rainy season.

For the next few weeks, Flipper became a surveyor and engineer as one cavalry troop dug for six days, then was relieved by another unit. Digging, singing, sweating, troop after troop arrived to do the hard labor, always black soldiers.

"Ain't right," Corporal King told Flipper. "We be better soldiers than any of dem white boys, sir. We can fights. I knows that's a fact, sir. But what dey gots us doin'? Diggin' a latrine ditch."

"It's not exactly a latrine ditch, Corporal," Flipper corrected.

"Maybe. But I's seen plenty of white soldiers buried. Seems to me dey could do their share of the diggin'."

"Carry on, Corporal. And don't let the men hear you complain."

"Yes, sir."

He had done his share of the digging, too, to show the raw recruits how to do it, to make sure they didn't dig too deep or too wide in a spot. So he was filthy when Lieutenant Colonel Davidson and a party of officers arrived shortly before Flipper completed the project. Wiping his sweaty, dirty face with a rag, Flipper walked toward the white officers and orderlies, brushing off his blouse the best he could as he neared the men.

Davidson and the others dismounted, and Flipper explained his accomplishments to the commanding officer while Whitall jumped into the canal, cut loose with a loud oath, and exclaimed: "You dumb Jim Crow! You got this thing running uphill."

The group fell silent. Flipper held his temper, and the group silently walked to the ditch as Whitall climbed out. Davidson climbed down himself and looked up at Flipper with sad eyes. "It certainly appears that way, Lieutenant. This won't do us any good."

Yelling for Corporal King to bring his instruments, Flipper dropped into the ditch beside Davidson. "Begging the general's pardon, sir," he said, using Davidson's brevet rank from the war as a matter of respect, military etiquette, and, to a degree, brown-nosing, "it's an optical illusion. If you look down a city street, sir, it appears to rise and fall and get narrower, even though you know the street's flat and the same width."

"Hmm." Davidson sounded uncertain.

The drainage did work. Flipper used his instruments to prove that the ditch went downhill, and, when the rains came later that spring, the water flowed away, the ponds no longer remained stagnant, and the health problems at Fort Sill diminished greatly. They called it "Flipper's Ditch." Flipper didn't get to enjoy his engineering marvel, though, because the campaign against Victorio and his Apaches intensified down south, and that May several troops of the 10th Cavalry were ordered to Fort Concho, Texas.

Chapter Twenty-One

November 19–23, 1881

Up until the time he got into this mess, Flipper had liked
First Lieutenant Frank Heartt Edmunds. He had known the
man for a couple of years at West Point, where Edmunds
had served as a French instructor before leaving early in
1875 to go into field duty. They hadn't seen each other
again until this past March, when Edmunds had arrived
with the 1st Infantry at Fort Davis. He had replaced Flipper
as Acting Commissary of Subsistence, and, although their
relationship had never been more than one of professional
courtesy, Edmunds had been the voice of reason, perhaps
even compassion, during Flipper's arrest.

"*Herr* Edmunds, vat did you discover ven you and Lieutenant Vilhelmi searched da quarters of da accused?"

"A great deal of cash, piled indiscriminately on his desk
. . . currency and silver, some checks, nothing in any regular
order."

"And your reaction?"

Facing Flipper, the infantry officer answered: "I said . . .
'Goodness gracious, you don't keep all this money in your
quarters, do you?' Lieutenant Flipper said he did."

Flipper leaned toward Barber and whispered: "That's
true. I asked Colonel Shafter if I should put the funds in his
safe, but he told me to keep them in my quarters."

The defense counsel nodded, and Flipper straightened
to listen to the rest of Edmunds's testimony. Flipper had
usually kept that money in his trunk. Sure, when he was in
a rush, he might leave some of it on his desk to be logged

218

later. He thought of the old Comanche word he had learned years ago—*Suapuat*. Well, he certainly had been stupid: leaving his trunk unlocked, trusting Lucy Smith, trusting his fellow officers. He'd be the first to admit that he was a lousy bookkeeper, a horrible A.C.S., and he'd be the first to admit that he had no one to blame but himself for being in this predicament. They had warned him, Sergeants Watts and Ross, a few others, had told him to watch his back, that Nordstrom and others were gunning for him. He should have listened to them.

Testimony was kept short that Saturday, and the court adjourned until Monday morning. The prosecution was wrapping up its case. Barber said that the defense would likely begin its presentation shortly after Thanksgiving.

"If it pleases da court, I wish to introduce dis letter from da accused to Lieutenant Vilhelmi, dated da Seventeenth of August, dis year." Holding up the piece of stationery, the judge advocate rose and waved the letter at Flipper and Barber. Clous grinned with delight.

Captain Barber crossed the room and snatched the paper from the German's giant paws. As he scanned the letter, Clous explained the letter's merits to the court-martial board. In the letter, Flipper had asked Wilhelmi to return his personal possessions, as well as some Mexican currency, that had been confiscated during searches of his quarters.

"Let me see the letter," Colonel Pennypacker said, and Barber gave the paper to Clous who walked to the front of the court. Barber quickly sat beside Flipper for a quick conference.

"It's your handwriting," he said quietly.

"I wrote the letter. They had my ring, my watch, a lot of my stuff. I just wanted to make sure I got it back."

They had confiscated a lot of stuff at the time of his arrest, although some of it, mostly furniture, had been returned after Flipper's release from the stone guardhouse.

"What about the Mexican money?"

"It's a curiosity. I like to collect foreign money. Captain Nolan gave me some Irish coins. Even Wilhelmi once sold me a Prussian note."

"All right," Barber said, and stood. "I object to this letter being introduced. It illustrates nothing."

Clous shook his head. "I find dis very refreshing, very amusing. Dis letter I vill use to introduce testimony regarding da lieutenant's intentions."

Barber waved off the argument. "Why don't you bring his horse into court? It might with just as much propriety come in here. . . ."

"Ach!"

Flipper and Barber had to step outside while Pennypacker closed the court to deliberate. Neither man was surprised that the court overruled Barber's objection.

Clous argued that Flipper's deceit dated as far back as May. Barber objected, pointing out that nothing in the charges and specifications dealt with May, but was overruled.

"You found several statements during your search of da accused's quarters?"

"I did," Edmunds answered.

"Vat did you determine?"

"I compared the statements against the commissary books. Some figures had been erased."

"I have one further remark. Is it possible, *Herr* Edmunds, for Lieutenant Flipper to have made two copies of statements, one clean, one covered *mit* his mistakes? He vould present da clean book to Colonel Shafte. . . ."

"Captain Clous," Pennypacker said, sighing, "you're speculating. Confine your examination to the facts."

Clicking his heels, Clous bowed to the court and smiled. "I have nothing further."

"What did you think of Lieutenant Flipper as an officer?" Merritt Barber asked when he began his cross-examination of Edmunds on November 22nd.

"Up to the Thirteenth of August, his character, in my opinion, had been above reproach."

"The judge advocate yesterday submitted into evidence a letter Lieutenant Flipper had written in which he asked for certain property to be returned. In regard to the articles on his person, were any articles taken?"

Edmunds thought a moment before answering. "I think his ring was taken, his watch and chain. That's about all I remember."

Barber nodded. "You said his ring. His class ring?"

"His class ring. Yes, sir."

"You took it off his finger?"

"I, nor Lieutenant Wilhelmi, pulled it off. Lieutenant Flipper probably took it off himself and gave it up with the other articles."

The captain turned to the court-martial board, addressing them and not the witness. "You took an officer's West Point ring, you took his watch and chain, and other personal items. And for what purpose? Humiliation. I submit to you that a white officer would not have been treated this way."

"Save that for your closing arguments, Captain," Colonel Pennypacker scolded, and Barber whirled around to face Edmunds.

"After leaving the quarters, Mister Edmunds, you sealed up Lieutenant Flipper's desk?"

"No, sir. I did not."

"Was it not sealed up in your presence?"

"Yes, sir."

"Well, Lieutenant, in the presence of whom?"

"I think Captain Nolan and Captain Bates, possibly Colonel Shafter and myself. And Lieutenant Wilhelmi. He sealed up the desk."

"Wilhelmi." Barber nodded. "You searched the quarters again, after Lieutenant Flipper's arrest, is that correct?"

"Yes, sir."

"Did you discover anything else?"

"We found more currency and the like, checks that had been reportedly sent to San Antonio. And we confiscated a few more personal items."

"I see. Did you find anything else in the desk?"

"Some of the checks, yes."

"But you did not find those items during the original search . . . only after Lieutenant Wilhelmi had sealed up the desk?"

"Yes, that's right, sir. I guess we missed them the first time."

"Yeah. I guess you did. Or Mister Wilhelmi planted them. . . ."

Clous exploded out of his chair and objected. Merritt Barber looked pleased as he walked back to his chair.

Captain Kinzie Bates took the stand Wednesday. Clous only asked him one question—to the relief of Barber, who feared the judge advocate would bring up that ridiculous burro race again—and that was if he had signed any of Flipper's statements when Colonel Shafter was not on the post?

Bates replied that he had, and Clous thanked him.

"Cross, Captain Barber?" Pennypacker asked.

"I have no questions at this time, but might call Captain Bates as a witness for the defense."

"Very well. Captain, you are excused for the moment. Captain Clous, call your next witness."

Commissary Sergeant Carl Ross entered the chapel a minute later. Flipper was not worried about his testimony, even if Clous brought up the forty-six-dollar loan Ross had extended him. The judge advocate didn't, however, confining his questions to the commissary books and statements. Ross was an honest man, a top soldier, and told the truth, as Flipper knew he would. Early that afternoon, Colonel Pennypacker halted the questioning and adjourned the court until after Thanksgiving.

Flipper spent the rest of the afternoon at the stables, grooming Abraham, losing his thoughts by working the curry comb and hoof pick until he was sweating despite the November chill. He could have Walter Cox or some other stable hand do the work, but he liked to do it himself, liked the smell of horse sweat and dust. He always had. Most officers wouldn't be caught dead doing something they could have a striker do for them, even though current Army policy frowned on the use of turning an enlisted man into a *de facto* manservant.

Finished, he gave the stallion a sugar cube and apple, then washed his face and hands. He should get back to his quarters, see what Barber wanted to do for supper, discuss any plans or strategy. Hell, it hit him. Tomorrow's Thanksgiving. He stepped out of the stall and into the light, just in time to see the buggy making its way down the old Overland Trail toward town. He would recognize that heavy Concord "Piano Box" anywhere, and knew the pas-

sengers just as easily: Lieutenant Charles Nordstrom and
Mollie Dwyer.

"Son-of-a-bitch," he said softly, having figured out finally how and why his world had spun out of control.

Chapter Twenty-Two

Fort Concho, 1880

Light tapping on the door to his quarters caught him by surprise. "Just a moment," he said when he found his voice. He had been unpacking that morning, so he buttoned his blouse, donned his cap, and opened the door. A white infantry officer, kepi tucked underneath his arm, stood, smiling, on the porch.

"My respects, Lieutenant Flipper," said the lieutenant, a short, squat man with thinning hair and a pockmarked face. "I'm Wallace Tear, Twenty-Fourth Infantry, and on behalf of the other officers of Fort Concho I bid you welcome and invite you to a supper Friday night in your honor. Six o'clock, if that meets with your approval." Tear put on his kepi and extended his hand.

They shook, and Flipper smiled. "I accept," he said, bowing slightly. Beaming, Tear clicked his heels, returned the bow, and walked across the parade grounds and underneath Old Glory, flapping in the West Texas wind. Flipper closed the door and went back to work, still smiling.

Another celebrity dinner. He had grown accustomed to that. He had arrived at Fort Concho in a rather somber mood, still disappointed over the troop's transfer from Fort Sill. But his new post impressed him. Almost every building here had been made of stone, and his quarters on the south end of the parade grounds, like most of the structures, had a stone floor with rafters and beams constructed of pecan. Much of the fort, he had been told, had been built by German stonemasons and carpenters from Fredericksburg, perhaps one hundred and fifty miles to the southeast. He compared that to his first post in Texas, Fort Elliott, built haphazardly by bored, unskilled soldiers, resulting in a fort that a modest summer thunderhead might blow out of the Panhandle.

The following morning, Captain Nolan ordered Flipper to lead a patrol, circling the nearby town of San Angelo and the county seat of Ben Ficklin, and scout the area for Apache signs. "It's unlikely Victorio will come this far north or east, me lad," Nolan told him, "but we must get our troops ready. This row has been going on for nigh two years now, but we've been kept out of it. But if I don't miss me guess, we'll be in a running fight with those Apaches for quite a spell. And soon, Henry, soon." Nolan put both hands on Flipper's shoulders, squeezing gently, and said softly in Gaelic, affectionately: *"Ádh mór ort, cara. Slán."*

He made it back early Friday morning, weary, dirty, hungry, like the rest of his men. They had seen scorpions, rattlers, longhorns, jack rabbits, and acres of prickly pear, but nothing resembling an Apache or any other kind of Indian. Back in his quarters after making his report to Captain Nolan, Flipper stripped off his filthy duds and washed. He had just finished dressing when someone knocked on his door.

"Lieutenant Flipper," Wallace Tear said, forcing a smile after Flipper invited him inside. "Glad to have you back."

"Well, Lieutenant, I couldn't very well miss a party in my honor."

The smile vanished. Tear stared at the stone floor and shuffled his feet. "Well, Lieutenant, that's the thing. I . . . well. . . ." He sighed, looked up, and got it out: "Lieutenant, I am forced to tell you that the supper tonight has been canceled." He swallowed, shaking his head, and added: "By orders of Major Anson Mills, commanding. I'm sorry, Lieutenant."

"Thanks for the ride, Henry."

"My pleasure, Miss Mollie," he said, collecting the reins to both horses and leading them to the stone corral on the north side of the post. He handed the reins to a stable hand, gave the trooper orders for the caring of the animals, and returned to walk Mollie back to her quarters.

They chatted easily that late Sunday afternoon about the article she had read in *Frank Leslie's Ladies' Journal*, the friends they had left behind at Fort Sill, the weather, and the stark beauty of West Texas, avoiding subjects such as Victorio and the Apaches, the barbarous town called San Angelo, and the treacherous stares Flipper noticed whenever he took Mollie for a Sunday ride. Annie Dwyer Nolan invited him inside for tea and cookies, and he stayed, enjoying the company and food, for an hour before returning to his quarters.

He dined alone in the officers' mess on bouillon, peas, oranges, and coffee, ignoring the whispers, shaking heads, and soft curses from the group of officers at a nearby table. Flipper retired early that evening, thumbing through a copy of *Freedman's Friend* magazine before blowing out the lantern. He slept fitfully, rose early, dressed, and was on his way to report for duty when a brutish voice stopped him.

"Hey, boy!"

Flipper whirled, furious. He expected to face some rake of a civilian, but saw instead a hulking 10th Cavalry lieutenant. The officer walked to him slowly, looked him over, and said stiffly: "Major Mills sends his compliments, and requests that you report to him as soon as possible."

Flipper looked the man over. He was a first lieutenant,

so Flipper couldn't scold a higher-ranking officer, but he could file a complaint with Major Mills—not that it would do any good. Mills, after all, had been the one to cancel Flipper's supper, so he would have to handle this matter on his own. He waited for a company of infantry to drift by, then spoke to the lieutenant in a steady voice.

"Lieutenant, I don't think I have had the pleasure." His eyes locked on the tall ogre.

"Nordstrom" came the reply. "First Lieutenant Charles Nordstrom."

"Well, Lieutenant. I'm Second Lieutenant Henry Flipper." Nordstrom didn't have the look of a West Pointer, so he added: "Class of 'Seventy-Seven."

Nordstrom stood silently, a cold stare voicing his true feelings. Flipper held out his hand, forcing the man to shake. To fail to do so would be disrespectful, conduct unbecoming an officer and a gentleman, although it would be Nordstrom's word against Flipper's. The lieutenant studied Flipper's hand, then jerked a cream gauntlet from inside his belt, and pulled it on. With his right hand now protected by the leather glove, Nordstrom gripped Flipper's hand with a vise-like grip.

"The pleasure's mine," he said through a clenched jaw.

Nordstrom broke the grip, surprised at Flipper's strength, and wheeled around. Flipper smiled. "One more thing, Lieutenant." The officer stopped but didn't face him again. "The name is Flipper. Lieutenant Flipper, H. O. Not boy. Do we understand each other?"

"Perfectly, Lieutenant Flipper," Nordstrom answered, and stormed away.

A Yankee by birth and education, Anson Mills had spent most of his life in West Texas, after being dismissed from

West Point for academic deficiencies in 1857. He had left Texas and served without distinction with Union volunteers during the war and earned a commission in the regulars after the surrender, working his way up the ranks. He had transferred to the 10th Cavalry a few years back, after serving in one of the white cavalry regiments, the 3rd or maybe the 4th, Flipper wasn't certain. What he was sure of, however, was that the years in West Texas had made Major Mills as hard as the brackish water they were forced to drink out here. He expected Mills to be some polished-boots martinet. He found him to be just a corncob-rough bastard.

"Lieutenant Flipper," he said from his roll-top desk after the adjutant left the officers alone, "I'm Major Mills." He rifled a shot of tobacco juice across the room toward the brass spittoon in the corner. He missed, and the dark stains on the stone wall informed Flipper that Mills had missed often, and didn't care.

Flipper stood at attention, waiting for the commanding officer to put him at ease. Anson Mills didn't. Wiping his mouth with the back of his hand, the major worked the tobacco into a comfortable position, and said: "Allow me to get straight to the point, Mister Flipper. I ain't got a bigoted bone in my body. Jews. Micks. Darkies. Bean-eaters. Secesh trash. Red niggers. Eastern politicians or Army goldbrickers. I don't give a damn who you are. The only thing I care about is keepin' the peace. On this post. Across West Texas. Wherever I'm in command."

"Yes, sir." Flipper didn't know what else to stay.

"I ordered that party in your honor canceled not because you're colored, but because it wouldn't be good for morale. And the Texicans in that hell town wouldn't care for it. I'm a peace-keeper, you see."

"Yes, sir. I see."

Mills spit again. This time his aim proved true. "No, you don't see, mister. This ain't Fort Sill, Lieutenant. This is the meanest part of Texas there is. A few years back, some dumb sons-a-bitches in Morris's Saloon got in their cups and cut a sergeant's chevrons off his sleeves. Thought it was pretty funny, till the sergeant came back here, got a bunch of troopers and carbines, and went back to that dram shop. Them Texans wound up buryin' one of their own, and Doc Schneider pulled some Forty-Five-Seventy slugs out of two others. We planted one trooper and kept another in the post hospital for two months. Also lost a good first sergeant named Goldsby, who lit a shuck for Mexico when the Rangers came here with arrest warrants. Nine soldiers were indicted for murder, Mister Flipper, and one of those was sentenced to hang. Won on appeal, but that don't matter. The point is this is Texas. San Angelo is filled with nigger-haters, and I can't protect you if you go there."

"I have no plans to go to town, sir, unless duty requires it."

Mills waved off the comment. "Yeah, but San Angelo ain't frettin' me right now. It's Fort Concho."

"Sir?"

"Your rides with Mollie Dwyer, Lieutenant. White woman. Colored man. You're beggin' for trouble."

"Sir, Miss Dwyer and I are friends. We enjoy riding together. We've been doing that since she arrived at Fort Sill, sir."

"Mister Flipper, you ain't been listenin'." He spit, and missed, again. "I'm tellin' you this ain't Fort Sill. This is Fort Concho, deep in Texas, and out here folks keep to their own kind if they know what's good for 'em. You go ridin' around this part of the country with a white woman, Lieutenant, and you'll get your neck stretched. Then I'll get my hide burned by Washington, Colonel Grierson, and those Republican newspapers. Like I said, I'm a peace-keeper, and this is my post, my command. So for your own good, don't go ridin' with Miss Dwyer any more."

He wanted to spray Mills with curses and arguments the way the major splashed the walls with tobacco juice, but Flipper held back, waiting for his anger to subside before speaking again.

"Is that an order, Major?"

Mills wiped his mouth again. "Not written, mister. Not by a damn' sight. Call it friendly advice. Dismissed."

Anson Mills wasn't lying about San Angelo. Flipper found that out soon enough. Trooper William Watkins, E Troop, was drunk. It being payday, he had plenty of company. Black and white soldiers rushed to San Angelo to spend their money freely on cards, whores, and forty-rod lightning. Cowhands from the various Tom Green County ranches, sheepmen, hide hunters, gamblers, and various parasites also packed the town that night.

Already out of money, Watkins was singing and dancing in McDonald's Saloon for drinks. White patrons laughed as the trooper belted out "Camptown Races" and danced unevenly. Two A Troop soldiers stuck their heads through the batwing doors, saw what was going on, and turned away. "You boys!" Tom McCarthy shouted. "Come on in and form us a trio." The soldiers quickly fled, and McCarthy, also well in his cups, laughed. He ran sheep on the San Saba River and spent his money freely whenever he came to town to have his rope pulled and his insides washed out with liquor. McCarthy picked up a bottle of rye and splashed some into Watkins's shot glass as soon as the trooper finished his song and dance. Watkins had been at it for more than an hour now. His eyes were bloodshot, his face covered with sweat, his shirt drenched.

"Whoa," McCarthy said. "You're startin' to stink like a nigger."

"He *is* a nigger, Tom!" someone hollered, and the saloon erupted with laughter.

"Sing us, 'Oh, Dem Golden Slippers,' boy," came another request, and Watkins downed the whisky and began another routine, this time crashing wearily over a chair and sprawling on the floor—to the delight of onlookers. McCarthy weaved over to the worn-out soldier and splashed Watkins's face with rye. "On your feet, soldier boy," he said, slurring his words. "Finish your song."

The men howled as Watkins pulled himself up. His voice was hoarse now, and he shuffled his feet weakly. Finished with the song at last, he leaned against the table and tried to catch his breath. Tom McCarthy refilled the glass, smiled, and said: "Sing 'The Bonnie Blue Flag,' trooper. Only lift your feet when you dance to this one, boy."

Watkins looked up and shook his head. "Massah Tom, suh . . . I be . . . tuckered out. Can't . . . sing an' dance . . . no more."

McCarthy took a pull of rye, and set the bottle on the table. "I said, 'Bonnie Blue Flag,' you uppity charcoal. You too good to sing a Johnny Reb song?" The sheepman's eyes blazed.

"No, suh . . `. Massah Tom. It's just . . . I'm gwine die . . . if I . . . dance an' sing . . . another song . . . suh."

"You got that right, boy. You're gonna die if you *don't* do as you're told." McCarthy put his hand on the old .44 Army Colt stuck in his waistband. "Now do like I say."

Closing his eyes, Watkins shook his head and pleaded: "I can't, Massah Tom."

The gun came out.

Watkins opened his eyes.

The saloon fell silent.

Watkins didn't move.

McCarthy pulled back the hammer.

"Boy," the sheepman said, "you gonna sing me my song?"

"Please," Watkins began.

Tom McCarthy shot him in the forehead.

We, the undersigned soldiers of the United States Army, do warn for the first and last time all citizens and residents of San Angelo and vicinity to recognize us as just and peace-loving men. If these terms are not met, and we do not receive justice, someone will suffer—guilty or innocent.

This has gone too far.

Justice or death!

The sheriff waved the poster in Flipper's face. "That's a threat. We don't take kindly to threats."

Flipper looked across the major's office, saw Mills wasn't going to help him, nor would the other officers in the room. "They had the courage to sign their names," Flipper said, studying the handbill. "I suppose it is a threat, Sheriff Spears, but you can't blame our men."

"I'll blame 'em if anyone gets hurt. I'll make you boys wish you was at Fort Pillow. That's how bad it's gonna get."

Now Major Mills stood up. "Jim, we don't take kindly to threats, either."

"Well, this is your damn' fault. Last night, a bunch of your darkies shot the Nimitz Hotel to pieces. Miracle nobody got hit. Then I find this"—Spears ripped the handbill

233

in half and dropped it at Flipper's feet—"tacked up on my door. Now. . . ."

"Sheriff Spears," Flipper said. "Tom McCarthy murdered a United States soldier in San Angelo. He was fleeing town when apprehended by two soldiers. My men showed restraint, sir, by not cold bloodedly killing the man as he did William Watkins. We put him in the post guardhouse that night, released him the following morning to you. And what did you do, Sheriff? You set him free. Let him walk about town as if he had done nothing. I can control my men, Sheriff, but only to a point. They demand justice. That's their right."

"Well, here's my right." Instead of addressing Flipper, the Texan whirled to face Mills. "If one of your niggers crosses the North Concho again, you'll fetch him back in a box. The Rangers will back my play, Major. All twenty of 'em."

Anson Mills sprayed Jim Spears's boots with tobacco juice. The sheriff reached for his revolver, thought better of it when Captain Nolan, Lieutenant Tear, and Flipper did the same, and stood shaking with rage, ears and neck turning a brilliant red. "You got twenty men," Mills said evenly, wiping his mouth. "I've got two hundred soldiers. Who you think's gonna win that fight, Jim?"

After the sheriff stormed out of the office, Mills stared at Flipper. "I put Spears in his place because he threatened my command. But I've told you, Mister Flipper, that I'm responsible for peace. That's all I care about. You make sure you keep that peace, Lieutenant. If any soldier from my post fires upon civilians, unprovoked, again, I'll have your bars, and let Jim Spears take in the men responsible. Understood?"

"Yes, sir."

* * * * *

A week later, Tom McCarthy was rearrested. Fearing a lynching, Sheriff Jim Spears ordered the prisoner transferred to Ben Ficklin. Fearing the prisoner's convenient escape, Major Anson Mills ordered Captain Nolan, Lieutenant Flipper, and six troopers to accompany the sheriff's posse and prisoner to the county seat. No one spoke during the four- or five-mile ride that seemed to take all day. The soldiers didn't speak until they were well out of Ben Ficklin, out of sight of angry, well-armed citizens.

"I hear McCarthy's lawyer has already put in for a change of venue," Flipper said.

"Aye. But that's fair, for both parties. He'd never see the rope were he tried in Tom Green County."

Flipper shook his head. "I'm not sure he'll hang anywhere in this state."

"I pray you're wrong, Henry."

Tom McCarthy was tried for first-degree murder in Austin. It took the jury two-and-a-half minutes to return a verdict of not guilty.

Chapter Twenty-Three

Thanksgiving, November 24, 1881

Coffee and tamales at a Newtown café were not exactly the Thanksgiving feast Flipper had wanted, but with Captain Nolan in the field, his wife visiting a sick friend at Fort Concho, Wade Hampton at the Fort Quitman sub-post, and Mollie Dwyer avoiding him, he ate alone. Maybe he could have dined with some of the town merchants, but he didn't feel like skulking around the stores, waiting for an invitation out of guilt, then feeling like an intruder. Even Barber had been celebrating the holiday elsewhere, forced to dine with Colonel William Rufus Shafter.

"Military protocol, Henry," Barber had explained. "I can't say no."

"I understand," Flipper had answered honestly. "No sense in ruining your career." Shafter had insisted that Barber dine with his staff, Flipper thought, so he'd be all alone.

"Hey, maybe that fat jackass will say something incriminating," Barber had gone on, trying to lighten the mood. "You'll be all right?" he then had said seriously.

"Sure," Flipper had said. "I'm dining with a good friend anyway."

Barber's face had gone blank. "Who?"

"Captain John Clous," Flipper had lied and relished the look on Barber's face before the lawyer realized he had been had.

"You scoundrel!" The two men had roared with laughter.

But now Flipper sat alone in the dusty café. Even the Mexican waitress avoided him, probably wishing he'd leave so she could celebrate the holiday with her family. He looked across the room, saw her staring at him, and realized that's exactly what she wanted. He quickly husked the last tamale, stuffed it in his mouth, and washed it down with coffee. He dropped a few coins on the table, put on his hat, and hurried out the door, mumbling a *"gracias"* and a "Happy Thanksgiving" to the waitress as he left.

The wind chilled him. The afternoon had been surprisingly warm, but evening had turned cold. A norther might be blowing in. That would certainly fit his mood. He mounted Abraham and rode back to the fort, grooming the stallion himself before walking back to his duplex. Nordstrom's side was dark. The lieutenant must still be celebrating with Mollie Dwyer, and Flipper fought back jealousy as he entered his quarters. Merritt Barber sat inside the living area, reading THE GILDED AGE.

"Didn't expect to find you here," Flipper said, hanging up his hat and unbuttoning his coat, glad to see his counsel, his friend, inside, glad to have someone to talk to on this night.

"Colonel Shafter is not much of a host. A pig, yes. Just watching him eat spoiled my appetite. How was your Thanksgiving turkey?"

"Pork tamales," Flipper corrected. "Highly recommended."

They fell silent. Flipper finished removing his coat and blouse. Barber turned back to his novel.

Tomorrow Carl Ross would finish his testimony. Captain Clous would begin winding up the prosecution's case, recalling any witnesses to clear up questions regarding their testimony. Soon Flipper would have a chance to tell his story. He sat on his bed, took a deep breath, exhaled, waited.

"How do you think the case has been going, Merritt?" he asked after a minute. "Honestly."

Barber closed the book. "Courts-martial are a funny thing, Henry." He patted his blouse for a cigar, realized he was out, and sighed. "I think we've done a good job. I don't know if that'll be enough. It should be. And I think we have a strong defense. I don't want you worrying, Henry, but I am going to be forthright with you. You're a man of color, and I don't think this country, this Army of ours, wants any men of color wearing an officer's shoulder straps."

"Yes, sir." Flipper felt his stomach turning. He stood, crossed the room, looked out the window into the darkening night. The wind began to moan. *Lousy damned holiday*, Flipper thought.

Barber came to stand beside him, putting an arm around Flipper's shoulders. "Don't give up, Henry. I just want you prepared for the worst. You've gone through hell these past few months, and there's a lot more hell you have to face. But no matter what happens . . . court-martial, prison, even an acquittal . . . you have to be strong. I've defended soldiers on murder charges, Henry, and watched two die. This isn't life or death."

Flipper nodded. Barber was right. If he won, he'd still be fighting this battle the rest of his career. And if he lost . . . ? Well, he didn't want to think about that yet. But he'd go on. This wasn't life or death. He knew that. He had seen death before.

Chapter Twenty-Four

In the Field—Summer, 1880

Apaches had hit troopers of the 9th Cavalry hard in New Mexico Territory, with Victorio's Mimbres warriors cutting a destructive swath across the south. General Sheridan ordered the 10th Cavalry out of Texas to help stop the bloodshed, but Colonel Grierson protested, arguing that West Texas would then be ripe for Apache plunder. Sheridan agreed, and Grierson had arrived at Fort Concho ready to implement his own plan of action. A short time later, Nolan, Flipper, and the rest of A Troop found themselves riding across this broken, brutal country east of the Pecos River with a supply train, heading for the low mountains near the Big Bend of the Río Grande.

"I'm not sure this land's worth fighting for," Flipper said at a water hole, looking at the vast expanse of dust and thorny mesquite. He let the stallion drink before filling his canteen with the iron-tasting water. "I wouldn't fight for it, if I were a settler or an Apache."

Nicholas Nolan smiled. "Aye. It's not Ireland, that's the truth. But the land changes farther west. The Davis Mountains are just a wee less beautiful than the Connemara back in me motherland, Henry. You'll love it."

"From what I've heard about Victorio, we'll wear out a lot of horses chasing him."

"I think not, my friend. Colonel Grierson's got another plan in mind."

No one would ever mistake the Pecos River for the Mississippi, Flipper thought, or the Hudson, or Chattahooche, or Ochlockonee for that matter. Yet, flooded, it had stopped A Troop and the supply wagons for three days. Although not wide, the dark river looked ominous. Horses could make it across, but the deep river flowed swiftly, its current too strong for the wagons. A rattler bit one trooper on the second day. He lived, but wouldn't be fit for service for a while. On the third day, two civilian teamsters decided they had had enough, stole two mules, and disappeared.

"I don't think this river's ever going to recede," Nolan said wearily, late that morning.

"Begging the captain's pardon," Flipper said, "but I think I have a solution."

"I'm all for solutions."

Smiling, Flipper pointed to a pair of mesquites on the far side of the Pecos. "I think we can rig a makeshift ferry, Captain, using those two trees. I can have two men swim the river and secure two guide ropes to those mesquites."

"What'll we do for a boat, me lad?"

Flipper turned, nodding at one of the wagons. "We unload that wagon, sir, take off the wheels and tongue, wrap the canvas tarp around its body. Turn it into a boat. I think it'll float. And we just ferry the supplies and men across. It'll take a few times across to get everything on the other bank. Then while we're reassembling the first wagon, we'll do the same with another wagon. And another. Keep it going until all the wagons are across and ready to roll."

"Horses and mules?"

"We can swim them across, sir. The river's not stopping A Troop, Captain, just the wagons."

The captain nodded. "You think this'll really work, Henry?"

"Only one way to find out, sir."

* * * * *

Coyotes woke him. At least he thought they had, hearing their incessant yipping in the desert night. But as his head cleared, he heard something else, saw the form of a man inside his tent, slowly recognized the baritone of Sergeant Watts.

"Lieutenant, sir, you awake now, sir?"

Flipper sat up quickly. "Yes, Sergeant, what's going on?"

"Captain wants you, sir. *Muy pronto*. It's Victorio. He's crossed into Texas."

Nicholas Nolan stood with a stranger to Flipper, both men studying a map stretched out over a table in the dimly lit crumbling adobe building at Fort Quitman. The subpost, some seventy miles from El Paso, sat so close to the Río Grande that even a poor shot like Anson Mills could spit into it. Quitman had never been much of a military establishment, even during its heyday in the late 1850s, and, since the last permanent troops had withdrawn three-and-a-half years ago, the adobe buildings had fallen into disrepair. The worst duty a soldier could pull, veterans often said, was to be sent to the end of the earth known as the Fort Quitman sub-post.

Colonel Benjamin Grierson hadn't sent A Troop here for punishment, though. No, the colonel had praised the soldiers up at Eagle Springs, had promised Flipper a commendation for his quick thinking at the Pecos River, action that resulted in no casualties and avoided a longer delay. Flipper had liked Grierson immediately. Even-tempered, well-educated, with a strong face and thick beard, the colonel acted more like a teacher—indeed, he had been a music instructor back in Indiana before the war—than a professional soldier.

241

Victorio had left New Mexico Territory and disappeared somewhere in Mexico, but the Apaches would return. Grierson had no doubt about that. They would cross the Río Grande and kill and steal in Texas, cut and slash, like Confederate guerrillas. The 9th Horse had lost plenty of horses, and a good number of men, chasing the Mimbres all over southern New Mexico. South of the border, Colonel Valle had garnered no success pursuing the hostiles—and the Mexican had four hundred soldiers at his disposal.

"Pursuit doesn't work against the Apaches," Grierson had told his officers back at Eagle Springs. "To beat an Apache, you have to think like an Apache. And what do Apaches know best?"

"Ambush," Charles Nordstrom had barked.

"Exactly," Grierson had said.

"Beggin' the colonel's pardon," Lieutenant Leighton Finley had said in his rich Southern drawl. "But how do we ambush Victorio? How do we even find him?"

Grierson had produced a map, which the officers gathered around. "Even an Apache can't survive without water, Mister Finley," the colonel had said. "So we stake out every water hole we know with cavalry and infantry."

Grierson had gone on, stressing how it was imperative soldiers hold their ground, to keep the Apaches from water at all cost. The eyes and ears of the campaign, he had added, would be the scouts and couriers. Captain Nolan had promptly suggested that Lieutenant Flipper serve as a courier. "He has the only stallion in the entire regiment," Nolan had said. "And it's one fine horse."

I hope I'm a good enough horseman, Flipper had thought back then, and again now as he waited for Captain Nolan's orders.

The stranger looked up. A bristly salt-and-pepper beard

covered his coppery face, and the lantern's glow illuminated black eyes and a wicked scar across the man's forehead. He wore a dirty sombrero, loose-fitting dark shirt, black flared trousers tucked inside calf-high moccasins. The man said something to Nolan, whose face was grim as he motioned to Flipper to join them.

"Mister Flipper," Nolan said formally, and kept the introductions short. The stranger was a scout named José Madrid. He had been watering his horse in the river when he had seen an Apache. They had exchanged shots, the Apache had disappeared, and Madrid had galloped to Quitman.

"*Señor* Madrid believes this Apache was part of an advance party. I agree. Undoubtedly, Victorio crossed the river quickly, as soon as the Apache reported back to him."

"What about Colonel Valle?" Flipper asked.

The Mexican laughed mirthlessly. "*Valle vale nada. Sus hombres son enfermos y muerto de hambre, sus caballos cansados. Se puede hacer nada, el pendejo.*"

"*Comprendo,*" Flipper answered, and Madrid's eyes registered surprise, and respect, that the lieutenant understood Spanish. Flipper had even smiled at Madrid's calling Colonel Valle a *pendejo*. Flipper had picked that up back at Concho. It certainly wasn't something Patrice de Janon had taught at West Point. "*¿Por si acaso los Apaches están a Tejas, por dónde próximo va Victorio?*"

Madrid jabbed a finger on the map. "*Tinaja de los Palmos,*" he said, and switched to English. "Nearest water."

"That's about fifteen miles west of Eagle Springs," Nolan said after briefly studying the map. He looked at Flipper. "Lieutenant, pick two good men and tell Colonel Grierson that we expect the Apaches to head for *Tinaja de los Palmos.*"

They saluted, and Flipper turned to go. *"Vaya con Dios, teniente,"* Madrid said softly.

A few minutes later, the strong Andalusian carried Flipper through the forest of yuccas, with Sergeant Watts and Trooper Scipio trying desperately to keep up. The stallion brought him without faltering all the way to the makeshift camp at Eagle Springs. Flipper leaped from the saddle, handed the reins to an infantry private, and stumbled toward the group of white officers, waiting curiously. He heard the worn-out mounts of Scipio and Watts lumber into camp while he fired a salute to Captain J. C. Gilmore.

"Captain Nolan's . . . compliments . . . sir," he said between breaths. "I must report . . . to Colonel Grierson."

Gilmore returned the salute nonchalantly. "Grierson's not here, Mister Flipper. He took his son, Lieutenant Colladay and six boys from G Troop over to *Tinaja de los Palmos* yesterday."

Flipper blinked. The words registered slowly. *Tinaja de los Palmos?* "Colonel Grierson's holding that water hole himself? With only eight men?" Flipper scarcely recognized his own voice.

"That's what I said."

Flipper practically leaped into his saddle. The stallion fought the bit, ready to run again, but he couldn't give him the reins, not yet. He bounced in the saddle, trying to control Abraham, and said: "Captain Gilmore, Victorio . . . crossed the border . . . sometime last night. We believe he's heading . . . straight for . . . *Tinaja de los Palmos.*"

"Mother of Mary," someone whispered.

Gilmore uttered something else. "Mister Flipper, is your horse played out?"

"No, sir!"

"I didn't think so. Best horse in the damn' regiment,

they say. Better than anything we've got here. But those horses that came with you aren't going much farther. You'll have to go it alone. Ride to Colonel Grierson at a gallop, Mister Flipper. Tell him we'll send reinforcements with due haste, but I can't leave Eagle Springs unprotected."

"I understand, sir."

"Due west, Lieutenant." He spun around, found a non-com, and barked: "Sergeant Higginson, draw Mister Flipper a map. Move it, man!"

Midnight had just passed. Abraham was lathered with salty sweat, and Flipper's legs were numb. After reining the stallion to a halt, he pulled out Higginson's map and checked it in the moonlight. That's when he heard the heavy click of a Spencer carbine being cocked. He froze. If it had been an Apache, he decided, he wouldn't have heard the click. He'd be dead now.

He found his voice. "It's Lieutenant Flipper," he said dryly.

Nothing. And then: "Lieutenant Flipper, suh, dat you?"

He could breathe again, felt his heart stop pounding, and watched as G Troop's Martin Davis stepped out from behind a juniper. The sentry had been as scared as Flipper. It was a miracle he had not simply blown out his brains.

"Where's the colonel, Davis?" Flipper asked.

"Think he's sleepin', suh. Jus' ahead."

Flipper nodded and eased Abraham into camp. The colonel's son, Robert, waited. Everyone else, except the sentry, slept. When he swung from the saddle, his legs couldn't support him, and Flipper crashed to the ground. That woke everyone, including Benjamin Grierson.

Robert helped Flipper to his feet, even supported the

lieutenant until the blood circulated through his legs once more, while Flipper gave his report.

"All right, Mister Flipper," Grierson said. "Excellent job. Let's hope those reinforcements beat Victorio here." He doubled the guards, told the rest of the camp to get some sleep, then disappeared inside the tent with his son. Flipper saw that someone had taken Abraham to the picket line and rolled out a blanket near his saddle on the ground. He pulled off his gun belt, placed the revolver within easy reach of his bed, and lay down. When he had time to think about it, he would realize he had ridden ninety-eight miles in twenty-two hours. Right now, however, he didn't want to think about anything, except tomorrow. He was dead tired, but he doubted if he could sleep a wink.

Lieutenant Flipper was softly snoring ten seconds after he rested his head on the McClellan saddle.

The sun woke him. He rose stiffly, buckled on his gun belt, and tried to get his bearings. Colonel Grierson stepped out of his tent and handed Flipper a tin cup.

"Coffee, Mister Flipper," Grierson said. "Cold. Can't help that. I've ordered no fires. Not even cigarettes."

He drank the bitter stuff down quickly.

"Mister Finley arrived at four this morning with ten troopers," the colonel explained. "I sent another trooper back to Eagle Springs with orders for Captain Gilmore to send more men here immediately as well as on to Rattlesnake Springs. I'm sure they're on the way."

"Where's Lieutenant Finley?" Flipper asked.

"Deployed lower on the ridge with some of the men. After you eat, Mister Flipper, I want you to take a message to Mister Finley. Tell him no smoking, no talking, nothing. Keep his men well hidden. I should have given him those instructions this morning. I'm sure Finley knows this already . . . he's a good soldier . . . but I want no mistakes. Understood?"

"Yes, sir."

"Grab something to eat, mister."

"I'm not hungry, sir," he lied, saluted Grierson, and trotted down the slope. He didn't see the colonel smile.

Waiting. That was the hard part. He squatted behind a pile of lava rocks, hat at his side, Colt revolver in his right hand. Sweating, he wiped his face and brow with a stained neckerchief. Nine o'clock, and it felt like someone had opened the gates to Hades. Or maybe it wasn't that hot. Maybe Henry Flipper was just scared.

"Lieutenant!" came a hoarse whisper.

Flipper blinked, saw Leighton Finley from his position just up the ridge, gesturing with the barrel of his carbine. Flipper hugged the largest boulder, risked a glimpse over the shelter, and saw them. The Colt felt heavier. He filled his lungs, held his breath, and pulled back the hammer of the .45, although the Apaches were well out of pistol range.

Their glistening hair flowed in the wind, sunlight reflecting off rifle barrels, *conchos*. . . . Flipper had no idea how many there were, not an army, but more than the twenty or so soldiers guarding this water hole. Victorio's Mimbres were experienced fighters. Henry Flipper certainly wasn't.

They didn't move, those Apaches, for an eternity. One man finally kicked his pinto into a trot, heading for the water. He wore a yellow silk headband, calico shirt, cotton trousers, and buckskin moccasins, a gun belt around his waist and Winchester rifle in his arms. His black hair hung past his shoulders, and a crooked white stripe ran across his cheeks and nose.

Out of the corner of his eye, Flipper caught Trooper Davis, raising the carbine. He tried to stop the trooper, but his mouth had gone completely dry. The Apache saw Davis's movement. The pinto whirled. A trumpet blared in the distance.

The world exploded. Flipper ran, crouched, firing. A bullet whined off a boulder. Another tore the hat off his head. He didn't even remember jamming on his hat when the shooting started. Flipper dived, ripping his trousers and skinning both knees. Gunshots exploded, echoing all over *Tinaja de los Palmos*. Whoops. Shouts. Orders. Horses screaming. He shoved the Colt into its holster, and lifted Trooper Davis's head, cradled the boy in his arms. Davis's eyes fluttered, found Flipper, stared. Blood seeped from his mouth. Flipper loosened his neckerchief and pressed it against the bloody hole through Davis's lung.

"Easy, soldier," he said. He heard the trumpet again. Someone yelled: "It's Captain Viele and C Troop!"

He forced a smile. "C Troop! You hear that, Davis?"

The smile vanished. Martin Davis heard nothing.

A horse crashed through the brush, snapping Flipper from his trance. He whirled, reached for his Colt, knew he was too late. He saw the fear in the mare's eyes, the empty Mexican saddle, blood covering the pinto's withers. The horse rode on, stumbled, rose quickly, continued to flee.

By then Flipper had lowered Davis to the ground and grabbed the dead man's carbine and Blakeslee Quickloader, a leather and wood case that held ten metal tubes, each filled with seven .56-.50 cartridges for quick reloading. Flipper stumbled through the clearing, saw the Apaches in the dust. Dropping to a knee, he brought the weapon to his shoulder, aimed, and fired.

Dust, sweat, and black powder burned his eyes. He shot

the carbine empty, jerked open the Quickloader, withdrew a tube, and rammed it through the opening in the carbine's stock. A shrill cry commanded his attention, and he sighted a lone Apache charging, firing a repeater over the horse's head. Two bullets *spanged* against the rocks near Flipper, and he dived for shelter, rolled over, fired blindly, slammed a fresh cartridge in the chamber, watched the Indian's horse crash to the ground, throwing the warrior into the rocks just below him.

The Indian didn't move. He shot the Spencer empty again, reloaded. And again.

Lieutenant S. R. Colladay stood by his side now, firing a Winchester. Not military issue, but Flipper welcomed the firepower. Others came down the ridge, firing, driving the Apaches back.

They watched the Indians mill, then break in a gallop toward a cañon to the south. Flipper and Colladay stepped into the clear, recognized C Troop at last.

Flipper sighed with relief. He had survived his first battle, and he hoped it would be his last. Colladay leaned the Winchester against a juniper and waved his hat at Viele's charging soldiers.

"Hurrah!" the lieutenant shouted. "Hurrah for C Troop!"

The next thing Flipper knew, S. R. Colladay was flying back against the rocks, blood spurting from his thigh.

"Stupid bastards!" Colladay spit out the words, grimaced, groaned. Flipper dropped by his side, felt bullets whining over his head, splintering the juniper, ricocheting off the rocks. He pulled Colladay behind cover, used the lieutenant's bandanna and revolver barrel to make a tourniquet, flinching as bullets still reined from Viele's men.

One of G Troop's troopers fired back.

"Hold your fire!" Flipper barked. "It's C Troop!"

He saw the determined face of G Troop's sergeant. "Beggin' the lieutenant's pardon, sir," Sergeant Josiah Brand said, "but if they shoot at me, damn it, I'm shootin' back!"

"One dead," Grierson said, shaking his head. "Ten horses killed. Mister Colladay shot by our own men . . . two enlisted men wounded."

"Yes, sir," Captain Charles Delavan Viele said, unsure of himself. "Sir, I'm terribly sorry about Mister Colladay, but my men had no idea those were our boys, sir. We thought they were Apaches."

"Put it in your written report, Mister Viele. Right now, we need to keep Victorio on the run. I want scouts sent out immediately. Let's find the Apache camp. They can't get far, not as long as we hold the water."

"Very good, sir."

After saluting, Grierson ran his fingers through his thick beard, spoke briefly to his son, then called for Flipper.

"Mister Flipper," Grierson said, "I've got a lousy job for you."

He watched as they lowered Martin Davis's body, wrapped in his bedroll, into a shallow grave as Trumpeter Thomas played "Taps." Finding his place, Flipper read the Episcopal services over the dead man. Joseph was the preacher in the Flipper family, not Henry. He read without emotion, his body drained. They had found seven dead Apaches over the battleground and thrown them in an arroyo, collapsing a wall of dirt over the bodies, then dragged the dead horses away and burned the already bloating bodies.

Flipper would oversee Davis's funeral, then report back

to Captain Nolan at Fort Quitman. He had no way of knowing it at the time, but the war was over for him. Grierson's tactical campaign would send Victorio's Apaches back into Mexico, and on October 14th, Chihuahua commander Colonel Joaquín Terrazas and his *asesinos* would surround the Mimbres camp and massacre Victorio and sixty of his warriors—not to mention eighteen women and children.

Closing the book, Flipper shut his eyes and said a silent prayer before looking up at the sergeant and giving a quick nod. The first shovelfuls of dirt began to cover Private Martin Davis.

"It be all rights," one of the troopers said. "You goin' home now, Martin. You goin' home."

Chapter Twenty-Five

November 25–26, 1881

What was the goal he had set a while back? Survive until Thanksgiving. Well, he had done it. Even a day longer. Now time for another goal, just as he had done back at the Academy during horseback drill. *I'll make one more circle, then I'll fall off.* And once he completed that circle—*I'll make one more circle, then I'll fall off.* On and on, changing the goal, putting it just a little further, until—excepting those times when he did actually lose his seat and spill into the arena dust with other unfortunate would-be cavalrymen—the drill had ended, and he had survived.

Survive until Christmas, Flipper told himself, as he and Merritt Barber walked to the post chapel. *Survive until Christmas.*

Sergeant Ross finished his testimony, saying nothing damning, nothing the court had not heard before. Court was adjourned early, and Flipper headed straight for the stables while Barber rode into town to interview the civilians he planned to call as defense witnesses.

After checking Abraham's hoofs, Flipper went to work with his brush and curry comb. Sergeant Watts once said Flipper's stallion was better groomed than all of the enlisted men of the 10th, even on payday. He hummed as he worked, occasionally singing a few bars of "I'll Take You Home Again, Kathleen," one of Captain Nolan's favorite songs. One of Mollie's, too. He felt sad again. Sunday was just around the corner, but there would be no afternoon ride with Mollie Dwyer. There hadn't been for some time.

Lost in his work and thoughts, Flipper didn't hear the horse arrive, or the officer's instructions to a stable hand after he had dismounted. In fact, Wade Hampton had to call Flipper's name twice before he was heard. Flipper saw the lieutenant, his good friend, and smiled.

"Hello, Wade. How was Fort Quitman?" Flipper hung up the grooming tools, gave the stallion a sugar cube, and left the stall, shaking the Southerner's hand warmly.

"Tolerable," Hampton answered. "How you been? Captain Barber started the defense yet?"

Flipper answered the first question with a shrug. "Clous is wrapping things up. Should finish the prosecution tomorrow. Glad you're back."

"Glad to be back. Quitman's not exactly Eden."

He understood, remembering his brief stay at the subpost during the Victorio campaign. They crossed the road and passed between the enlisted men's barracks, Flipper summing up the testimony Hampton had missed while they walked across the parade grounds, underneath the flagpole, and toward Flipper's duplex.

"I need to report back, Henry," Hampton said at Flipper's door.

Flipper nodded, and held out his hand once more. "I'm glad you're back," he said again.

Clous recalled Colonel Shafter the following morning. Listening to the dull testimony, Flipper figured that, if he had been a trial lawyer, he would always close with a bang, save the strongest witnesses for last. But that wasn't the case here or during Flipper's duties as a judge advocate; it never seemed to happen in courts-martial. Shafter said nothing much, just clarified a few statements. Barber didn't bother to cross, and the court members had no questions, either. *No*, Flipper thought, *Clous was closing his case with a bore.*

J. A. Tilley read back the transcripts, the witnesses made their corrections, and, satisfied, at two o'clock on Saturday afternoon, November 26th, Judge Advocate Clous rested the government's case. Pennypacker adjourned the court until Monday, November 28th, at which point Merritt Barber would begin his defense, and Henry O. Flipper would have to prove that he was an excellent soldier, an officer and a gentleman—and an innocent man.

Again, Flipper found himself alone. Barber had to ride back to town to get his witnesses in order, and Hampton would be with his troop. He headed to his duplex, staring at the dusting of snow that covered Sleeping Lion Mountain. He remembered Captain Nolan's fondness for this country. *What was it he had said? "The Davis Mountains are just a wee less beautiful than the Connemara . . . you'll love it."*

To begin with, he had loved his posting, the people in town, the mountains and valleys, Wild Rose Pass and Limpia Creek, Fort Davis itself. Quitman and Elliott had been hellholes. Concho had a beauty about it, but was really empty, and San Angelo quickly soured his feelings. Impressions of places like Fort Stockton and Fort Griffin during brief stops there, had not been overly romantic. After arriving at Fort Davis, Flipper had thought this to be an officer's dream, better even than Fort Sill. Now, he wished he had never set foot here.

Chapter Twenty-Six

Fort Davis, 1880–1881

> **Follow the drinkin' gourd,**
> **Follow the drinkin' gourd.**
> **'Cause the old man is a-waitin'**
> **To take you to freedom,**
> **If you follow the drinkin' gourd.**

Standing alone outside his tent, Flipper listened to the sweet harmony from the squad of A Troop soldiers sitting around the campfire, tired after a long, weary ride escorting a supply train to Fort Stockton and now halfway back to Fort Davis, but never, it seemed, too tired to sing. Flipper didn't have much of a singing voice—Joseph and Festus, Jr., had been the Flipper sons to inherit that trait from Isabella Buckhalter Flipper—but he always loved music. It pained him that he couldn't walk over to the troopers and join them, but he was an officer and couldn't fraternize with enlisted men. A black man in a black regiment, yet as an officer he found himself alone, unable to socialize with, even sing with, men of his own race. So he stood in the shadows, thinking about the slaves back in Georgia, how they sang as well in the fields as they did in church. Anna White had a beautiful voice, also, regularly performing solos in church on Sundays. On the frontier, white soldiers sang, too, but Flipper found their tunes all too often bawdy, downright lewd. The men of the 10th finished "Follow the Drinking Gourd" and followed it with "No More Auction Block for Me". Then "Amazing Grace" and "Swing Low, Sweet Chariot".

They'd sing all night if Sergeant Watts would let them, but Flipper knew he would make them turn in before long. Flipper ducked inside the canvas tent, pulled off his boots and blouse, and settled onto his bedroll. With the death of Victorio, A Troop had been transferred to Fort Davis in late November. Nestled in a rugged cañon in the Davis Mountains, the post had been everything Captain Nolan had said it would be, and more. He remembered one of his first assignments, a routine reconnaissance, when he had camped in a cañon a few miles west of the fort. He had sat on a boulder watching an eerie glow illuminate the top of a mountain. The light had brightened and brightened until finally a giant, shimmering full moon rose above the mountain. Flipper could make out the craters, and the moon had seemed so close he swore, if he climbed to the top of the ridge, he'd be able to touch the lustrous white ball. It had lit up the entire countryside. An owl had hooted, a coyote had wailed, and Henry Flipper had stayed awake half the night, amazed at the tranquility and beauty of this patch of Texas.

Now, he closed his eyes, fighting the loneliness enveloping him, and listened to his men:

> **Gonna lay down my sword an' shield,**
> **Down by the riverside,**
> **Down by the riverside,**
> **Down by the riverside.**
> **Gonna lay down my sword an' shield,**
> **Down by the riverside.**
> **Ain't gonna fight war no more.**

He had purchased the military-issue tent at Fort Stockton. Not that he would have much need for it back at Davis. For some reason Flipper couldn't grasp, Major Napoleon Bonaparte McLaughlen, commanding during Colonel Grierson's absence, had appointed him Assistant Post Quartermaster and Acting Commissary of Subsistence. Flipper didn't know a damned thing about either job. They hadn't trained him to be a pencil-pusher back at West Point, and, although he certainly enjoyed math, he was by no means a bookkeeper. Keeping track of hay, salt pork and hardtack bored him tremendously. But maybe if he could show a little initiative, the job would work to his advantage. A promotion, perhaps, somewhere down the road: First Lieutenant H. O. Flipper . . . Captain. . . .

Shortly after his appointment, he had received a letter from Lieutenant Charles Ward, Quartermaster and A.C.S. at Fort Stockton. Ward had complained that he was short four wagons, asked if Flipper had them, and pointed out that, if the wagons did not turn up, Lieutenant Ward would have to pay for them himself.

"That's this man's army," Captain Nolan had said with a smile after Flipper informed him of Ward's letter. "The Army misplaces four wagons and asks a wee lieutenant to pay for them. It's Ward's problem, Henry. Don't worry yourself none."

Yet Flipper had worried. He hadn't known Charles Ward, but he saw no reason that lieutenant should pay for wagons most likely lost to war, nature, or military paperwork during the Victorio campaign. Flipper had walked up and down the rows at the post wagon yard, looking at the decrepit vehicles already condemned and awaiting destruction. His father had not only been an excellent cobbler, he had been a pretty good carriage repairman, and Flipper had also learned a few things from wheelwright Johnny Quarles. So he had picked out four of the condemned wagons, had them repaired and painted by the post wheelwright, and brought them along with the supply train to Stockton. Captain Nolan had given the guard duty detail to Flipper so he could personally deliver the wagons to Lieutenant Ward. The ever-so-thankful subsistence officer had thanked Flipper profusely for saving his pay, then had sold him a tent at a modest discount.

Mollie Dwyer had arrived. During the Victorio campaign, she and Annie had remained at Fort Concho, but the ladies, this week, had finally made it to Fort Davis—although it irked Flipper that the scoundrel Nordstrom had been in charge of their escort—and Flipper looked forward to resuming his Sunday afternoon rides. No Fort Concho meant no Anson Mills, and, therefore, no *de facto* orders prohibiting those casual jaunts. He was lost in his thoughts, staring out his window at the winter landscape. Snow continued to fall, and Flipper hoped it would let up by Sunday. Then he saw the flames.

He grabbed his gloves, coat, and hat, and raced outside, slipping on the frozen porch, sailing, sprawling in the foot-deep snow. Rising quickly, he yelled, spreading the alarm, and raced to the burning haystacks. He heard the commotion behind him, the clanging of bells, the pounding of boots. By the time the first troopers had arrived, Flipper was already emptying a bucket of water onto the flaming rick. Flames warmed his face one second, then he felt the stinging snow as he ran for more water.

Wade Hampton was there now, pouring water into Flipper's bucket.

" 'Evenin', Lieutenant," Hampton said easily.

He had known the South Carolinian only a little more than a month now, but he liked Hampton immensely. The man was a rock.

Captain Nolan couldn't hide his fear, barking out orders, screaming that they had to put the fire out. The haystacks provided the only livestock feed available at Fort Davis—the Army had used up its supply of grain chasing Victorio. If it all went up in smoke. . . .

"Drown that hay!" Nolan shouted, trying to organize a bucket brigade.

Flipper emptied his bucket, turned, was handed another bucket. The soldiers had the brigade going now, one line fighting the burning rick, others dousing the closest stacks, keeping them wet, preventing the fire from spreading. He became a machine, ignoring the searing heat, his cramping muscles, the freezing water that splashed his boots and trousers.

Dawn came, and the fire died. He caught his breath, examined his gloves, blackened by soot, tried to flex his fingers. The snow had stopped. He hadn't noticed it till now. His pants were frozen stiff. He hadn't noticed that, either. They had lost the one haystack, and nothing more. Flipper started back toward his quarters to change clothes.

Major McLaughlen stopped him. "Not so fast, Mister Flipper."

"Sir?" He turned, saw the other officers gathering around, most of them, like the commander, in unsoiled clothes. Only Hampton, Nolan, and Flipper had fought the fire. The remaining officers, those who had not slept through the night, had simply shouted orders or watched, standing far from the flames and smoke.

"I want to know how hay starts to burn during a snow-storm," the major said acidly.

"So do I." Flipper glanced at the officer who had spoken those words and recognized Charles Nordstrom.

The clerk, Flipper thought. McLaughlen and Nordstrom

were right. The fire had been set, accidentally or arson? Any soldier could have dropped a cigarette or match unintentionally, but arson? The clerk, a pockmarked white man named Bisbee who showed up too often in his cups, if he showed up at all. Flipper had fired him two days ago, and the man had stormed off to one of the local saloons, but Flipper didn't want to put the blame on someone without proof. He didn't have to.

"Walter Bisbee," Wade Hampton said. Flipper had mentioned Bisbee's incompetence to Hampton. In fact, Hampton had suggested that Flipper fire the cad, and now he was coming to Flipper's defense when McLaughlen's and Nordstrom's eyes accused the Assistant Post Quartermaster and A.C.S.

"What?" McLaughlen asked, then coughed.

Flipper felt chilled, wanted desperately to get out of his clothes, to drink a cup of scalding coffee, anything rather than stand here in the freezing wind. "I fired a civilian clerk named Walter Bisbee," Flipper explained. "I have no proof, sir, but if this is arson, then Bisbee would be my first suspect."

Nordstrom scowled. "Bisbee. He's a white man."

That brought Nolan into the showdown. "Watch your tongue, Mister Nordstrom."

No one spoke.

The blaring of "Assembly of Trumpeters" broke the silence. "Reveille" would soon follow, although almost everyone at the post was wide-awake by now.

"Sir," Flipper said, addressing the major, "I'd like to request a board of survey to clear up this matter."

"That's a good idea, Mister Flipper." McLaughlen finally relaxed, perhaps realizing just how cold it was this morning. "Get cleaned up, report to headquarters after 'Fatigue Call.' "

★ ★ ★ ★ ★

He shook off the chill, let the dizziness subside, and led Abraham and the gelding out of the stables. Mollie smiled at him.

"It's been much too long, Henry," she said excitedly, taking the reins and leaping into the saddle. "Race you to town!" She took off down the road while Flipper labored to climb into the saddle.

He shuddered, shook his head, looked at the dust. He didn't get sick, refusing to admit it could happen to him, although he recognized these symptoms. He had seen it enough back at Fort Sill before he drained those cesspools and stinking ponds. He had buried soldiers there, too, but, no, he wasn't sick. He was just tired, maybe weak from fighting the hay fire. He kicked the stallion into a trot and followed Mollie Dwyer.

"What do you think of Charlie Nordstrom, Henry?" she asked as he nibbled a drumstick on the banks of Limpia Creek.

"I really don't know the man," Flipper lied, feeling suddenly sick again. He tossed the meat away.

Frowning, Mollie rose and put both hands on her hips. "Annie will have a fit, Henry Ossian Flipper. You barely touched that chicken. And you haven't spoken ten words to me today. First, you stopped riding with me back at Fort Concho, always coming up with some stupid excuse, and now you act like I've got the plague."

I'm the one who has the plague, he thought. He looked up, putting on his best shamed face, and watched Mollie's smile return.

"That's better. Anyway, I want to know if you'd be jealous if I went for a ride with Charlie Nordstrom? He

261

keeps asking me. And I had to ride with him a lot while you were off fighting those Apaches. Well, Henry, what do you think?"

She waited. "Henry?"

Nothing.

"Henry?"

Her smile vanished. He was shivering now, sweating, and the world spun violently, wickedly.

"HENRY!"

The words came to him slowly. Words he had heard before, spoken by men like his brother Joseph . . . and John Quarles . . . chaplains . . . preachers. . . .

He restoreth my soul: he leadeth me in the paths of righteousness for his name's sake. Yea, though I walk through the valley of the shadow of death, I will fear no evil: for thou art with me; thy rod and thy staff they comfort me. Thou preparest a table before. . . .

He must have said something, because the voice stopped. A chair leg scrapped against the floor, and the face appeared.

"Lieutenant?"

Flipper blinked, refocused his eyes, said weakly: "Major McLaughlen?"

The officer nodded. His eyes were bloodshot. "You gave us quite a scare, son. Picked a wrong time to get sick, Mister Flipper. We didn't have any medicine . . . ran out fighting the Apaches, and the requisitions hadn't been filled." McLaughlen grinned. "I supposed I should complain to the A.C.S., but I won't. Let me get Doctor Kingslie, tell him you're awake. You need anything, Mister Flipper?"

"I'm thirsty."

* * * * *

"So what do you remember?" Wade Hampton asked.

"Not much."

"God's been with you, my friend. Our ol' sawbones didn't expect you to live, and he told McLaughlen . . . the major's been at your bedside . . . him, me, or Capt'n Nolan . . . typhoid malarial fever. That's what Doc Kingslie called it."

Flipper took a drink from his cup. "I thought the major hated me."

"Maybe he did. Maybe he's feelin' guilty. While you was supposed to be dyin', gettin' force-fed morphine every night . . . once the medicines finally got here . . . the board of survey came back and cleared you of any wrongdoin' 'bout that hay fire. You do remember the fire, don't you?"

"Vaguely."

"Well, you won't be spendin' no time bustin' rocks at Leavenworth. And Walter Bisbee's disappeared. Not that we found any proof that he set that fire. Anyway, I wouldn't be surprised if the major put you in for the Medal of Honor." Hampton shook his head. "You make me mighty jealous, Mistah Flipper. Hell, I'm kinda wishin' that I burned that rick, practically froze to death tryin' to put it out, got myself accused of startin' the damn' thing, then went picnickin' with a pretty Irish gal and come down with typhoid malarial fever and had her all distraught that I might up and die. . . ."

It hurt to laugh, but it also felt great.

He made two troopers fetch a stretcher, and had them carry him to the quartermaster's office. Captain Nolan found him there, lying on his back, writing payment vouchers for the civilian teamsters, packers, and smithy.

"Mister Flipper," Nolan said through clenched teeth, "just what do you think you're doing?"

"My job, sir," Flipper answered weakly, longing to take another of those Sappington's Quinine Pills, but not wanting his captain to realize how sick he remained.

Nolan started to say something, maybe order the troopers to carry the A.C.S. back to the post hospital and keep him there, but thought better of it and shook his head in defeat.

Chapter Twenty-Seven

November 28, 1881

"Da accused asks me to summon W. S. Chamberlain of Fort Davis as a vitness," John Clous addressed the court on a brutally cold morning, "but does not give me any information to satisfy me under da Article of da Codified Regulation dat he is a necessary vitness."

More cat-and-mouse games, Flipper thought, as Barber shot out of his chair and stood in front of the court-martial board. "Mister President," Barber began, "I have the right to defend my client. And Mister Chamberlain isn't the only civilian on my witness list."

Clous clucked his tongue. "Civilians must have permission to be on military property. I do not tink dey should be allowed to set foot on dis post as character vitnesses. Da accused can certainly call Army personnel to speak for da accused's character. I ask da court's indulgence."

"Mister Chamberlain was on the post at the time of Lieutenant Flipper's arrest," Barber fired back. "He had permission then, and he certainly should be allowed to testify on my client's behalf."

Colonel Pennypacker huddled briefly with the other officers, turned and said: "The order of the court is that the witness be summoned."

The chapel door opened, and Flipper heard the unmistakable sound. He stared ahead for what seemed like hours as old W. S. Chamberlain dragged his right foot slowly across the floor. A frail, balding Negro with thick glasses, Chamberlain wore Flipper's old brogans—about three sizes too large for the tiny watchmaker—and other hand-me-downs, although the coat and cravat looked new, probably donated by J. B. Shields for today's court appearance. He took the oath and collapsed into the chair.

Chamberlain had been a good friend. Next to Wade Hampton, and now Merritt Barber, he was likely the best friend Henry Flipper had at Fort Davis. The old-timer had been the one to plead to Shields, Keesey, Sender, Siebenborn, and other town merchants, raising money after Flipper's arrest. He could picture Chamberlain's dragging his bum leg up and down the dusty town all day and half the night.

"Mister Chamberlain," Barber began after the perfunctory name, residency, occupation questions, "at the time of Lieutenant Flipper's arrest were you boarding with him?"

"I was," came a hoarse whisper.

Pennypacker cleared his throat. "Mister Chamberlain, you will have to speak up, sir."

"I was."

"Why was that?"

"I met Lieutenant Flipper in town. He was good to me. Offered to give me a place to stay till I gots back on my feet." Chamberlain forced a smile, thought of something else, and added quickly: "He gots permission. I weren't here illegally."

"Thank you. Did you also know Lieutenant Flipper's housekeeper, Lucy Smith?"

"Yes, sir."

"Did you ever hear the lieutenant discuss safety precautions with Miss Smith?"

He nodded vigorously. "Yes, sir. Lots o' times, sir. On the very day Henry gots arrested, that morn he tells her she had to make sure she locked everything up. Gived her a key even. Think it was a key. Likely to his trunk. She ax for it, and he given it to her. Told 'er to make sure she locks it up."

"But you were not on this post at the time of the arrest, correct? When did you learn of Lieutenant Flipper's arrest?"

"Later that day. Was at my shop in town." He looked directly at Flipper. "I wouldn't been able to have that shop if it weren't for Henry. He was awful goods to me."

"Thank you, sir. And what did you do after learning of the lieutenant's arrest?"

"I come back here as fast as I could. They wouldn't let me see 'im, though, so I wents to Colonel Shafter's office. He told me abouts the missing money, and I ax him if I could raise enough money to cover what was missin', iffen that would help."

"What did Colonel Shafter say?"

"Well, he says it'd save 'im from the penitentiary. He also saids something like . . . 'I will buck up a hunnerd dollars myself'."

"So you went about raising money in town?"

"I did. Shafter never gives me nothin', though. But when I brung 'im the money I'd raised, he said he thought Henry was an honest man, didn't believe 'im guilty, and said . . . I think he put it this way . . . 'There was some other damned nigger at the bottom of it'."

"He used the word 'nigger' in front of you, a man of color yourself?"

"Yes, sir. I used to it."

"You said Lieutenant Flipper helped you get back on your feet, gave you money, a place to stay, helped you set up your business in town. Did he ever strike you as a man living above his means?"

"Oh, no, sir. Not a-tall. He like to go to the *bailes,* but wouldn't spend no more'n a dollar or two each week on hisself. No, sir, I'd say Henry was always frugal for hisself. But he was mighty nice to me."

"Thank you, Mister Chamberlain. I have no more questions for this witness."

Clous stood shortly after Barber sat down. "*Herr* Chamberlain, you testified dat Lucy Smith asked da accused for something on da morning of his arrest. You thought it might be a key. To his trunk. Are you sure of any of dis?"

"I don't rightly knows. Thought it was a key. Could have been to his trunk. I didn't sees it clearly."

"So it could have been anyting, *ja?*"

"Yes, sir."

"Or it could have been a key to da trunk, and Lucy could have been helping herself to stolen money *mit* da accused's permission!"

"Oh, no, sir. Henry wouldn't done nothing like that. He's a good man."

"*Ja.* Dat is vye he is on trial. I have no more questions of dis vitness."

Other witnesses were quickly disposed of: Lieutenant S. L. Woodward, who had overseen the transfer of funds from Fort Quitman, Sergeant William J. Jean and merchants John B. Shields and Whittaker Keesey, who praised Flipper's integrity. Captains Bates and Viele admitted that they had in fact organized the burro race, and then Walter David Cox, a former trooper who now worked in the post corrals and took care of Flipper's horse.

"Mister Cox," Barber asked, "did Lieutenant Flipper ever remove his saddlebags?"

"Only one time to my recollection," Cox answered, "and that was when he took them off to be fixed. Straps were broken."

"How long ago was that?"

"It has been some time."

"How long were they off?"

"Three or four days."

"So, anyone who had known Lieutenant Flipper for some time would not be suspicious because he rode to town with his saddlebags?"

"That's correct."

"Did you ever seen the lieutenant put anything in those bags, or take anything out?"

"No, sir. He didn't put anything in 'em. He'd just put his boots in the stirrups and ride off."

"Please state your name, place of residence, and occupation for the court."

"John M. Dean, Presidio County, former district attorney for the same and now just a humble attorney-at-law." The words came out in a rich Georgia drawl as the slender man with a handlebar mustache crossed his legs. He looked more like a cowhand than an attorney.

Barber used his first questions to set up Dean's relationship with Flipper and to bring out the point that the lawyer had represented Lucy Smith at her hearing.

"Do you have any opinion of Lieutenant Flipper's habits?"

"I'd say they were remarkably good for any man his age in this section of the country."

"How about Colonel Shafter?"

"Well, I can't rightly say much good about his character."

"Why is that?"

"Well, suh, at first I thought the colonel was a fair man. But I overheard him say that he would get Flipper, or made some remark like that, that he was gettin' more evidence against'm.' "

" 'Getting more evidence' isn't necessarily incriminating, Mister Dean. Were those his actual words?"

"No, suh. As I recollect, he used the phrase 'piling it up on'm'."

"Do you know whether or not Lieutenant Flipper at that time had confidence that Colonel Shafter was acting in a friendly and fair manner towards him?"

"Yes, suh. I think that Flipper was puttin' considerable faith in the colonel. In fact, I'd been led to believe that Colonel Shafter was actin' as Lieutenant Flipper's friend. But when I heard Shafter make that remark . . . about 'pilin' it up on'm' . . . I came to the conclusion that he was playin' him double."

"You told this to Lieutenant Flipper?"

"Yes, suh. I went to see the lieutenant in his cell while I was workin' on obtainin' a writ of *habeas corpus* for Lucy Smith. I told'm that I thought it would be in his best interest to conduct this matter without the colonel's assistance."

"What was Lieutenant Flipper's reaction?"

"He was hurt."

Back in the duplex, Merritt Barber pumped his fist. "That was a good day, Henry. It's always a good day when Captain Clous can't think of much to ask. Tomorrow, we'll bring Mister Hampton to the stand, then Lucy Smith." He found a cigar, clipped the end, and searched his pockets for a match.

"Clous didn't keep his mouth shut all day," Flipper said quietly.

Barber, now holding a flaming match to the cigar, lifted

his eyes toward Flipper. He waited till he had it fired up, then withdrew the cigar, and asked: "You mean his questioning of Mister Shields?"

Flipper nodded. The Irish merchant had sung Flipper's praises on Barber's direct, said Flipper had no bad habits that he knew of, that he had given Chamberlain fifty dollars to help the cause, that he liked the man, and was testifying simply because he thought the lieutenant innocent. But on cross-examination, Judge Advocate Clous had suggested that Flipper sold the merchant government supplies for resale.

"Shields held his own, Henry. Colonel Pennypacker and the court saw that."

"Did they?"

"It was a drought, for heaven's sake, Henry. You gave the man two cans of peaches and a sack of flour, some corned beef. And they came from your own provisions, not the Quartermaster Department. Any officer worth his rank would have done the same thing. In fact, I bet a lot of officers here helped out civilians. It was a hard, long, and brutally hot summer. What you did was a Christian act, Henry, not criminal."

Flipper sighed, accepting Barber's rebuttal. He had not done anything wrong. He had just wanted to help the man and his family, and Shields, he was so proud, he wouldn't take food without offering some sort of payment, so he repaired Flipper's cavalry boots.

They had been friends—Shields and Keesey, Sender and Siebenborn, others—at first, anyway, although the money had dried up shortly after Flipper's arrest. At least they had testified on his behalf, and Barber was right. John Shields had told the truth. Clous had tried to suggest that the merchant and Flipper had conspired to defraud the government, but Shields said they had done nothing wrong, and they hadn't.

The day's testimony played through his head again. He thought about Colonel Shafter, how he had trusted the louse, hoping his commander would be fair, remembering his reaction, the pain, when Dean told him Shafter was "playin' you double, son." Flipper had originally hoped Dean would serve as his attorney, but the Georgian turned him down, saying it would be a conflict of interest since he was serving as Lucy's attorney.

"What time is it?" Barber asked.

Flipper pulled out his watch, which had finally been returned to him after being confiscated during his arrest. "Quarter till six," he answered, and stared at the hand counting off the seconds.

"You hungry?" Barber asked, but Flipper didn't hear him.

Chapter Twenty-Eight

Fort Davis, March 1881

"You made this?" Flipper asked, stunned as he hefted the pocket watch in his right hand.

It was heavy, open faced, with large Roman numerals, and a smaller second hand at the bottom marked with Arabic numbers. The stem-wind piece was silver, with five-point stars engraved around the edge of the heavy, bevel-edged glass. Stunning, beautiful, a masterpiece, the connecting chain itself was a work of art.

"Two dollars," the black man said, already dropping the price four bits.

Flipper looked up. The watch had to be worth ten times that, probably even more. He had been stopped by the panhandler while walking toward George Bentley's adobe compound on Chihuahua Creek. At first Flipper had thought the man had stolen the watch, but as he looked into the man's weary eyes, he had realized this wasn't some pickpocket or sneak thief, or a tramp looking for a mark to supply him with scamper juice. Still, he had asked the man where he got the watch and studied the expression as the bum dropped his gaze, shuffled his feet, and muttered: "Made it."

"You made this?" Flipper repeated.

The old-timer nodded his head slightly, still shuffling his feet, and looked up again. "Yes, sir. Was a watchmaker and engraver in Saint Louis some time back."

Flipper looked back at the watch, turned it over, and studied the engraving on the back.

"I've never seen anything quite like this," he said softly, and looked up when the elderly gentleman shot back: "A dollar seventy-five."

George Bentley was a former buffalo soldier, a distinguished veteran with the 9th Cavalry who had left the service and retired to Fort Davis. He had invited Flipper for Sunday supper. Flipper looked the old man up and down once more and decided that Bentley wouldn't mind if he brought along a guest.

The man who called himself Chamberlain held a spoonful of stew in his trembling hand and brought it to his mouth. He ate slowly, deliberately. That surprised Flipper, who expected the ancient watchmaker to gorge himself like a ravenous coyote. He wondered when the man had last eaten.

Flipper sipped his coffee, standing near the fireplace in the flat-roofed Bentley Hall, George Bentley to his right, puffing on a clay pipe.

Chamberlain appeared to be in his fifties—fifty-some hard years—his beard unkempt, thinning silver on the sides of his head and the top bald. His shoes were nothing more than leather scraps wrapped tightly with filthy woolen rags, and he wore no hat. He carried a pair of glasses in his vest pocket, and, when he pulled them out to fetch a handkerchief, Flipper noticed that both lenses were cracked. His hands were delicate, the kind you would expect for a jeweler, a watchmaker. Flipper set his cup on the hearth and withdrew the silver watch from his coat pocket.

"You really think that ol' cripple made that timepiece?" Bentley asked.

"I do," Flipper said.

"Where did he say he was from?"

"Saint Louis."

"Far piece from here. He tell you how his leg got so stoved up, or how he come to be beggin'?"

"No. Not yet. And I'm not asking him. If he wants to tell me, he will."

Bentley tapped his pipe against the stone fireplace. "How much you pay him for that watch?"

"He was asking a dollar seventy-five," Flipper said. "I gave him twenty dollars."

That caused Bentley to cough and swear. "You give a rummy twenty bucks. Henry Flipper, what's gotten into you?"

"He's not a drunk, George. Just hungry and tired. And it's a beautiful watch," Flipper said, holding it out for Bentley's inspection.

The retired soldier had to agree. "What you plan on doin' with him, Henry?" Bentley asked.

"I'm not sure," Flipper answered, although he knew exactly what he had in mind.

Major McLaughlen tried to suppress a cough, failed, and turned away from Flipper to let loose with another awful hacking spell. The commanding officer, sick most of the winter, had already dropped maybe twenty pounds, and his health showed no sign of improving. He wiped his mouth and nose with a handkerchief before turning back to the second lieutenant.

"Just what are you asking, Mister Flipper?" McLaughlen inquired, and picked up the silver watch.

"I was hoping to hire Mister Chamberlain . . . as a clerk. We haven't replaced Walter Bisbee, sir."

The major examined the watch Flipper had shown him, sighed, and returned the timepiece to Flipper. "It's a rather handsome watch, I'll admit. But Mister Flipper, you just met that man. You know nothing of his character."

"Begging the major's pardon, sir, but I think I do know his character. Some people you know immediately. Chamberlain is one of those people. He was a watchmaker, jeweler, and engraver in Saint Louis, lost his family in a wagon accident, almost died himself. He let his business slide, lost it, and has been living hand-to-mouth ever since, drifting West. He told me this last night. Sir, I'm sure, if he can save up some money, get a steady job, he can go back to doing what he does best. He doesn't drink hard liquor, Major. He's started putting the death of his wife and children behind him. All he needs is a chance."

McLaughlen coughed again, shook his head, and took a deep breath. "You also want this man to share your quarters?"

"Yes, sir. But just temporarily. Six months maybe. No longer than eight. That'll give him time to save up money for a place of his own in town."

The room fell silent as McLaughlen considered Flipper's proposal. At last he nodded, and Flipper let out a sigh of relief. "All right, Mister Flipper, I'll grant your request. Six months, though. That's all. This man is not family. Chamberlain can board with you as long as he is employed as a civilian clerk but no longer than September First. Understood?"

"Yes, sir. Very good, sir. And thank you kindly, sir."

McLaughlen smiled. "I hope you're right about judging a man's character, Lieutenant. I've made a few mistakes in character myself."

Their eyes locked, reaching a silent understanding. Flipper realized McLaughlen was apologizing for the way he had treated him in the past, the suspicion after the hay fire, things like that. Flipper stepped back and offered a crisp West Point salute. McLaughlen rose. He remained weak, looked gaunt, but his return salute was strong.

As Flipper turned to leave, the major stopped him. "Mister Flipper. In a few days Colonel Shafter will arrive to assume command of this post."

"Yes, sir. I've heard, sir."

"A lot of the Tenth will likely be transferred elsewhere, to join Colonel Grierson at Fort Concho, man the Quitman sub-post, perhaps be sent out of the States."

"Yes, sir. I've told Chamberlain that, if I'm transferred, he can't come with me, that he'll have to make out for himself here in town and can't stay on the post. He understands, sir."

"That's not my point."

"Sir?"

"You don't know William Shafter, Mister Flipper. He's a hard man, a tough soldier, and one spiteful son-of-a-bitch. And so are most of his junior officers. Watch your back, Lieutenant. Watch your back. Dismissed."

The regimental staff of the 1st Infantry arrived on March 11th with the banners flapping, every soldier at attention in dress uniforms, and the Fort Davis band playing "Battle Hymn of the Republic." At the head of the column rode William Rufus Shafter on a blue roan gelding. Obese, out of breath, and looking haggard from the ride, the colonel still forked a saddle as well as many cavalry troopers. He dismounted, waited for the band to finish its number, and offered a lazy salute to the 10th Cavalry delegation greeting the new post commander.

Shafter kept the fanfare short, said he would assume command the following day, and would meet with various staff personally. After telling the sergeant to dismiss A

Troop, Flipper returned to the quartermaster storehouse.

"That new colonel, he be a big fellow," Chamberlain said from his desk.

"He's not skinny," Flipper answered.

"I hear he don't like colored folks."

"Don't listen to rumors," Flipper said.

"No, I won't. I'll give the colonel my respect. But what it be like, Henry? New command and all. Will things change here?"

Flipper shrugged. "We'll wait and see. But usually things stay the same. That's the Army for you." Yet, deep down, he wondered. Most of the posts where he had served had been commanded by officers of his own black regiment. Yet the 1st was an all-white unit, and, although William Rufus Shafter had once led the black 24th Infantry, word going around the barracks said "Pecos Bill" despised the command and felt relief to be rid of his "darkies in blue."

His stomach fluttered as he entered the new commander's office. William R. Shafter sat behind his desk, snacking on pralines while reading a file. The colonel's face was jowlly, eyebrows thick as a forest, and his graying hair resembled a bird's nest after a tornado. He swallowed the candy, brushed crumbs onto the floor, and took a quick sip of coffee before looking up.

The officer who had escorted Flipper from the quartermaster office to Shafter's desk stepped forward and said in a nasal whine: "Colonel, this is Second Lieutenant Flipper, H. O., Company A, Tenth Cavalry."

Shafter grunted something and addressed Flipper: "Mister Wilhelmi just made one big damned mistake. Can you tell me what the hell it was, Lieutenant?"

Flipper thought. Had Wilhelmi broken some military etiquette? He ran the introduction through his head again, but before he could answer Shafter went on: "Cavalry companies are called troops, Mister Wilhelmi. See that you don't make that damned mistake again. And you should have known that immediately, Mister Flipper. You are a damn' cavalry officer, aren't you?"

Wilhelmi stepped back, shamed. Flipper straightened, held his breath, realized that everything he had heard about "Pecos Bill" must be true. The man was a martinet, a by-the-book commander with no tolerance or humor. Company or troop? Those were simply words. Cavalry officers often interchanged the two. Company A or A Troop. Who cared?

"At ease, Flipper. You too, Wilhelmi." Shafter glanced at the papers in front of him. "Colonel Grierson gives you high marks, Flipper. Says your a damned fine soldier."

"Thank you, sir."

"Thank Grierson, Flipper. Not me. I'll judge your abilities for myself, by God."

"Yes, sir."

"First things first, Flipper. I'm relieving you of your duties as post quartermaster. Louis Strother will take over immediately. I'm also having you replaced in the damned commissary, though that might take a while."

"Very good, sir."

"I don't have any damned complaints, Flipper. Hell, from all I see here, you've done well in those jobs. But you're a cavalry soldier, and I want you back with your damned troop. Understand?"

"Yes, sir. What should I do with the commissary funds, Colonel?"

"Where do you keep them?"

"They've been in my quarters, sir."

Shafter shook his head. "Your quarters. Good God,

Mister Flipper, those funds should be kept in the damned safe at headquarters."

"I agree, sir. I don't even have a safe. But Major McLaughlen asked me to keep them in my quarters, so I've been keeping them in my trunk. He wanted to keep the commissary funds separate from. . . ."

Shafter waved him off. "McLaughlen's sickness must have affected his damned judgment. Jesus! Your trunk, Flipper? How secure can a damned trunk be?"

Lieutenant Wilhelmi stepped forward as Shafter caught his breath. "Colonel, sir?"

"What is it?"

"Perhaps Lieutenant Flipper should carry on, sir, as he has been doing. Keep the commissary funds in his trunk until he is replaced as A.C.S. There's no need in changing his routine."

"All right." Shafter nodded, took another swig of coffee. "Lieutenant Wilhelmi has been appointed post adjutant, Flipper. You will keep him . . . and me . . . informed of your temporary duties as A.C.S. until I find your damned replacement. Carry on."

Flipper saluted, and left. As he crossed the parade grounds, heading for his quarters, he smiled. Shafter and Wilhelmi had done him a huge favor. He hated his work as Quartermaster and Commissary of Subsistence, and definitely didn't want the job with "Pecos Bill" the C.O. Soon Flipper would be back with A Troop as a cavalry officer, working with his men, doing what he longed to do. He was a soldier, not an accountant. William Shafter might be one hard-ass, a tough s.o.b. who used profanity in every sentence, but for the moment he had earned high marks from Henry Ossian Flipper—relief. His smile widened. Henry Flipper simply felt relieved.

Chapter Twenty-Nine

November 29, 1881

A carpet of ankle-deep snow covered the parade grounds as Flipper and Barber made their way to the post chapel. Although the snow had stopped falling, gray clouds obscured the peak of Sleeping Lion Mountain, and a bitter wind swept down the cañon. Reporters shivered underneath the awning of the post headquarters next door, while Lieutenant Wade Hampton, a wool overcoat loosely covering his dress uniform, waited by the chapel door, leaning against the adobe wall and chewing tobacco. The brown-stained pocket at the edge of the stone doorstep revealed that Hampton had been waiting a while.

After shaking hands, they glanced at the herd gathered in front of headquarters, but none of the journalists seemed inclined to leave the shelter from the blustery wind. Barber angled his head toward the door. "It's likely warmer inside," he said.

Hampton nodded. "One of the First Infantry boys lit the stove shortly after 'Assembly'."

"You've been here since 'Assembly'?" asked Flipper, hands thrust underneath his great coat and deep inside his trouser pockets.

His friend offered a weak smile. "Actually since five-thirty. Couldn't sleep."

The counsel shook his head, gestured again to the door. "You could have waited inside."

"My mama raised me better than to go about chawin' 'baccer in church, Capt'n."

Barber put a gloved hand on the doorknob. "Gentlemen, since neither of you can take a hint, I'll meet you indoors."

The door closed behind him. Flipper chuckled and started to follow. Hampton's jaw pounded the tobacco furiously. "You coming, Wade?"

"Best wait here," he said. "Till the court calls me."

"You could wait at HQ. Get some coffee. Stay warm."

Hampton shook his head, leaned over the railing, and let a stream of tobacco juice melt more snow and ice. "I'll wait here," he said, and Flipper opened the door. Wade Hampton had always been the rock of the 10th Cavalry. He had been the calmest soldier during the hay fire back in February, the voice of strength for Flipper the past two months, and had been commended for his bravery against the Apaches at Rattlesnake Springs, months before the two officers ever met. Yet today he seemed as nervous as a groom on his wedding day, jittery, shaking not because of the freezing temperature. Flipper could understand that to a degree. Testifying in a court-martial could always be hard on one's nerves, but at stake was Flipper's career, not Hampton's.

Inside the warm chapel, Flipper shed his overcoat and joined Barber at the front. They went over the attorney's notes as others slowly arrived. Major Schofield was first, then Captain Fletcher, the stenographer, and Judge Advocate Clous. Fletcher and Tilley joined Schofield by the stove while Clous sat at his table and pulled papers from his satchel. Captains Walker and Heiner showed up, finishing their coffee and discussing the trial in Washington of Charles Guiteau, President Garfield's assassin. Others filed through the door one at a time, letting in cold air. The last to arrive was Colonel Pennypacker, who walked straight to his chair and said: "Gentlemen, let us get to business."

They dispensed with the oaths and other formalities quickly before Pennypacker instructed Barber to call his next witness.

"Please state your name, rank, regiment, command, and station."

"Wade Hampton, Second Lieutenant, Tenth Cavalry, B Troop, Fort Davis, Texas." Hampton had spit out the quid before entering the chapel, but specks of tobacco remained stuck between several teeth and along his gum line.

"Lieutenant, do you know the defendant?" Barber asked easily.

"Yes, sir." Flipper noticed the "sir." Hampton almost always pronounced the word suh. He had shucked his Carolina accent, either intentionally or, as Flipper suspected, due to nerves. "I met Lieutenant Flipper this past New Year's Day. I had seen him around the fort since my transfer here last November after the Victorio campaign, but didn't meet him personally until I joined him at his quarters to share New Year's dinner."

"Did the two of you strike up a friendship?"

"Yes, sir. I was new here, and Lieutenant Flipper didn't have many friends. But I found him to be intelligent, honest, and a good friend. And an excellent soldier."

"In fact, you took a leave of absence, did you not, and returned East to try to drum up financial support for Mister Flipper after his arrest?"

"Yes, sir."

"At your own expense?"

"Yes, sir."

"Why would you do that for a man you had known less than a year, Lieutenant?"

Hampton swallowed before answering. "We were good

friends, Captain. Sure, I had known him only seven months or so, but there are some people you meet and feel like you've known all your life. I trusted Hen . . . Lieutenant Flipper. He would have done the same for me. He's that kind of person, sir. And I knew in my heart that Lieutenant Flipper was innocent of the charges against him."

"You had occasion to visit Mister Flipper often in his quarters, is that correct?"

"Yes, sir."

"You were aware that he kept commissary funds in his quarters?"

"Yes, sir."

"Did he have any bad habits regarding the security of those funds?"

"Henry . . . er, the lieutenant told me he didn't enjoy the job, said he didn't like bookkeeping, but he worked hard to do the best he could. At first he kept the funds in his trunk, and kept the trunk unlocked. He was too trustin', that's how I looked at him. But by late spring, he had started locking the trunk. I heard him tell his housekeeper to make sure she kept the trunk locked. He even started locking his desk. He told Mister Chamberlain, while he was boarding with him, not to let anyone in his quarters if he wasn't home."

"When did the change come about?"

"Shortly after Colonel Shafter took command."

"But didn't the colonel relieve Mister Flipper of his duties in the Quartermaster and Commissary Departments?"

"Yes, sir, but he had not replaced Lieutenant Flipper as A.C.S., and told him to keep the money in his quarters until he was notified to do otherwise."

"Did that strike you as strange?"

Clous barked out an objection. "*Herr* Hampton is not

qualified to answer dat question. He has never served in any capacity in da quartermaster or commissary."

Pennypacker nodded. "Sustained."

Barber had expected the objection and ruling and didn't let the decision interrupt his flow. "Did Mister Flipper tell you why he began stressing security?"

"Yes, sir. Well, actually, I warned him. So did some of the non-commissioned officers."

"Warned him? About what?"

"We heard that some officers were out to get Lieutenant Flipper. They were going to set him up."

Clous objected again, pointing out that rumors were nothing more than hearsay, and Pennypacker agreed with the judge advocate. But Barber seemed satisfied. He had made his point and sat down without asking more questions.

Wiping his glasses with a handkerchief and smiling at Hampton, the judge advocate remained seated as he began the cross-examination.

"Your uncle is da famous Wade Hampton of da Confederacy, *ja?*"

"Yes, suh." The Southern accent slipped out now.

"And you vould have dis court believe dat a Southerner like yourself, blood kin to a man who led da late Rebellion to keep coloreds in bondage . . . you vould have us believe dat you could befriend a Negro?"

Merritt Barber's fist shook the table. "Objection!" he shouted. "I object to this offensive line of questioning!"

"Captain Clous," Pennypacker said sternly, and the judge advocate smiled, still cleaning his glasses.

"My apologies. Lieutenant, you testified to da accused's increased security. Did Lucy Smith have a key to dis trunk?"

"No, sir. She would ask for the key when she needed it, and the lieutenant would give it to her."

Clous laughed. "And dis is 'increased security'?"

Hampton didn't respond.

"Lucy Smith vas arrested, vasn't she? For possession of government property?"

"Yes, sir."

The counsel chuckled and donned his glasses. "Such security," he said.

Barber rose, leaned on the table, and said: "The judge advocate isn't asking questions, Mister President. He's delivering his summation."

"Save it for your closing argument, Captain," Pennypacker told Clous. "Ask the witness questions. Don't make statements."

"*Ja.* I have only one more question for dis vitness." He stood and walked directly in front of Hampton, who turned suddenly pale. Clous stared at the lieutenant for a full minute, still smiling, before he stepped back, lost his grin, and said: "You testified dat you first met da accused on New Year's Day. Vhy?"

Flipper leaned forward, wondering at the point of this question. Barber objected, but this time Pennypacker overruled him and told Hampton to answer.

"I don't understand the question," Hampton said nervously.

"Is simple, Lieutenant. Vhy did you pick dat particular date to visit *mit* da accused?"

Hampton swallowed. "It's customary . . . ," he began, but Clous interrupted him, raising his voice.

"*Entschuldigen Sie, bitte.* It is customary for officers to visit da ladies of da post, *Herr* Hampton. Ach! Lucy Smith vas not employed by da accused at dat time, and a darky housekeeper is not considered a 'lady' for dat matter. And it is not customary for officers to visit other officers on da First of January. Vhy did you visit da accused? Answer me."

The lieutenant looked down, and Clous stepped back, beaming once again. "Perhaps I can refresh your memory, Lieutenant. On New Year's Day, vere you not at Lightner's Saloon in town *mit* Lieutenants Nordstrom and Woodward and *Kapitän* Viele?"

"Yes, suh," Hampton answered in a hoarse whisper.

"And *Kapitän* Viele suggested a vager, a bet, *ja?*"

Hampton nodded, still looking down. "Yes."

"You cut cards, and you lost?"

"Uhn-huh." He looked up, stared blankly at the far wall. His eyes welled with tears. So did Henry Flipper's.

"So, you lost da bet and had to join da accused? Isn't dat how you came to be *mit* him?"

Hampton's "yes" was barely audible.

Clous's large head bobbed happily. "*Ja.* You are a fine friend, *Herr* Hampton. No more questions."

The room fell silent. Hampton's gaze dropped to the floor again. Pennypacker asked Barber if he cared to redirect, but he simply shook his head, stunned by Hampton's revelation. He could have asked Hampton to explain his actions, perhaps say that, yes, it had started out as a bet, but the friendship proved something stronger. That's why he continued seeing Henry Flipper. That's why he went East to drum up support. But Flipper knew Barber couldn't ask those questions, because he couldn't be certain how Wade Hampton would answer.

Flipper put both elbows on the table, locked his fingers, and rested his head against his hands. He closed his eyes, holding back tears, and bit his bottom lip to fight the pain.

"Does the court have any questions of this witness?" Pennypacker asked.

Silence again.

"Then Mister Hampton, you are excused."

The chair legs scraped the floor, and footsteps sounded as Wade Hampton made his way out of the chapel. The hinges squeaked, the wind moaned, and a blast of frigid air caused Flipper to open his eyes. He let out a sigh as the door slammed shut.

"This court is adjourned," Pennypacker announced, "until two o'clock this afternoon." The gavel fell.

Flipper felt oblivious to the cold as he and Barber walked in silence. Flipper fumbled with the key and unlocked the door. He realized he had left his overcoat in the chapel, but didn't care. Once inside, Merritt Barber sank in a chair while Flipper stared out the window.

"You think . . . ?" Barber shook his head. "You think Hampton set us up?"

"No," Flipper said with a sigh. "You saw how he looked. He didn't want to say what he did."

It had started snowing again. He heard the door to Nordstrom's quarters open and close, saw him walking with Mollie Dwyer, arm-in-arm, heading toward the post trader's compound. Flipper's jaw and fists clenched. He felt sick, betrayed.

"Wade's testimony didn't hurt us, really," Barber said. "It. . . ." His voice trailed off.

The snow fell harder.

Maybe Wade Hampton's testimony didn't damn Flipper to Leavenworth's penitentiary, but it certainly hurt. It hurt like hell.

Chapter Thirty

Fort Davis, April–May 1881

"You need a servant, Henry," Wade Hampton said, to which Flipper had to nod in agreement.

Having a guest boarder had taken a toll on his bachelor quarters. Not that W. S. Chamberlain lived like a pig, but this side of the duplex definitely lacked a woman's touch. Chamberlain spent six days at the commissary or quartermaster depot and Sundays working on watches and jewelry in town at the Sender and Siebenborn Mercantile. Flipper split his duties between A Troop and the commissary, and divided his Sundays between chapel services, the Nolans, and a ride to town or through the countryside, sometimes with Mollie Dwyer but, more frequently, without her company. Mollie was seeing more and more of Charles Nordstrom these days, especially after the Swede bought that Concord "Piano Box" to carry her around in style.

Hampton shot another quick glance around the quarters, smiling and shaking his head as he handed Flipper a personal check. Flipper grunted something and sat at his desk. He rescued a pencil from underneath piles of paperwork, read the check again, and scribbled something down on a note pad. He collected some other cash strewn about the desk, jotted down more notes, and knelt beside his trunk that he quickly opened, withdrawing a wooden box. Inside this he filed Hampton's check, the other cash, and his note pad, then put the box back in place, and closed the trunk.

"I'll be mighty glad when the colonel finds my replacement," Flipper said.

"Don't blame you," Hampton added.

They walked out the back door, past the cistern, and into the cramped kitchen where Flipper let the B Troop adjutant sample his pitiful coffee. Hampton was polite enough not to make a face or spit out the bitter drink.

"Wanna ride to town, grab a bite to eat?" Hampton asked.

Flipper shook his head. "Not today. I'm supposed to meet Miss Mollie at the stables. Promised to take her toward Mitre Peak." He grinned. "Nordstrom's in the field. Not expected back till Tuesday."

Hampton stared at his coffee cup, saying nothing.

"What's the matter?"

"Nothin'."

"Wade. This is me, Henry Flipper. Talk to me."

The lieutenant looked up, tasted the coffee again, and let out a sigh, setting the cup on a counter top. "I just hear talk, Henry. That's all."

He understood. Some of that talk managed to get back to him, sometimes even to Mollie. "Miss Mollie and I have been friends for a long time. I don't see anything wrong with us going for Sunday rides."

"She's practically engaged to Nordstrom."

Flipper tossed out the dregs. Nordstrom, what in God's name did Mollie see in that lecher? Why couldn't two people, an Army officer and a lady—sister-in-law to a cavalry captain, for that matter—take a friendly ride together? There had never been any problems back at Fort Sill, or at least the talk and sneers never made their way back to Flipper. This was Fort Concho all over again. Flipper wondered if Colonel Shafter would eventually order him not to accompany Mollie Dwyer. He studied his friend, wondering.

"Wade, do you have a problem with Miss Mollie and me?" There. He had gotten it out.

Hampton looked up, hurt. "No, Henry. 'Course not." Their eyes held for several seconds. Hampton looked away first, found a spot to stare at on the ceiling, shook his head, and sighed once more before facing Flipper again. "All right. I'm from a hotbed of secession. Until I met you, I wasn't used to seein' Negroes and whites together socially. Definitely wasn't used to me socializin' with a man of color. But I've changed. The problem, Henry, is that others here ain't changed. I hear what they say when you and Miss Mollie go for a ride. The colonel, he can't stand it. And his whole staff hates your guts . . . worse than Nordstrom or any of our boys in the Tenth. I just want you to watch yourself, Henry. I got a bad feelin' 'bout all this."

Smiling reassuringly, Flipper placed both hands on Hampton's shoulders and gave them a gentle squeeze. "I appreciate your concern, Wade. I'll be careful."

He waited at the corral for an hour. After checking his Chamberlain-made watch a final time, he led Abraham back to his stall, told Cox to unsaddle the stallion, and hurried across the road, past the enlisted men's barracks, and across the parade grounds toward the Nolan residence. Maybe Mollie had taken ill. Hat in hand, he knocked on the door and waited, expecting Annie or maybe the captain to open it. Mollie did, however, and quickly stepped onto the porch.

She didn't look sick, but she had been crying.

"Miss Mollie . . . ," Flipper began, but she held up her hand to stop him.

"Henry, I'm sorry." She looked away.

He knew what was happening then. His heart sank. He

saw himself on the banks of the Chattahooche River in Atlanta, saw Anna White, heard those painful whispers: "Henry, I'm sorry. . . . Henry, this is hard to say. . . ."

"I should have told you, Henry," she said, not looking at him, just staring at the flag popping in the West Texas wind. "But I didn't know how. I didn't want to hurt you, but Charles and I are going to be married. And he . . . well . . . he . . . he just said I shouldn't be seen with you alone. Said folks might get the wrong impression."

Flipper nodded dumbly. He felt stupid out here, hat in hand, listening to Mollie Dwyer's justification. She had once defended him, had been his friend and confidant. Now she was shucking him for the likes of a racist swine like Charles Nordstrom. For the first time in his life, he really wanted a drink. He wanted to find Wade Hampton and split a bottle of Taos Lightning, or whatever they served in the worst saloons of Newtown or Chihuahua.

"Henry, I don't want to hurt you, but I love Charles. And. . . ."

He looked at her now, saw the tears flowing down her cheeks. "I guess I love you too, Henry. I guess I have for years. But . . . but that can't happen, Henry." She sobbed. "You know why."

Her words shocked him. He had never expected to hear this from Mollie, always telling himself their relationship was platonic, nothing more. Somehow, he managed to nod again.

"I know why you stopped riding with me at Fort Concho. And I know what some of the officers have been saying about us, about our Sunday rides. Henry. . . ." She closed her eyes tightly, shuddered. "You're a good man, Henry. You've been a wonderful friend. But if we continued riding, it would destroy your career. Those bigoted sons-of-bitches would see to that. That's why I can't see you any more. It's for your own sake. Do you understand?"

His answer came in a dead undertone, a slight bob of his head. He pulled on his hat and left Mollie Dwyer standing on the porch.

"That Mistah Williams come by, Henry," Chamberlain said. "Told me to give you this here check, said it's for the commissary bill for the bakery for the month."

Flipper saw the name on the check and corrected his boarder. "Wilhelmi, W. S. Not Williams. Lieutenant Wilhelmi."

"Yes, sir. I's sorry."

"Don't worry about it." Flipper opened the trunk, pulled out his box of funds, and logged Wilhelmi's payment.

"I don't like that fella, Henry."

"Who's that?"

"Wil . . . Wil-hel- . . . that lieutenant."

Flipper didn't like the post adjutant, either, but nothing could be done about that. He returned the box, closed the trunk, and dropped onto his bed, closing his eyes.

"He ax where you kept the funds, looked around an awful long time. I told'm I didn't know nothin'. Told'm he would have to see you 'bout that. Then I hears him tell Mistah Nordstrom outside that he can't believe how us colored folks live. He says that loud enough that he knowed I hears. Shameful. He acts shameful if you ax me."

"Well, we could use a servant," was all Flipper said.

She was a small woman with a delicate, round face and mesmerizing black eyes accentuated by a nearly perfect nose and full lips. *Almost beautiful,* Flipper thought, as he motioned Lucy Smith to take a seat in his quarters. She handed him the letter of reference, and Flipper noticed her small but strong hands, hardened from years of work as a post laundress. Her skin was much darker than Flipper's, her muslin dress shabby and worn, her shoes dirty and scuffed beyond recognition. Lucy Smith reminded Flipper of neither Anna White nor Mollie Dwyer.

"You're boarding with Miz Olsup in Chihuahua," Flipper said, reading the letter.

"Yah, suh." He placed the accent from the deep South, Alabama perhaps, maybe Mississippi.

Her eyes locked on the dirty floor. Flipper waited for Lucy to look up, wanted her to make eye contact. He had never understood why so many blacks seemed scared to look white folks in the eye—only Flipper wasn't white, and Lucy wasn't a slave any more. He was of her race, with his uniform the only thing separating them.

She finally lifted her head. Their eyes met. Flipper wished they hadn't. "I . . . I . . . you're. . . ." He studied the letter again. "I . . . Miz Olsup speaks highly of you, and, as you know, I need a . . . need help with cooking, cleaning, ironing."

"Yah, suh. I cooked for Lieutenant Ward when I lived at Fort Stockton, suh. He'd tell you I works hard iffen you ax him. I can helps you, Lieutenant Flipper."

"Call me Henry," he said, and from the corner of his eye saw her smile.

Captain Nicholas Nolan's eyes sparkled as he lifted the green calico dress draped over the trunk. Flipper waited, embarrassed, as the Irishman shook his head and said laughingly: "Mister Flipper, I hope you don't plan on wearing this out of these quarters. I dare say 'Pecos Bill' would consider it out of uniform."

"Lucy asked if she could keep some of her clothes here," Flipper said in defense, realizing just how that sounded, and quickly adding, "to wear while cleaning."

"I see," the captain said, but Flipper thought he couldn't. In fact, he wasn't certain that he understood Lucy's reasoning himself.

He decided it best to proceed to other grounds. "Can I interest you in a cup of coffee, Captain?"

"Certainly," Nolan said. "Miss Smith, I hope, made it."

"She did," Flipper said, and led his friend and commander to the kitchen out back.

They sat on the back porch, sipping the chicory Lucy had brewed earlier that day. Too potent for Flipper—he had grown accustomed to his own awful brew—but Chamberlain, Hampton, and the other infrequent visitors liked the stuff, so Flipper learned to drink it without complaint, although he often watered his cup down a mite.

Nolan nodded with satisfaction and smacked his lips. They watched the clouds drift over the cañon wall for a while, listening to the noise around the post: sergeants barking orders, hoofs pounding, axles squeaking, soldiers grunting, horses snorting, trace chains jingling.

"Annie and I have missed your company, Mister Flipper," Nolan said at last. "We haven't seen you off-duty for a few weeks now."

"Yes, sir. I've been busy, sir. Commissary. Vouchers. You know."

The captain's head bobbed slightly. "Well, we were hoping you might join us for Sunday dinner."

Flipper drank. He tried to think of some excuse, but couldn't.

"Henry," Nolan said, "I know you're upset. What Mollie sees in Mister Nordstrom I'll never understand. He's kind to her, though. Not the bastard he is with the troops. But it's her decision, her life. I'll not butt my thick Irish skull in her business."

"I'm not angry or upset at Miss Mollie," Flipper said. A half lie. He wasn't angry. He could never been angry at Mollie Dwyer, but he was upset. She had hurt him. But he wouldn't look back. He had put Anna White behind him, and he'd do the same with Nolan's sister-in-law. Mollie's words wouldn't kill him.

"Well, if it makes things easier, Mollie won't be here this Sunday. She's leaving for Fort Stockton."

With Nordstrom? Flipper almost asked bitterly. He caught himself, though, as Nolan went on: "Visiting a friend of hers who has taken ill. She left this morning. And I have it on good authority that Mister Nordstrom has orders to deliver supplies to Quitman. He leaves at first light. So. . . ." His voice trailed off.

Who was Flipper fooling? He had missed the company of the Nolans. He smiled and said: "Tell Miz Annie that I would be delighted to join you both after services. Can I bring anything?"

The gleam returned to Nolan's eyes. "Well, you could bring Miss Smith if you'd like."

Flipper laughed. "Captain, she's my laundress and cook. Nothing more."

He explained that Lucy, anyway, spent her Sundays at Mrs. Olsup's in Chihuahua. He'd come alone, and would try to pick up a bottle of wine, although he didn't drink. They shook hands, and Nolan finished his coffee. Flipper stared at Shafter's private stable between Officer's Row and the post hospital, although if anyone had asked him to tell him what he saw, he'd be hard pressed to answer. He sat lost in thought. *She's my laundress and cook. Nothing more.*

That was a half-truth as well. There was nothing between Lucy and Flipper—not yet—but he felt a soldier's crush or some similar attraction to the dark beauty.

Chapter Thirty-One

November 29, 1881

Wringing her hands, eyes focused on the chapel floor, Lucy Smith sat in the witness chair that afternoon as Merritt Barber gently began coaxing her through testimony. She nodded when the defense counsel asked if she still roomed with Mrs. Olsup in Chihuahua, and Barber explained that he needed a verbal answer. She looked up with those haunted eyes. Lucy didn't know the meaning of "verbal." They got through the routine questions, and then the tougher ones. Was she awaiting federal trial herself? Yes. Was she free from jail on personal recognizance? Yes.

"Lucy," Barber asked, "why did you keep some of your personal items in Lieutenant Flipper's quarters?"

" 'Cause I had no place to put my things after I moved out of Mizzus Olsup's. See, I was livin' in a tent on the post then. So I ax him could I keep some things in his trunk."

Barber nodded. "Very good, Lucy. Did he keep his trunk locked?"

"Yah, suh. Need be I gots to fetch somethin' out, I has to ax him for the keys and give'm back when I's finished."

Flipper studied the faces of the court-martial board, saw how they were riveted. Judge Advocate Clous was the same. They reminded Flipper of spectators at some carnival, eyes fixed unashamedly on the freaks of nature. They leaned forward, focusing on her words, wondering if she would say something scandalous, maybe hoping she would, but also transfixed by her beauty. They likely found her a paradox, a woman with a face like Helen of Troy's and a full body, but nothing more than an overworked scullery maid with threadbare clothes and shabby English. They loathed her, yet they longed for her—forgetting that she was black and they were white.

"Lucy, what happened on the morning of Lieutenant Flipper's arrest?"

"I don't recollects," she said, her voice faster, nervous fidgeting worsening.

Barber remained patient. "Perhaps I can refresh your memory. Mister Chamberlain testified that you asked the lieutenant for keys to the trunk. Is that right?"

She nodded, and Barber pointed out that she had to say so. "Yah, suh. I thinks I was doin' his laundry and needed to put his shirts away in his trunk."

"Did you take out any papers and envelopes?"

Another nod, but this time she remembered to speak. "I taken out two envelopes, hid 'em in my bosom."

"Why?"

"There was this other cleanin' woman workin' at Lieutenant Nordstrom's that morn, and I was a-feared that she might sneak into where I was at and take to thievin'."

Now Flipper leaned forward. This was the first he had heard about that. He tried to remember, tried to picture Nordstrom's house servant? No luck. Was Lucy lying? Shifting suspicion? Barber didn't expand on this line of questioning. Maybe he thought Lucy wasn't telling the truth, or maybe he simply hadn't expected the answer and wasn't prepared.

"Did Lieutenant Flipper ask you to lock the trunk and return his key?"

"Yah, suh. He often times tells me . . . 'Lucy, don't go away and leave that trunk open. You be very careful and keep it locked and always given me back the key.' He always tolds me that."

"Did he ever tell you why he was so careful?"

"Naw, suh."

"Those papers and envelopes you took. If I understand, you took them out without his knowledge?"

"Yah, suh."

"What happened next?"

"I don't rightly remember. He was gone by the time I finished, and I think I puts the key on his table."

"He . . . you mean Lieutenant Flipper?"

"Yah, suh."

"Did you lock the trunk?"

She shook her head. "I can't remember, Capt'n."

Barber smiled reassuringly. "That's all right, Lucy. Do you remember if Colonel Shafter came to the quarters that day?"

"I don't remembers nothin' 'bout it."

"Did you see the colonel that morning?"

"I don't remember iffen I seen him or not. I was so scared."

"What scared you?"

"I can't tell you that. I don't know what scared me. I was scared through."

"Lucy," Barber asked, "in your employment, did you find Lieutenant Flipper to be an honest and trustworthy man?"

"Yah, suh. He was mighty good to me. He wouldn't steal nothin' from nobody."

"Thank you, Lucy. I have no more questions."

Clous began his attack before Barber was seated. "May it please da court, I vould like to avoid bringing any scandal to dis case, but I have to examine dis vitness. *Fräulein,* do you remember your own arrest? An arrest on federal charges? Do you remember da statement you gave to Commissioner Hartnett? Answer me. Don't nod your damned black face!"

"Calm down, Captain Clous," Pennypacker said. "Give the witness time to answer your questions one at a time."

Lucy wiped her eyes and said meekly: "I kinda recalls bein' arrested. I don't remembers what I said to the commissioner, though."

"Did not you on the Twentieth day of August, vhile you were in jail in Chihuahua go before Judge Hartnett, that is U.S. Commissioner Hartnett, and make an affidavit before him?"

"An affidavit? What dat?"

"My God, you ignorant. . . . Ach! Do not you remember anyting dat led to your release from jail?"

"Naw, suh. I was frightened to death. How could I remember?"

"You vere still frightened on da Twentieth of August?"

"Yah, suh. I be frightened yet."

Shaking his head, the angry Clous moved forward. "Ven you saw Colonel Shafter in his office, didn't you tell him you had no papers on your person? But ven you vere searched, those papers vere found, *ja?*"

"I don't knows, Capt'n. I was frightened to death."

"Ach! You don't remember anything, do you?"

"Naw, suh. I ain't gotten over my scare yet."

Clous waved his bear-like fist at her and whirled around, muttered something in German underneath his breath, and fired out: "How about da accused? You remember him, *ja?*"

"Yah, suh."

"He messes vith you?"

"He don't do no such thing. He don't mess with me. I

do his cleanin', his ironin'."

"*Ja.* And perhaps other vork? Do you remember telling a soldier after your own arrest dat nothing could be done for da accused because he had fixed everything?"

"I don't remembers that."

"Of course, you don't. You still live with da accused, don't you?"

"Naw, suh. I ain't never. I pitched my tent behinds his place for a while. But now I lives with Mizzus Olsup. I still do his cleanin' some, but that's all."

Clous shook his head. "Dis is a tainted vitness," he told the court. "She vould lie to protect da accused, and her memory is horrible. I am finished *mit* her."

When the judge advocate had settled in his chair, Colonel Pennypacker looked at Barber. "Redirect?"

Nodding, Barber rose. "Thank you, Colonel. Since my colleague has tried to bring scandal to this case, after all, I do have a few more questions. Lucy, did you ever spend the night in Lieutenant Flipper's quarters?"

Flipper froze.

"Naw, suh." She finally looked at Flipper. "Once we went dancin' and didn't get back till three in the morn. He likes to go to them Mexican dances. He made some coffee, and I went home. That was afore I pitched my tent behind his place. But naw, suh, I ain't never spent the night in his quarters."

"Thank you, Lucy," Barber said as he sat down. The court had no additional questions for Lucy, but only after Pennypacker dismissed the witness, and only after Lucy closed the chapel door behind her, did Flipper let out his breath.

Chapter Thirty-Two

Fort Davis, June–July 1881

They stumbled into the kitchen, too giddy to be tired after a night at the Mexican *baile* over in Newtown. Flipper had escorted the Widow Olsup, Lucy, and Chamberlain to the dance. Mrs. Olsup had bowed out around eleven-thirty, and Chamberlain called it a night after midnight, but Lucy and Flipper stayed and danced until well past two-thirty. It had been Lucy's first *baile,* and she hadn't missed a song. Everyone there—Mexican laborers, *vaqueros,* sheepherders, even one or two merchants—had shaken a leg with the alluring Lucy Smith. Flipper, the only officer present, had cut the rug with her four times himself. She was bewitching on the dance floor.

While she stepped on a chair to reach a can of Arbuckle's ariosa—being out of her chicory concoction and forced to drink Flipper's former brand—he turned up the lantern just a tad, found the coffee pot, and fired up the stove. He toppled two tin cans, and Lucy snickered and told him to be quiet, that he'd wake the dead. She handed him the can, which he put it aside to take her hands and help her down.

She slipped, but Flipper caught her, and eased her feet to the floor. They laughed for a second, but, when she looked up, both smiles vanished. He held her close, not intentionally—at least, not at first—and took in her smell, the contours of her face. He swallowed nervously, wanting to pull back, to play the part of the officer and the gentleman, to play the part of her employer, but somehow couldn't.

Nor did she pull away. In fact, she leaned closer, pressing her breasts against his pounding chest.

He looked down at her, started to say her name, to tell her this wasn't right, but instead found himself closing his eyes and kissing her. A light kiss at first, then harder, and then his eyes popped open, embarrassed and shocked to feel her tongue. He stumbled back against the stove, cursed at being burned, and fell against the counter. Lucy licked her lips and giggled.

"It's all rights, Henry," she said, and moved closer.

She kissed his burned palm, reached up, grabbed his neck, and found his mouth.

"It's all rights," she whispered again. "This be your first time, but I be gentle with you."

It wasn't his first time. He wanted to tell her that. He also wanted to tell her as she kissed him hungrily that this wasn't what he would consider gentle. He wanted to tell her a lot of things, but after another minute the only thing he wanted was for W. S. Chamberlain or Charles Nordstrom not to come inside the kitchen.

She was gone when he woke up Sunday morning. He looked around, saw he was in his own bed, wondered how he had gotten there. He dressed quickly and walked outside to the kitchen, where Chamberlain was nibbling on bacon and sipping coffee.

" 'Mornin'," the watchmaker said. "What time you get home?"

Flipper filled his own cup and stared dreamily at the counter. He seemed to smell Lucy's rose-scented soap everywhere. "Three or so," he finally answered. "You working today?"

Chamberlain answered with a nod. "After church, I

reckon. What be your plans?"

"I don't know," Flipper said, but he thought he might call on Lucy Smith. He thought he might ask her if she would like to pitch her tent out back as other servants and laundresses did. It would save her from paying room and board at Mrs. Olsup's.

"You seem uncomfortable, Mister Flipper," Shafter said, lifting his eyes from the account books Flipper had submitted for his weekly approval. "Malaria acting up?"

"No, sir. Had trouble sleeping is all."

A half-truth. He also had trouble getting the statements to add up, scribbling, erasing, adding, erasing, adding, until finally the accounts looked to be in order. He wished the colonel would hurry up and relieve him of this tedious job to which he was ill-suited. Besides, the figure he came up with and the money for which he was responsible didn't match. Somewhere he had botched up everything. That was easy to understand, too. Collecting money owed by soldiers stationed all over West Texas could be taxing, downright impossible.

To make matters worse, in early May, Commissary Agent Michael Small had telegraphed Flipper that he would not be at headquarters for the rest of the month and not to send funds until notified. At first Flipper had thought this a Godsend. It would give him time to collect more of the money the Army was owed. But now it just seemed to add to his headaches as he tried to figure out how the books had become so far off, to find his mistakes, and correct them before Shafter and others discovered something was amiss. For the first time, Flipper thought they might accuse him of embezzlement.

He glanced at the others in Shafter's office. Captain

Bates and Lieutenant Wilhelmi. Maybe they already suspected him. The back of his neck dampened with sweat.

"Very well," Shafter said at last, and signed the statement. "But since Major Small has said not to send any
funds until he is back at headquarters, let's suspend this
damned weekly meeting until Small's back. It's a pain in
the arse. Carry on, mister."

Shafter handed the ledger to Flipper and didn't bother
saluting. Flipper left in a hurry, surprised to see Lieutenant
Nordstrom and Charles Ward waiting in the anteroom. As
Flipper walked out the door, Wilhelmi told the two men to
come inside. Ward, the former A.C.S. at Fort Stockton,
what was he doing at Fort Davis? Hadn't he been court-
martialed and dismissed from duty a few months back because of habitual drunkenness? He shrugged off the questions. He had more important things to think about—A
Troop's drill and getting those accounts settled, and Lucy.

He entered the duplex and opened the trunk, placed the
account ledger and statement inside, and closed the lid.
Staring at the little brass padlock, he thought about
Nordstrom and Wilhelmi, recalled Chamberlain's conversation: *He ax where you kept the funds, looked around awful long
time.* A few days earlier after "First Sergeants' Call," Watts
had approached Flipper and said: "Lieutenant, sir, permission to speak frankly?" Flipper had readily agreed. "Something's up, sir. They's tryin' to get you?"

"Who?" Flipper had asked.

"Them white officers."

He had heard that before, practically every week since
West Point. He hadn't locked his trunk since the Academy
or when traveling. Now he found himself moving to his
desk, rooting out the key from underneath foreign coins and
notes, spent bullets, arrowheads, and plenty of things he

should have thrown away a long time ago. He slipped the key onto the ring, knelt by the trunk again, and went to work, tugging on the lock to make sure it held. Lucy kept her cleaning clothes in the trunk. He'd have to make sure she could get to them when necessary.

Stepping out of Abraham's stall after brushing the stallion, he spotted some infantry corporal throw an empty can of peaches into the corral. A barrel-chested man with graying red hair and a pockmarked face, the soldier folded his pocket knife, dropped it into a trouser pocket, and wiped his mouth. He glanced at Flipper, frowned, and began walking down the road.

"Excuse me, Corporal," Flipper said, trying to keep his anger in check.

The soldier stopped, turned.

Flipper marched to the corral and pointed at the empty tin. "There are places for trash on this post, soldier, and the cavalry corral isn't one of them."

With a shrug and a wink, the corporal said: "Figured one of your nigger troopers'll pick it up when he's policin' the grounds, Lieutenant."

Blood rushed to Flipper's head. His fists clenched. "What's your name, soldier?" he barked.

"Wiley Arrington, First Infantry, Comp'ny D."

"A horse could cut its leg on that, Arrington. You're going to pick that trash up, Corporal, and dispose of it properly . . . or you're going on report."

"Like hell. I ain't one of your niggers. You don't give me no orders."

Flipper started for him, stopped himself. Arrington smiled.

"Go ahead, boy. Hit me. Do it. I can whup you good."

"You're under arrest, Arrington."

"Ain't no darky man enough to send me to the stockade. You're gonna have to carry me there. If you can."

It would have been easy. The infantry soldier had a few pounds on Flipper, but was short, probably well in his cups, and lacked Flipper's reach. He started to swing, wanted to, but stopped himself. Lieutenants Wilhelmi and Nordstrom and a 1st Infantry sergeant stood across the road, watching, waiting. He hadn't spotted them until now. They could hear everything being said. Why weren't they doing anything? Silly question. They were hoping for a fight, wanting Arrington to throttle the Negro officer. He would never expect them to come to his aid.

He looked again at Arrington, saw the man gleaming, licking his lips, not in a defensive position, just waiting. The clopping of a horse's hoofs on the road sounded behind Flipper. Arrington's smile vanished.

"What's going on here?" Captain Nolan said, reining to a stop and swinging from the saddle.

"I've ordered Corporal Arrington to pick up an empty tin of peaches that he tossed into the corral, sir," Flipper answered stiffly. "We're having a difference of opinion."

Nolan handed the reins to an orderly who had appeared out of nowhere. As the stable hand led Nolan's gelding away, the Irishman peered over the corral wall.

"Is that yours, Corporal?" Nolan asked.

"Yes, sir." Arrington's bluster had disappeared.

"Did Mister Flipper tell you to pick it up?"

"Yes, sir."

"Did you obey his order?"

"No, sir."

"Any particular reason?"

"None, sir."

Flipper looked across the street. Wilhelmi, Nordstrom, and the sergeant were gone.

"You have a name, Corporal?"

Arrington answered.

"Do you know where the post guardhouse is?"

"Yes, sir."

"*Go maith!* Good, good. Because I want you to march your *tóin* over there double-quick. But first, you shall tell the Officer of the Day that Captain Nolan has placed you under arrest on a whole slew of charges that I'll think of by the time I get to headquarters. And when you get out of The Mill, if you ever do, I think we can arrange all sorts of unpleasant duties for you, *Private* Arrington. Now get out of my sight."

Wade Hampton shook his head as Flipper finished his story, sighed, and sipped his coffee. "Sounds like they were tryin' to set you up, Henry. You strike an enlisted man with Wilhelmi an' Nordstrom servin' as witnesses against you. The first sergeant, too. Did Capt'n Nolan prefer charges against this Arrington?"

"Oh, yeah." Flipper smiled. "He's facing general court-martial."

"Good. Maybe that'll stop anything else like this from happening."

"I don't think so."

He stared at his coffee cup as they stood just outside the duplex kitchen. On top of all this, he had been busy helping Captains Viele and Bates with the burro race for Independence Day. That had been rather fun duty even if his only duties had been printing up posters in Spanish and talking to some Mexicans about competing. At least that had gotten off without any hitches. Hampton had even taken a few dollars from Captain Bates on friendly wagers. But the Fourth of July had passed, and troubles seemed to torment Flipper even more.

He had kept his accounting woes to himself for so long. Maybe he should have discussed the matter with Captain Nolan, but he would have felt awkward, afraid he might see Mollie, or afraid Mollie might learn just how stupid Henry O. Flipper could be. But he had to tell someone, and Wade Hampton was his friend. "My commissary statements are a hopeless mess," he said at last. "I'm missing a lot of money."

Hampton swallowed and emptied the dregs onto the ground. Nordstrom walked outside and passed in silence, carrying his dirty clothes toward the laundresses set up behind the hospital. Neither Flipper nor Hampton spoke until certain Nordstrom was out of earshot.

"How much?" he asked.

"A lot." He felt tears welling, but held them back. "Hell, Wade, I'm on tick for a few months' salary myself."

"My God, Henry."

"I've been supporting W. S. Chamberlain and, now, Lucy . . . on a second lieutenant's pay. Even gave some folks in town food and supplies to help them through this drought. If Mister Markland would ever send me my royalty check, I can cover my bill. But I don't know where some of the money has gone. It's missing."

"Missin'?"

Flipper nodded.

"You mean stolen?"

"I don't know how, Wade. I've been locking up the funds in the trunk. Last night I locked my desk."

Another round of silence.

"I'll see what I can find out for you, Henry. And if you

need some money, I'll do my part. You know that."

"It's appreciated, Wade. I mean that."

"We've got some time."

The mirthless laugh surprised Hampton. Shaking his head, Flipper laughed again and looked into his friend's eyes. "Not as much time as you think. I met with Colonel Shafter this morning. Major Small's back in San Antonio. He wants all subsistence money as of June Thirtieth sent to headquarters promptly."

He stood before Shafter again, along with Wilhelmi and Bates, showed the colonel the smudged statement ledger, and informed him that several hundred dollars were still out because the debtors were in the field or in service elsewhere. Shafter rose irritably and barked: "Mister Flipper, I'm not inspecting this until all damned funds are here."

"Yes, sir, but that could be some time." He felt himself sweating, wishing it were malaria. "Perhaps I could write a personal check to cover the funds still out."

He regretted this as soon as he had said it. His pathetic bank account couldn't cover that much money.

"That's a damned right smart of money for a second lieutenant," Shafter said.

Wilhelmi spoke up. "The lieutenant is a famous author."

Flipper caught the sarcasm, but Shafter didn't. The colonel eased his bulky frame into the squeaking chair. "Very well," a much calmer Shafter said. "See that it's done, mister, and report to me first thing tomorrow morning."

"Yes, sir."

His quarters would never pass inspection at the Academy. In fact, he could not remember ever having his room look this way. It would have brought about his dismissal from the Point, would have brought out his father's razor strop at home.

He had gone through everything, emptying the contents of the trunk on the floor, turning over the mattress, rifling through his desk, and he had found some money. Fourteen dollars and sixty-three cents, plus a check from Captain Viele for eleven dollars. He had written a check himself for one thousand, four hundred forty dollars, and forty-three cents, but didn't plan on mailing it. Major Small was on another trip and wouldn't be back until the end of the month or early August. He still had some time.

"Henry? Goodness gracious, Henry, what happened here?"

He looked up, wiped his eyes, forced a grin as Lucy entered the room, picking up items from the floor—*ever the housekeeper,* he thought, and smiled genuinely this time. She sat beside him.

"Did somebody breaks into here? They steals anything?"

"No," he said, putting his arm around her. She shivered. From nerves, he guessed. "No, I couldn't find something. Guess I went a little loco."

"Musta been mighty important to you," she said.

He nodded. "Mighty important."

After repositioning the mattress, she climbed on the bunk behind him, putting both hands on his shoulders, squeezing gently. It felt good. "I helps you, Henry. You know I do anything for you."

He mouthed—"I know."—although she couldn't see his face. He felt so wound up he might explode. "I should start cleaning up this mess," he said absently. "Before W.S. gets back."

"You hush."

She pulled him around, kissed his forehead, caressed his

thigh. He felt suddenly exhausted, homesick, alone. He buried his head into her breasts as she stroked his head, wanting to believe her murmurs that everything would be all right, that Lucy would fix everything.

"She's a whore and a thief."

Flipper jumped up, almost tripped over the stones on the bed of parched Limpia Creek. The fingers from his balled fists ached as he stepped closer to Hampton. "You watch yourself, Wade." Flipper almost spat out the words.

They had ridden from the post and up the road toward Wild Rose Pass, stopping to rest their mounts on the banks of the meandering creek, where the horses could slake their thirsts at one stagnant pool of water that would dry up within a couple of weeks if the rains never came.

Hampton had told Flipper he had learned something, something that might explain why he was suddenly so short of commissary funds. He suggested they go for a ride, away from the post so no one could hear. Five or six miles from the fort, they stopped to sit on a toppled dead cottonwood while the horses drank and pawed the ground. Hampton had asked what Flipper really knew of Lucy Smith. Now Flipper was a fraction of a second from breaking his friend's jaw.

"She's a whore, Henry," the Southerner said again without flinching. Flipper drew back his fist. Hampton held his ground, suddenly acting like his famous Confederate namesake. "She worked for Lieutenant Ward back at Fort Stockton. As a housekeeper. But word around Stockton was that Ward also hired her out. He caught her stealin' . . . not the first time, from what I hear . . . and, instead of firin' her or turnin' her over to the authorities, he blackmailed her. Made her whore for him. She'd done that before, too. Also spent time in other jails."

The fist caught Hampton solidly on his right cheek, sending him over the dead tree. Flipper leaped over the cottonwood, no longer thinking, hands gripping Hampton's blouse, tearing buttons, pulling the lieutenant to his feet. He fired another punch, felt the cartilage in Hampton's nose give way, saw him fall hard, face down, among the rocks. Hampton rolled over slowly. Blood poured from his broken nose.

Seeing what he had done, Flipper felt sick. He stood numbly, staring in disbelief. His legs trembled, and he almost collapsed, stopping himself by using the tree for support.

"What do you know about her, Henry?" asked Hampton, sounding more like Louis Wilhelmi because of the busted nose. "She shows up here when you need a servant. Who recommended her to you?"

"Miz Olsup. She was boarding with her."

"And who told you to ask the Widow Olsup?"

"Nordstrom . . . in one of his nicer moments."

"Nicer. Just springin' the trap."

"I can't believe that. You're wrong, Wade. You've got to be wrong."

The nausea passed. Flipper extended his hand to Hampton, but Hampton shook his head.

"I'll sit here a spell. You go on."

Flipper turned, climbed over the tree, walked to the horses, and gathered the reins to Abraham. "I'm sorry," he said softly. He mounted, saying again, this time loud enough for Hampton to hear: "I'm sorry."

Sorry because he had hit his best friend? Or sorry because he couldn't believe him? Flipper wasn't certain.

"She's just part of the trap," Hampton said from behind the fallen tree.

★ ★ ★ ★ ★

After turning Abraham over to Walter Cox at the stables, Flipper walked with a purpose toward his duplex. A voice stopped him between the privies and the enlisted men's barracks. Flipper turned, recognized Sergeant Carl Ross.

"You all right, Lieutenant?

"Yeah," he answered brusquely.

Ross shuffled his feet, looked over his shoulders, and moved closer. He spoke in a whisper. "Lieutenant, I heard Lieutenant Wilhelmi say something yesterday that I thought you should know."

"Go on." He was impatient. He wanted to get back to his quarters.

"Well, sir, he was talkin' to this hide inspector. They was talkin' about you."

"And?"

"He said . . . Wilhelmi said, I mean . . . he says . . . 'I've found a way to get the nigger'."

Flipper had heard that before, too. He thanked Ross and hurried across the parade grounds, unlocked his door, and collapsed onto the bunk. He was grateful to be alone, hoped that Chamberlain would work late this day. He visualized Hampton's battered face. Nausea returned. Flipper shot up, darted out back, fell to his knees, and vomited next to Lucy's tent. He was thankful she wasn't here, either. He rose weakly after a bout with the dry heaves, wiped his mouth, looked around to see if anyone had seen him. He was alone. His housekeeper's and lover's tent loomed before him. He pictured Wade Hampton again. Leaning against the wall, he tightly closed his eyes.

I've found a way to get rid of the nigger.

Well, so had Second Lieutenant Wade Hampton if he

315

wanted to: striking an officer, breaking his nose, consorting with—could it be true?—a lewd woman. Hell, Wade Hampton could put Flipper behind bars at Leavenworth for several years.

Chapter Thirty-Three

November 30–December 3, 1881

But Hampton didn't say anything.

"He told everyone he fell off his horse," Flipper informed Barber that evening in his quarters. "Lot of jokes told at his expense. Cavalry officer falling from his horse, breaking his nose, those kinds of things. He could have nailed my hide to the wall."

"Maybe," Barber admitted. "Maybe not. No witnesses."

"Who the hell would need a witness, Merritt? A white man's word against mine?"

The attorney nodded, trying to placate his client. "All right, Henry. But this doesn't help us with the charges you're facing." He fell silent, thinking for a few minutes. "Who was there when you and this . . ."—Barber checked his notes—"Corporal Arrington almost tangled?"

Flipper told him. Barber tugged on the ends of his mustache for a moment, again lost in thought. He found a cigar and match, raised both, slowly lowered them. "I wonder if we could get Arrington to talk. He's the only one who could testify about a conspiracy. I thought Lucy might, but she's too scared, if she was involved. But this corporal. He could be looking at a lengthy spell in federal prison."

Flipper shook his head. "He pled guilty and was cashiered. Shot dead over a card game a few weeks later in town."

"Killed? Convenient. You think . . . ?"

"No." Flipper cut Barber off, shaking his head. "Arrington was killed because he was an ill-tempered ass. It wasn't murder."

Barber sighed, forgetting his cigar and match. "Well," he said, "I guess we had better get to court."

A frail, bespectacled man in a dusty woolen suit entered the chapel to testify, but before Joseph Sender was administered the oath, Captain Clous asked a question: "*Herr* Sender. You are an Israelite, I believe?"

The merchant nodded and affirmed that he was Jewish.

"What's the meaning of this?" Barber shouted from his chair. "Mister President, I must protest. . . ."

Now facing Colonel Pennypacker, Clous explained: "Dis vitness does not recognize da faith. . . ."

"He recognizes God," Barber shot back. "This is outrageous. We administer oaths to agnostics and atheists. . . ."

"Calm down, Captain," Pennypacker said. "Mister Sender, is an oath biding on your conscience as administered here?"

"Yes, sir."

"Swear in the witness, Captain, and let's proceed."

Preliminaries finished, Sender said that he had been the sole owner of the Sender and Siebenborn Mercantile since his partner passed away in October. He had been in business for seven years in town and knew Henry Flipper since shortly after the lieutenant was posted at Fort Davis.

"Would you consider him some sort of rascal?" Barber asked.

"No, sir."

"You have supported him during this whole affair, correct?"

"Yes, sir. If I didn't believe him innocent, I would not have helped him."

"He spent a lot of time at your store, sir. Did he spend a lot of money?"

"No, sir. I wouldn't call him a skinflint, but he was provident."

"Thank you, Mister Sender. I have no more questions."

Clous removed his glasses and leaned back in his chair. *"Herr* Sender, da accused may have been as you say, 'provident,' at your mercantile. But he could have spent a lot of cash at other places in town, *ja?"*

"No, sir. I don't think so."

The judge advocate snorted. "Vhy?"

"Well, sir, Fort Davis ain't such a large city. I think I would have known it, Captain."

Barber grinned. It was a good blow against Clous. The prosecutor lost his cadence, asking a few more meaningless questions before the court excused Sender. Barber next called Major Napoleon Bonaparte McLaughlen to the stand as another character witness. The ailing major testified to Flipper's good name, raved about the lieutenant's exceptional character and outstanding service as an officer. Clous didn't bother with any cross-examination, and court was adjourned for the day.

"May it please the court," Barber began the following morning. "The defense has no more witnesses to call, but I would like to read, for the record, a letter written at Fort Concho by Colonel Grierson."

Clous objected. This wasn't evidence, he said. If the commander of the 10th Cavalry wished to testify, he should be present. The judge advocate could not cross-examine a letter, he railed. Barber and Flipper were excused as the court discussed the matter in closed session. When they returned ten minutes later, to both men's surprise, Colonel Pennypacker told Barber to read the letter.

May it please the Court:

As an officer and a gentleman, Lieutenant Flipper's integrity and veracity have never been questioned, and his character and standing have been beyond reproach.

Lieutenant Flipper came under my immediate command in 1880 during the campaign against Victorio and his hostile Apaches. From personal observation, I can testify to his efficiency and gallantry in the field. Others under whom he has served have spoken of him to me in the highest terms. He has been selected for many special and important duties. In each case, he discharged them faithfully.

Being the only officer representative of his race in the Army, Lieutenant Flipper has, under most unfavorable and discouraging circumstances and surroundings, steadily won his way by sterling worth and ability, by manly and soldierly bearing, earning the confidence, respect and esteem of all with whom he has served or come in contact.

I have no personal knowledge as to Lieutenant Flipper's alleged offenses, but my confidence in his honesty has not been shaken. If he's guilty of anything, it is poor judgment or carelessness. My faith in his final vindication is as strong as ever.

As his Commanding Officer, I believe in his great promise. His restoration to duty would give me, and the entire regiment, great satisfaction. I most heartily recommend his acquittal of these charges, or at least the leniency of the Court and reviewing authorities.

> Benjamin Henry Grierson
> Colonel, 10th Cavalry
> Commanding
> Fort Concho, Texas
> November 1, 1881

All the witnesses had been called. The stenographer read back the previous day's testimony on Friday morning. Corrections were made. Flipper and Barber had discussed the merits of his testimony and had decided against it. Instead, Flipper would read an argument. Barber, of course, would have his own summation, but, if the court allowed Flipper to make his own case as well, then the defense would in effect have two closing arguments, not that Flipper had any hope that the judge advocate would allow this.

"I wish the judge advocate to distinctly understand," Barber said, "that the accused desires to submit an argument for the record."

Clous nodded. That surprised Flipper. The way the two attorneys had been bickering since the trial began, Flipper thought an objection was certain, but the judge advocate simply said: "Da next thing in order vill be to determine how much time is needed."

Pennypacker spoke up: "It's been a long, complicated case. I don't want the closing arguments to be rushed."

"Yes, sir," Barber said. "I will ask the court to give me until Tuesday." Clous, again, did not object.

"Granted," Pennypacker said. "This court will reconvene at ten o'clock Tuesday, December Sixth." The gavel fell.

He hadn't written a word. Well, that wasn't true. He had started several times, as the wastebasket in his quarters proved, but he hadn't found any of his attempts satisfying. This argument had to be close to perfect.

That's why Flipper found himself walking alone to the post chapel. Since mid-September he had dreaded making this walk. The adobe walls of the church had caused his stomach to churn, caused him to sweat despite the chill of autumn and, now, winter. He hesitated at the door, finally pulled it open, and stepped out of the cold.

It no longer looked like a courtroom. It was a church again. Flipper suddenly realized that he had not been to Sunday services since this whole mess began. Too busy, he figured, trying to save his skin. He looked up and saw that he wasn't alone. An officer knelt, head bowed, in front of the pulpit. The man's words were barely audible, but Flipper could tell he was sobbing. He felt like an intruder here, thought that he should leave, come back another time, but he wasn't sure he would be able to muster up the courage. So he quietly moved to the end of a pew, sat, and bowed his own head.

Where to begin? His brother Joseph would know. Flipper should know, too. *Dear God.* . . . He stopped, sighed. He heard the footsteps, and waited for the praying soldier to leave. But the sound stopped. No door opened.

"Henry?"

Flipper unclasped his hands, opened his eyes, and looked up. "Wade." He choked out the name.

They stared at each other until Flipper blinked, stood, and crossed the room. "How you been?" he asked.

Hampton shrugged. "Fine. You?"

"All right, I guess. Little warmer today."

"Yeah. Well, reckon I'll leave you alone. Good luck."

He started for the door, but stopped when Flipper called out his name, but Hampton didn't turn around.

"You didn't do anything wrong, Wade."

The Southerner's shoulders slumped. Hampton turned, tears rolling down his cheeks, and blurted out: "I did plenty wrong, Henry."

"Nothing you said hurt my case."

"It sure hurt our friendship."

Flipper shook his head. "No, it didn't." He stepped forward and offered his hand.

"Henry. . . ." The tears cascaded now. "Henry, the only reason I went to your quarters was because I cut the low card. Ten of clubs. Figured I was off scot-free when I showed that card."

"The first time," Flipper said, "we met was because of that bet. But you came back. You stuck by me. You didn't have to do that."

He nodded. "Maybe."

Hampton bit his trembling lip. Flipper waited patiently as the tears slowed and finally stopped. Hampton found a handkerchief, wiped his face, and blew his nose. Flipper realized he had been crying, too, and reached for his own handkerchief. Both men smiled awkwardly.

"You've always been there for me, Wade," Flipper said after a pause. "I know you meant well about Lucy. I. . . ." He paused. Flipper still couldn't believe she had been part of it all, had set him up, had stolen money. Their relationship had cooled, of course. She still cleaned his quarters—but only that—and they seldom spoke to one another. Maybe she had not stolen from him, but she had been a prostitute. Flipper was sure of that. She would probably wind up in prison. But Hampton had meant well. Although Flipper couldn't admit it right now, perhaps Hampton had been right about everything. "I'm sorry I hit you. . . ."

"I fell off my horse, Lieutenant."

Their smiles were genuine this time.

"The luckiest thing that ever happened to me," Hampton said, "was when I lost that bet on New Year's Day, when I had to go over to your quarters. . . ." He sniffled, but no tears came. "You've been the best friend I ever had, Henry, and I'll make everythin' up to you. I swear it."

Their hands clasped. Then they embraced. "You're a good friend," Flipper whispered. "You're a fine officer and gentleman. The best thing that ever happened to me in this man's army was meeting you."

Hampton pulled away. "Best get goin'," he said. "Leave you be for a spell. Good luck to you, Lieutenant Flipper."

"Thank you kindly, Lieutenant Hampton."

They offered each other salutes, and Hampton left.

Flipper stood alone. He faced the pulpit and walked slowly down the aisle. The words spoken in this building for almost three months echoed hauntingly.

Embezzlement in violation of the Sixtieth Article of War . . . conduct unbecoming an officer and a gentleman. "How does the defendant plead?" "Not guilty, to all charges."—"The detectives you sent took anything they could lay their hands on. Tell me, Colonel, who looks like the thief here?"—"I had no reason to be dissatisfied with his administration of the post subsistence affairs."—"I said . . . 'Goodness gracious, you don't keep all this money in your quarters, do you?' Lieutenant Flipper said he did."—"And you vould have dis court believe dat a Southerner like yourself, blood kin to a man who led da late rebellion to keep coloreds in bondage, you vould have us believe dat you could befriend a Negro? . . . *Ja*. You are a fine friend, *Herr* Hampton. No more questions."—"He was mighty good to me. He wouldn't steal nothin' from nobody."—My faith in his final vindication is as strong as ever. . . ."

Kneeling, Flipper tried to remember the last time he had prayed, really prayed.

Chapter Thirty-Four

Fort Davis, August, 1881

FUNDS STILL NOT ARRIVED. STOP. PLEASE CHECK ON STATUS. STOP. WIRE IMMEDIATELY. STOP. COMMISSARY AGENT MAJOR SMALL.

Closing his eyes, he wadded up the telegraph and tossed it into the trash can. His mind raced back to a summer afternoon in Atlanta. He could almost hear the Army locomotive pulling out of the depot.

Thick clouds of black smoke shot skyward as the engine picked up speed. He was ten years old, if that, darting out of the trees and running along the side of the track, brother Joseph already trailing by a few yards, struggling to keep up.

The soldiers of the 2nd Massachusetts watched from their perches on the flatbed cars. One stood, squinting, and recognized the two oldest Flipper brothers.

"What are you boys doing?" Private Henry Hartsell shouted above the metallic sound of the wheels and the coughing locomotive.

"Coming with you!" Henry Flipper answered, trying to run faster.

Joseph Flipper tripped, sprawled on the gravel, and started crying. Henry didn't glance back. He caught up with the flat car, reached out for the soldiers. Why wouldn't they help him up? The train picked up speed. He fought to stay alongside. Behind him, Joseph wailed, pleading for him to come back. He hadn't wanted his brother to come anyway, but the pest had tagged along. Private Hartsell moved through the sitting soldiers

until he reached the edge of the car, where he knelt but didn't ex-
tend a hand to lift the running boy onto the train.

"Henry," the soldier said. "You go back home."

"I want to go with you! I want to be a soldier!"

"Your brother needs you, son. Your parents will miss you."

"Help me! Pull me up." Tasting the salty tears, he tried to
tell himself they came from the cinders and soot of the churning
locomotive. But he knew better.

"You need to wait, Henry. You'll be a soldier someday. But
you gotta take care of your parents, your brothers."

He was beginning to tire. Tripping, he fought to stay upright
as Private Hartsell and the Union soldiers inched farther ahead.
"Help me up!" he cried one last time.

A gray-bearded sergeant with a leather patch over his right
eye spoke up: "Boy, you get on this here train, there ain't no
turnin' back."

Private Hartsell sat down, waving good bye. "So long, Top
Soldier. Take care of yourself."

Henry Flipper stumbled again, slowing to a trot as the train
pulled away. Finally, realizing defeat, he stopped and bent over,
resting on his knees, waiting for his labored breath to slow, the
pain in his ribs to diminish. When he looked up, the train had
rounded a curve. All he could see was smoke. "Henry!" Joseph
wailed, and he straightened and walked back toward his
younger brother.

Flipper walked out of the commissary office. He would
send a wire, but not to Major Small. Instead, he would ask
Mister Jonathan James Markland of Homer Lee & Company about his royalties. He had already lied to Colonel
Shafter about the missing funds. He could cover those, if
only he got paid. As he passed the old Quartermaster Storehouse, he thought about that nameless sergeant's warning
back in Atlanta: *Boy, you get on this here train, there ain't no*

turnin' back. Well, he had gotten on a train by not telling Shafter the truth, and now he couldn't get off.

"What the hell were you thinking, mister?" "Pecos Bill" Shafter's voice rocked the room. "You didn't record the checks or letter of transmittal?"

"No, sir," Flipper answered. The room started to spin. After not receiving a reply from Flipper, Major Small had sent a wire to Colonel Shafter. Flipper knew that would have to happen sooner or later. He wished, naturally, that he could have bought a little more time, so he told the volcanic colonel not a lie exactly, but not the whole truth and nothing but the truth.

"That's damned stupid of you, Mister Flipper. Damned inexcusable. I'm going to have to stop payment on those checks, those you can remember since you forgot to record the damn' things."

"Yes, sir."

Shaking his massive head, Shafter opened a drawer and pulled out a pewter flask. He took a quick pull, swallowed, and looked up. "Mister Flipper, your damned carelessness in this matter has left me no choice. Son-of-a-bitch! I'm relieving you as A.C.S. and putting Mister Edmunds in charge as of tomorrow morning."

"Very good, sir." Why couldn't Shafter have done that a month or two sooner? "I understand, and apologize for my negligence in this matter."

The colonel waved him off and stared at his flask. "Dismissed."

Wade Hampton grimaced. The two officers stood at the corral. The road seemed quiet this hot day, and only a handful of soldiers worked the stables and corrals. "What you gonna do now, Henry?" his friend asked, his nose still swollen from Flipper's punch. They had made their peace shortly after their fight. Flipper was thankful for that.

"I can't wait for that damned publisher any longer. I'm riding into town. See Mister Sender, Mister Siebenborn, maybe John Shields. They might loan me some money." The thought sickened him. He wasn't sure if he could muster the courage to ask those men for help. White men. What if they said no? The drought had hurt everyone in town this summer. Siebenborn was sick. Someone said he had uremic poisoning, wouldn't live to see the new year. There was always George Bentley. He was a man of color like Flipper and had some money put aside. But that wouldn't be easy, either. Flipper sighed. The train seemed to be picking up speed now, screaming out of control down a steep grade.

"What about Capt'n Nolan?"

Flipper shook his head. "He's out with A Troop on the Pecos. And I couldn't ask him for help. He's got a family to look after, and Mollie as well."

"I could wire home. The Hamptons of South Carolina ain't exactly po' dirt farmers."

"Couldn't get it in time, Wade. And what if they asked you why you needed the money?"

Hampton chuckled. "Why, suh, I'd tell them the management at Lightner's Saloon have asked me to settle my bill."

Walter Cox brought out the saddled Andalusian. Flipper thanked the stable hand, mounted quickly, waved good bye to both men, and took off at a lope toward town.

Once the sergeant left to send a wire to Major Small, William Shafter took another drink before capping the flask and returning it to the drawer. "What do you think, Mister Wilhelmi?" he asked.

The adjutant hid his smile. "Well, sir, you've said it to me a hundred times. You really can't trust a nigger to do anything right."

"Yeah. But by all accounts, Flipper's been an excellent soldier. Honesty above reproach."

"Yes, sir. But. . . ." Wilhelmi focused on a crack in the wall behind Shafter's desk.

"But what, mister?"

"Well, sir, it's just that. . . ." Wilhelmi slowly exhaled. "Well, Colonel, he was speaking a lot to those damned greasers at the burro race last month. And he's been working with all that money for a long time. That's a fortune to a darky, sir. I just think he might have stolen the money and is planning to go to Mexico."

Shafter grunted. "Maybe. But I just can't see Flipper doing that. Hell, I should have relieved him months ago."

"You couldn't have known, sir. And there's the matter of that darky strumpet who has been cleaning his quarters. I talked to Charles Ward, sir, and he says she's nothing more than a whore and a gyp."

The colonel raised his eyebrows. "She could have stolen the money. But would Flipper lie for her?"

"They are both niggers, sir. Can't be trusted. And she could be Flipper's accomplice, Colonel."

Shafter looked at the drawer again, debating on having another drink. He decided against it—at least for right now—and Wilhelmi excused himself. The seeds had been planted.

He stepped outside to see Lieutenant Charles Nordstrom waving at him from the commissary storehouse. The two men walked briskly toward each other and met behind the post guardhouse.

"Flipper just rode to town," Nordstrom said.

Wilhelmi's eyes danced. "With his saddlebags?"

"Of course."

"And where's his black wench?"

"Cleaning his place. And I mentioned to that bitch that my cleaning lady isn't exactly honest, told the fool she needs to be careful, watch out for Flipper's money."

"From what Charlie Ward said, I figured Lucy would steal the stuff for herself."

Nordstrom shrugged.

"Where do you think Flipper's going?"

"Where else?"

"Sender and Siebenborn's store."

"His home away from home."

"Thanks, Charles." Wilhelmi smiled. "We've got us one dead darky now." He spun around and hurried back inside headquarters, barging into Shafter's office.

"Colonel, sir," he said, trying to catch his breath. "I just saw Lieutenant Flipper ride to town."

"Why in hell should I give a tinker's damn about that?"

"He had his saddlebags, sir."

Shafter looked on hollowly.

The adjutant calmly explained: "Why would he bother to take his saddlebags with him, sir, for a one-mile ride?"

The chair squeaked as the colonel leaned back and tugged on the ends of his mustache. "You think . . . ?"

"Sir, it's a relatively short ride to Mexico, especially on a stallion as strong as his."

Both fists slammed onto the desk. Shafter's face turned bright red as he shot out of his chair and swore vehemently. Wilhelmi bit his lip to contain his glee. Seeds sowed, and now the crops were being reaped. "Mister Wilhelmi," Shafter spat out, "I want you to bring that black bastard back to this damned post immediately. Find Mister Edmunds at once. Have him meet you at Flipper's quarters where you'll conduct a thorough search. If he's stolen that money, I'll skin his black hide alive."

In his own room, Flipper stood in a daze, watching Edmunds and Wilhelmi look through his trunk, desk, everything. Wilhelmi held up a copy of THE COLORED CADET AT WEST POINT, shaking it violently to see if any papers fell out, breaking the book's spine, then tossing it across the room. Somehow Flipper held his temper. This was part of the snare, he thought. Blow up, lose control and they'd just tack on some other charge. He peered through the window at the armed detail of 1st Infantry soldiers waiting on the porch, chewing tobacco, smoking cigarettes, telling jokes.

"Christ A'mighty, Lieutenant," Edmunds said from Flipper's desk. "You don't keep all this money in your quarters, do you?"

"No choice," Flipper answered. "I was told not to use the safe at headquarters."

Wilhelmi stepped in front of Flipper. "Empty your pockets," he ordered. He was enjoying this.

Flipper withdrew a handkerchief from his inside blouse pocket. "Let me see that," Wilhelmi said, snatching it. He opened it, and to Flipper's amazement a piece of paper fell and floated to the floor.

"Frank!" the adjutant shouted. Edmunds turned from the desk, saw the paper as it landed on the floor, and walked over. Wilhelmi's gaze never left Flipper while the new A.C.S. squatted and unfolded the paper.

"It's a check. Good God, Louis, it's yours."

"Let me see that." Wilhelmi took the check, barely considered it, and waved it in Flipper's face. "You remember this!" he shouted. "My commissary bill for July, you son-of-a-bitch!"

"Louis," Edmunds said cautiously, a voice of reason, the nearest thing to a friend Flipper had right now.

"He stole the money, Frank," Wilhelmi shot back. "I think we should arrest him."

Edmunds shuffled his feet, his gaze dropping from the damning check—to Flipper—to Wilhelmi—to the ransacked quarters. With a sigh, he walked outside to the guard detail. Flipper never looked away from Wilhelmi.

"You planted that," Flipper said icily.

The post adjutant grinned. "So you say. I'm placing you under arrest, Lieutenant Flipper."

Flipper nodded. This was hopeless, for now. "Very well," he said.

An infantry soldier, armed with Springfield rifle and a cartridge belt, followed Edmunds inside. "Sergeant Dean," Wilhelmi said, "Lieutenant Flipper has been placed under arrest. He is to be confined to his quarters until Lieutenant Edmunds and myself report our findings to Colonel Shafter. He is to talk to no one. Nothing in this room is to be touched. If Lieutenant Flipper tries to remove something, if he even touches anything, even looks at a broom, you are to stop him. Shoot him if necessary."

"Louis,"—caution returned to Edmunds's voice—"you're taking this too far."

"I don't think so, Frank. An embezzler. A liar and a brigand."

Frank Edmunds glanced apologetically at Flipper. He turned around, looked at the fireplace, and moved closer. "Something's been burned," he said, and Wilhelmi whirled around.

"Too hot for a fire." Wilhelmi became curious. "Maybe he was trying to burn evidence."

"Maybe." Edmunds sounded defeated.

Flipper shook his head. Lucy had burned some trash a week ago. He thought about mentioning this, but they wouldn't believe him anyway. Hell, let them find out for themselves.

"How about his servant?" Edmunds asked. "We probably should question her. I'd bet if anyone's stolen anything it's her, not Flipper."

Wilhelmi shrugged. "Likely in on it together. But you're right. We should question her. Sergeant, have your men find Lucy Smith and bring her to Colonel Shafter's office. She's probably out back in her smelly tent."

"Yes, sir."

"But you stay with the lieutenant. And you have your orders."

Outside, the wind picked up. Thunder rolled in the distance.

They returned in force two hours later. Two 1st Infantry privates nailed the windows shut, while others walked out with just about everything: typewriter, table and chairs, clothes (Lucy's and his own), saber, trinkets, the desk, even Flipper's West Point ring.

Captain Bates had joined them, joking with Wilhelmi in whispers about the search conducted on Lucy Smith. Flipper held his anger in check. He had to. They left him again after a few hours. He spent the night in the sweltering room, under guard, a lantern burning in the window, by orders, with the shades open so Sergeant Dean or his relief could see inside at all times.

The following morning, Charles Nordstrom came with a

detail of 10th Cavalry troopers. The final shame, making his own men, soldiers of his own color, march Flipper to the post guardhouse.

They walked outside in a drizzling rain, down Officers' Row, across the parade grounds, underneath the limp American flag, took a hard left in front of the barracks, a right before post headquarters, and there loomed the stone walls of the guardhouse. The Mill, the soldiers called it. Inside, through the officer's and guards' rooms and into the dark, damp prison, Nordstrom opened the cell door, smiled as Flipper walked inside. He slammed the door shut, locked it, and said: "Enjoy your stay, Lieutenant. I don't think Mollie will be visiting you here."

"That's what this is all about, isn't it, Nordstrom?"

The fiend left without replying. Did he need to?

Flipper was alone. Cramped in a malodorous coffin, six-and-a-half feet by four-and-a-half feet, stone walls, ticky mattress, and a leaking bucket for a chamber pot. He had never heard of an officer being confined to The Mill. House arrest, sure. But in the guardhouse? They would never treat a white officer like this.

No one visited him that first day. Not W. S. Chamberlain, not Wade Hampton, not the Nolans, Sender, Shields, or Siebenborn. Only the 10th Cavalry trooper who brought his hardtack and water. "Dey says a couple of folks from town tried to see you," the guard told Flipper in a whisper. "But Colonel Shafter, he says ain't no one allowed to visit a thievin' nigger. Lieutenant Flipper, you ain't done nothin' wrong, is you?"

"I'm innocent," Flipper answered.

"Yea, suh, but I seen lots of innocent colored boys court-martialed, flogged, and worser."

"It'll be all right, Trooper. You best get back. Don't

want the colonel putting you in here with me for talking to the prisoner."

"Yea, suh. I' be prayin' for you, Lieutenant."

Alone again. He didn't eat, wasn't hungry. Instead, he sat on the cot, leaning his bare head against the stone wall. He had grown used to the gagging stink inside The Mill. The rain had stopped, the sun reappeared, and the guardhouse turned sweltering, foul, inhumane. Dusk brought welcome relief. He tried to sleep, but couldn't.

Outside, he heard the trumpeter playing "Taps." Then silence.

Yeah, Flipper said to himself. *You pray for me, Trooper.*

Silence again.

At last Flipper crawled out of the uncomfortable bunk. He fell to his knees, closed his eyes, clasped his hands.

Dear God . . . , he began.

Chapter Thirty-Five

December 6–8, 1881

The cottonwoods had lost their leaves. Strange how he hadn't noticed it until now. He had missed most of the fall, the vibrant yellow of the cottonwoods, the soldiers singing as they raked and burned the fallen leaves. He thought about making another goal for himself, recollected that he hadn't reached his earlier target, survive until Christmas. Maybe he should change that, make it a little more realistic: survive until . . . tomorrow?

Court was called to order. The turkey vultures had returned to his stomach. Flipper pulled out his papers, was sworn in, and began: "I declare to you in the most solemn and impressive manner possible that I am perfectly innocent in every manner, shape, or form," he said, his voice trembling at first. As he continued, he became more confident, and it showed as he sounded stronger, defiant, innocent.

He talked about Lucy Smith, Colonel Shafter, and others. He admitted his own fallibilities. It wasn't the letter he had hoped to write, but the best he could do. He looked up and concluded: "Of judgment, I am human. Of crime, I am not guilty."

After folding the letter, he handed the pages to Colonel Pennypacker, snapped a crisp West Point salute, turned on his heel, soldier to the last, and took his seat beside his defense counsel. Now, it was Merritt Barber's turn.

"Lieutenant Henry Ossian Flipper said it right," Barber

began humbly as he slowly pushed away from table and rose. "He's human. He doesn't say his actions under the second charge are blameless. He simply asks that you understand his foibles and motives so that they may be weighed together. Now, on the first charge, he denies that *in toto*. And my esteemed colleague, the judge advocate, has not come close to proving that Lieutenant Flipper embezzled anything."

Barber stepped forward, alternating his focus on the court-martial board and Captain Clous.

"Let's look at some of this testimony. Colonel Shafter? He couldn't remember anything. The government blames Lieutenant Flipper, but if the commanding officer had done his job, none of this would have likely happened. Lieutenant Wilhelmi? He's a bitter man. His little injections of gratuitous suspicions are so manifest as to justify a suspicion on our part of unkindness toward the accused. Let me explain this further . . . Lieutenant Flipper succeeded in winning laurels at West Point, which Mister Wilhelmi's"— Barber coughed intentionally—"sickness prevented him from ever obtaining. His testimony cannot be believed in full."

This was the kind of letter Flipper had hoped to write. After Barber had read the final draft, he had said it was a fine letter, firm, forceful, but also realistic, believable. Barber said the letter and his own closing summation would be a powerful double charge of buckshot.

"A shortage in funds does not establish the intent to embezzle," Barber continued. "Under the Sixtieth Article of War . . . no matter what Captain Clous wants you to believe . . . the accused is not required to prove that he did not embezzle the money, but it is for the government to prove that he did embezzle it, and that he did knowingly and willfully misappropriate the money and apply it to his own use. But have they done so?" Barber shook his head and directed his stare at Clous. "Where, when, and by what testimony? There is not one syllable of proof."

Flipper studied the faces of his so-called peers. Barber commended Flipper's service, at West Point and in Texas and Indian Territory, "a spotless career over nine arduous years." Nine? Not quite. Flipper smiled. Well, Merritt Barber wasn't a mathematician.

"I want you to think about this," Barber said, now resting against the table beside Flipper. "I want you to think of a mere boy who stepped upon our platform and asked the privilege of competing with us for the prize of success. I want you to think of Henry O. Flipper, who has had to fight the battle of life all alone. He has had no one to turn to for counsel or sympathy.

"Is it strange then, when he found himself in troubles which he could not master, trapped in a mystery he could not solve, that he should hide in his own breast, endeavor to solve this problem alone? After all, he has had to work out problems alone for most of his life."

Shaking his head, Barber looked directly at each member on the board. "We've proved our case," he said. "The government hasn't proved theirs. I don't think you can understand or appreciate all that Lieutenant Flipper has accomplished. You were not born into slavery. You have not had to fight persecution all of your life. It saddens me to say this, but I don't think Henry Flipper is really on trial here. I think the United States Army is. What you decide here isn't just Lieutenant Flipper's fate. It's the Army's. Because the question before you is this . . . is it possible for a colored man to secure and hold a position as an officer of the Army?"

Barber sat down. Clous began his closing argument, but Flipper barely heard. He, too, studied the faces of the court-martial board. Deep down, he knew. He had lost—not because they believed the case presented by Clous, but because they didn't want a man of color to serve as an officer in their Army.

When Clous had finished, no one spoke for a few minutes. The only sound came from Clous, who shuffled his papers and grunted as he sank in his chair. After the attorneys and court went through a few formalities, Clous cleared his throat and said: "*Herr* Flipper, your presence before dis court is no longer required at dis time."

At 10 a.m., December 8th, the court met, without Flipper and Barber, for one final time, and adjourned at half past noon. While Pennypacker, Clous, and the others finalized their decision, Flipper rode with Barber to the Newtown café.

"Now what?" Flipper asked after they had ordered coffee, tortillas, and enchiladas.

"Now we wait. They've made their ruling. We just have to see what the review boards say. I'm optimistic, Henry. No news is good news."

Flipper shook his head. "I've served as judge advocate before," he said, addressing his coffee cup more than his friend. "No news is bad news. If they had voted for an acquittal, we would have heard something."

"Maybe." Barber sipped his coffee.

They ate in silence.

Flipper escorted Barber to the corral the following morning, where an Army ambulance waited. "It's going to be strange," Flipper said lightly. "I've gotten used to having you for a roommate."

Barber laughed. "You'll miss my snoring."

"You don't snore."

"You sure as hell do."

Barber held out his hand. Flipper shook it warmly. "This is the hardest part of my job, Mister Flipper," Barber said. "You fight for your client, then have to leave him alone."

Flipper nodded. He tried to think of something to say, but couldn't. He was used to being alone, though, and had been since 1873.

"I did do some research," Barber went on. "Nine years ago, a paymaster was convicted of embezzling more than twenty-three thousand dollars. He was reprimanded in General Orders and suspended from rank and command for four months. That's not what I would call a harsh sentence. You were accused of embezzling only three thousand or so. So, if the worst happens, and you are convicted, I. . . ."

"Merritt?"

"Yeah?"

"That paymaster . . . he was white."

Barber looked away. "Good luck, Henry," he said, and climbed aboard the wagon. "You're one hell of an Army officer and an outstanding young man. I'd serve under you anytime."

"Thanks."

He stopped almost immediately after he turned away, watching an orderly carry Captain John Clous's bags to the ambulance, the bear-like judge advocate close behind. Clous smiled, after spotting Flipper, took off his glasses to clean the lenses, and said: "Ah, *Herr* Flipper, I vas hoping to see you before I left."

Flipper said nothing.

"I vanted you to know dat I hold no ill vill toward you. It

vas my duty, is all. You understand, *ja? Auf Wiederseh'n*."
He donned his glasses and extended his hand.

Hold your tongue, Flipper told himself, but found that he
couldn't. He had been keeping silent for more than eight
years now, letting white officers walk all over him because
he knew he couldn't fight them, couldn't win. Now he had
nothing to lose. He ignored Clous's hand. "It's wasn't a job
to you, Captain. It wasn't a job to anyone on that court-
martial board. I saw your faces. You didn't prove a damn'
thing against me. You just don't want any Negro officers in
this man's army. Most of you don't even want any colored
enlisted men."

Clous lowered his hand angrily. "*Ach!* You are one uppity. . . ."

"Listen to me, Captain. We're not talking soldier-to-
soldier, just man-to-man. No newspaper reporters. No witnesses. I don't know how the court voted, but I have a fair
idea. And I don't know how this will all turn out. I hope for
the best. But I want you to admit it. You don't want me in
your Army."

He waited.

"Captain!" the ambulance driver called out, "we're
ready to ride."

"A minute, Corporal." Clous smiled at Flipper. "I did
my duty, Lieutenant. Is all. I do not despise you. But, *ja,*
you are correct. I do not tink da Negro race is ready for
command in da Army. You vere graduated from Vest Point.
Bully for you. But no one has followed you. Da coloreds
simply cannot handle da regimen. Now, I must go. *Es ist
gern geschehen.*"

Cadet Johnson C. Whittaker had been dismissed from
the Academy a year or so ago. No Negro had taken his
place. Democratic newspapers, even the *Army and Navy*

Journal, were reporting that blacks lacked the mental faculties and fortitude to survive West Point. Many predicted there would never be another colored cadet at West Point, and certainly not another Henry Flipper in the Army.

"Mark my words, Captain,"—Flipper was talking to the large man's back as a soldier helped the judge advocate into the ambulance—"you may get rid of me, but more will be coming. And you won't be able to run all of us out of your Army."

He opened the door to his quarters to let Captain Nolan inside. "My wife was wondering if you would care to join us for supper, Mister Flipper," the Irishman said formally.

"Thank you, but I've already eaten," Flipper lied.

Nolan nodded. "Well. . . ."

Flipper felt guilty. The Nolans had been his friends, practically family, since Fort Sill. "Perhaps tomorrow evening," he suggested. "Or I could come by for tea tonight."

The captain nodded. "Henry," he said softly, "I've exchanged wires with Colonel Grierson. He seems to think, and I agree, that you might be better off at a different post. So I'm sending you to Quitman. For a change of scenery, if nothing else. At least until all of this mess is cleared up."

"Very good, sir. When do I report?" All military.

"I'll draw up the orders. You can leave in a couple of days. Annie would tan my britches if I sent you packing before you dined with us. Come by for tea. Say seven-thirty?" Flipper nodded. "And tomorrow at six. We'll talk about old times."

"Sounds great."

Nolan started to leave, but stopped and slowly looked at Flipper. "Henry, no matter what happens, you are a top soldier, a grand friend. And you must remember this. You are a success. They can't take that away from you. Don't ever let them. You're the first colored graduate of West Point, the first Negro officer in the United States Army. You're a fine man and a champion friend. Annie and I love you dearly. So does. . . ." He didn't finish, couldn't finish, and hurried away.

A success? Flipper closed the door, unbuttoned his blouse, and dropped onto his bunk. Success at what? This was what he had always wanted, and they were trying to take it away from him. Yes, he would always be West Point's first black graduate, but if they convicted him, cashiered him . . . ? He had failed at just about everything but West Point. THE COLORED CADET AT WEST POINT hadn't been the great seller of which he had dreamed. He had certainly proved to be one lousy Acting Commissary of Subsistence. If he had not been so determined to make the military a career, he probably could be anywhere but here— commanding General of the American Colonization Society's Liberian Exodus Army, teaching at a Negro college in Atlanta, sitting beside his parents and successful brothers in church, listening proudly to Joseph's sermon, watching his children play underneath the sweet gum trees while he and Anna laughed on their porch on a cool Atlanta evening. Anna? Yes, he had failed at love—with Anna White, Mollie Dwyer, Lucy Smith. Not that he loved Lucy, and he had certainly never realized that Mollie loved him. He had loved Anna, yet he had left her behind—for what?

Chapter Thirty-Six

Summer, 1882

Dust rose along the road leading to Fort Quitman, whipped by a furious, scalding wind. Flipper removed his weathered campaign hat, untied the calico bandanna, and soaked both in the murky Río Grande. He rinsed his mouth, spit, donned his hat, and retied the kerchief around his neck, enjoying the coolness as he stood and took the dusty trail back to his post. Post? More like a prison. For six months he had been here, waiting. Each time he saw the rising white plumes in the distance, he thought he might soon receive the news. Sometimes it was a cavalry detail, sometimes a stagecoach or Army ambulance, once a horse herd driven by *vaqueros,* and quite a few times just the beginnings of a dust storm.

No news had come, except one letter, and that was only a note from Presidio County attorney John M. Dean, thanking Flipper for his letter-affidavit used as a character reference for Lucy Smith in her federal trial. Dean informed Flipper that, although Lucy had been convicted, he thought he had an excellent chance of a reversal on appeal. Lucy had moved to Presidio the day before Flipper had left for Quitman. She was probably in prison by now. Prison or Presidio, what did it matter? He'd never see her again.

When he arrived at the crumbling adobe fort this time, he spotted Lieutenant Wade Hampton handing the reins to a 10th Cavalry trooper. The South Carolinian began feverishly pounding his trail-worn clothes, trying to remove most of the dirt and grime. He pulled on his hat, admitting defeat, and looked up. He recognized Flipper, and Flipper read Hampton's face. His heart sank.

Having maturely considered all the evidence, the court finds Second Lieutenant H. O. Flipper of the 10th Regiment of U.S. Cavalry as follows:

As to the first specification of the first charge: Not guilty.

As to the first specification of the second charge: Guilty.

As to the second specification of the second charge: Guilty.

As to the third specification of the second charge: Guilty.

As to the fourth specification of the second charge: Guilty.

As to the fifth specification of the second charge: Guilty.

He had expected that: acquittal of embezzlement, conviction of conduct unbecoming an officer and a gentleman. He had tried to steel himself for the rest, but seeing it in front of him, he could hardly breathe.

The Court does therefore sentence Second Lieutenant H. O. Flipper of the 10th Regiment of U.S. Cavalry to be dismissed from the service of the United States.

More followed: reviews from Generals Augur and Swaim, Secretary of War Lincoln, and finally President Chester Arthur, who succinctly wrote: **The sentence in the foregoing case of Second Lieutenant H. O. Flipper, 10th Regiment of U.S. Cavalry, is hereby confirmed. And: At 12 o'clock noon, 30 June 1882, Second Lieutenant H. O. Flipper is to be dismissed from the United States Army.**

Flipper slowly knelt on the ground. He felt sick, weak, dead. He wanted to read the verdict again, find some mistake, discover his eyes had played a nasty trick on him, but he didn't. He dropped the dispatch Hampton had brought, letting the bitter wind take it away.

"I'm sorry," Hampton said painfully.

Flipper didn't hear.

"Capt'n Nolan figured it might be best if I brought you the news. They say even Colonel Shafter's stunned. No one expected them to kick you out, Henry."

"I guess I did," Flipper said numbly.

"Capt'n Nolan's got most of your gear. Says you're welcome to stay with him till you fight this thing out."

Flipper shook his head. "I'm done fighting, Wade. Hell, the President of the United States approved the verdict and sentence. Not much I can do. For now, at least."

Hampton started to argue, thought better of it, and simply bowed his head.

"What day is it, Wade?" Flipper asked.

"June Twenty-Seventh."

"Three days."

"Yeah."

"Damn it all to hell."

"Yeah."

June 30th, 1882 came and went without fanfare. Flipper packed his bags, dressed in canvas trousers and a blue shirt, and rode back to Fort Davis as a civilian, seldom stopping, pushing his mount. Wade Hampton traveled with him, but talked little. What was there to say? They reached Fort Davis on July 2nd.

Instead of staying with the Nolans, Flipper boarded with

George Bentley in town. If he stayed with the captain, Annie, and Mollie, he felt for certain he would collapse. So he only went to the fort to get his things, settle affairs, bid farewell to Sergeant Watts and a few others, pay off his forty-six-dollar debt to Sergeant Ross, getting everything done quickly. He wanted to leave here as soon as possible. That's why he had ridden so hard from Quitman to Davis. He packed up a few keepsakes, some clothes and personal items, and mailed them to an El Paso hotel. He wasn't sure where he was going after El Paso but knew it couldn't be Atlanta. He would stay out West, put his military education to some use, try to forget the Army and the men who had ruined his life, ended his career. He needed money, of course, so he sold his tack and other items. Charles Nordstrom even bought a few things, maybe for Mollie. Flipper didn't ask. Maybe they would be trophies to remind him of his greatest Army victory.

His tent went to John B. Shields. Charles Ward, dismissed from the Army earlier but now a civilian clerk at Fort Davis, came by later and took it back, saying it was government property and that Flipper had no right to sell it, especially not to a civilian. "Ward," Flipper told the drunk icily, "you sold me that yourself when you were at Stockton. You know it's mine."

"Got a receipt?"

"You bastard!"

Maybe he should have hit the cheat. What else could the Army do? They weren't officers any more, just lowly civilians, Flipper convicted of conduct unbecoming an officer and gentleman, and Ward drummed out for drunkenness on duty. They could lock him up in the county jail maybe. Hell, it might even be worth it, but Flipper simply refunded Shields the money and apologized.

* * * * *

He knocked on the door of the Nolans' house, expecting the captain or Annie to open it. Mollie did. Flipper stepped back, removed his hat, and stammered out her name. She looked past him, saw Abraham tethered out front.

"You're leaving?" she said.

"Nothing for me here," he said. "I was hoping to say good bye to Annie and the captain."

"She's in town. I don't know where Nicholas is."

Flipper felt crestfallen. "I told Captain Nolan I'd be by this afternoon."

"Well," she said, hesitating, "you know how soft he really is. Hates good byes. Especially. . . ." Her voice trailed off. A tear rolled down her cheek.

"Yeah." He looked away, thought he might cry yet. Abraham snorted. "Well," he said, "tell them I'll write." When he looked back, Mollie's tears streamed.

"I will. Take care of yourself, Henry," she said between sniffles.

"You, too, Mollie." He had at last dropped the Miss.

She reached for him, but he had already turned. Mollie watched him gather the reins. She held the door open momentarily, but couldn't bear to watch him ride away. The door clicked closed.

Flipper pulled himself into the saddle. There was nothing left for him. He had said his farewells to Wade Hampton last night at Lightner's Saloon. Biting his lower lip, he kicked the Andalusian into a walk. He wouldn't cry. He would just ride past headquarters, hit the road and leave, taking it easy once this hellhole was behind him, letting Abraham rest a bit on the trail. El Paso wasn't going anywhere. Soldiers assembled in front of the barracks across the parade grounds. What were they doing? Well, that wasn't his concern any more. He pulled his hat lower and swallowed the lump in his throat.

A few officers had gathered in Shafter's office. Most of them were 1st Infantry men, but Lieutenant Nordstrom was there at Wilhelmi's invitation. The regiment's sergeant-major popped the cork on a bottle of wine and filled the glasses. Shafter raised his goblet in a toast.

"To the United States of America on this glorious Fourth of July," he said. "And to the United States Army and all it stands for."

"There goes Flipper," Nordstrom said absently, looking out the window.

"Good riddance," someone remarked. A few chuckles followed.

Then they heard it. A rifle volley. And another. Finally, a third.

"What the hell!" Shafter said, slamming his empty goblet on his desk. "Mister Wilhelmi, find out what the hell's going on."

"Sounds like a twenty-one gun salute," Frank Edmunds suggested.

The adjutant returned in a less than a minute. "Carbine practice," Wilhelmi reported.

"By whose authority?" Shafter belted.

"Captain Nolan's."

The colonel nodded, appeased, but when no other shots sounded, his fury returned. "Carbine practice hell! That was a twenty-one gun salute. For a convicted nigger, for Christ's sake."

He shoved his way outside, intent on lambasting the A Troop commander. Instead, he stopped dumbfounded as Flipper rode past headquarters. "Jesus, Mary, and Joseph,"

Shafter stammered, looking beyond the black man on the gray stallion.

Flipper might have been oblivious to the makeshift honor guard, the secretive twenty-one gun salute, but there was no ignoring the line of 10th Cavalry troopers standing at attention in front of the barracks. Sergeants, corporals, every Negro enlisted cavalry trooper on this post—except those at the rifle range. A few yards in front of rows of troopers, wearing his dress uniform, stood Second Lieutenant Wade Hampton. Scattered across the fort, soldiers, of the 10th, 1st and, other regiments, as well as civilians, stopped to stare in awe.

"Eyes right!" Hampton barked.

The black soldiers obeyed.

Then, in unison, the men saluted as Flipper rode past. Blood rushed to Shafter's head. He knuckles whitened as he clenched both fists. His lips trembled. Behind him, Wilhelmi and Nordstrom cursed. Wade Hampton stood at attention, erect and proud, also offering a sharp salute.

Flipper, dressed in a rose-colored shirt, striped trousers, and matching vest, returned the salute until he was out of their sight, riding past the guardhouse and toward the old Overland Trail.

Shafter trembled with fury. "Mister Hampton! On the damned double. Now!"

Nordstrom filed off the porch, barking orders, running toward the rows of troopers. "You damned darky sons-of-bitches! You don't salute that man, damn you. I'll have every one of you in The Mill for this. . . ."

Stopping in front of headquarters, Lieutenant Hampton offered Shafter a lame salute. "You need me for somethin', Colonel?" he asked easily.

"Pecos Bill" wanted to strangle him. His eyes bulged.

"I'll have you up on charges, you nigger-loving jackass." He stepped toward Hampton, kicked up dust, spit, and screamed out myriad curses. "What the hell do you think you're doing, mister? That man is not an Army officer any more. You don't salute him, damn your hide!"

"With all due respect," Hampton said, holding his ground, refusing to yield to Shafter's intense stare. "I wasn't salutin' an officer, Colonel." He turned slowly, watching the gray stallion carry Henry Flipper out of Fort Davis. Flipper kept his back straight, proud, and never looked back. He paused briefly at the main road, letting a freight wagon pass, then rode west, disappearing in the thick dust.

"What do you mean, mister?" Shafter barked, his entire body shuddering. "Damn your hide, I will not tolerate insubordination!"

"We weren't salutin' an officer," Hampton repeated, and added softly, respectfully, sadly: "We were salutin' a man."

Author's Note

This novel is based on the true story of Lieutenant Henry Ossian Flipper, the first black graduate of West Point who was court-martialed and dismissed from the service as depicted in the preceding pages. My main sources for this novel were two memoirs written by Flipper—THE COLORED CADET AT WEST POINT: AUTOBIOGRAPHY OF HENRY OSSIAN FLIPPER, U.S.A., FIRST GRADUATE OF COLOR FROM THE U.S. MILITARY ACADEMY, originally published in 1878, and reprinted by the University of Nebraska Press with an introduction by Quintard Taylor, Jr., in 1998 and BLACK FRONTIERSMAN: THE MEMOIRS OF HENRY O. FLIPPER, originally written in 1916, edited by Theodore D. Harris, and published by Texas Christian University Press in 1997; the court-martial transcripts, courtesy of Fort Davis National Historic Site; THE COURT MARTIAL OF LIEUTENANT HENRY FLIPPER by Charles M. Robinson III (Texas Western Press, 1994); HENRY OSSIAN FLIPPER: WEST POINT'S FIRST BLACK GRADUATE by Jane Eppinga (Republic of Texas Press, 1996); and AN OFFICER AND A GENTLEMAN: THE MILITARY CAREER OF LIEUTENANT HENRY O. FLIPPER by Lowell D. Black and Sara H. Black (The Lora Company, 1985).

I am indebted to the staffs at the Fort Sill Museum, Fort Concho and Fort Davis National Historic Sites, the National Archives, and the Combined Arms Research Library of Fort Leavenworth, Kansas, as well as William H. Leckie's THE BUFFALO SOLDIERS: A NARRATIVE

OF THE NEGRO CAVALRY IN THE WEST (University of Oklahoma Press, 1967). I'm equally appreciative of my agents, Vicki Piekarski and Jon Tuska, and my wife, Lisa, who serves as my first proofreader, sounding board, and copy editor. John Duncklee helped out with the border Spanish, and I must also thank the editor/publisher of *The Shootist* magazine, George Glenn, who planted the seed that somehow sprouted into this piece of fiction.

For the purpose of narrative, I expanded and contracted some incidents, invented and deleted others, and changed the location of a few. The murder of E Troop's William Watkins in San Angelo, Texas, for instance, actually occurred in January 1881, after Flipper had been transferred to Fort Davis. Most of this novel's characters were actual people, and I have relied on the court-martial records for many—but certainly not all—quotations. Of course, this being a historical novel, the characterizations of everyone depicted here are my own invention.

One bit of literary license is Lieutenant Wade Hampton. In his 1916 memoirs, Flipper wrote that the only visitor he had on New Year's Day, 1881 was Lieutenant Wade Hampton, the nephew of famed Confederate General Wade Hampton. Wrote Flipper: "Lieut. Hampton was a splendid, nice fellow. Some years afterwards another nephew worked with me in Chihuahua as a surveyor."

Lieutenant Hampton, if he even existed, did not testify at the court-martial. In fact, according to Fort Davis National Historic Site historian Mary L. Williams, "we cannot say one way or the other if he was actually at Fort Davis on New Year's Day, 1881." There was no Hampton serving as an Army officer in the last quarter of the 19th Century, Williams said. Interestingly enough, I did uncover a Wade Hampton stationed at Fort Davis, but it's highly unlikely he was related to the Confederate hero and post-Civil War governor and senator from South Carolina.

Wade Hampton enlisted in the 25th Infantry, Company I, on September 8, 1876, and reënlisted on March 1, 1880. He was a sergeant, and the 25th Infantry, like the 24th Infantry and 9th and 10th Cavalry regiments, was composed of black enlisted men and predominantly white officers. Could Flipper, writing of events more than thirty years later, have been confused? Would a black non-commissioned officer have secretly fraternized with a black second lieutenant? Who knows? I thought the character of a white Lieutenant Hampton was too good to abandon.

After his court-martial, Flipper didn't just fade away from history. Although "thoroughly humiliated, discouraged, and heart-broken," he traveled first to El Paso and found work as a clerk. Later, he put his military background and education to use as a mining engineer and surveyor across the Southwest. He also served as a newspaper correspondent, researcher, and, to some extent, a published historian. From 1893 to 1910, he worked as a Justice Department special agent, then returned to engineering, became a translator because of his fluency in Spanish, was an assistant to Secretary of the Interior during the Harding Administration and worked in Venezuela for an oil company. In 1918, he renewed his relationship with Anna White, whose husband, Augustus Shaw, had died four years earlier. Although engaged, the relationship was broken off by one party, more than likely Anna. Henry Flipper retired in 1930 and returned to Atlanta to live with his brother Joseph.

In 1898, Flipper began a fruitless attempt to have his court-martial reviewed and his name cleared. Nothing happened, however, and on May 3, 1940, at age 84, Henry O. Flipper suffered a fatal heart attack. As one Georgia newspaper wrote, he died "unwept, unhonored, unsung." But Flipper's family, and others, took up the cause to clear a good man's name. It took thirty-six more years.

In December 1976, the United States Army at last reversed the court-martial and gave Flipper an honorable discharge, and the U.S. Military Academy created a memorial scholarship named after Flipper. On February 11, 1978, Second Lieutenant Henry Ossian Flipper, 10th United States Cavalry, was reinterred with full military honors in Thomasville, Georgia. Maybe the most fitting testimonial came eleven years later when President Bill Clinton praised the "extraordinary American," saying: "He did all his country asked him to do."

The Lightning Warrior

The Indians call the great white wolf the Lightning Warrior because of the swiftness of his attack. But even the giant Colbolt isn't interested in the massive wolf until Sylvia Baird makes the beast's pelt the one condition for her hand in marriage. She thinks she is safe, but when he returns with not only the pelt, but the wolf itself, and demands his prize, Sylvia's only hope is a desperate flight for freedom. Colbolt sets out in determined pursuit, but he's forgotten Sylvia's newest ally. . .the Lightning Warrior.

___4420-X $4.50 US/$5.50 CAN

Dorchester Publishing Co., Inc.
P.O. Box 6640
Wayne, PA 19087-8640

Please add $1.75 for shipping and handling for the first book and $.50 for each book thereafter. NY, NYC, and PA residents, please add appropriate sales tax. No cash, stamps, or C.O.D.s. All orders shipped within 6 weeks via postal service book rate. Canadian orders require $2.00 extra postage and must be paid in U.S. dollars through a U.S. banking facility.

Name_____
Address_____
City_____State_____Zip_____
I have enclosed $_____ in payment for the checked book(s).
Payment <u>must</u> accompany all orders. ☐ Please send a free catalog.
    CHECK OUT OUR WEBSITE! www.dorchesterpub.com

OUTLAWS ALL

From Alaska to the Southwest, Max Brand, the master of the Western tale, brings the excitement of the frontier to life like no one else. His characters live, breathe, struggle and triumph in a world so real you can hear the creaking of the saddle leather. Gathered in this collection are three classic short novels by Brand, all filled with the adventure and heroism, the guts and the gunsmoke, that made the West what it was.

___4398-X $4.50 US/$5.50 CAN

Dorchester Publishing Co., Inc.
P.O. Box 6640
Wayne, PA 19087-8640

Please add $1.75 for shipping and handling for the first book and $.50 for each book thereafter. NY, NYC, and PA residents, please add appropriate sales tax. No cash, stamps, or C.O.D.s. All orders shipped within 6 weeks via postal service book rate. Canadian orders require $2.00 extra postage and must be paid in U.S. dollars through a U.S. banking facility.

Name_____
Address_____
City_____ State_____ Zip_____
I have enclosed $_____ in payment for the checked book(s).
Payment <u>must</u> accompany all orders. ☐ Please send a free catalog.
      CHECK OUT OUR WEBSITE! www.dorchesterpub.com

THE WHITE WOLF

MAX BRAND

"Brand is a topnotcher!"
—New York Times

Tucker Crosden breeds his dogs to be champions. Yet even by the frontiersman's brutal standards, the bull terrier called White Wolf is special. With teeth bared and hackles raised, White Wolf can brave any challenge the wilderness throws in his path. And Crosden has great plans for the dog until it gives in to the blood-hungry laws of nature. But Crosden never reckons that his prize animal will run at the head of a wolf pack one day—or that a trick of fate will throw them together in a desperate battle to the death.

_3870-6 $4.50 US/$5.50 CAN

Dorchester Publishing Co., Inc.
P.O. Box 6640
Wayne, PA 19087-8640

Please add $1.75 for shipping and handling for the first book and $.50 for each book thereafter. NY, NYC, and PA residents, please add appropriate sales tax. No cash, stamps, or C.O.D.s. All orders shipped within 6 weeks via postal service book rate. Canadian orders require $2.00 extra postage and must be paid in U.S. dollars through a U.S. banking facility.

Name_____
Address_____
City_____State_____Zip_____
I have enclosed $_____ in payment for the checked book(s).
Payment <u>must</u> accompany all orders. ☐ Please send a free catalog.

WILD BILL

DEAD MAN'S HAND

JUDD COLE

Marshal, gunfighter, stage driver, and scout, Wild Bill Hickok has a legend as big and untamed as the West itself. No man is as good with a gun as Wild Bill, and few men use one as often. From Abilene to Deadwood, his name is known by all—and feared by many. That's why he is hired by Allan Pinkerton's new detective agency to protect an eccentric inventor on a train ride through the worst badlands of the West. With hired thugs out to kill him and angry Sioux out for his scalp, Bill knows he has his work cut out for him. But even if he survives that, he has a still worse danger to face—a jealous Calamity Jane.

___ 4487-0 $3.99 US/$4.99 CAN

WILD BILL

JUDD COLE

THE KINKAID COUNTY WAR

Wild Bill Hickok is a legend in his own lifetime. Wherever he goes his reputation with a gun precedes him—along with an open bounty of $10,000 for his arrest. But Wild Bill is working for the law when he goes to Kinkaid County, Wyoming. Hundreds of prime longhorn cattle have been poisoned, and Bill is sent by the Pinkerton Agency to get to the bottom of it. He doesn't expect to land smack dab in the middle of an all-out range war, but that's exactly what happens. With the powerful Cattleman's Association on one side and land-grant settlers on the other, Wild Bill knows that before this is over he'll be testing his gun skills to the limit if he hopes to get out alive.

___4529-X $3.99 US/$4.99 CAN

WILDERNESS

Fang & Claw
David Thompson

To survive in the untamed wilderness a man needs all the friends he can get. No one can battle the continual dangers on his own. Even a fearless frontiersman like Nate King needs help now and then and he's always ready to give it when it's needed. So when an elderly Shoshone warrior comes to Nate asking for help, Nate agrees to lend a hand. The old warrior knows he doesn't have long to live and he wants to die in the remote canyon where his true love was killed many years before, slain by a giant bear straight out of Shoshone myth. No Shoshone will dare accompany the old warrior, so he and Nate will brave the dreaded canyon alone. And as Nate soon learns the hard way, some legends are far better left undisturbed.

___4862-0 $3.99 US/$4.99 CAN

WILDERNESS

#28
The Quest
David Thompson

Life in the brutal wilderness of the Rockies is never easy. Danger can appear from any direction. Whether it's in the form of hostile Indians, fierce animals, or the unforgiving elements, death can surprise any unwary frontiersman. That's why Nate King and his family have mastered the fine art of survival—and learned to provide help to their friends whenever necessary. So when one of Nate's neighbors shows up at his cabin more dead than alive, frantic with worry because his wife and child had been taken by Indians, Nate doesn't hesitate for a second. He knows what he has to do—he'll find his friend's family and bring them back safely. Or die trying.

___4572-9 $3.99 US/$4.99 CAN

Dorchester Publishing Co., Inc.
P.O. Box 6640
Wayne, PA 19087-8640

Please add $1.75 for shipping and handling for the first book and $.50 for each book thereafter. NY, NYC, and PA residents, please add appropriate sales tax. No cash, stamps, or C.O.D.s. All orders shipped within 6 weeks via postal service book rate. Canadian orders require $2.00 extra postage and must be paid in U.S. dollars through a U.S. banking facility.

Name_____
Address_____
City_____State_____Zip_____
I have enclosed $_____ in payment for the checked book(s).
Payment <u>must</u> accompany all orders. ☐ Please send a free catalog.
CHECK OUT OUR WEBSITE! www.dorchesterpub.com

KIT CARSON

BLOOD RENDEZVOUS
DOUG HAWKINS

The high point of any trapper's year is the summer rendezvous, the annual gathering where mountain men from all over the frontier meet to trade the pelts they risked their lives for. But for Kit Carson, the real danger lies in getting to the rendezvous. He is leading a party of trappers, all of them weighed down with a year's worth of furs. That is enough to make them a tempting target for any killer on the trail—especially when the trail leads through Blackfoot territory.

___4499-4 $3.99 US/$4.99 CAN

Dorchester Publishing Co., Inc.
P.O. Box 6640
Wayne, PA 19087-8640

Please add $1.75 for shipping and handling for the first book and $.50 for each book thereafter. NY, NYC, and PA residents, please add appropriate sales tax. No cash, stamps, or C.O.D.s. All orders shipped within 6 weeks via postal service book rate. Canadian orders require $2.00 extra postage and must be paid in U.S. dollars through a U.S. banking facility.

Name_____
Address_____
City_____State_____Zip_____
I have enclosed $_____ in payment for the checked book(s).
Payment <u>must</u> accompany all orders. ❑ Please send a free catalog.
CHECK OUT OUR WEBSITE! www.dorchesterpub.com

KIT CARSON

KEELBOAT CARNAGE
DOUG HAWKINS

The untamed frontier is filled with dangers of all kinds—both natural and man-made—dangers that only the bravest can survive. And so far Kit Carson has survived them all. But when he sets out north along the Missouri River he has no idea what lies ahead. He can't know that the Blackfeet are out to turn the river red with blood. And when he hitches a ride on a riverboat, he can't know that keelboat pirates are waiting just around the bend!

___4411-0 $3.99 US/$4.99 CAN

BORDER TOWN

LAURAN PAINE

Nestled on the border of New Mexico since long before there was a New Mexico, the small town of San Ildefonso has survived a lot. Marauding Indians, bandoleros, soldiers in blue and raiders in rags have all come and gone. Yet the residents of San Ildefonso remain, poor but resilient.

But now renegades from south of the border are attempting to seize the town, in search of a rumored conquistador treasure. With few young men able to fight, the village women and even the priest take up arms. But will it be enough? Will the courageous townspeople survive to battle another day?
